A Book Of

ORGANIC CHEMISTRY

T.Y.B.Sc. CH-343 : Semester IV
As Per New Revised Syllabus w.e.f. June 2015

Dr. V. D. Bobade
Reader in Chemistry
H.P.T. Arts
R. Y. K Science College
NASHIK

Dr. A. D. Natu
Ex. Head
Department of Chemistry
Abasaheb Garware College
PUNE

Dr. P. C. Mhaske
Assistant Professor
Department of Chemistry
S.P. College
PUNE

NIRALI ™
PRAKASHAN
ADVANCEMENT OF KNOWLEDGE

N1858

T.Y.B.Sc. Organic Chemistry (CH-343) (Semester - IV)   ISBN 978-93-5164-918-2

First Edition : **December 2015**

© : **Authors**

Published By :
NIRALI PRAKASHAN
Abhyudaya Pragati, 1312, Shivaji Nagar,
Off J.M. Road, PUNE – 411005
Tel - (020) 25512336/37/39, Fax - (020) 25511379
Email : niralipune@pragationline.com

✦ DISTRIBUTION CENTRES

PUNE

Nirali Prakashan : 119, Budhwar Peth, Jogeshwari Mandir Lane, Pune 411002, Maharashtra
Tel : (020) 2445 2044, 66022708, Fax : (020) 2445 1538
Email : bookorder@pragationline.com, niralilocal@pragationline.com

Nirali Prakashan : S. No. 28/27, Dhyari, Near Pari Company, Pune 411041
Tel : (020) 24690204 Fax : (020) 24690316
Email : dhyari@pragationline.com, bookorder@pragationline.com

MUMBAI

Nirali Prakashan : 385, S.V.P. Road, Rasdhara Co-op. Hsg. Society Ltd.,
Girgaum, Mumbai 400004, Maharashtra
Tel : (022) 2385 6339 / 2386 9976, Fax : (022) 2386 9976
Email : niralimumbai@pragationline.com

✦ DISTRIBUTION BRANCHES

JALGAON

Nirali Prakashan : 34, V. V. Golani Market, Navi Peth, Jalgaon 425001,
Maharashtra, Tel : (0257) 222 0395, Mob : 94234 91860

KOLHAPUR

Nirali Prakashan : New Mahadvar Road, Kedar Plaza, 1st Floor Opp. IDBI Bank
Kolhapur 416 012, Maharashtra. Mob : 9850046155

NAGPUR

Pratibha Book Distributors : Above Maratha Mandir, Shop No. 3, First Floor,
Rani Jhanshi Square, Sitabuldi, Nagpur 440012, Maharashtra
Tel : (0712) 254 7129

DELHI

Nirali Prakashan : 4593/21, Basement, Aggarwal Lane 15, Ansari Road, Daryaganj
Near Times of India Building, New Delhi 110002
Mob : 08505972553

BENGALURU

Pragati Book House : House No. 1, Sanjeevappa Lane, Avenue Road Cross,
Opp. Rice Church, Bengaluru – 560002.
Tel : (080) 64513344, 64513355,Mob : 9880582331, 9845021552
Email:bharatsavla@yahoo.com

CHENNAI

Pragati Books : 9/1, Montieth Road, Behind Taas Mahal, Egmore,
Chennai 600008 Tamil Nadu, Tel : (044) 6518 3535,
Mob : 94440 01782 / 98450 21552 / 98805 82331,
Email : bharatsavla@yahoo.com

niralipune@pragationline.com | www.pragationline.com

Also find us on f www.facebook.com/niralibooks

Preface ...

The new approach to the subject matter in chemistry in well defined manner introduced as per new Revised Syllabus w.e.f. June 2015 is a welcome step. We are happy to place this text book of **"Organic Chemistry" (CH-343)** in the hands of students of T.Y.B.Sc. Semester - IV.

This book has been written according to the new revised syllabus introduced from June 2015 for Semester - IV. We have tried our best using our versatile experience to make this book quite informative as well as simple and lucid. Wherever possible an attempt is made to provide additional information to raise the standard of education.

Topics like Carbanions and their reactions, Retrosynthetic Analysis and Applications, Rearrangement Reactions, Spectroscopic Methods in Structure Determination of Organic Compounds, and Natural Products have been revised as per new revised syllabus.

The concepts are illustrated with examples wherever necessary. A large number of exercises have been given at the end of each topic. We are sure that this book will be equally useful to the teachers and students. We are confident that this book will cater to the exact requirements of students.

We are grateful to our dynamic publisher Shri. Dineshbhai Furia, Shri. Jignesh Furia of Nirali Prakashan for publishing this book with utmost care in a very short time. We are also thankful to the entire staff of Nirali Prakashan, especially Mr. Akbar Shaikh, Mr. Kiran Velankar and Mrs. Anjali Muley for making completion of this book as early as possible. We are also thankful to all marketing staff especially Mr. Nilesh Deshmukh and others for co-ordinating the matter well in time.

Any comments, criticism and suggestions from the readers for improving the book will be highly appreciated.

December 2015   **Authors**

Syllabus ...

1. Carbanions and their Reactions (06)

Introduction, Formation and Stability of Carbanion. Reactions involving carbanions and their mechanisms: Aldol, Claisen, Dieckmann and Perkin condensations. Synthesis and Synthetic applications of Malonic ester, Acetoacetic ester and Wittig reagent.

Aims and objectives: Students should know:

1. Definition and formation of carbanions.
2. Possible mechanism of some known name reactions involving carbanions.
3. Synthetic applications of some reagents.
4. To predict product/s or supply the reagent/s for these reactions.

2. Retrosynthetic Analysis and Applications (05)

Introduction, Different terms used – Disconnection, Synthons, Synthetic equivalence, FGI, TM. One group disconnection, Retrosynthesis and Synthesis of Target molecules: Acetophenone, Crotonaldehyde, Cyclohexene, Benzylbenzoate, and Benzyl diethyl malonate.

Aims and objectives: Students should learn:

1. Meaning of terms: Disconnection, Synthons, Synthetic equivalence, Functional Group Interconversion, Target Molecule.
2. What is retrosynthesis?
3. Various steps involved in the synthesis of some molecules (detailed mechanism is not expected).

3. Rearrangement Reactions (06)

Introduction, Mechanism of Rearrangement reactions involving carbocation, nitriene and oxonium ion intermediate. Beckmann, Baeyer-Villiger, Pinacol-Pinacolone, Curtis, Favorski, Claisen rearrangement.

Aims and objectives: Students should understood:

1. What is rearrangement reaction?
2. Different types of intermediates in rearrangement reactions?
3. To write mechanism of some named rearrangement reactions.

4. Spectroscopic Methods in Structure Determination of Organic Compounds (24)

Introduction, Meaning of spectroscopy, Nature of electromagnetic radiation, Wave length, Frequency, Energy, Amplitude, Wave number, and their relationship, Different units of measurement of wavelength, frequency, Different regions of electromagnetic radiations. Interaction of radiation with matter. Excitation of molecules with different energy levels, such as rotational, vibrational and electronic level. Types of spectroscopy and advantages of spectroscopic methods.

Aims and objectives: Students should know:
1. What is spectroscopy?
2. Different regions of electromagnetic radiations.
3. Various terms used in spectroscopy.
4. What is the interaction of radiation with matter?
5. Types of energy levels with diagram.
6. Brief idea about the advantages of spectroscopic methods.

(A) Ultra Violet Spectroscopy: Introduction, nature of UV, Beer's law, absorption of UV radiation by organic molecule leading to different excitations. Terms used in UV Spectroscopy: Chromophore, Auxochrome, Bathochromic shift (Red shift), Hypsochromic shift (Blue shift), Hyperchromic and Hypochromic effect. Effect of conjugation on position of UV band. Calculation of λ_{max} by Woodward and Fisher rules for dienes and enone systems, Colour and visible spectrum, Applications of UV Spectroscopy - Determination of structure, Determination of stereochemistry (Cis and trans).

Aims and objectives: Students should learn:
1. What is UV spectroscopy and Beer's law?
2. Different types of electronic excitations.
3. Various terms used in UV spectroscopy.
4. What is the effect of conjugation on UV band?
5. To calculate λ_{max} for dienes and enone systems.
6. Define colour.
7. What is the range of vision region?
8. Applications of UV spectroscopy.

(B) Infra Red Spectroscopy: Introduction, Principle of IR Spectroscopy, Fundamental modes of vibrations (3N-6, 3N-5), Types of vibrations (Stretching and bending), Hooke's law, Conditions for absorption of IR radiations, Vibration of diatomic molecules. Regions of IR Spectrum: Fundamental group region, finger print region, aromatic region, Characteristics of IR absorption of functional groups: Alkanes, alkenes, alkynes, alcohol, ethers, alkyl halides, carbonyl compounds (–CHO, C=O, –COOR, –COOH), amines, amides and aromatic compounds and their substitution patterns. Factors affecting on IR absorption: Inductive effect, resonance effect, hydrogen bonding. Applications of IR spectroscopy in determination of structure, chemical reaction and hydrogen bonding.

Aims and objectives: Students should understood:

1. What is IR spectroscopy?
2. To calculate fundamental modes of vibrations for a given molecule.
3. Which factors affect IR band position?
4. To distinguish compounds by this spectroscopic method.
5. To determine structure and follow the course of reaction by IR spectrum.

(C) PMR Spectroscopy: Introduction, Principles of PMR Spectroscopy, Magnetic and nonmagnetic nuclei, Precessional motion of nuclei without mathematical details, Nuclear resonance, chemical shift, shielding and deshielding effect. Measurement of chemical shift, delta and tau-scales. TMS as reference and its advantages, peak area, integration, spin-spin coupling, coupling constants, J-value (only first order coupling be discussed).

Aims and objectives: Students should know:

1. What is the principle of PMR?
2. Various terms used in PMR spectroscopy.
3. Why TMS is used as a reference compound?
4. To distinguish compounds by PMR

(D) Problems based on U.V., I.R. and PMR.

5. Natural Products   (07)

Terpenoids: Introduction, Isolation, Classification. Citral - Structure determination using chemical and spectral methods, Synthesis of Citral by Barbier and Bouveault synthesis.

Alkaloids: Introduction, extraction, Purification, Some examples of alkaloids and their natural resources. Ephedrine - Structure determination using chemical methods. Synthesis of Ephedrine by Nagi.

Aims and objectives: Students should learn:

1. What are terpenoids and alkaloids?
2. Various methods of isolation/extraction of these natural products.
3. Synthesis of Citral and Ephedrine by Barbier-Bouveault and Nagi methods, respectively.
4. To determine the structure of above compounds by chemical methods.

■■■

Contents ...

4. Spectroscopic Methods in Structure Determination of Organic Compounds
4.1 - 4.79

■■■

Chapter 1 ...

Carbanions and their Reactions

Contents ...

1.1 Introduction

- Theoretically, any organic compound containing a C-H bond, can function as an acid by donating its proton to a suitable base and the resultant conjugate base is called as a *carbanion* (an organic compound in which carbon atom carries negative charge). Thus,

$$R_3C - H + B: \quad \rightleftharpoons \quad R_3C^{\ominus} + BH^{\oplus}$$

Organic compound   Carbanion

- There are other methods also for generation of carbanions than by proton removal, which will be discussed later. Carbanion formation is important because of its involvement in a variety of synthetically useful reactions. Many of these reactions result in the formation of carbon-carbon bonds.

1.2 Formation of Carbanions

- The most general method of forming carbanions is by removal of an atom or group X from carbon, X leaving its bonding electron pair to carbon.

$$R_3C - X + \overset{..}{Y} \rightleftharpoons R_3C^{\ominus} + XY^{\oplus}$$

(a) The most common leaving group is X = H, where it is a proton that is removed as shown above. Other leaving groups are also known but will be discussed later.

(i) The tendency of **alkanes** to lose proton and form carbanions is not marked, as they possess no structural features that either promote acidity in their H atoms or stabilize the carbanion with respect to the undissociated alkane.

However, carbanion can be obtained from triphenylmethane $Ph_3C–H$ by the action of sodamide $NaNH_2$ in liquid ammonia.

$$Ph_3\overset{\oplus}{C} – H \ + \ \overset{\oplus}{Na} \ \overset{\ominus}{NH_2} \ \underset{\rightleftharpoons}{\overset{liq.\ NH_3}{}} \ Ph_3\overset{\ominus}{C} \ \overset{\oplus}{Na} + NH_3$$

Triphenylmethane   Sodamide   Triphenylmethyl sodium

The carbanion generated is stabilized due to delocalization of negative charge over the three benzene rings and hence triphenylmethyl sodium is a very strong organic base.

(ii) **Alkenes** are slightly stronger acids than alkanes, but the **alkynes** are much more strongly acidic and the carbanion may be generated from alkynes with $NaNH_2$ in liquid ammonia.

$$R – C \equiv C–H + \overset{\oplus}{Na} \ \overset{\ominus}{NH_2} \underset{\rightleftharpoons}{\overset{liq.\ NH_3}{}} R – C \equiv \overset{\ominus}{C} \ \overset{\oplus}{Na} + NH_3$$

Alkyne   Acetylenic anion

These acetylenic anions are of synthetic importance.

(iii) The introduction of electron withdrawing substituents also increases the acidity of hydrogen atoms on carbon. Thus, the action of strong bases on chloroform forms the corresponding carbanion $\overset{\ominus}{C}Cl_3$.

(iv) The effects with *substituents that can delocalize a negative charge, as well as having an electron-withdrawing inductive effect* are even more pronounced. Thus nitromethane, CH_3NO_2, by the action of $\overset{\ominus}{O}Et$ in EtOH or even of $\overset{\ominus}{O}H$ in H_2O results in the formation of corresponding carbanion $\overset{\ominus}{C}H_2 \ NO_2$.

(b) Other leaving groups are also known. Thus,

(i) CO_2 as the leaving group from the decarboxylation of carboxylate ion $RCOO^{\ominus}$.

(ii) $Cl^{\ominus}$ as the leaving group from triphenylmethylchloride $Ph_3C - Cl$.

$$Ph_3C - Cl \xrightarrow{\text{Na/Hg}} Ph_3C^{\ominus} \overset{\oplus}{Na}$$

1.3 Stabilization of Carbanions

- The main features that serve to stabilize carbanions are as follows:

(a) Increase in 's' character at the carbanion carbon:

From alkane to alkyne the acidity of hydrogen atoms increases

$$CH_3 - CH_3 < CH_2 = CH_2 < HC \equiv CH$$

This reflects the increasing 's' character of the hybrid orbital involved in the σ bond to H i.e. $sp^3 < sp^2 < sp^1$. The 's' orbitals are closer to the nucleus than the corresponding 'p' orbitals and are at a lower energy level. The electron pair in an sp orbital is held closer to and more tightly by, the carbon atom than an electron pair in an sp^2 or sp^3 orbital. This makes the H atom more easily donated without its electron pair i.e. more acidic and also stabilizes the resultant carbanion.

(b) Electron-withdrawing inductive effect:

Consider the acidity in the following sequence:

$$CH_4 < HCF_3 < HC(CF_3)_3$$

pK_a values   43   28   11

The powerful electron-withdrawing inductive effect of the fluorine atoms, makes the H atom in HCF_3 and $HC(CF_3)_3$ more acidic than the H atom in CH_4. The resultant carbanions $^{\ominus}CF_3$ and $^{\ominus}C(CF_3)_3$ are also stabilized by electron withdrawal. The effect is more prominent in $HC(CF_3)_3$ where nine F atoms are involved, compared with only three in HCF_3. Formation of $^{\ominus}CCl_3$ from $HCCl_3$ is mentioned earlier, where a similar electron-withdrawing effect operates. This may be less effective with Cl than with the more electronegative F. This deficiency may be overcome to some extent by delocalization of the carbanion electron pair into the vacant d orbitals of second row element chlorine, which is not possible with the first row element fluorine.

On the contrary, the electron-donating inductive effect of alkyl groups destabilizes the carbanion. Thus, the observed carbanion stability sequence is:

$$\overset{\ominus}{C}H_3 > R\overset{\ominus}{C}H_2 > R_2\overset{\ominus}{C}H > R_3\overset{\ominus}{C}$$

(c) Conjugation of the carbanion lone pair with a polarized multiple bond:

This is the most common stabilizing feature, e.g. with $-CN, - C = O, - NO_2, - CO_2Et$ etc.

B: ⟶H
$$CH_2 \cdots C \equiv N \rightleftharpoons \left[\overset{\ominus}{CH_2} - C \equiv N \longleftrightarrow CH_2 = C = \overset{\ominus}{N} \right] + \overset{\oplus}{BH} \quad pK_a = 25$$

B: ⟶H
$$CH_2 \cdots \overset{Me}{\underset{\delta+ \quad \delta-}{C}} = O \rightleftharpoons \left[\overset{\ominus}{CH_2} - \overset{Me}{C} = O \longleftrightarrow CH_2 = \overset{Me}{C} - \overset{\ominus}{O} \right] + \overset{\oplus}{BH} \quad pK_a = 20$$

B: ⟶H
$$CH_2 \cdots \overset{\oplus}{N} = O \rightleftharpoons \left[\overset{\ominus}{CH_2} - \overset{\oplus}{N} = O \longleftrightarrow CH_2 = \overset{\oplus}{N} - \overset{\ominus}{O} \right] \overset{\oplus}{BH} \quad pK_a = 10.2$$
(with $O^{\ominus}$ substituents on N)

In each case, an electron-withdrawing inductive effect increases the acidity of the H atoms, but the stabilization of the resultant carbanion by delocalization is of greater significance. As expected, NO$_2$ group is most powerful. The effect of introducing more than one such group on a carbon atom is more prominent. Thus, CH(CN)$_3$ and CH(NO$_2$)$_3$ are as strong acids in water as HCl, HNO$_3$ etc.

The carboxylate group e.g. CO$_2$Et is less effective in carbanion stabilization than the $\diagup$C = O group in simple aldehydes and ketones. This may be seen from the following sequence of pK$_a$ values.

$$CH_3-\overset{O}{\overset{||}{C}}-OEt \qquad EtO-\overset{O}{\overset{||}{C}}-CH_2-\overset{O}{\overset{||}{C}}-OEt \qquad CH_3-\overset{O}{\overset{||}{C}}-CH_2-\overset{O}{\overset{||}{C}}-OEt \qquad CH_3-\overset{O}{\overset{||}{C}}-CH_2-\overset{O}{\overset{||}{C}}-CH_3$$

pK$_a$ 24   13.3   10.7   8.8

This is due to the electron-donating conjugative ability of the lone pair of electrons on the oxygen atom of the OEt group.

B: ⟶H
$$CH_2 \cdots \overset{\delta+ \quad \delta-}{C} = O \rightleftharpoons \left[\overset{\ominus}{CH_2} - C = O \longleftrightarrow CH_2 = C - \overset{\ominus}{O} \longleftrightarrow H_2\overset{\ominus}{C} - C - O^- \right] + \overset{\oplus}{BH}$$
(with :OEt substituents)

(d) Aromatisation:

Consider the case of cyclopentadiene, which has a pK$_a$ value of 16 when compared with pK$_a$ ≈ 37 for a simple alkene. This is due to the resultant carbanion, the cyclopentadienyl anion being a 6π electron delocalized system i.e. $4n + 2$ Huckel system, where $n = 1$.

Cyclopentadiene   Cyclopentadienyl anion

The 6π electrons can be accommodated in three stabilized π molecular orbitals, like benzene and the anion thus shows quasi-aromatic stabilization, it is stabilized by aromatisation.

1.4 Reactions Involving Carbanions

- Carbanions can take part in most of the main reaction types e.g. addition, elimination, displacement, rearrangement etc. Many of these reactions are synthetically useful, because they result in the formation of carbon-carbon bonds.

(i) Addition:

Carbanions which are the effective nucleophiles can undergo nucleophilic addition reaction with a carbonyl compound like an aldehyde or a ketone. Thus,

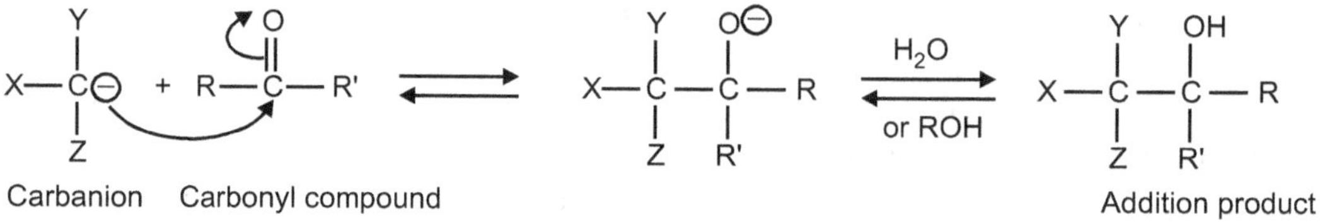

Carbanion   Carbonyl compound   Addition product

In the nucleophile $^{\ominus}CXYZ$, one or more of X, Y and Z are usually electron withdrawing in order to stabilize it. The initial adduct acquires a proton from the solvent (often H_2O or ROH) to yield the simple addition product. Examples of addition reaction are Aldol condensation, Dieckmann reaction etc. which will be discussed later in detail.

(ii) Elimination:

Carbanions are involved as intermediates in elimination reactions i.e. those that proceed by the E1cB mechanism. Thus

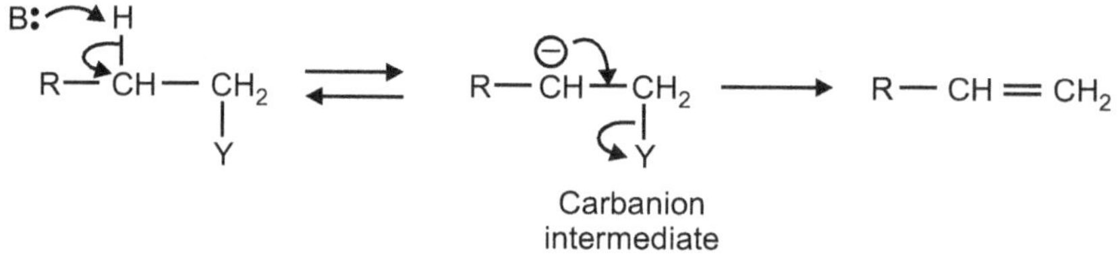

Carbanion
intermediate

(iii) Displacement:

Carbanions are involved in variety of displacement reactions either as intermediates or as attacking nucleophiles. Carbanion intermediates are involved in reactions such as *Deuterium exchange.*

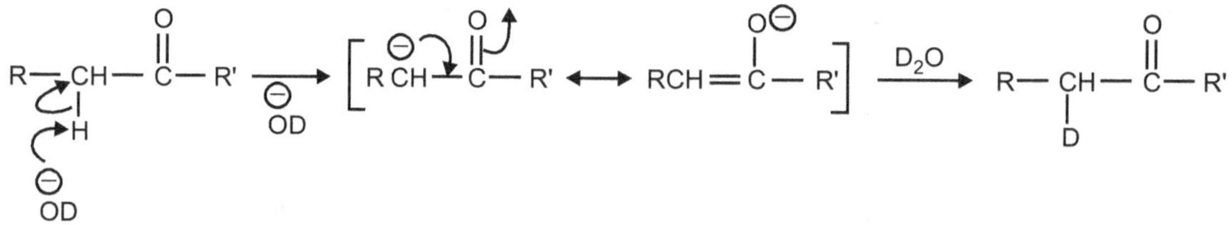

Carbanions are used as nucleophiles in synthetically useful alkylation reactions. Thus,

$$HC \equiv CH \xrightarrow{\quad NaNH_2 \quad} HC \equiv C^{\ominus} \overset{\oplus}{Na} \xrightarrow{\quad R-Br \quad} H-C \equiv C-R + NaBr$$

acetylide anion

(iv) Rearrangement:

Rearrangements involving carbanions are less commonly observed because of the unstable transition state. e.g. 1, 2-alkyl shift involving a carbanion.

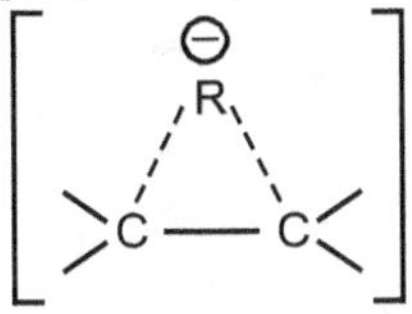

Carbanion T.S.

However, 1, 2-shifts of aryl/phenyl groups are known, where some stabilization of the carbanion T.S. is possible through delocalization of the extra electrons by the migrating phenyl group. Thus,

$$Ph_3C-CH_2Cl \xrightarrow{Na} Ph_2\overset{Ph}{\overset{|}{C}}-\overset{\ominus}{C}H_2\overset{\oplus}{Na} \longrightarrow Ph_2\overset{\ominus}{C}-\overset{Ph}{\overset{|}{C}H_2} \xrightarrow{ROH} Ph_2\overset{H}{\overset{|}{C}}-CH_2Ph$$

Carbanion Rearranged product

Some of the well-known reactions involving carbanions are as discussed below.

1.4.1 Aldol Reaction / Condensation

- In this reaction, the carbanion obtained from the action of base (usually $\overset{\ominus}{OH}$) on an α–H atom of one molecule of a carbonyl compound adds to the carbonyl carbon of another molecule to give a β-hydroxy carbonyl compound. Thus, with ethanal (or acetaldehyde) CH_3CHO, the product is 3-hydroxybutanal or aldol (containing an aldehyde and an alcoholic –OH as functional groups).

$$\underset{\text{Ethanal}}{CH_3-\overset{O}{\overset{\|}{C}}-H} + H-CH_2-\overset{O}{\overset{\|}{C}}-H \overset{\overset{\ominus}{O}H}{\rightleftharpoons} \underset{\text{3-Hydroxybutanal (Aldol)}}{\overset{4}{C}H_3-\overset{3}{\underset{\underset{H}{|}}{\overset{\overset{OH}{|}}{C}}}-\overset{2}{C}H_2-\overset{1}{C}HO}$$

Mechanism:

Step I: α-H atom from the aldehyde is abstracted by base $\overset{\ominus}{O}H$ to form the carbanion or enolate ion.

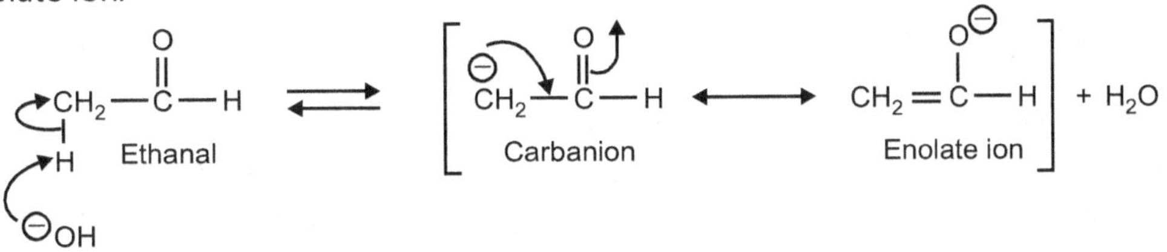

Step II: The enolate ion attacks the carbonyl carbon of another molecule of aldehyde to form a new carbon-carbon bond and an anion results.

Step III: The anion formed in earlier step picks up a proton from water to form β-hydroxy aldehyde (aldol).

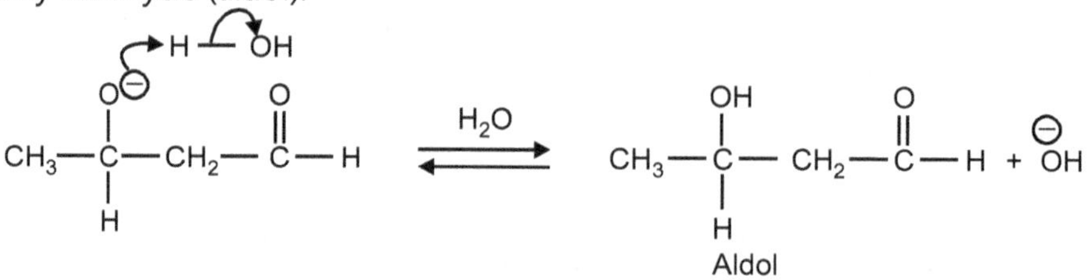

- All the steps shown are reversible, but in case of ethanal the equilibrium is found to shift to the right in favour of aldol. When the reaction is carried out in D_2O, deuterium is not incorporated into the CH_3 group of as yet unchanged ethanal. This indicates that step II is more rapid than the reverse of step I, which makes step I almost irreversible.
- Aldol thus formed, readily loses a molecule of water (dehydration) when heated with aqueous acid to give α, β-unsaturated aldehyde.

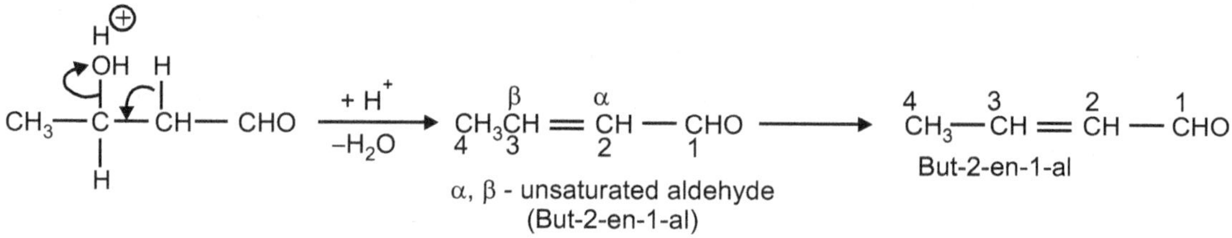

α, β - unsaturated aldehyde
(But-2-en-1-al)

But-2-en-1-al

- Dehydration of aldols may also be effected under the influence of base e.g. with aldol formed from ethanal.

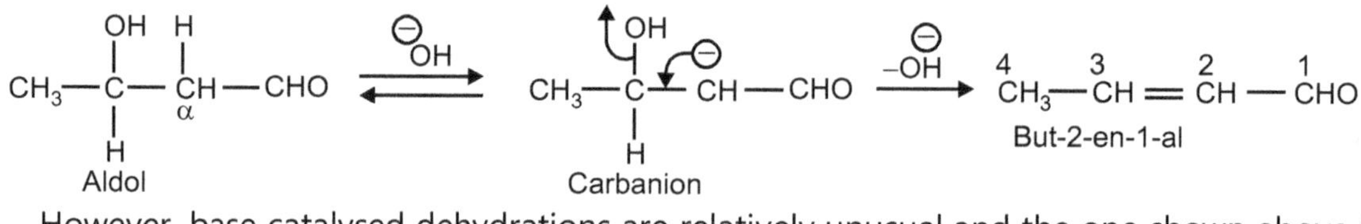

But-2-en-1-al

- However, base catalysed dehydrations are relatively unusual and the one shown above is due to the facts that (i) the aldol contains α-H atoms removable by base to yield ambient concentration of carbanion and (ii) this carbanion possesses a good leaving group $^{\ominus}OH$ on the adjacent carbon atom.
- The possibility of such an elimination may displace the equilibrium to the right in a number of simple aldol additions, where it would otherwise lie far over to the left. However, it should be remembered that the overall process of aldol formation and dehydration is reversible.

- Similar to aldehydes, simple ketones can also react with base to generate a carbanion which on reaction with second molecule of ketone can give a β-hydroxyketone. e.g. propanone (acetone).

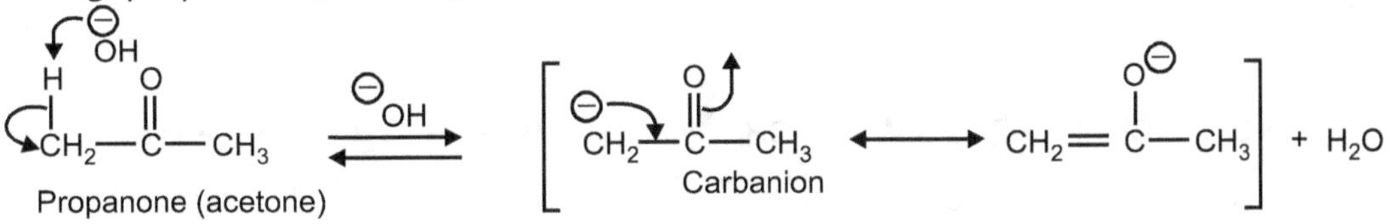

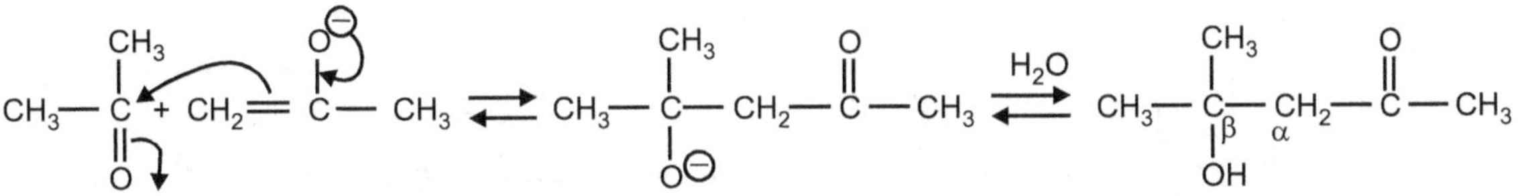

Propanone (acetone) → Carbanion + H_2O

β-hydroxy ketone
(Diacetone alcohol)

- But here, the equilibrium is found to lie far over to the left (~2% of β-hydroxyketone) reflecting the less readily attack of the carbanion on a 'keto' rather than on an 'aldehydro' carbonyl carbon atom. Thus, in case of propanone, carrying out the reaction in D_2O results in the incorporation of deuterium into the CH_3 group of as yet unchanged propanone.

- However, this reaction can be made efficient for the preparation of β-hydroxyketone by a continuous distillation/siphoning process in a Soxhlet apparatus. The details of this process will not be discussed here.

Crossed Aldol Condensation:

- Condensation between two different aldehydes (or other suitable carbonyl compounds) having α-H atoms are synthetically not useful because a mixture of four different products can result. e.g. reaction between ethanal (acetaldehyde) and propanal (propanaldehyde).

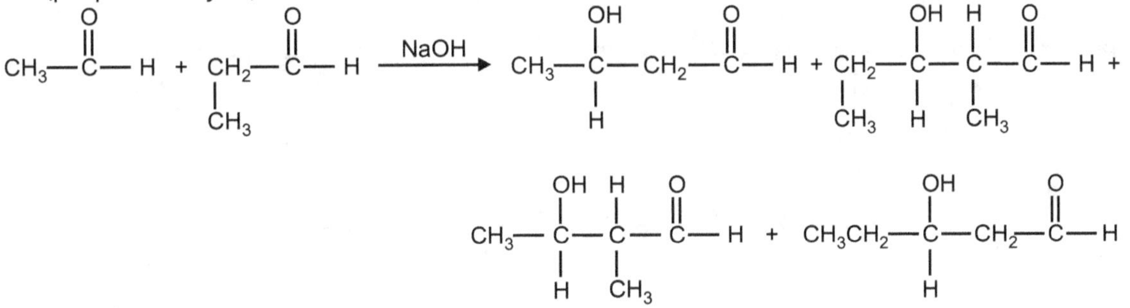

- However, such reactions can be synthetically useful, when one aldehyde (or a carbonyl compound has no α-H atoms, and can thus act as a carbanion acceptor. Examples of such aldehydes are benzaldehyde, formaldehyde etc. In such cases, this aldehyde is mixed with base and the carbonyl compound having α-hydrogen is added slowly to the above mixture (to avoid self condensation).

- **Mechanism** for reaction between ethanal (acetaldehyde) and formaldehyde is given below:

Step I:

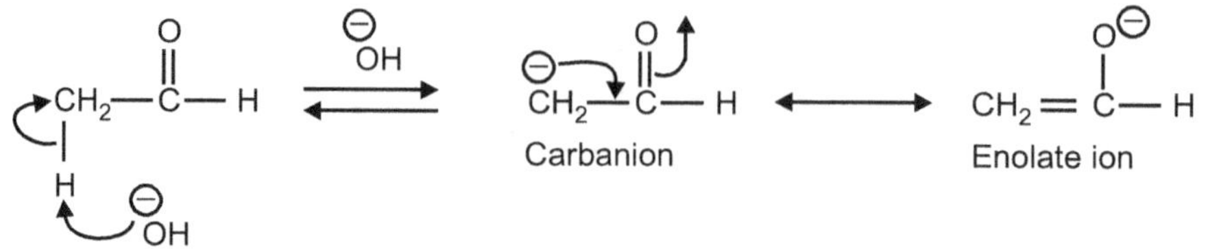

Carbanion Enolate ion

Step II:

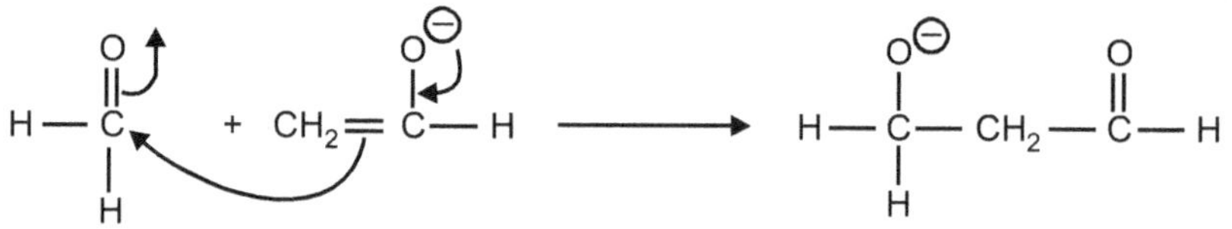

Formaldehyde (no α-H) Enolate ion

Step III:

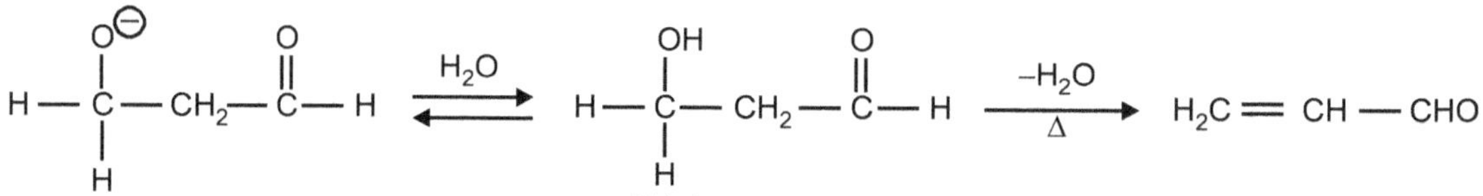

Aldol Propenal

- Many times dehydration takes place under the reaction conditions itself or just by heating.

Other examples of crossed aldol reactions:

(i)

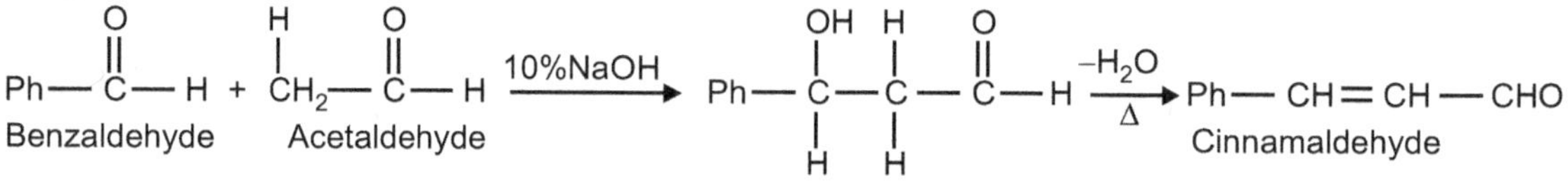

Benzaldehyde Acetaldehyde Cinnamaldehyde

(ii)

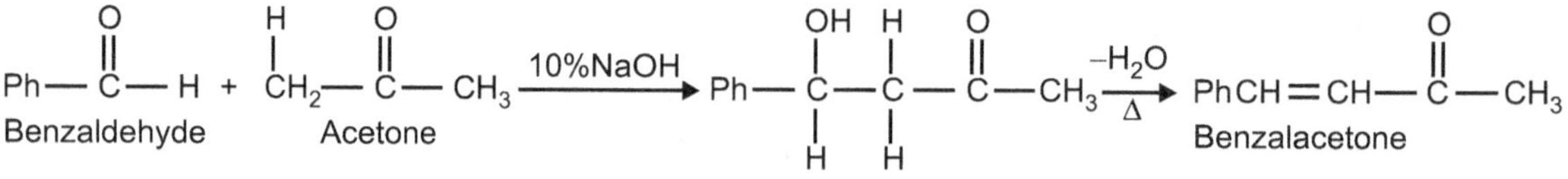

Benzaldehyde Acetone Benzalacetone

(iii)

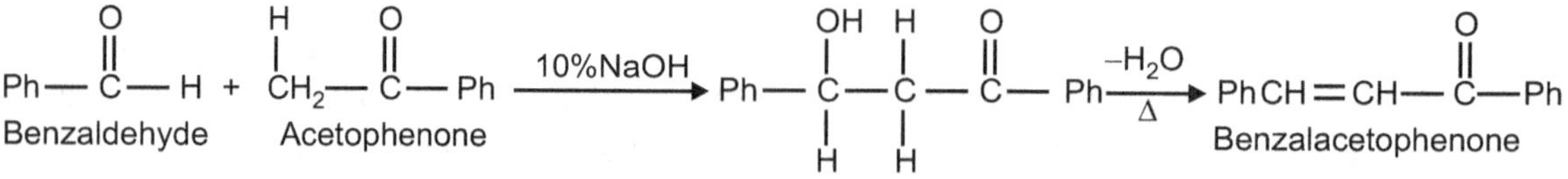

Benzaldehyde Acetophenone Benzalacetophenone

Intramolecular aldol condensation:

- Suitable dicarbonyl compounds when treated with base undergo intramolecular aldol condensation leading to cyclisation.

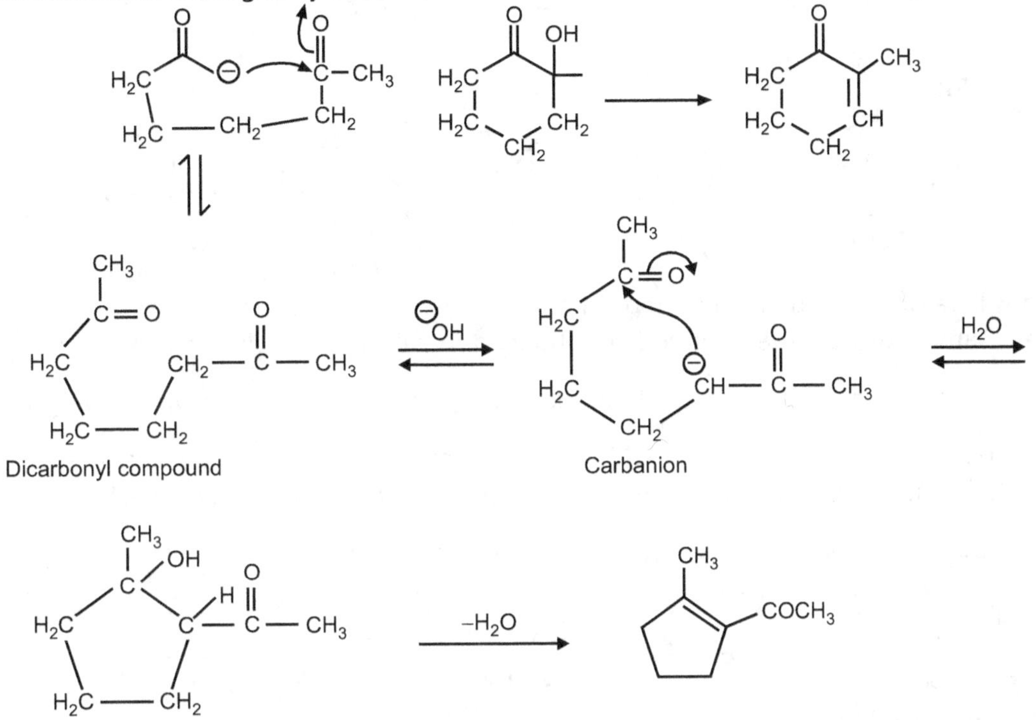

Dicarbonyl compound   Carbanion

1.4.2 Claisen Ester Condensation

- This is another reaction that involves carbanion derived from esters. This carbanion adds to the carbonyl carbon atom of another ester molecule.
- Thus, concentration of an ester molecule having α-hydrogen atom with another molecule of same or different ester is known as Claisen condensation. It can be considered as a reaction of esters similar to aldol condensation of aldehydes. Thus,

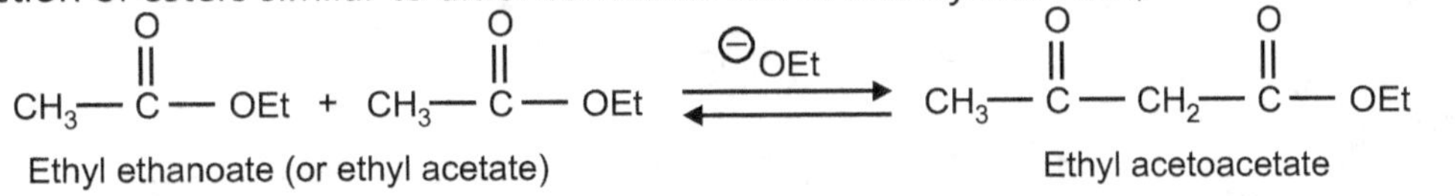

Ethyl ethanoate (or ethyl acetate)   Ethyl acetoacetate

Generally the base used is sodium ethoxide NaOEt or ethoxide ion $\overset{\ominus}{OEt}$.

Mechanism:

Step I:

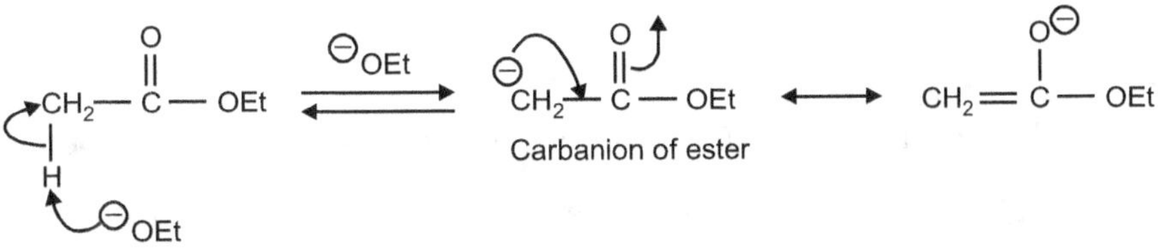

Carbanion of ester

Step II:

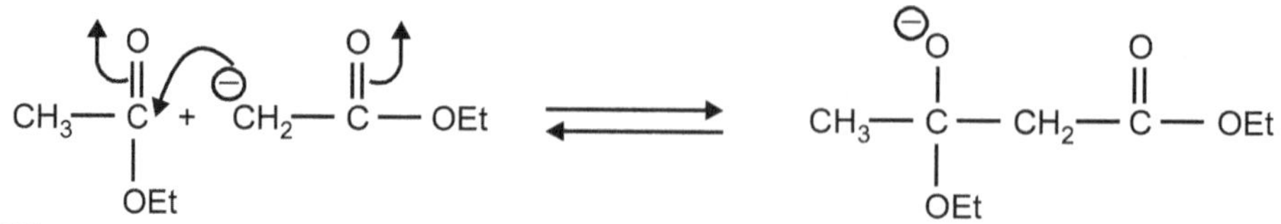

Step III:

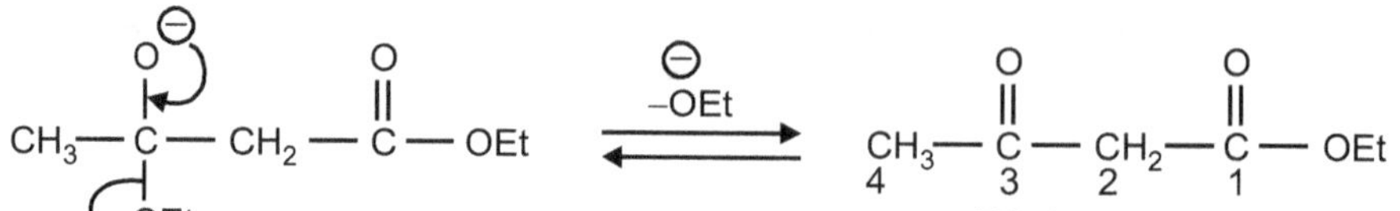

Ethylaceto acetate
(or ethyl-3-ketobutanoate)

- It will be observed that initial steps in aldol condensation and Claisen ester condensation are same, but now the intermediate obtained in step II is having a good leaving group $\overset{\ominus}{O}Et$. Hence, in step III instead of picking up a hydrogen from water (as in aldol condensation), $\overset{\ominus}{O}Et$ is lost to yield a β-ketoester, ethyl-3-keto-butanoate. It should be noted that the product β-ketoester (ethylacetoacetate) itself contains α-H atom which can be removed in presence of base $\overset{\ominus}{O}Et$ into a stabilized carbanion.

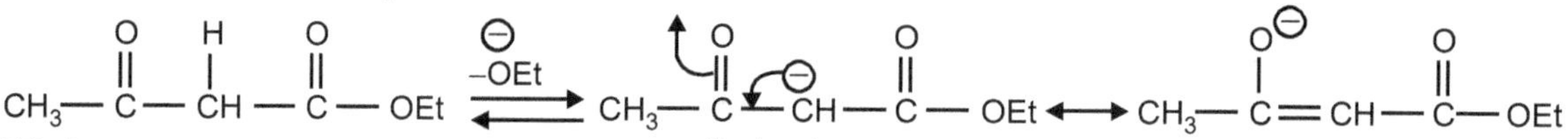

Ethylaceto acetate Carbanion

Important Features:

(i) The carbanion of ester is less effectively stabilized than the carbanion of aldehyde in aldol condensation.

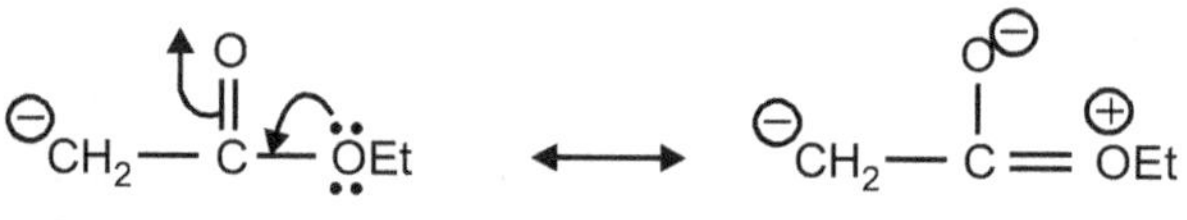

Less effective stabilization of carbanion

Carbanion of ester

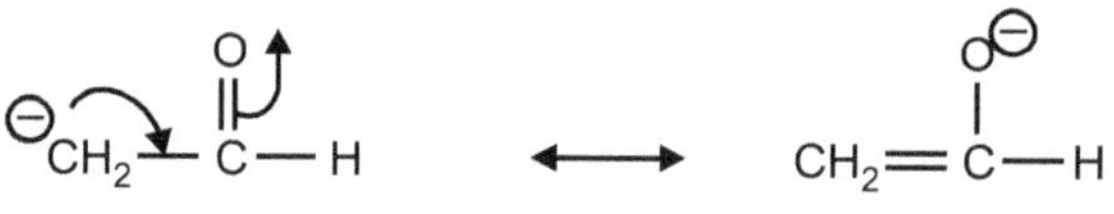

Effective stabilization of carbanion

Carbanion of aldehyde

(ii) No reaction occurs with R_2CHCO_2Et (contains only one α-H) in the presence of $\overset{\ominus}{O}Et$, even though the β-ketoester $R_2CH - \overset{\overset{O}{||}}{C} - CR_2 - \overset{\overset{O}{||}}{C}-OEt$ is expected to be formed. It should be observed that this β-ketoester has no α-H atom and hence cannot be converted to a carbanion similar to that in ethylacetoacetate in the presence of $\overset{\ominus}{O}Et$.

- However, use of a base like $Ph_3\overset{\ominus}{C}\overset{\oplus}{Na}$ which is sufficiently strong to make step I almost irreversible in the forward direction is found to induce a normal Claisen reaction in R_2CHCO_2Et.

$$R_2CHCO_2Et + Ph_3\overset{\ominus}{C}\overset{\oplus}{Na} \rightleftharpoons R_2\overset{\ominus}{C}CO_2Et$$

$$R_2CHCO_2Et + R_2\overset{\ominus}{C}CO_2Et \rightleftharpoons R_2CH-\overset{O}{\overset{||}{C}}-CR_2-\overset{O}{\overset{||}{C}}-OEt$$

Crossed Claisen reaction:

- Claisen condensation with two different esters, each of which is having α-H atoms results in the formation of four possible products and hence synthetically not much useful.

- However, when one of the two esters has no α-H atoms e.g. HCOOEt, ArCOOEt, $(COOEt)_2$ etc. then crossed Claisen condensation is very useful. This is because, such acids can act only as a carbanion acceptor and the side reaction of the self condensation of the other ester RCH_2COOEt does not create problem. Thus,

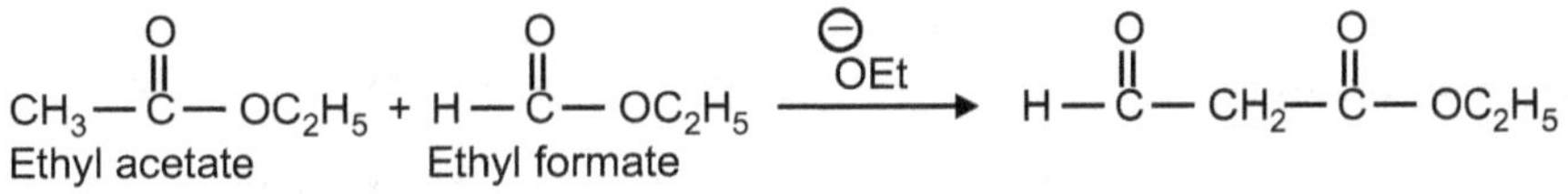

$$CH_3-\overset{O}{\overset{||}{C}}-OC_2H_5 + H-\overset{O}{\overset{||}{C}}-OC_2H_5 \xrightarrow{\overset{\ominus}{OEt}} H-\overset{O}{\overset{||}{C}}-CH_2-\overset{O}{\overset{||}{C}}-OC_2H_5$$
Ethyl acetate   Ethyl formate

Mechanism:

Step I:

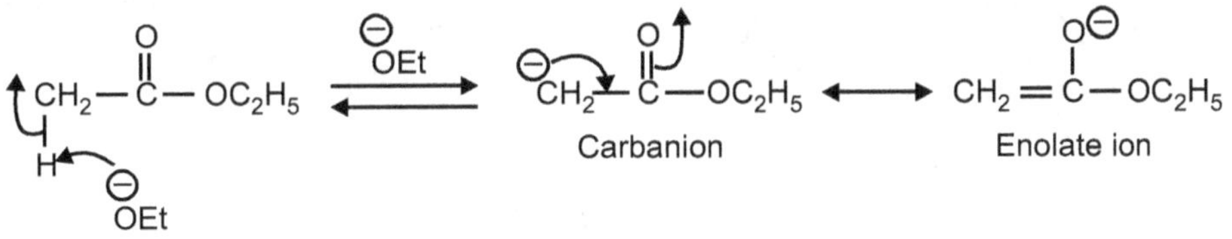

Carbanion   Enolate ion

Step II:

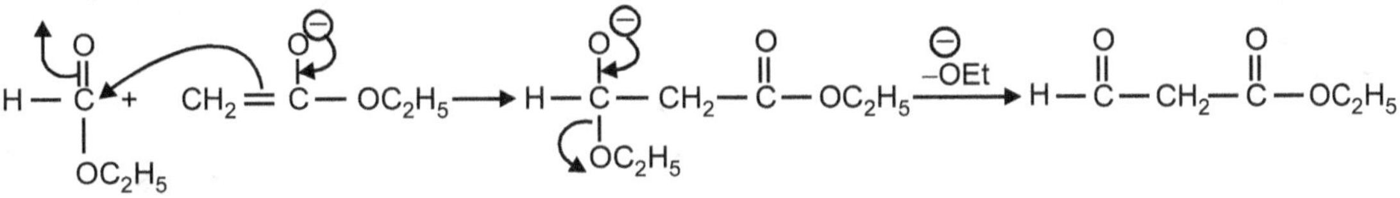

Other examples are:

(i)

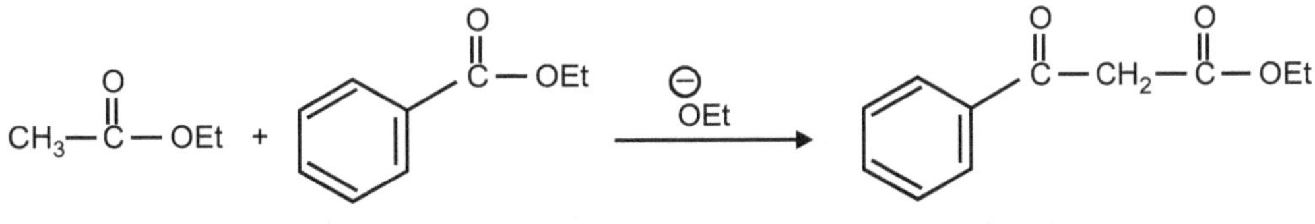

(ii) $H–\overset{\displaystyle O}{\overset{\displaystyle \|}{C}}–OEt + CH_3CH_2–\overset{\displaystyle O}{\overset{\displaystyle \|}{C}}–OEt \xrightarrow{\overset{\ominus}{OEt}} H–\overset{\displaystyle O}{\overset{\displaystyle \|}{C}}–\underset{\underset{\displaystyle CH_3}{|}}{CH}–\overset{\displaystyle O}{\overset{\displaystyle \|}{C}}–OEt$

(iii) $EtO–\overset{\displaystyle O}{\overset{\displaystyle \|}{C}}–OEt + PhCH_2–\overset{\displaystyle O}{\overset{\displaystyle \|}{C}}–OEt \xrightarrow{\overset{\ominus}{OEt}} EtO–\overset{\displaystyle O}{\overset{\displaystyle \|}{C}}–\underset{\underset{\displaystyle Ph}{|}}{CH}–\overset{\displaystyle O}{\overset{\displaystyle \|}{C}}–OEt$

1.4.3 Dieckmann Cyclisation

- Intramolecular Claisen reactions, where both CO_2Et groups are part of the same molecule, are referred to as Dieckmann cyclisations. Under simple conditions, these work best for the formation of anions of 5-, 6- or 7- membered cyclic β-ketoesters i.e. with $EtO_2C(CH_2)_nCO_2Et$ where n = 4, 5, 6. Here, carbanion formed preferentially attacks ester carbonyl carbon atom at the other end of the chain of the molecule (intramolecular) rather than ester carbonyl carbon of another molecule (intermolecular).

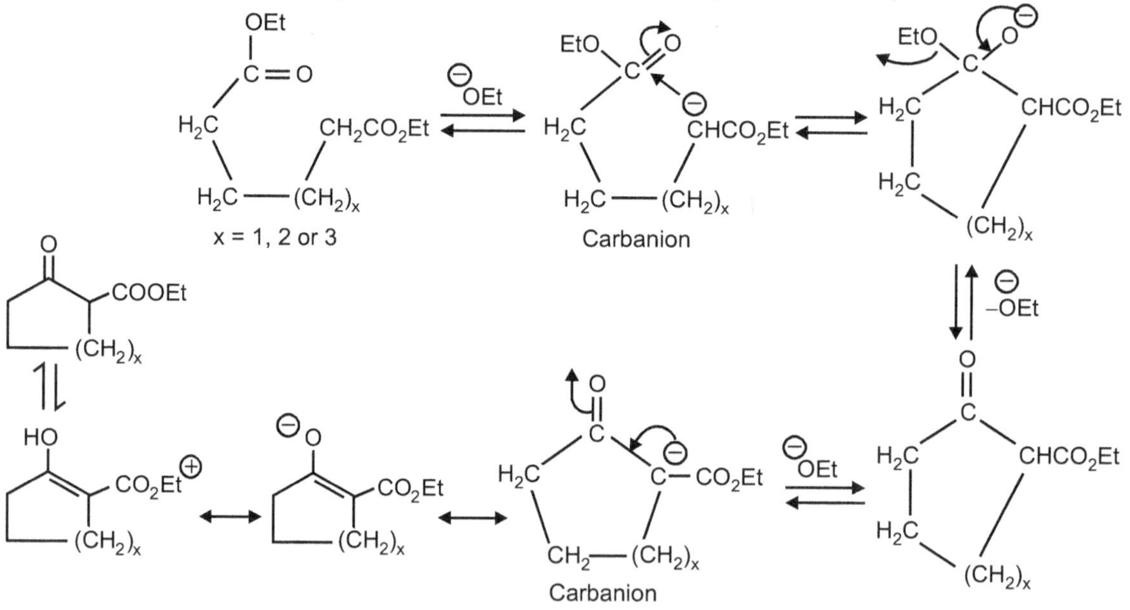

- Large ring ketones may also be obtained by using high dilution when chances of intramolecular reaction are more rather than intermolecular reaction.

1.4.4 Perkin Reaction

- Perkin reaction is the condensation of an aromatic aldehyde and an aliphatic acid anhydride containing at least two α-hydrogen atoms, in the presence of sodium or potassium salt of corresponding acid to form α, β-unsaturated acid. Thus,

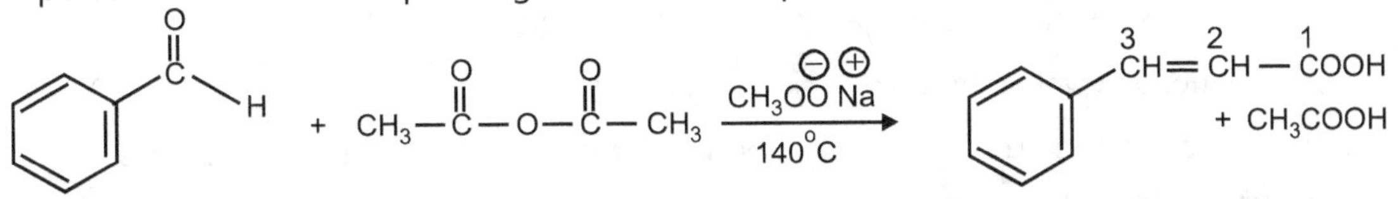

Benzaldehyde   Acetic anhydride   Cinnamic acid
                                                      or 3-phenyl propenoic acid

Mechanism:

- Here, the carbanion is obtained by removal of an α-H atom from a molecule of acid anhydride by base (in this case CH₃COO). The carbanion attacks the carbonyl carbon of the aldehyde to yield the alkoxide anion. Internal transfer of the acetyl group in this anion takes place from the carboxyl oxygen atom to alkoxy oxygen atom via the cyclic intermediate, thereby forming a more stable species. Removal of an α-H atom from this anion by CH₃COO results in the loss of the good leaving group CH₃COO from the adjacent β-position to yield the anion of the α, β-unsaturated acid. The reaction mixture on acidification with dilute acid leads to the product i.e. α, β-unsaturated acid.

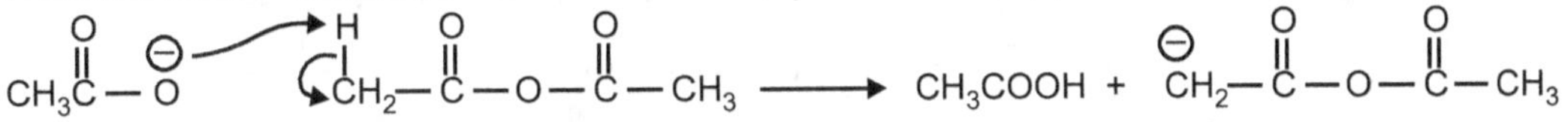

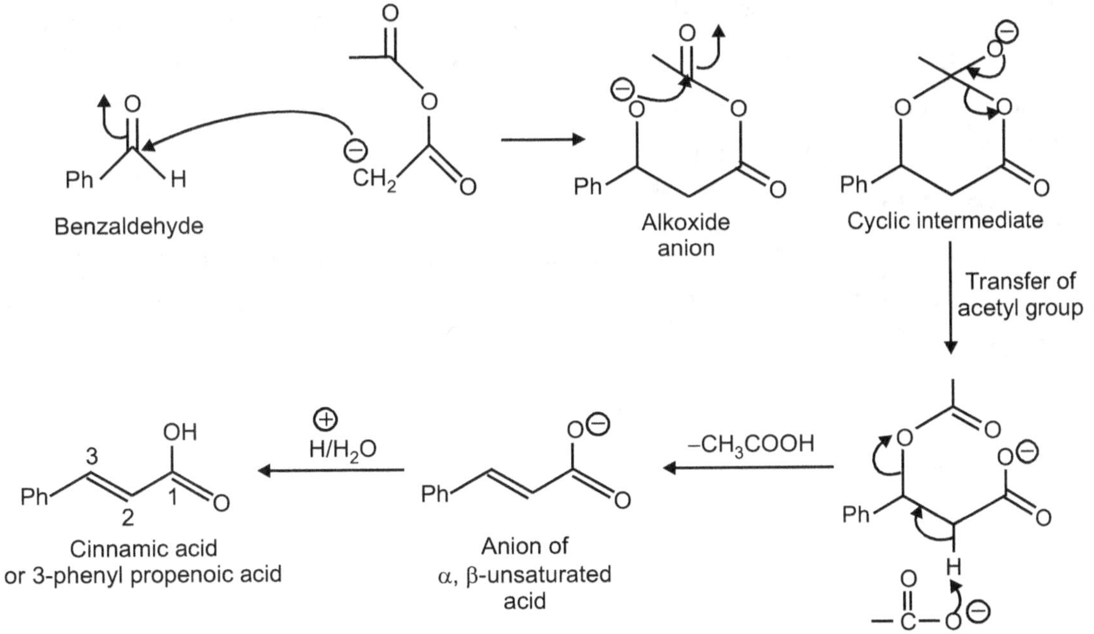

1.5 Synthesis and Applications of Synthetic Reagents

- Organic synthesis deals with building up of large complex molecules from simple easily available compounds. In synthesis, two main types of reactions are important:

  (i)   Reactions in which the functional group is changed.

  (ii) Reactions in which the carbon skeleton is built-up.

- In formation of new carbon-carbon bonds from small molecules, carbanions play an important role. In this connection, we are going to study applications of some synthetic reagents. They are:

  1.   Malonic ester (Diethyl malonate)

  2.   Acetoacetic ester (Ethylacetoacetate)

  3.   Wittig reagent.

1.5.1 Malonic Ester (Diethyl Malonate)

$$H_5C_2O - \overset{\overset{\textstyle O}{\|}}{C} - CH_2 - \overset{\overset{\textstyle O}{\|}}{C} - OC_2H_5$$

↑

Reactive methylene group

- In malonic ester, the methylene group is in between two carbonyl groups. Due to strong electron-withdrawing groups on both sides, hydrogen atoms of the methylene group (α-hydrogens w.r. to carbonyl) are highly acidic i.e. they can be easily removed by a base to form a carbanion which is stabilized due to two adjacent carbonyl groups. This can be further used to form new C-C bond.

Synthesis of Malonic Ester:

- Malonic ester is prepared by reacting sodium chloroacetate with a cyanide when first sodium cyanoacetate is formed, which is then heated with ethyl alcohol in the presence of H_2SO_4.

$$Cl - CH_2\overset{\ominus}{C}O\overset{\oplus}{O}Na \xrightarrow{\overset{\ominus}{C}N} \underset{CN}{\overset{\overset{\ominus}{C}O\overset{\oplus}{O}Na}{\underset{|}{\overset{|}{CH_2}}}} \xrightarrow[H_2SO_4, \Delta]{C_2H_5OH} \underset{COOC_2H_5}{\overset{COOC_2H_5}{\underset{|}{\overset{|}{CH_2}}}} + \overset{\oplus}{N}H_4$$

Sodium chloroacetate   Sodium cyanoacetate   Diethyl malonate

Synthetic Applications:

1. Synthesis of a substituted acetic acid – Alkylation:

- Malonic ester when treated with sodium ethoxide in absolute alcohol, is converted into its salt, sodiomalonic ester by removal of the acidic hydrogen from active methylene group.

Sodiomalonic ester

- Reaction of this salt with an alkyl halide yields a substituted malonic ester, often called as an **alkyl malonic ester**.

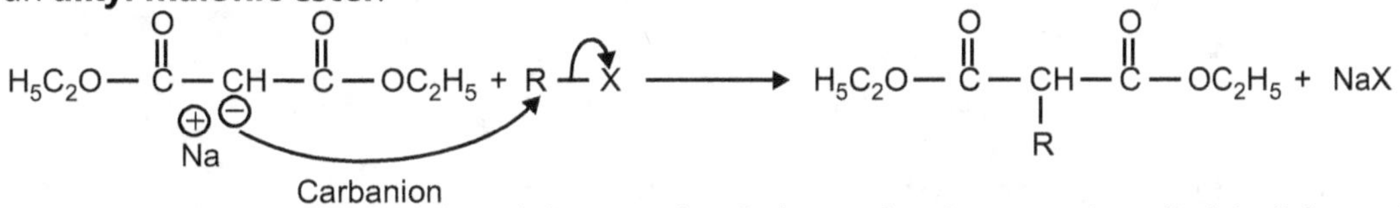

Carbanion

- This reaction involves nucleophilic attack of the carbanion on the alkyl halide and as expected gives highest yields with primary alkyl halides, lower yields with secondary alkyl halides, while for tertiary alkyl halides and aryl halides very poor yields.

- Malonic acid ($HOOC - CH_2 - COOH$), when heated above its melting point, readily loses carbon dioxide to form acetic acid. Similarly, substituted malonic acids readily lose carbon dioxide to form substituted acetic acids. The alkyl malonic ester prepared earlier is readily converted into monocarboxylic acid by hydrolysis, acidification and heat.

Alkyl malonic ester

Thus, with CH_3I (methyl iodide), propanoic acid CH_3CH_2COOH results.

Important features:

1. In the final product $-CH_2 - \overset{\overset{\displaystyle O}{\|}}{C} - OH$ part is coming from malonic ester.
2. Group R is coming from alkyl halide (CH_3 from CH_3I).
3. In hydrolysis step both –COOEt groups are converted into –COOH.
4. On heating only one –COOH is lost and α-substituted acid is formed.
5. In the final product one α-hydrogen atom comes from decarboxylation.

6. As there are two acidic hydrogens in diethyl malonate, two alkyl groups can be joined. Thus,

$$RCH(COOC_2H_5)_2 + C_2H_5\overset{\ominus}{O}\overset{\oplus}{N}a \underset{\leftarrow}{\longrightarrow} R\overset{\ominus}{C}(COOC_2H_5)_2\overset{\oplus}{N}a + C_2H_5OH$$

$$R\overset{\ominus}{C}(COOC_2H_5)_2 \xrightarrow{R'X} \underset{\underset{|}{\overset{|}{R'}}}{R-C(COOC_2H_5)_2} \xrightarrow[\text{(ii) } H^+]{\text{(i) } H_2O,\ \overset{\ominus}{O}H,\ \Delta} \underset{\underset{COOH}{\overset{|}{R-C-R'}}}{\overset{COOH}{\overset{|}{}}}$$

$$\underset{\underset{COOH}{\overset{|}{R-C-R'}}}{\overset{COOH}{\overset{|}{}}} \xrightarrow[\substack{140°C,\\ -CO_2}]{\text{Heat}} \underset{\underset{H}{\overset{|}{R-C-COOH}}}{\overset{R'}{\overset{|}{}}}$$

Disubstituted
acetic acid

Consider the **synthesis of 2-methyl butanoic acid:**

$$\underset{4}{CH_3}-\underset{3}{CH_2}-\underset{2}{\overset{\alpha}{\underset{|}{CH}}}-\underset{1}{\overset{O}{\overset{||}{C}}}-OH$$
$$CH_3$$

- It is a disubstituted acetic acid, C_1 and C_2 coming from malonic ester. The two groups attached to C_2 are $-CH_3$ and $-CH_2CH_3$, hence dialkylation is to be carried out using two halides CH_3Br and CH_3CH_2Br. The α-H is coming after decarboxylation.
- Thus, the steps involved in this synthesis are:

$$\underset{\text{Diethyl malonate}}{EtO-\overset{O}{\overset{||}{C}}-CH_2-\overset{O}{\overset{||}{C}}-OEt} \xrightarrow[\text{EtOH}]{\text{NaOEt}} \underset{\underset{\text{Carbanion}}{\overset{\oplus}{Na}}}{EtO-\overset{O}{\overset{||}{C}}-\overset{\ominus}{CH}-\overset{O}{\overset{||}{C}}-OEt} \xrightarrow[-NaBr]{CH_3Br}$$

$$\underset{\underset{CH_3}{\overset{|}{}}}{EtO-\overset{O}{\overset{||}{C}}-\overset{|}{CH}-\overset{O}{\overset{||}{C}}\!\!=\!\!OEt} \xrightarrow[\text{EtOH}]{\text{NaOEt}} \underset{\underset{CH_3}{\overset{|}{}}}{EtO-\overset{O}{\overset{||}{C}}-\overset{\overset{Na^\oplus}{\ominus}}{C}-\overset{O}{\overset{||}{C}}-OEt} \xrightarrow{CH_3CH_2Br}$$

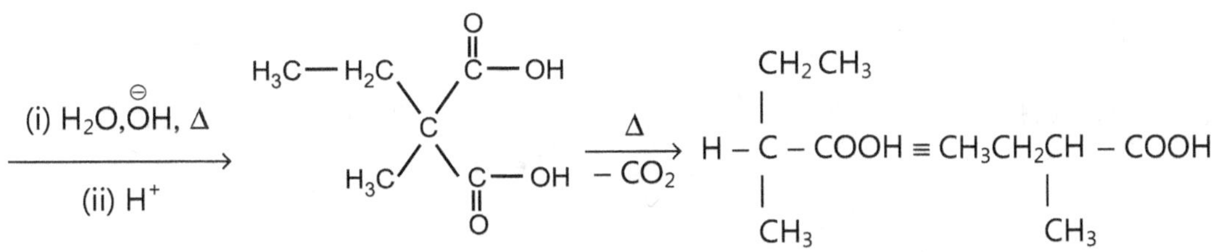

$$\xrightarrow[\text{(ii) H}^+]{\text{(i) H}_2\text{O},\overset{\ominus}{\text{O}}\text{H, }\Delta}$$

Dicarboxylic acid

$$\xrightarrow[-CO_2]{\Delta} \quad H - \underset{\underset{CH_3}{|}}{\overset{\overset{CH_2\,CH_3}{|}}{C}} - COOH \equiv CH_3CH_2\underset{\underset{CH_3}{|}}{CH} - COOH$$

2-methyl butanoic acid

2. Synthesis of succinic acid:

Succinic acid is

$$\underset{CH_2COOH}{\overset{CH_2COOH}{|}}$$

It is clear that instead of alkyl halide if we use α-haloester, we should get succinic acid.

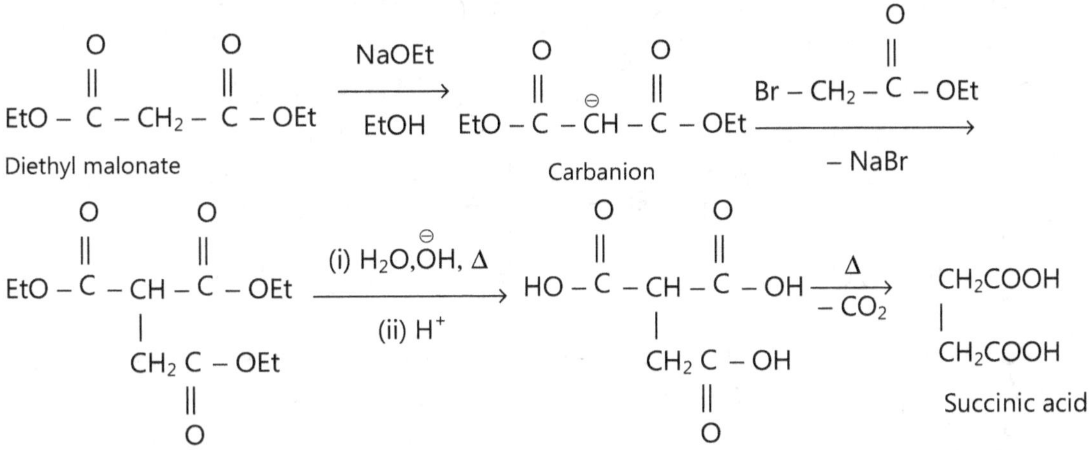

Diethyl malonate   Carbanion   – NaBr

Succinic acid

3. Synthesis of γ-dicarboxylic acid:

Two moles of malonic ester when condensed with CH_2X_2 in the presence of base, form a tetraester which on hydrolysis and decarboxylation produce γ-dicarboxylic acid.

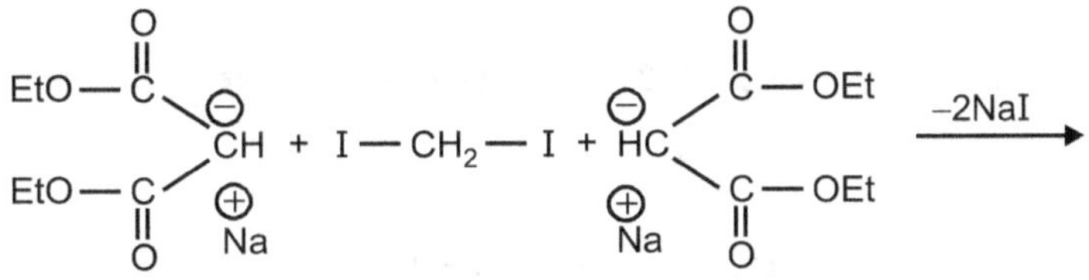

$$\underset{\substack{\text{COOEt} \qquad\qquad \text{COOEt} \\ | \qquad\qquad\qquad | }}{\text{EtOOC} - \text{CH} - \text{CH}_2 - \text{CH} - \text{COOEt}} \xrightarrow[\text{(ii) H}^+]{\text{(i) HOH, } \overset{\ominus}{\text{OH}}} \underset{\substack{\text{COOH} \qquad\qquad \text{COOH} \\ | \qquad\qquad\qquad | }}{\text{HOOC} - \text{CH} - \text{CH}_2 - \text{CH} - \text{COOH}}$$

Tetracarboxylic acid

$$\xrightarrow[-2\ CO_2]{\Delta} \overset{5\qquad\ 4\qquad\ 3\qquad\ 2\qquad\ 1}{\text{HOOC} - \underset{\gamma}{\text{CH}_2} - \underset{\beta}{\text{CH}_2} - \underset{\alpha}{\text{CH}_2} - \text{COOH}}$$

Pentane-1, 5-dicarboxylic acid or γ-dicarboxylic acid

(Glutaric acid)

4. Synthesis of cycloalkane carboxylic acid:

Instead of an alkyl halide, if a dihaloalkane is condensed with malonic ester in the presence of a base, cycloalkane dicarboxylic acid is first formed which on decarboxylation give cycloalkane carboxylic acid.

$$\underset{\substack{\text{O}\qquad\qquad\text{O}\\||\qquad\qquad||}}{\text{EtO} - \text{C} - \text{CH}_2 - \text{C} - \text{OEt}} \xrightarrow[\text{EtOH}]{\overset{\oplus\ \ominus}{\text{NaOEt}}} \underset{\substack{||\\ \text{O}}}{\overset{\substack{\text{O}\\||}}{\text{NaC}} \overset{\text{C} - \text{OEt}}{\underset{\text{C} - \text{OEt}}{\big\langle}}} \xrightarrow{\text{Br} - \text{CH}_2 - \text{CH}_2 - \text{CH}_2 - \text{CH}_2\text{Br}}$$

$$\underset{\substack{\text{O}\qquad\quad\text{O}\\||\qquad\quad||\\ \text{EtO} - \text{C} - \text{CH} - \text{C} - \text{OEt}\\|\\ \text{CH}_2\ \text{CH}_2\ \text{CH}_2\ \text{CH}_2\ \text{Br}\\ \text{COOEt}}}{} \xrightarrow{\overset{\oplus\ \ominus}{\text{NaOEt}}} \underset{\substack{\text{O}\qquad \text{COOEt}\\||\qquad\ |\\ \text{EtO} - \text{C} - \overset{\oplus}{\underset{|}{\text{C}}}\overset{\ominus}{} \text{Na}\\ \text{CH}_2 - \text{CH}_2 - \text{CH}_2}}{} \xrightarrow[\text{CH}_2\,\text{Br}]{- \text{NaBr}}$$

$$\underset{\text{HOOC}}{\equiv} \left[\ \text{pentagon}\ \right] \quad \text{Cyclopentane carboxylic acid}$$

1.5.2 Acetoacetic Ester (or Ethylacetoacetate)

$$\underset{\beta}{\overset{\substack{\text{O}\qquad\quad\text{O}\\||\quad\ \alpha\quad||}}{\text{CH}_3 - \text{C} - \text{CH}_2 - \text{C} - \text{OC}_2\text{H}_5}}$$

- In acetoacetic ester, methylene group is adjacent (or α-) to two carbonyl groups. The two hydrogen atoms on this carbon are therefore acidic and can be removed by base to generate a carbanion.

Synthesis:

- Acetoacetic ester or ethyl acetoacetate is a β-ketoester and its synthesis by a **Claisen ester condensation** is discussed earlier:

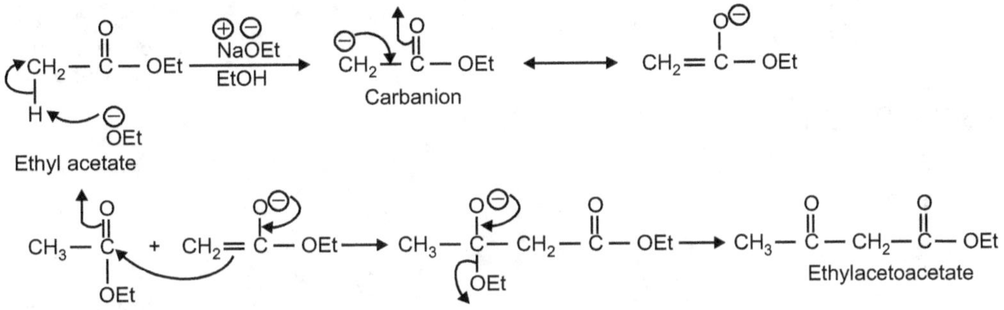

Synthetic Applications:

1. Acetoacetic ester synthesis of ketones:

- This synthesis is very similar to malonic ester synthesis of carboxylic acids.

- Acetoacetic ester is first converted by sodium ethoxide into the sodioacetic ester which is then reacted with an alkyl halide R–X to form an alkylacetoacetic ester $CH_3COCHRCOOC_2H_5$; if required the alkylation can be repeated using R'X to yield a dialkyl-acetoacetic ester, $CH_3COCRR'COOC_2H_5$. All alkylations are conducted in absolute alcohol.

- After hydrolysis by dilute aqueous alkali (or by acid), these monoalkyl acetoacetic or dialkylaceto acetic esters yield the corresponding acids $CH_3COCHRCOOH$ or $CH_3CORR'COOH$, which undergo decarboxylation to form ketones CH_3COCH_2R or $CH_3COCHRR'$. This loss of carbon dioxide occurs even more readily than from malonic acid, and may even take place before acidification of the hydrolysis mixture.

- Thus, acetoacetic ester synthesis of ketones yields an acetone molecule in which one or two hydrogen atoms have been replaced by alkyl groups.

- In planning an acetoacetic ester synthesis of a ketone, important thing is to select proper alkyl halide or halides. For this, we have to look closely the structure of the ketone to be synthesized.

$$CH_3COCH_2COOC_2H_5 \xrightarrow[C_2H_5OH]{\overset{\ominus}{C_2H_5}\overset{\oplus}{O}Na} CH_3\overset{\ominus}{C}OCHCOOC_2H_5 \xrightarrow{R-X}$$

Acetoacetic ester   Stabilised carbanion

$$CH_3COCHCOOC_2H_5 \xrightarrow{\overset{\ominus}{O}H,\ H_2O} CH_3COCHCO\overset{\ominus}{O} \xrightarrow{H_2O,\ H^+} CH_3COCHCOOH$$
$$\underset{R}{|} \qquad\qquad\qquad \underset{R}{|} \qquad\qquad\qquad \underset{R}{|}$$

Monoalkyl aceto acetic ester

$$\downarrow \overset{\overset{\ominus}{C_2H_5}\overset{\oplus}{O}Na}{C_2H_5OH}$$

$$CH_3CO\overset{\ominus}{C}\ COOC_2H_5$$
$$\underset{R}{|}$$

$$\downarrow R'X$$

$$\underset{R}{\overset{R'}{\underset{|}{\overset{|}{CH_3CO-C-COOC_2H_5}}}} \xrightarrow{\overset{\ominus}{O}H,\ H_2O} \underset{R'}{\overset{R}{\underset{|}{\overset{|}{CH_3CO-C-CO\overset{\ominus}{O}}}}} \xrightarrow{H_2O,\ H^+} \underset{R'}{\overset{R}{\underset{|}{\overset{|}{CH_3CO-C-COOH}}}}$$

For the monoalkyl branch:

$$\Delta \Big| -CO_2$$

$$CH_3COCH_2-R$$
A monosubstituted acetone

For the dialkyl branch:

$$\Delta \Big| -CO_2$$

$$\underset{R'}{\overset{R}{\underset{|}{\overset{|}{CH_3CO-C-H}}}}$$
Disubstituted acetone

- For example, consider the **synthesis of 3-ethyl-2-pentanone**.

$$\overset{1}{CH_3}-\overset{2}{\overset{O}{\overset{||}{C}}}-\overset{3}{CH}-\overset{4}{\overset{5}{CH_2CH_3}}$$ 3-ethyl-2-pentanone
$$|$$
$$CH_2CH_3$$

- It will be observed that this is a disubstituted acetone and the two substituents are the ethyl substituents. Hence, two moles of ethyl halide will be required. Thus, the sequence of reactions will be as follows:

$$\underset{\text{Ethylaceto acetate}}{CH_3-\overset{O}{\overset{||}{C}}-CH_2-\overset{O}{\overset{||}{C}}-OEt} \xrightarrow[\text{EtOH}]{\overset{\oplus}{N}a\overset{\ominus}{O}Et} \overset{\oplus}{N}a\ \overset{\ominus}{C}\Big\langle \begin{matrix} \overset{O}{\overset{||}{C}}-OEt \\ \\ C-OEt \\ \overset{||}{O} \end{matrix} \xrightarrow[-\text{NaBr}]{CH_3CH_2Br}$$

Carbanion

$$CH_3 - \overset{O}{\overset{||}{C}} - \underset{\underset{CH_2CH_3}{|}}{CH} - \overset{O}{\overset{||}{C}} - OEt \xrightarrow[\text{EtOH}]{\overset{\oplus \ominus}{NaOEt}} CH_3 - \overset{O}{\overset{||}{C}} - \overset{\ominus}{\underset{\underset{CH_2CH_3}{|}}{C}} - \overset{O}{\overset{||}{C}} - OEt \xrightarrow{CH_3CH_2Br}$$

$$CH_3 - \overset{O}{\overset{||}{C}} - \underset{\underset{CH_2CH_3}{|}}{\overset{\overset{CH_2 CH_3}{|}}{C}} - COOEt \xrightarrow[\text{(ii) H}^+]{\text{(i) } \overset{\ominus}{OH},\ H_2O} CH_3 - \overset{O}{\overset{||}{C}} - \underset{\underset{CH_2CH_3}{|}}{\overset{\overset{CH_2 CH_3}{|}}{C}} - COOH \xrightarrow[- CO_2]{\Delta} \overset{1}{CH_3} - \overset{O}{\overset{||}{\underset{\underset{CH_2CH_3}{|}}{\overset{2}{C}}}} - \overset{3}{CH}\ \overset{4}{CH_2}\ \overset{5}{CH_3}$$

3-ethyl-2-pentanone

Similarly, for the synthesis of 3-methyl-2-hexanone,

$$\overset{1}{CH_3} - \overset{O}{\overset{2\ ||}{C}} - \overset{3}{CH} \overset{4}{CH_2} \overset{5}{CH_2} \overset{6}{CH_3}$$
$$\underset{CH_3}{|}$$

two alkyl halides, n-propyl bromide and methyl bromide must be used.

2. Synthesis of methyl cycloalkyl ketone:

Use of dihaloalkane will result in the formation of methyl cycloalkyl ketone. Thus,

$$CH_3 - \overset{O}{\overset{||}{C}} - CH_2 - \overset{O}{\overset{||}{C}} - OEt \xrightarrow[\text{EtOH}]{\overset{\oplus \ominus}{NaOEt}} \overset{\oplus \ominus}{NaC} \underset{C-OEt}{\overset{C-CH_3}{<}} \xrightarrow[-NaBr]{Br-CH_2-CH_2-CH_2-Br}$$

Ethyl aceto acetate   Carbanion

$$CH_3 - \overset{O}{\overset{||}{C}} - \underset{\underset{CH_2-CH_2-CH_2-Br}{|}}{CH} - \overset{O}{\overset{||}{C}} - OEt \xrightarrow[\text{EtOH}]{\overset{\oplus \ominus}{NaOEt}} CH_3 - \overset{O}{\overset{||}{C}} - \overset{\ominus}{\underset{\underset{CH_2CH_2CH_2Br}{|}}{C}} - \overset{O}{\overset{||}{C}} - OEt \equiv CH_3 - \overset{O}{\overset{||}{C}} - \underset{\underset{CH_2CH_2CH_2-Br}{|}}{\overset{\overset{COOEt}{|}}{C}}\ominus$$

$$\xrightarrow{-NaBr} CH_3 - \overset{O}{\overset{||}{C}} - \underset{\underset{CH_2-CH_2}{|}}{\overset{\overset{COOEt}{|}}{C}}—CH_2 \xrightarrow[\text{(ii) H}^+]{\text{(i) } \overset{\ominus}{OH},\ H_2O} CH_3 - \overset{O}{\overset{||}{C}} - \underset{\underset{CH_2-CH_2}{|}}{\overset{\overset{COOH}{|}}{C}}—CH_2 \xrightarrow[-CO_2]{\Delta} CH_3 - \overset{O}{\overset{||}{C}} - \underset{\underset{CH_2-CH_2}{|}}{CH}—CH_2$$

Cyclobutyl methyl ketone

3. Synthesis of γ-keto acid:

Use of α-haloester instead of an alkyl halide will result in the formation of γ-keto acid.

$$CH_3-\overset{O}{\overset{||}{C}}-CH_2-\overset{O}{\overset{||}{C}}-OEt \xrightarrow[\substack{EtOH}]{NaOEt} CH_3-\overset{O}{\overset{||}{C}}-\overset{\ominus}{\underset{\oplus}{CH}}-\overset{O}{\overset{||}{C}}-OEt \xrightarrow[-NaBr]{BrCH_2-\overset{O}{\overset{||}{C}}-OEt} CH_3-\overset{O}{\overset{||}{C}}-\underset{\underset{O}{\overset{||}{CH_2-C-OEt}}}{CH}-\overset{O}{\overset{||}{C}}-OEt$$

Na
Carbanion

$$\xrightarrow[\text{(ii) } H^+]{\text{(i) } \overset{\ominus}{OH},\, H_2O} CH_3-\overset{O}{\overset{||}{C}}-\underset{\underset{O}{\overset{||}{CH_2-C-OH}}}{CH}-\overset{O}{\overset{||}{C}}-OH \xrightarrow[-CO_2]{\Delta} \overset{5}{CH_3}-\underset{\gamma}{\overset{O}{\overset{||}{\overset{4}{C}}}}-\underset{\beta}{\overset{3}{CH_2}}-\underset{\alpha}{\overset{2}{CH_2}}-\overset{O}{\overset{||}{\overset{1}{C}}}-OH$$

γ-keto acid (4-keto pentanoic acid)

4. Synthesis of β-diketone:

Instead of an alkyl halide if an acyl chloride or acid anhydride are used, the β-diketone is formed. Thus,

$$CH_3-\overset{O}{\overset{||}{C}}-CH_2-\overset{O}{\overset{||}{C}}-OEt \xrightarrow[\substack{EtOH}]{NaOEt} \underset{NaC}{\overset{\oplus}{\underset{\ominus}{}}}\overset{\overset{O}{\overset{||}{C}}-CH_3}{\underset{\underset{O}{\overset{||}{C}}-OEt}{}} \xrightarrow[\text{Acetyl chloride, } -NaCl]{CH_3-\overset{O}{\overset{||}{C}}-Cl}$$

Carbanion

$$CH_3-\overset{O}{\overset{||}{C}}-\underset{\underset{O}{\overset{||}{C}}-CH_3}{CH}-\overset{O}{\overset{||}{C}}-OEt \xrightarrow[\text{(ii) } H^+]{\text{(i) } \overset{\ominus}{OH},\, H_2O} CH_3-\overset{O}{\overset{||}{C}}-\underset{\underset{O}{\overset{||}{C}}-CH_3}{CH}-\overset{O}{\overset{||}{C}}-O-H \xrightarrow[-CO_2]{\Delta} CH_3-\overset{O}{\overset{||}{C}}-\underset{\beta}{CH_2}-\underset{\alpha}{\overset{O}{\overset{||}{C}}}-CH_3$$

β-diketone

5. Synthesis of γ-diketone:

Use of an α-haloketone will result in the formation of γ-diketone.

$$CH_3-\overset{O}{\overset{||}{C}}-CH_2-\overset{O}{\overset{||}{C}}-OEt \xrightarrow[\substack{EtOH}]{NaOEt} \underset{NaC}{\overset{\oplus}{\underset{\ominus}{}}}\overset{\overset{O}{\overset{||}{C}}-CH_3}{\underset{\underset{O}{\overset{||}{C}}-OEt}{}} \xrightarrow[\substack{\alpha\text{-Bromo acetone} \\ -NaBr}]{Br-CH_2-\overset{O}{\overset{||}{C}}-CH_3}$$

Carbanion

$$CH_3-\overset{O}{\overset{||}{C}}-\underset{\underset{O}{\overset{||}{CH_2-C-CH_3}}}{CH}-\overset{O}{\overset{||}{C}}-OEt \xrightarrow{H_2O,\, H^+} CH_3-\overset{O}{\overset{||}{C}}-\underset{\underset{O}{\overset{||}{CH_2-C-CH_3}}}{CH}-\overset{O}{\overset{||}{C}}-O-H \xrightarrow[-CO_2]{\Delta} CH_3-\overset{O}{\overset{||}{C}}-\underset{\gamma}{\overset{\beta}{CH_2}}-\underset{\alpha}{CH_2}-\overset{O}{\overset{||}{C}}-CH_3$$

γ-diketone

1.5.3 Wittig Reagent and Wittig Reaction

- This is a very important method for the synthesis of alkenes. It involves the addition of a phosphonium ylide (also known as a phosphorane) to the carbonyl group of an aldehyde or ketone. This ylide is actually a carbanion having an adjacent hetero atom. Such species are generated by the reaction of an alkyl halide, RR'CHX with a trialkyl or triaryl phosphine (usually triphenyl phosphine Ph_3P) to yield a phosphonium salt, followed by abstraction of a proton from it by a very strong base like phenyl lithium PhLi.

$$Ph_3\ddot{P} + R\overset{R'}{\underset{H}{-C-}}X \longrightarrow Ph_3\overset{\oplus}{P}\underset{X^{\ominus}}{-}CHRR' \xrightarrow{PhLi}$$

Phosphonium salt

$$Ph_3\overset{\oplus}{P} - \overset{\ominus}{C}RR' \longleftrightarrow Ph_3P = CRR'$$

Phosphonium ylide or a phosphorane or Wittig reagent

- Addition of the Wittig reagent to a carbonyl compound gives an alkene.

$$R_1 - \overset{\overset{\displaystyle O}{\|}}{C} - R_2 + Ph_3\overset{\oplus}{P} - \overset{\ominus}{C}RR' \rightarrow R_1R_2C = CRR' + Ph_3P = O$$

alkene   triphenyl phosphine oxide

Probable mechanism:

$$R_1R_2C = CRR' + Ph_3P = O$$

alkene   triphenyl phosphene oxide

- Because of the possibility of variations in the substituents of the original halide and in the carbonyl component, it becomes a very useful and versatile method for the synthesis of substituted alkenes. The presence of a double bond C = C or triple bond C ≡ C even when conjugated with the C = O group does not interfere. An ester group will react very slowly as compared to a carbonyl group and hence will not interfere in the reaction. The reaction is particularly valuable for forming a double bond into positions that are usually difficult e.g. exocyclic double bond and β, γ-unsaturated acids.

Some examples of Wittig reaction are:

1.

Cyclohexanone   Exocyclic double bond

$+ Ph_3\overset{\oplus}{P} - \overset{\ominus}{C}H_2$ $+ Ph_3P = O$

2.

$+ Ph_3\overset{\oplus}{P} - \overset{\ominus}{C}H - CH = CHPh \longrightarrow$ CH $=$ CH$-$CH$=$CH$-$ Ph

3. $R_2C = O + Ph_3\overset{\oplus}{P} - \overset{\ominus}{C}H$ $CH_2\overset{\ominus}{COO} \longrightarrow R_2\overset{\gamma}{C} = \overset{\beta}{C}H$ $\overset{\alpha}{C}H_2\overset{\ominus}{COO} + Ph_3P = O$

β, γ-unsaturated acid

Exercises

1. What are carbanions? Explain how carbanions can be generated from different substrates.

2. Discuss the factors affecting stability of carbanions with examples.

3. What is Aldol condensation? Discuss mechanism of Aldol condensation with a suitable example.

4. Explain crossed Aldol condensation and intramolecular Aldol condensation with suitable examples.

5. What is Claisen ester condensation? Discuss the mechanism of formation of ethyl acetoacetate from ethyl acetate.

6. What is Perkin reaction? Explain its use in the synthesis of cinnamic acid.

7. Explain Dieckmann cyclisation with a suitable example.

8. What are phosphorous ylide? How are they prepared? Explain the synthesis of 1, 1-diphenylethene from benzophenone with mechanism.

9. What is Wittig reaction? Explain its use in organic synthesis with suitable examples.

10. The diketone 2, 4-pentanedione is almost as acidic as phenol and much more acidic than acetone; explain.

11. Benzaldehyde and ethyl acetate give ethyl-3-phenylpropenoate $C_6H_5CH = CH$ $COOC_2H_5$ in the presence of sodium ethoxide. Show all steps in the probable mechanism of this reaction.

12. Write the structure of products obtained and complete equation for the reaction of benzaldehyde with

(i) acetaldehyde, dil. NaOH

(ii) acetone, dil. NaOH

(iii) acetophenone, NaOH

(iv) $Ph_3P = CH(OC_6H_5)$

(v) acetic anhydride, sodium acetate, heat

13. Outline the synthesis of each of the following from acetoacetic ester and any other reagents:

(i) Ethylmethyl ketone

(ii) 3-ethyl-2-pentanone

(iii) Methyl succinic acid

(iv) 3, 6-dimethyl-2-heptanone

(v) β-methylbutyric acid

14. Outline the synthesis of each of the following from malonic ester and any other reagents:

(i) Succinic acid

(ii) Phenylacetic acid

(iii) Cyclohexane carboxylic acid

(iv) 2-methyl butanoic acid

(v) Pentane-1, 5-dicarboxylic acid

15. Give the structure of Wittig reagent and a carbonyl compound from which each of the following could be synthesized.

(i) $C_6H_5CH = CHC_6H_5$

(ii) $CH_2 = CH \cdot CH = C(CH_3)COOCH_3$

(iii) $C_6H_5C(CH_3) = CH \cdot CH_2C_6H_5$

(iv) $CH_3CH_2CH_2CH = C(CH_3)CH_2CH_3$

(v) 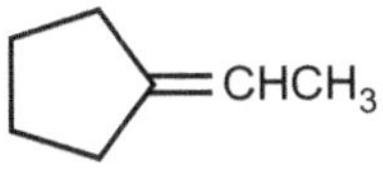 $=CHCH_3$

16. **Multiple Choice Questions:**

(i)   Increasing order of acidity of C–H among the following compounds is:

I. $\underset{\underset{H}{|}}{CH_2} - \overset{\overset{O}{\|}}{C} - N(CH_3)_2$

II. $\underset{\underset{H}{|}}{H_2C} - \overset{\overset{O}{\|}}{C} - O - CH_2 - CH_3$

III. $\underset{\underset{H}{|}}{H_2C} - \overset{\overset{O}{\|}}{C} - CH_3$

IV. $\underset{\underset{H}{|}}{H_2C} - \overset{\overset{O}{\|}}{C} - H$

(a) **I < II < III < IV**   (b) IV < III < II < I
(c) III < II < IV < I   (d) II < I < III < IV

(ii)   The decreasing order of stability among the following carbanions is:

I. $H_3C - C \equiv C - H$

II. $\underset{H}{\overset{H_3C}{>}} C = C \underset{H}{\overset{H}{<}}$

III. $H_3C - CH_2 - CH_3$

(a) I < II < III   (b) **I > II > III**
(c) I > III > II   (d) II > I > III

(iii)   The increasing order of acidity among the following dicarbonyl compounds is
(I) $H_3C - \overset{\overset{O}{\|}}{C} - CH_2 - \overset{\overset{O}{\|}}{C} - CH_3$ (II) $H_3C - \overset{\overset{O}{\|}}{C} - CH_2 - \overset{\overset{O}{\|}}{C} - OC_2H_5$

(III) $H_3C - \overset{\overset{O}{\|}}{C} - CH_2 - \overset{\overset{O}{\|}}{C} - H$ (IV)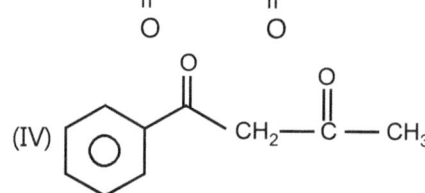

(a) I < II < III < IV   (b) II < I < IV < III
(c) II < IV < I < III   (d) II < I < III < IV

(iv)   Arrange the following compounds with increasing order of acidity:

(I) $H_3C - NO_2$ (II) $H_3C - \overset{\overset{O}{\|}}{C} - H$

(III) $CH_3 - \overset{\overset{O}{\|}}{C} - NH_2$

(a) I < II < III   (b) **III < II < I**
(c) II < I < III   (d) III < I < II

(v) How many products are formed when cross aldol condensation of propanaldehyde and 3-methyl butanaldehyde is carried out?

(a) One   (b) Two

(c) Three   **(d) Four**

(vi) The product formed by intramolecular aldol reaction of 2, 7-octane dione is

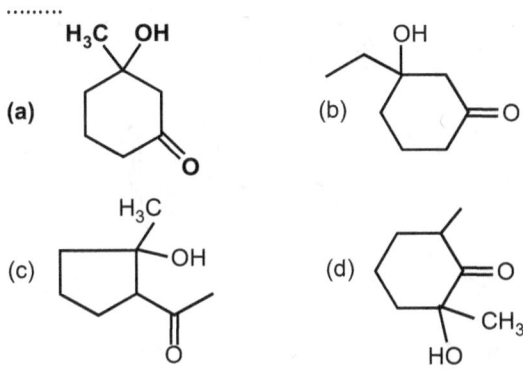

(vii) Which of the following compounds would be expected to decarboxylate when heated?

(I)

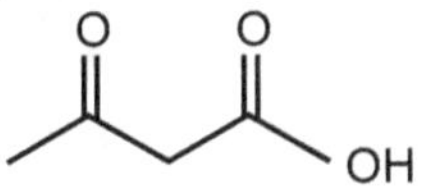

(II)

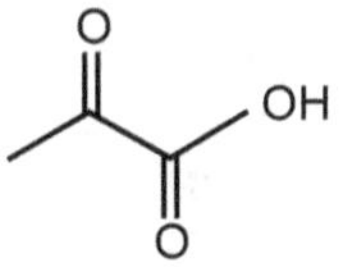

(III)

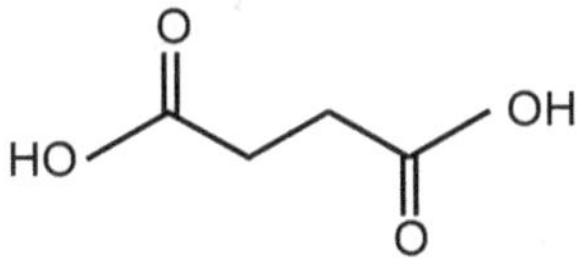

(IV)

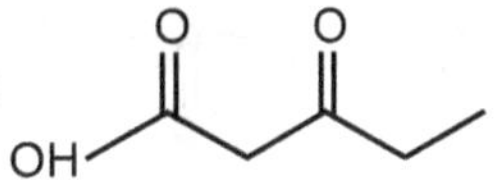

(a) Only I   (b) Only II and IV

(c) Only I and III   **(d) Only I, III and IV**

(viii) Which of the following products is formed when 1, 5-dibromo pentane and diethyl malonate are treated with sodium ethoxide?

(a)

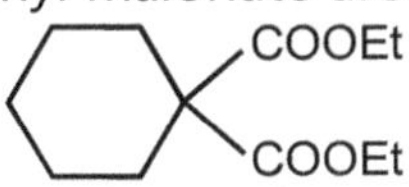

COOEt

COOEt

(b)

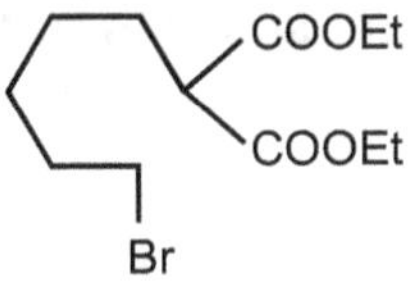

COOEt

COOEt

Br

(c)

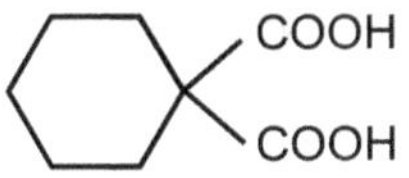

COOH

COOH

(d)

COOH

COOH

Br

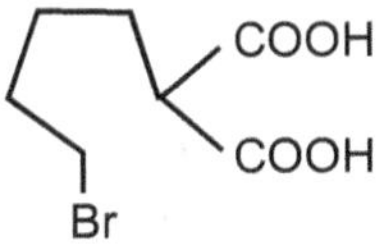

(ix) The major product formed in the following reaction is ....

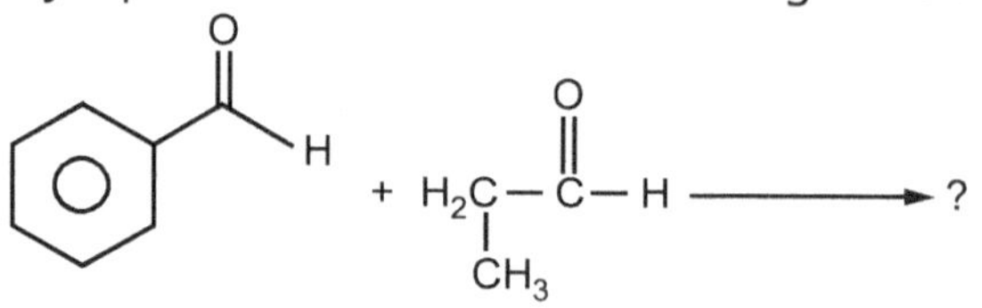

(a) 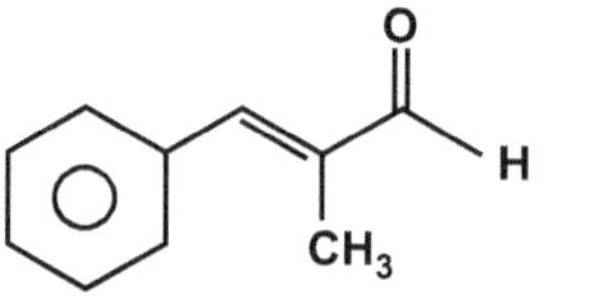 (b)

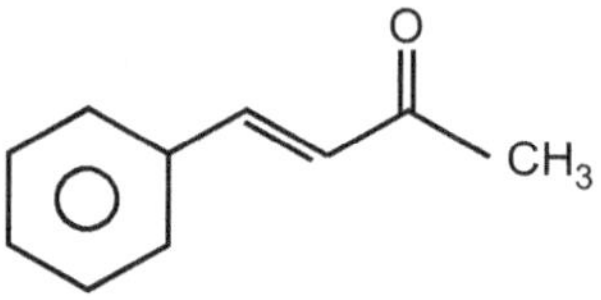

(c) $H_3C - CH_2 - C = C$ 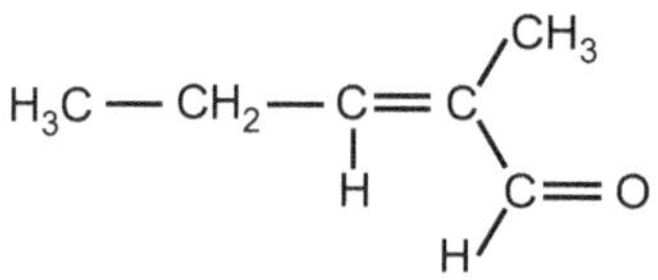 (d)

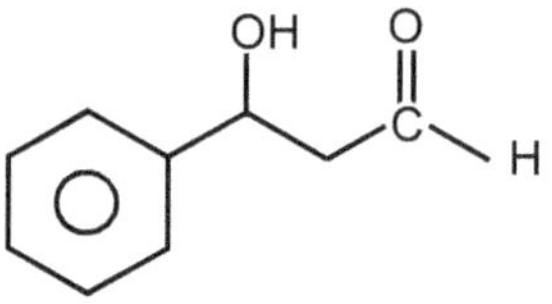

(x)   The stable intermediate formed in the following conversion is

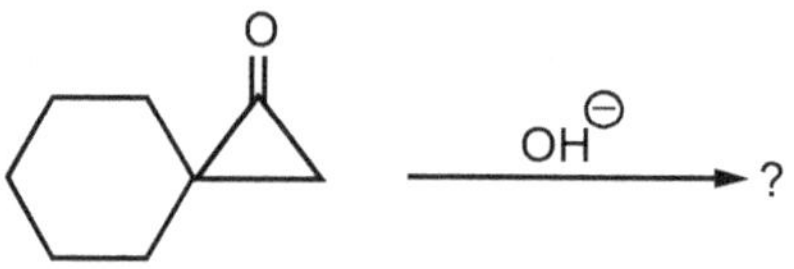

(a) 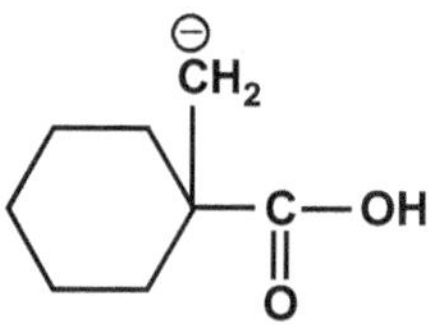 (b)

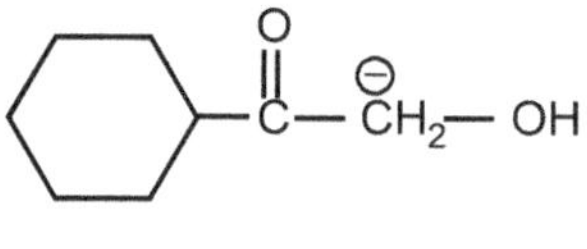

(c) 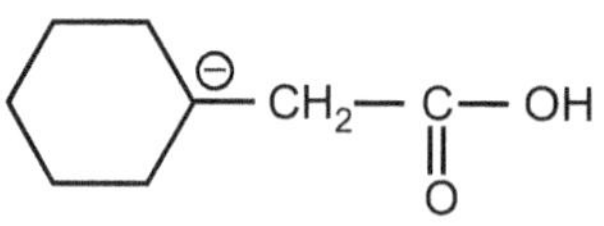 (d)

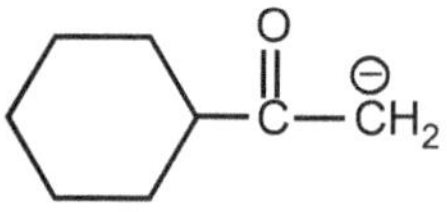

(xi) Which of the following products is formed when ethyl acetate and ethyl benzoate are treated with sodium ethoxide?

(a) 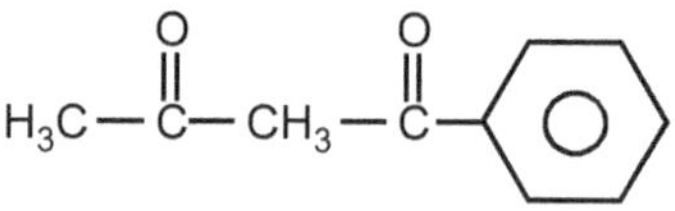 (b)

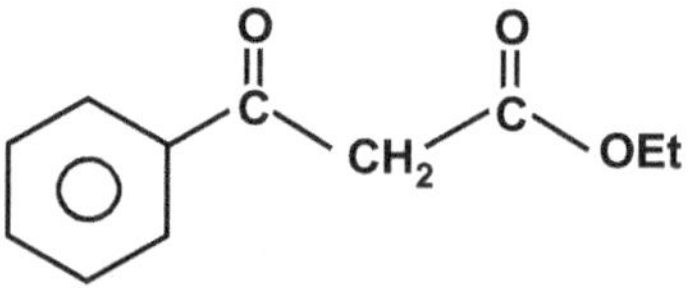

(c) 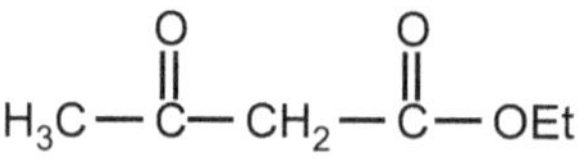 (d)

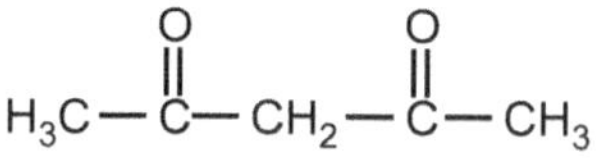

(xii) The product formed in the following reaction is ....

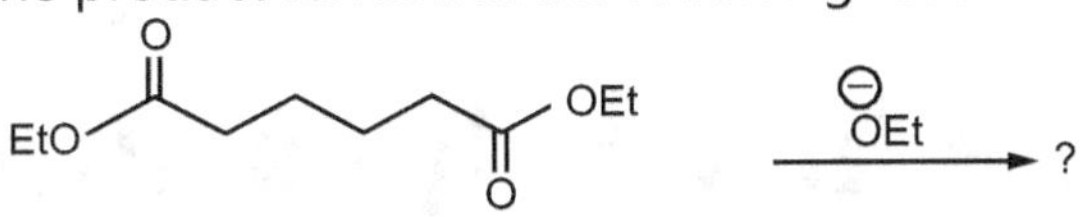

(a) 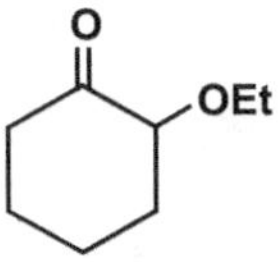   (b)

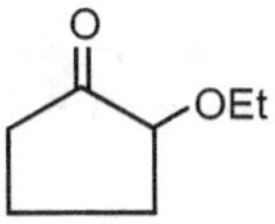

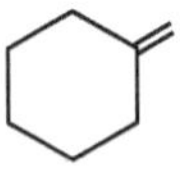

(c) 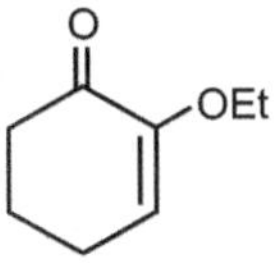   (d)

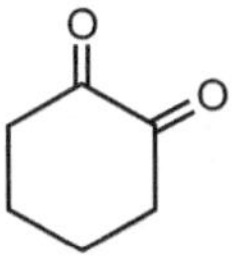

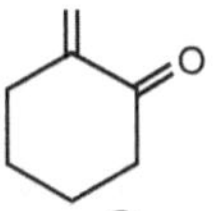

(xiii) The product formed in the following reaction is ....

+   Ph₃P = CH₂   ——→ ?

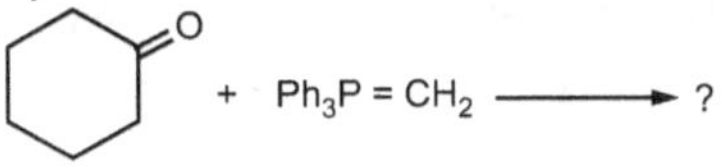

(a) 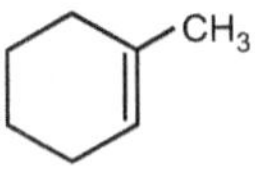   (b)

(c) 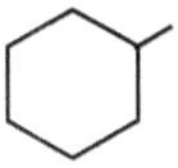   (d)

(xiv) How can you synthesize

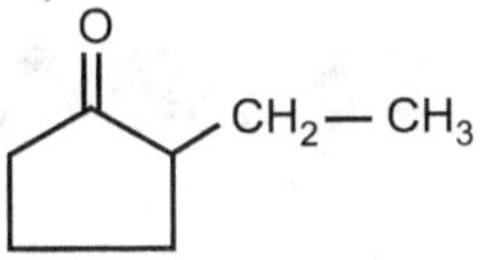

(a) 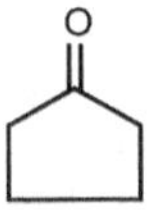   + CH₃—CH₂—Br + LDA

(b) 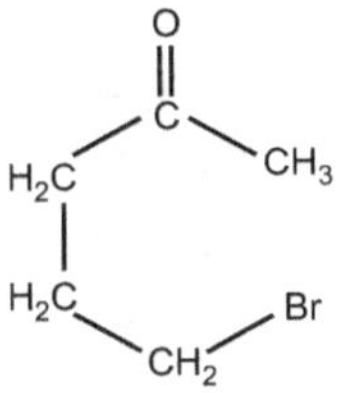   + LDA

(c) 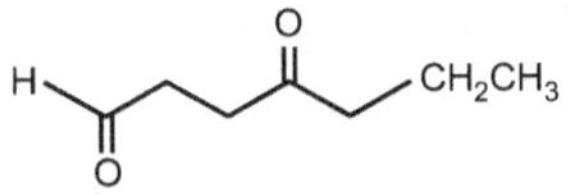   CH₂CH₃ + LDA

(d) 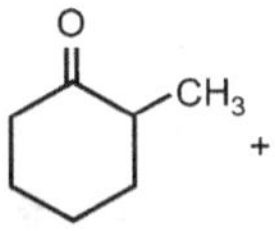   + I—CH₃ + LDA

■■■

Chapter 2...

Retrosynthetic Analysis and Applications

Contents ...

2.1 Introduction

- Mankind is always curious about nature. This curiosity towards nature, different natural colours, flavours, fragrances and other properties ultimately resulted in isolation of different natural products. Once, they were isolated in pure forms, their structures were deduced by degradative reactions, because physical methods were not that developed at that time for determination of structure.

- After establishing the exact structure for a compound, the next step was confirmation of this structure by preparing or synthesizing this compound in the laboratory. Comparison of properties of the compound synthesized in the laboratory with the properties of the compound isolated from nature, finally confirmed the structure of the compound. Thus began the synthesis of organic compounds. The first organic compound synthesized in the laboratory was urea by Wöhler.

- This opened a new branch in organic chemistry i.e. organic synthesis. As the success and skill in organic synthesis was developed, many compounds not present in nature were also synthesized for variety of reasons. Synthesis of new drugs and pharmaceuticals or of new pigments and plastics are constantly undertaken in research laboratories and in chemical industries. This led to the invention of new drugs for the benefit of mankind.

2.2 Design of Organic Synthesis and Retrosynthesis

- Any given organic compound can be synthesized by many different routes. A synthetic route is a sequence of reactions designed to convert commercially available starting materials into the desired substance.

- In practice, number of different routes for synthesis of given organic molecule are devised and compared to select the best one. In general, the best synthesis of a substance involves conversion of the cheapest and readily available starting materials into the desired product by the least number of steps and in the highest possible overall yield.

- Formulation of syntheses of organic molecules usually involves a stepwise procedure of working backward from the structure of the final product to the structures of available starting materials. This is **retrosynthesis** ('retro' in Latin means "backward" or reverse). Possible reactions that might lead to the desired final product are considered first. Compounds needed for these final reactions are next examined and subjected to retrosynthesis. This procedure is repeated until simpler and easily available starting compounds are encountered. This process of converting an organic molecule into simpler precursor structures is **Retrosynthetic analysis.**

2.3 Terms Used in Retrosynthesis

(i) **Target Molecule (TM):** The molecule whose synthesis is being planned is termed as the target molecule and is usually written as (TM). e.g. if we want to synthesize tert-butyl alcohol $(CH_3)_3C-OH$ then tert-butyl alcohol is the target molecule.

(ii) **Disconnection:** It is an imaginary analytical operation, which breaks a bond and converts a molecule into a possible starting material or materials. Thus, it is the reverse of a chemical reaction. It is denoted by a symbol $\Rightarrow$ and a curved line is drawn through the bond that is imagined to be broken. Thus,

$$H_3C-\underset{\underset{CH_3}{|}}{\overset{\overset{CH_3}{|}}{C}}-O-H \implies H_3C-\underset{CH_3}{\overset{CH_3}{|}}C=O + \overset{\ominus}{CH_3} + \overset{\oplus}{H}$$

TM

Sometimes it is also called as dislocation.

(iii) **Synthon:** It is an imaginary fragment, usually an ion which is produced by a disconnection. This could be used to synthesize the molecule.

Example: $\overset{\ominus}{CH_3}$ produced in the disconnection shown earlier.

(iv) **Synthetic equivalent:** It is a reagent which can provide the required synthon (which cannot itself be used because many times it is too unstable). Thus, the synthon $\overset{\ominus}{CH_3}$ can be provided by the reagent CH_3MgX, a Grignard reagent. Here CH_3MgX is the synthetic equivalent of synthon $\overset{\ominus}{CH_3}$.

(v) Functional Group Interconversion (FGI): It is the operation of writing one functional group for another so that disconnection becomes possible. Again, it is the reverse of a chemical reaction. Here, FGI is written above the symbol $\Rightarrow$. Thus,

(i) 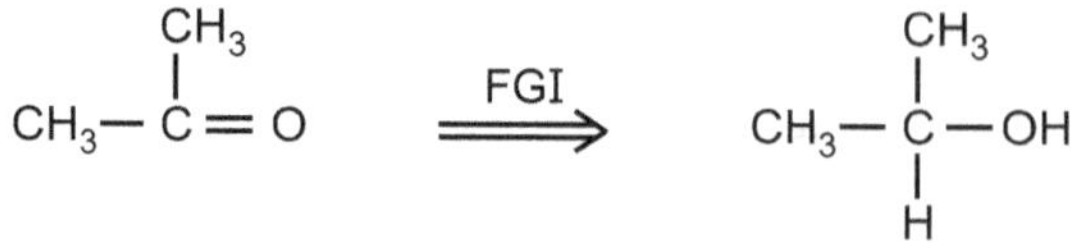 $CH_3 - \underset{\displaystyle CH_3}{\overset{\displaystyle CH_3}{C}} = O \quad \overset{FGI}{\Longrightarrow} \quad CH_3 - \underset{\displaystyle H}{\overset{\displaystyle CH_3}{\underset{|}{\overset{|}{C}}}} - OH$

(ii)  $Ph \diagdown \diagup \diagdown Br \quad \overset{FGI}{\Longrightarrow} \quad Ph \diagdown \diagup \diagdown OH$

As an example, consider retrosynthetic analysis and synthesis of tert-butyl alcohol. There may be more than one retrosynthetic approaches.

(a) Route a:

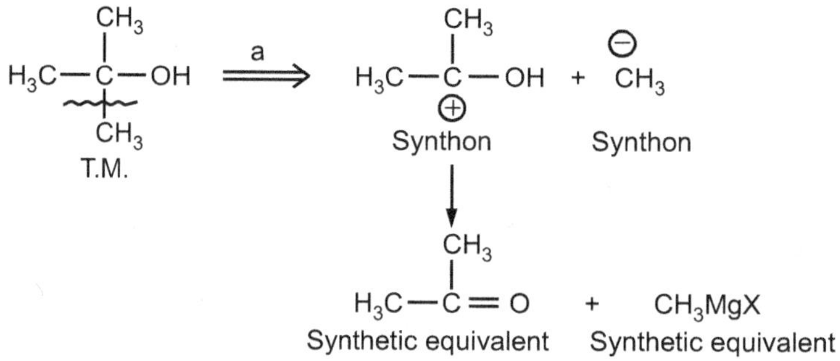

$H_3C - \underset{\displaystyle CH_3}{\overset{\displaystyle CH_3}{\underset{|}{\overset{|}{C}}}} - OH \quad \overset{a}{\Longrightarrow} \quad H_3C - \overset{\displaystyle CH_3}{\underset{\oplus}{\overset{|}{C}}} - OH \quad + \quad \overset{\ominus}{CH_3}$

T.M.   Synthon   Synthon

$\downarrow$

$H_3C - \overset{\displaystyle CH_3}{\overset{|}{C}} = O \quad + \quad CH_3MgX$

Synthetic equivalent   Synthetic equivalent

$CH_3MgX \Rightarrow CH_3X + Mg$

$CH_3X \quad \overset{FGI}{\Rightarrow} \quad CH_3OH$

Synthesis:

$CH_3OH \quad \underset{\text{or } SOCl_2}{\overset{PCl_5}{\longrightarrow}} \quad CH_3Cl \quad \underset{\text{ether}}{\overset{Mg}{\longrightarrow}} \quad CH_3MgCl$

Many times, instead of CH_3Cl, CH_3I is used because it is readily available.

$CH_3I \quad \underset{\text{ether}}{\overset{Mg}{\longrightarrow}} \quad CH_3MgI$

This Grignard reagent is then reacted with acetone

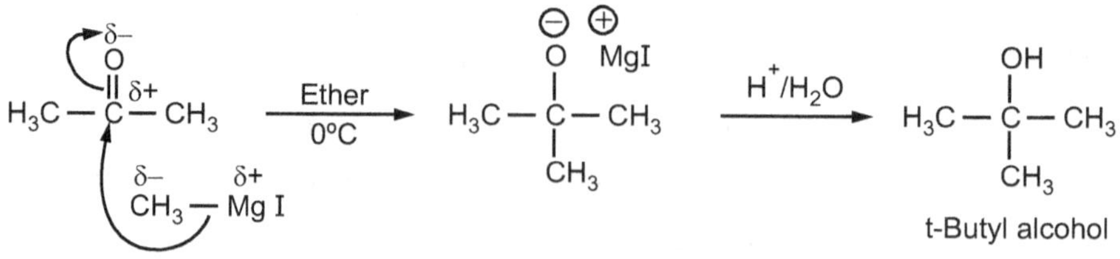

$H_3C - \overset{\delta-}{\underset{\underset{CH_3 - MgI}{\delta- \quad \delta+}}{\overset{\overset{\delta-}{O}}{\underset{\delta+}{C}}}} - CH_3 \quad \underset{0°C}{\overset{\text{Ether}}{\longrightarrow}} \quad H_3C - \overset{\overset{\ominus \quad \oplus}{O \quad MgI}}{\underset{CH_3}{\overset{|}{C}}} - CH_3 \quad \overset{H^+/H_2O}{\longrightarrow} \quad H_3C - \overset{OH}{\underset{CH_3}{\overset{|}{C}}} - CH_3$

t-Butyl alcohol

(b) Route b:

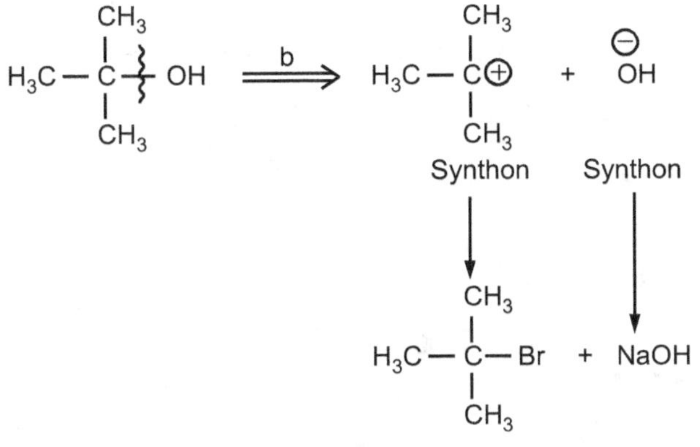

Synthetic equivalents

Synthesis: t-Butyl alcohol can be obtained from t-butylbromide by treatment with aq. NaOH through S_N^1 mechanism.

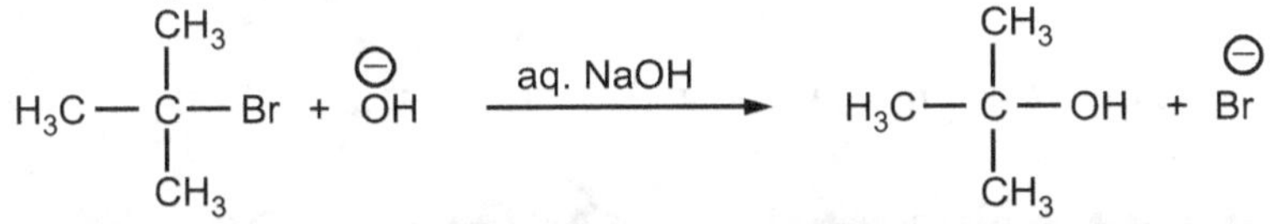

2.4 One Group Disconnections

1. Disconnection of Simple Alcohols:

(i) All simple alcohols can be disconnected in such a way that the most stable anion of the substituents and a carbonyl compound result. Thus,

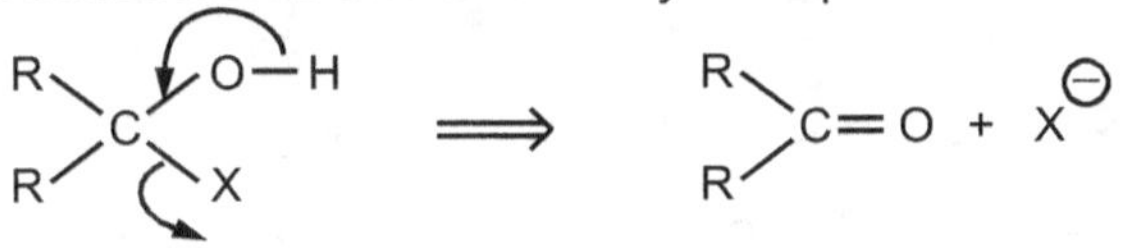

Synthons

Actual synthesis can be planned on the basis of this disconnection. e.g.

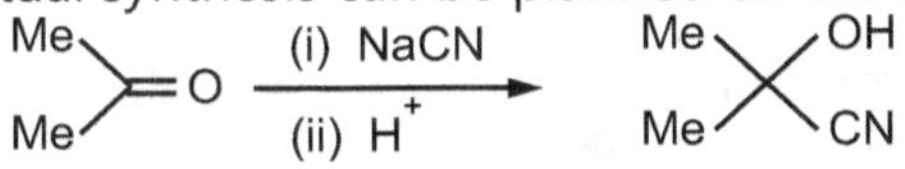

(ii) When none of the substituents gives a stable anion, then synthetic equivalent of the anion like Grignard reagent or alkyl lithium is used. Thus,

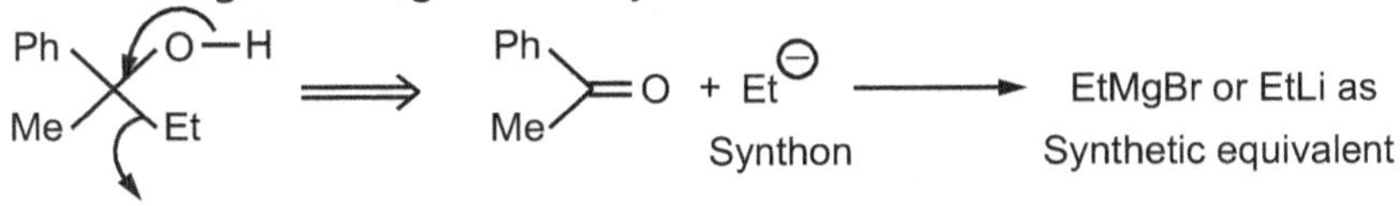

Hence, actual synthesis will be

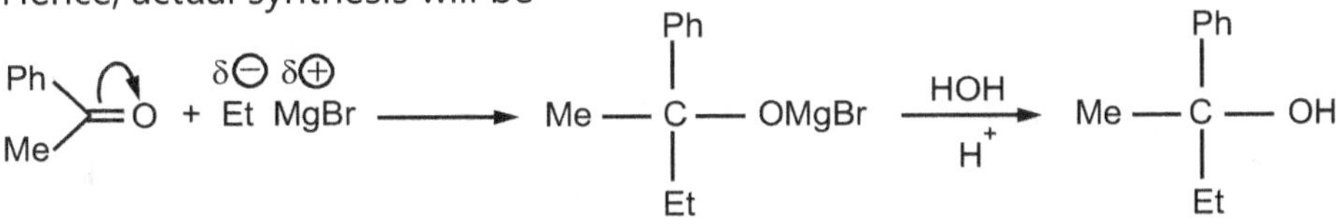

(iii) When two groups on a tertiary alcohol are same, then both are removed in a single disconnection to give an ester and two moles of the Grignard reagent. Thus,

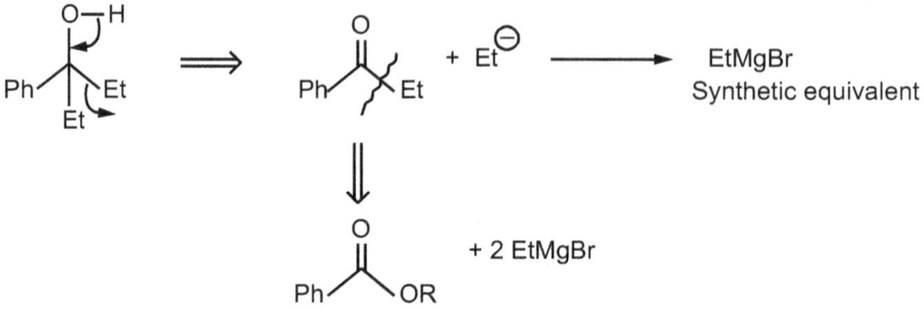

so the reaction becomes

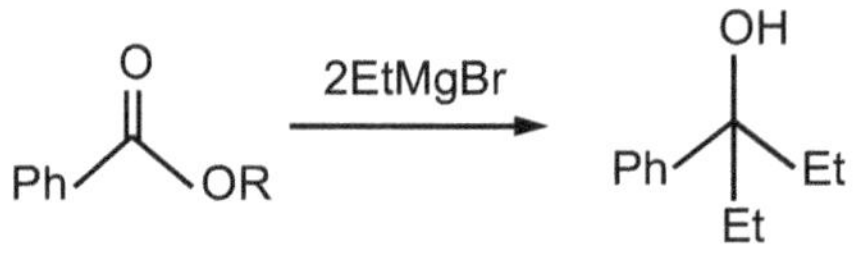

(iv) If one of the groups in the alcohol carbon is H, then a disconnection possible is

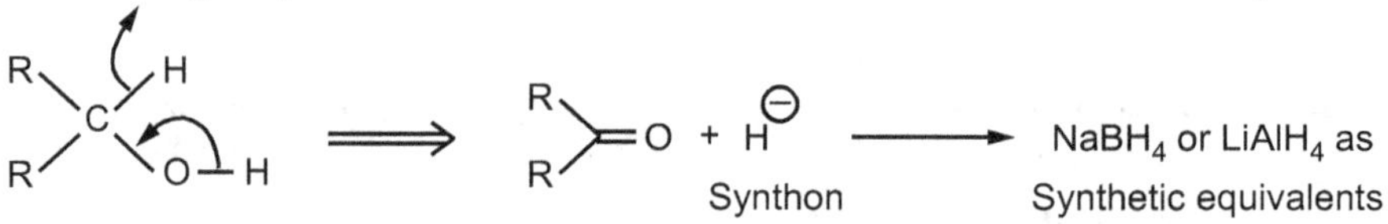

Here, carbon skeleton is not altered, hence this is not really a disconnection but it is a FGI.

2. Disconnection of compounds derived from alcohols:

Aldehydes, ketones, alkyl halides, ethers, olefins, esters, acids can be obtained from corresponding alcohols. Hence, in retrosynthetic analysis they are first converted to alcohols by FGI and then alcohols are disconnected. Thus,

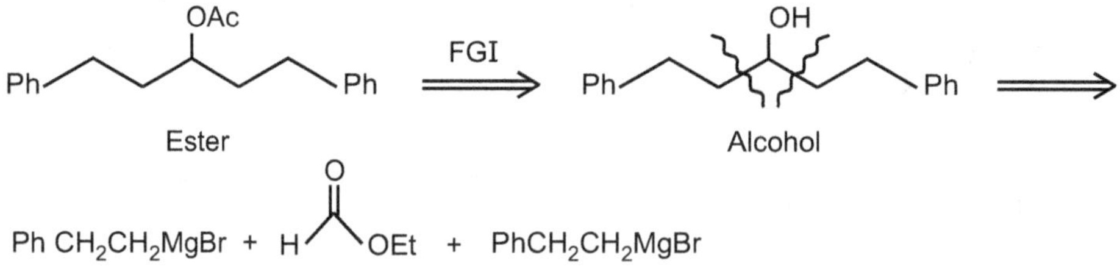

$Ph\ CH_2CH_2MgBr\ +\ H\overset{O}{\underset{}{\diagdown}}OEt\ +\ PhCH_2CH_2MgBr$

Synthesis

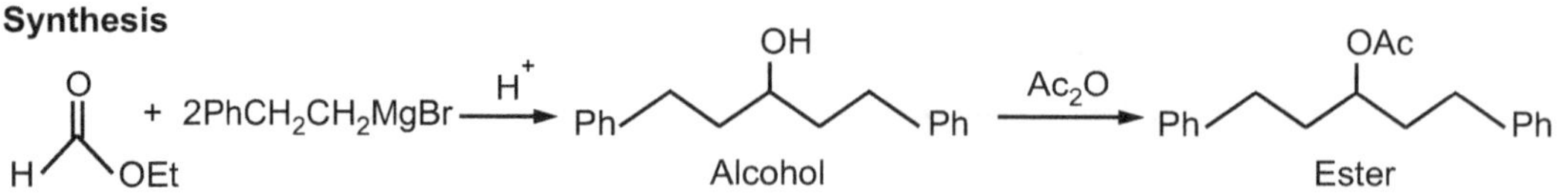

3. Disconnection of simple olefins:

(i)   Olefins can be made by the dehydration of alcohols. Hence, in designing an olefin synthesis, the FGI is obtained by adding water across the double bond. Thus,

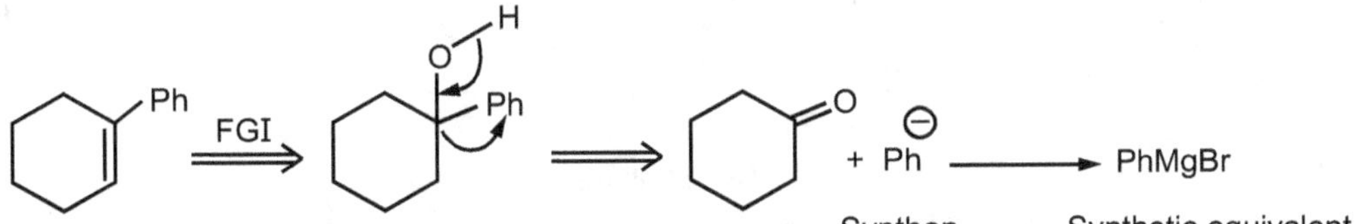

Synthesis   Synthon   Synthetic equivalent

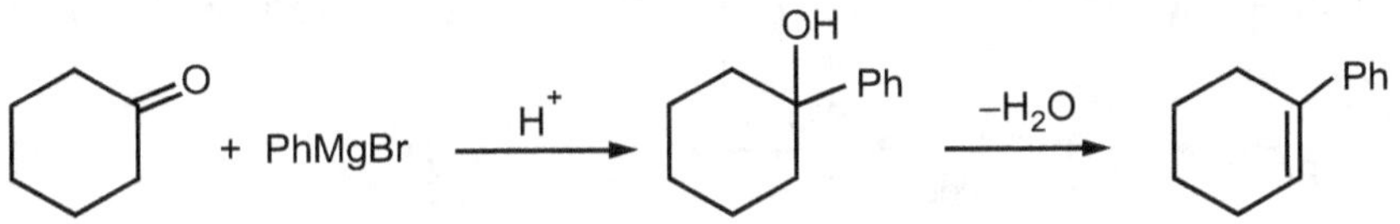

(ii) An alternative route to olefins is by an immediate disconnection of the double bond that corresponds to Wittig reaction. Thus,

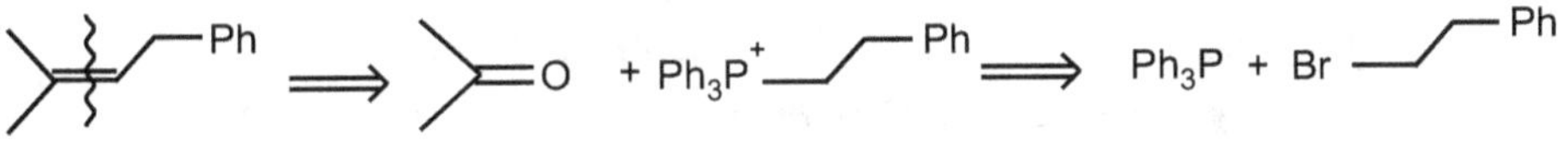

4. Disconnection of aryl ketones:

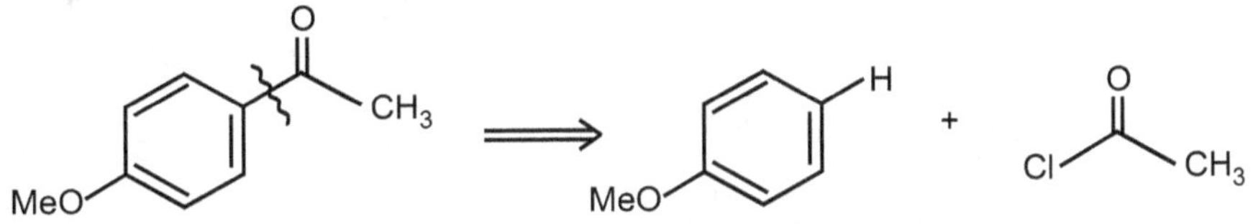

Thus, the synthesis will involve Friedel-Craft's acylation.

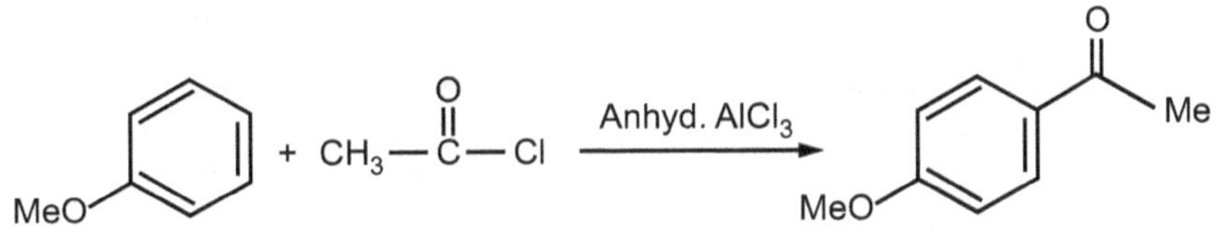

Friedel-Craft's acylation

5. Disconnection of simple ketones and acids:

(i)   **Ketones** are first converted to alcohols by FGI and then disconnected.

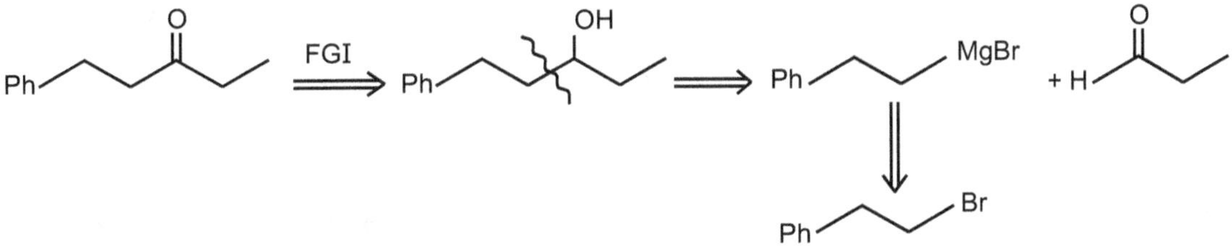

(ii) Acids can be prepared from primary alcohols.

$$R-\overset{O}{\underset{||}{C}}-OH \overset{FGI}{\Longrightarrow} R-CH_2-OH$$

But,

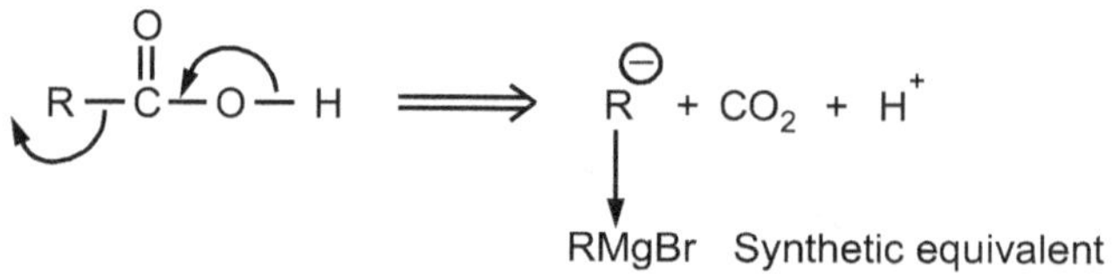

$$R-\overset{O}{\underset{||}{C}}-O-H \Longrightarrow \overset{\ominus}{R} + CO_2 + \overset{+}{H}$$

RMgBr   Synthetic equivalent

Thus, the reaction of appropriate Grignard reagent with CO_2 can form acid.

Acid derivatives are made directly from acids or by conversion from other acid derivatives. Thus,

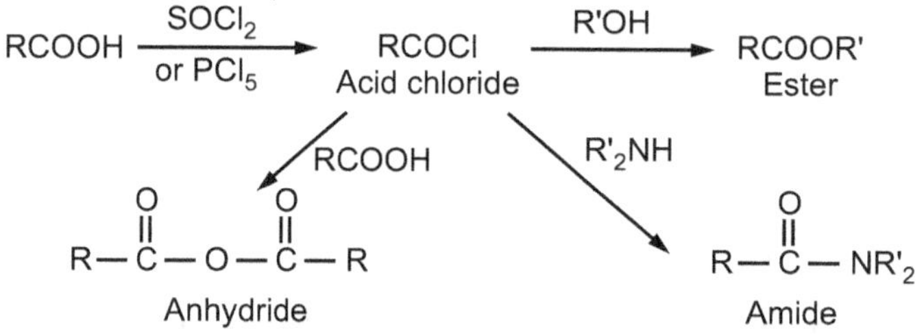

$$RCOOH \xrightarrow[\text{or } PCl_5]{SOCl_2} \underset{\text{Acid chloride}}{RCOCl} \xrightarrow{R'OH} \underset{\text{Ester}}{RCOOR'}$$

RCOOH   R'$_2$NH

$$R-\overset{O}{\underset{||}{C}}-O-\overset{O}{\underset{||}{C}}-R$$
Anhydride

$$R-\overset{O}{\underset{||}{C}}-NR'_2$$
Amide

6. Disconnection of fully saturated hydrocarbons:

These compounds have no functional group at all. These are many times made by hydrogenation of a double bond and then the disconnection can be made anywhere we want. Thus,

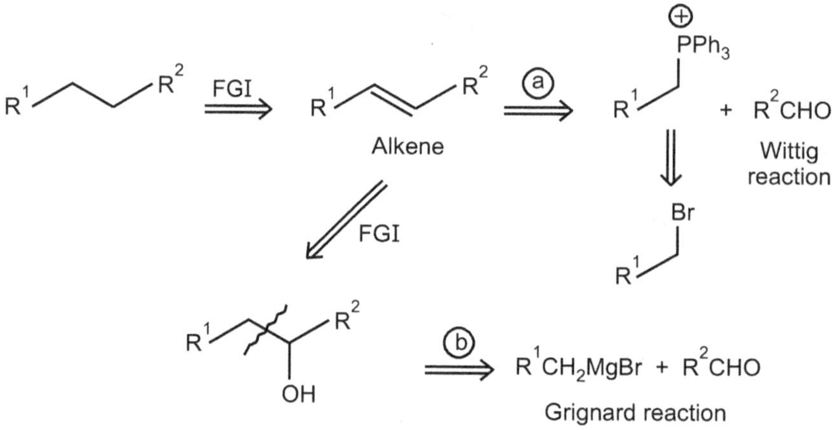

e.g.

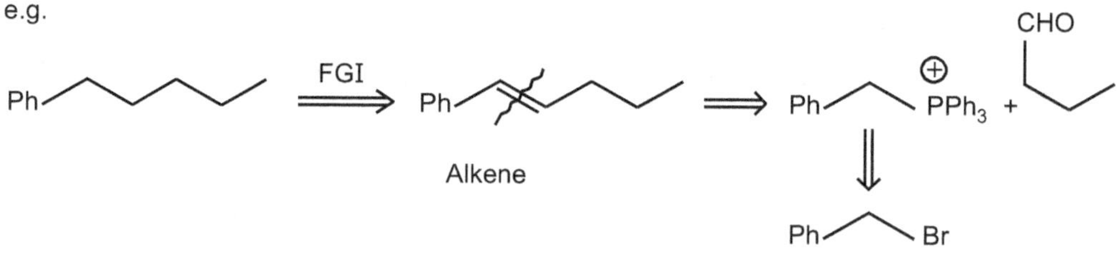

Synthesis:

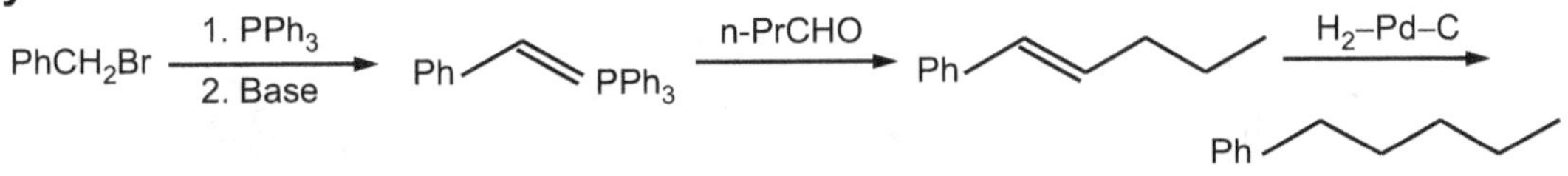

$$PhCH_2Br \xrightarrow[\text{2. Base}]{\text{1. } PPh_3} Ph\diagup\diagdown PPh_3 \xrightarrow{\text{n-PrCHO}} Ph\diagup\diagdown\diagup\diagup \xrightarrow{H_2-Pd-C}$$

Ph⌒⌒⌒

A good disconnection should have following:

(i) A good mechanism which will give the required product.

(ii) Greatest possible simplification.

(iii) It should give recognizable and readily available starting materials.

On the basis of retrosynthetic analysis, actual synthetic scheme is designed. This involves following steps:

(i) Writing the actual synthetic plan with reagents and reaction conditions.

(ii) Steps in the synthetic sequence should be in a rational order.

(iii) Aspect of chemoselectivity should be considered so that the unwanted reactions will not occur elsewhere in the molecule.

(iv) Protecting groups are used if necessary.

(v) The synthetic plan has to be modified in case of failure.

2.5 Retrosynthesis and Synthesis of Target Molecules

- When a target molecule is given for retrosynthesis, the first step is to find out the functional group in the TM and then start the retrosynthetic analysis. Observe the synthons obtained and consider possible synthetic equivalents. If necessary, FGI is also considered.

  Consider the retrosynthesis and synthesis of the following target molecules.

2.5.1 Acetophenone

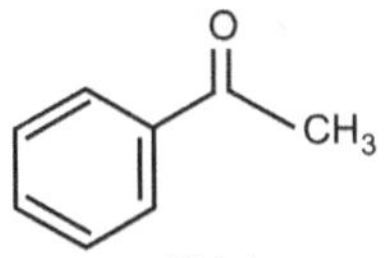

TM-1

- The TM-1 is an aryl ketone and its retrosynthetic analysis suggests that it can be easily obtained by the Friedel-Craft's acylation reaction.

- Thus, the retrosynthesis of TM-1 can be given as:

(A)

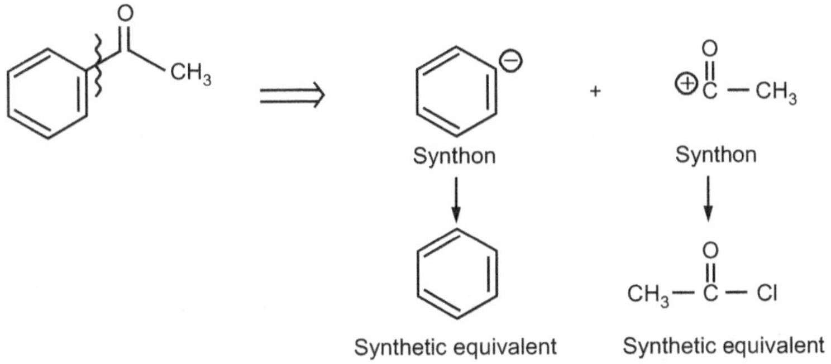

Synthon	Synthon
Synthetic equivalent	Synthetic equivalent

(B)

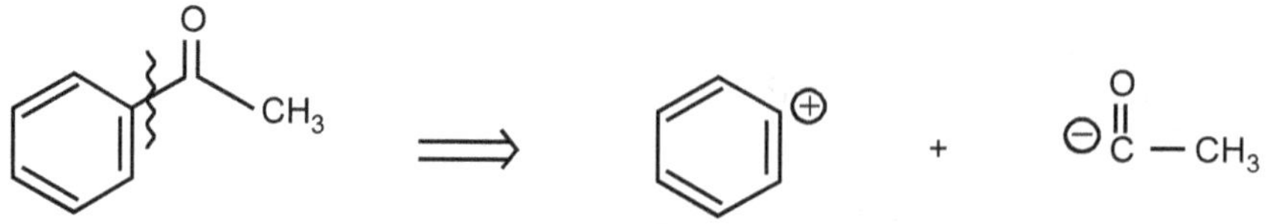

Synthon   Synthon

- As benzene is an electron rich species, positive charge cannot be accommodated on the benzene ring. Hence, as compared to route (B), route (A) will be the proper route for synthesis of TM-1 (acetophenone).
- **Synthesis:** The acetophenone (TM-1) is easily obtained by reacting benzene with acetyl chloride in the presence of Lewis acid AlCl$_3$.

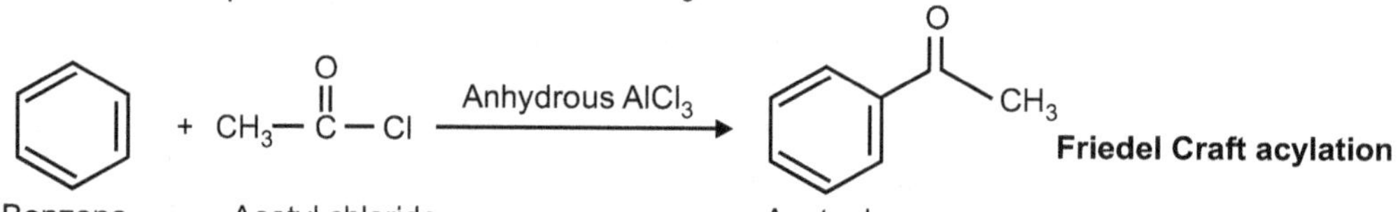

Benzene   Acetyl chloride   Acetophenone

Mechanism:

(i) $CH_3 - \overset{O}{\underset{||}{C}} - Cl$ + AlCl$_3$ ⟶ $CH_3 - \overset{O}{\underset{||}{C}}\oplus$ + $\overset{\ominus}{AlCl_4}$

Acetyl chloride

(ii)

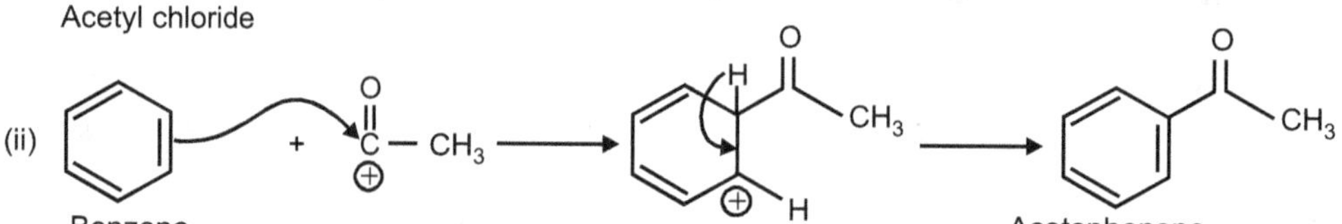

Benzene   Acetophenone
                                                    TM-1

2.5.2 Crotonaldehyde

$$CH_3 - CH = CH - \overset{\overset{H}{|}}{C} = O$$
TM-2

- The TM-2 is an α, β-unsaturated aldehyde. Hence, the disconnection will need FGI.
Retrosynthesis:

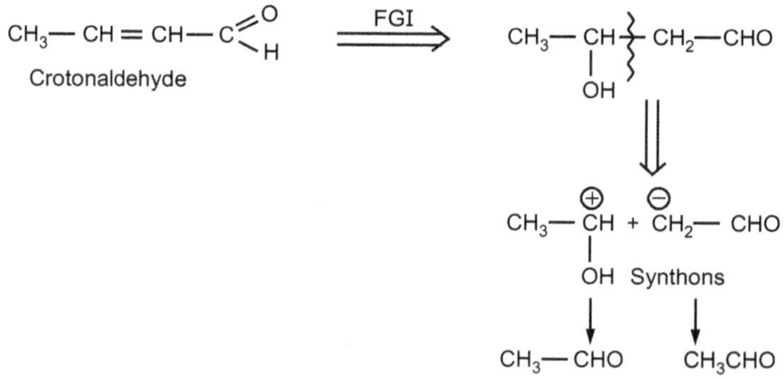

$CH_3 - CH = CH - C\overset{\nearrow O}{\underset{\searrow H}{}}$ $\overset{FGI}{\Longrightarrow}$ $CH_3 - \overset{}{\underset{OH}{CH}}\!\!\!\!\!\!\!\!\}CH_2 - CHO$

Crotonaldehyde

$CH_3 - \overset{\oplus}{\underset{OH}{CH}}$ + $\overset{\ominus}{CH_2} - CHO$ Synthons

$CH_3 - CHO$ CH_3CHO

Synthetic equivalents

Thus the TM-2 can be obtained by aldol condensation of acetaldehyde.

Synthesis:

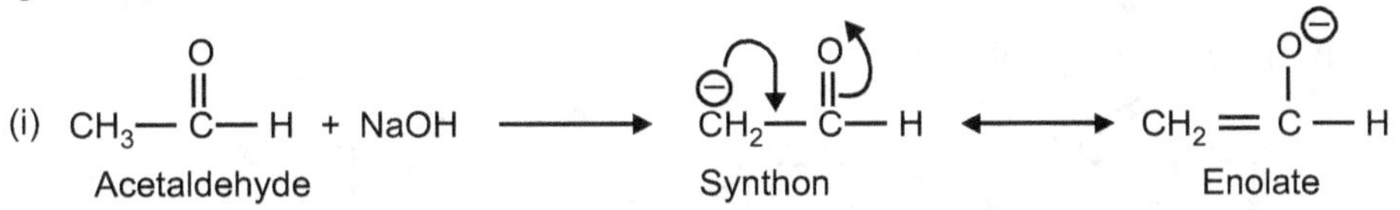

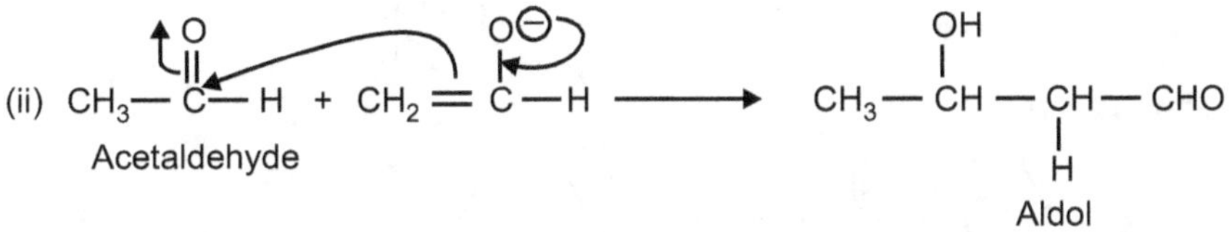

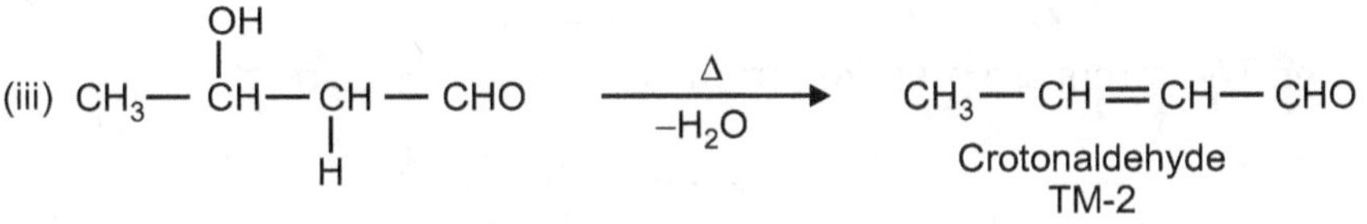

(i) $CH_3 - \overset{\overset{O}{\|}}{C} - H$ + NaOH $\longrightarrow$ $\overset{\ominus}{C}H_2 - \overset{\overset{O}{\|}}{C} - H$ $\longleftrightarrow$ $CH_2 = \overset{\overset{O^{\ominus}}{|}}{C} - H$

Acetaldehyde   Synthon   Enolate

(ii) $CH_3 - \overset{\overset{O}{\|}}{C} - H$ + $CH_2 = \overset{O^{\ominus}}{C} - H$ $\longrightarrow$ $CH_3 - \overset{\overset{OH}{|}}{C}H - \overset{\overset{|}{CH}}{\underset{H}{|}} - CHO$

Acetaldehyde   Aldol

(iii) $CH_3 - \overset{\overset{OH}{|}}{C}H - \overset{\overset{|}{CH}}{\underset{H}{|}} - CHO$ $\xrightarrow[-H_2O]{\Delta}$ $CH_3 - CH = CH - CHO$

                                                        Crotonaldehyde
                                                        TM-2

2.5.3 Cyclohexene

TM-3

Cyclohexene on retrosynthetic analysis suggests two different pathways and accordingly it has two different synthetic routes.

Retrosynthesis (1):

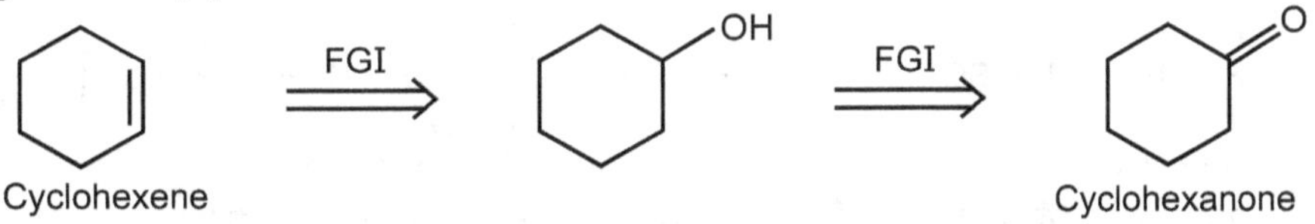

Cyclohexene   FGI   Cyclohexanone

Synthesis:

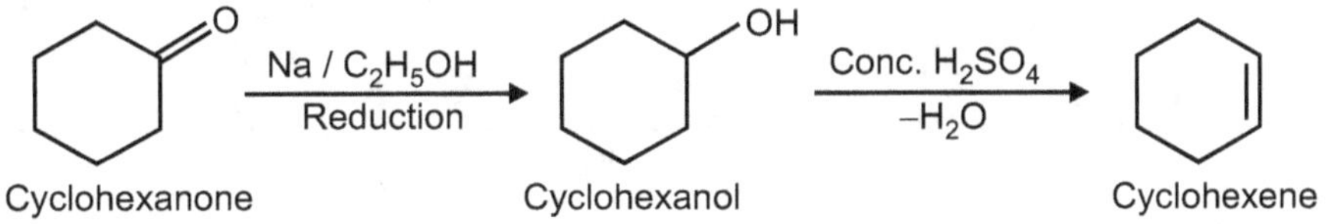

Cyclohexanone   Na / C_2H_5OH Reduction   Cyclohexanol   Conc. H_2SO_4 $-H_2O$ Cyclohexene

Retrosynthesis (2):

Retro Diels-Alder reaction   Ethylene   +   Butadiene

Synthesis: When butadiene and ethylene are heated, they undergo [4+2] cycloaddition (Diels-Alder reaction) to form cyclohexene.

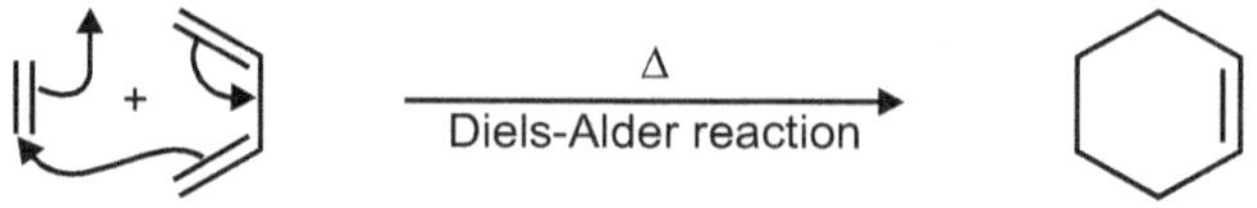

Cyclohexene
TM-3

2.5.4 Benzyl Benzoate

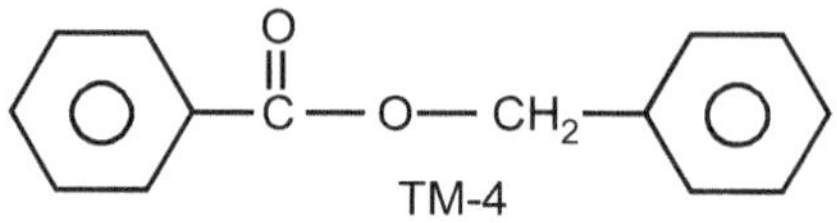

TM-4

The TM-4 is an ester. The esters are prepared from an alcohol and acid.

Retrosynthesis:

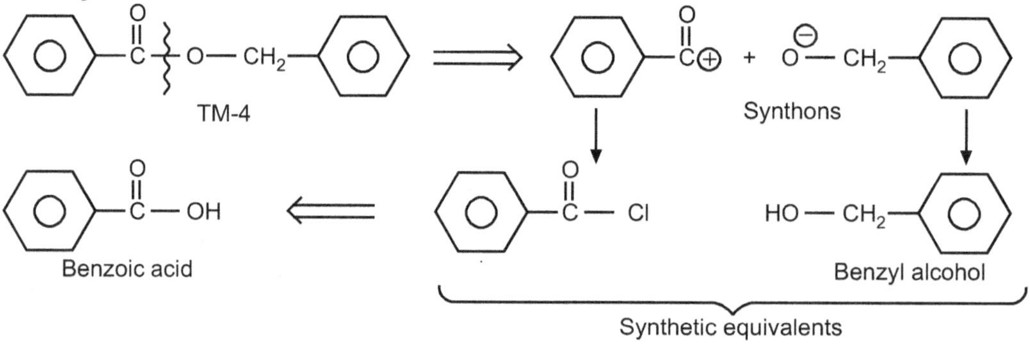

TM-4   Synthons

Benzoic acid   Benzoyl chloride   Benzyl alcohol

Synthetic equivalents

Synthesis:

(i)   Benzoic acid is treated with thionyl chloride to give benzoyl chloride.

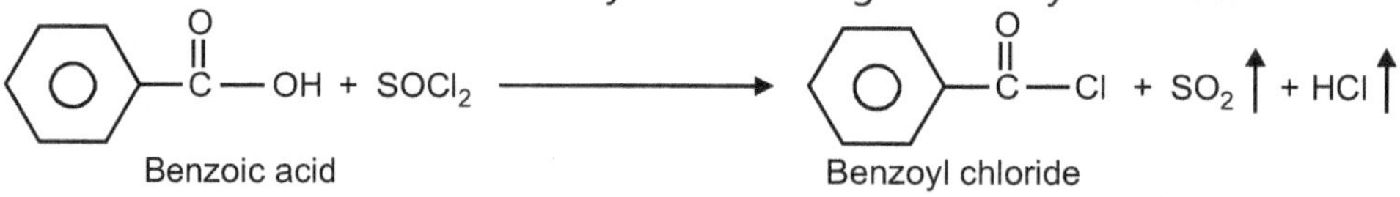

Benzoic acid   Benzoyl chloride

Then benzyl alcohol and benzoyl chloride are stirred in the presence of a base such as triethylamine $(C_2H_5)_3N$.

(ii)

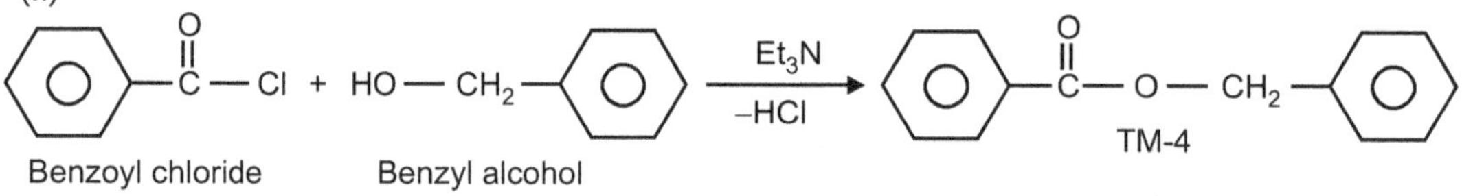

Benzoyl chloride   Benzyl alcohol   TM-4

Alternate synthesis: When benzoic acid is treated with benzyl alcohol in presence of catalytic amount of acid, it forms the corresponding ester.

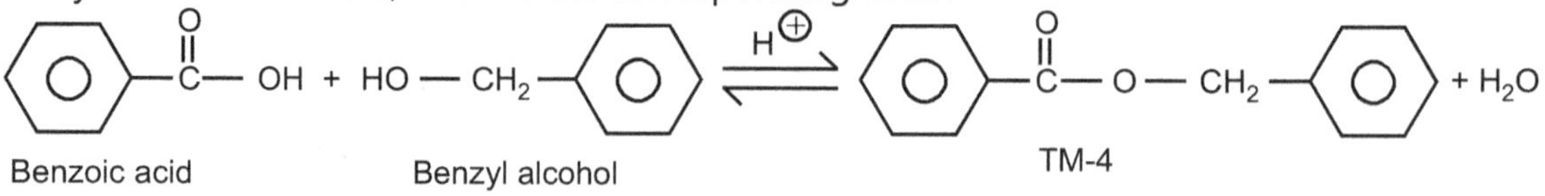

Benzoic acid   Benzyl alcohol   TM-4

2.5.5 Benzyl Diethyl Malonate

$Ph - CH_2 - CH(COOEt)_2$ TM-5

If we consider the breaking of $Ph-CH_2$ bond or $-CH_2 - CH$ bond, we can write three types of disconnections.

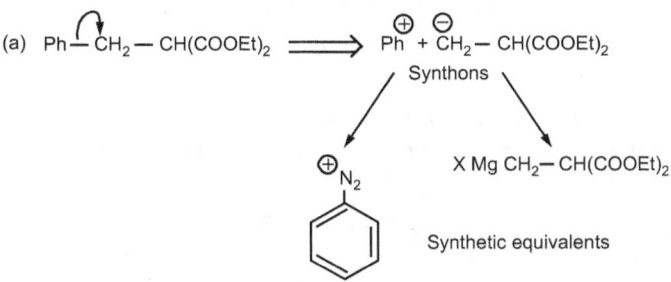

(a) $Ph - CH_2 - CH(COOEt)_2 \Longrightarrow \overset{\oplus}{Ph} + \overset{\ominus}{CH_2} - CH(COOEt)_2$

                   Synthons

     $\overset{\oplus}{N_2}$ X Mg $CH_2 - CH(COOEt)_2$

                Synthetic equivalents

(b) $Ph - CH_2 - CH(COOEt)_2 \Longrightarrow \overset{\ominus}{Ph} + \overset{\oplus}{CH_2} - CH(COOEt)_2$

                   Synthons

    PhMgBr $XCH_2 - CH(COOEt)_2$

               Synthetic equivalents

(c) $Ph\,CH_2 - CH(COOEt)_2 \Longrightarrow \overset{\oplus}{Ph\,CH_2} + \overset{\ominus}{CH}(COOEt)_2$

                   Synthons

    $PhCH_2X$ $CH_2(COOEt)_2$

    Benzyl halide   Diethyl malonate
                   Synthetic equivalents

           FGI

$Ph\ CH_2\ X \Rightarrow Ph\ CH_2\ OH$

Benzyl halide   Benzyl alcohol

A disconnection should always lead to simplification, out of the above three disconnections, the disconnection (c) is best, since it gives a good cation and a good anion. Moreover, the synthons correspond to easily available synthetic equivalents benzyl bromide and diethyl malonate. Benzyl bromide or benzyl chloride can be obtained from benzyl alcohol. Thus,

            PBr_3 PCl_5

$Ph\ CH_2\ Br \xleftarrow{\hspace{1cm}} Ph\ CH_2\ OH \xrightarrow{\hspace{1cm}} Ph\ CH_2\ Cl$

Benzyl bromide   Benzyl alcohol   Benzyl chloride

Synthesis : Diethyl malonate is first treated with base such as NaOEt to form the corresponding carbanion. This carbanion then attacks on benzyl halide to form TM-5.

           $CH_2(COOEt)_2$ $\xrightarrow[- EtOH]{NaOEt}$ $\overset{\ominus}{CH}(COOEt)_2$

           Diethyl malonate

                         $\downarrow$ $X - CH_2 - Ph$ X = Br or Cl

              $Ph - CH_2 - CH(COOEt)_2$

                   TM-5

Exercises

1. What do you mean by retrosynthesis? Discuss different steps involved in retro-synthesis.
2. Define and explain the following terms with suitable examples:
   (a) FGI (b) Retrosynthesis (c) Disconnection   (d) Target molecule (e) Synthon (f) Synthetic equivalent
3. Comment on one group disconnections.
4. Explain the retrosynthesis and synthesis of the following target molecules :

(i)

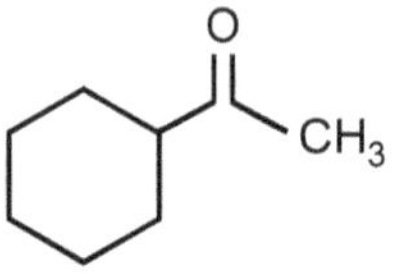

(ii)

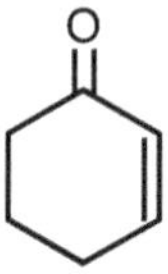

(iii) 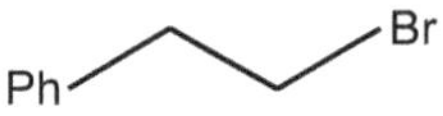   Ph$\diagup\diagdown\diagup\diagdown$Br

(iv) 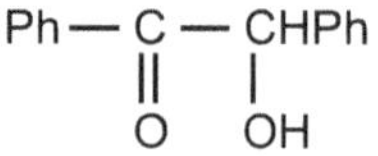 Ph—C—CHPh
       ‖ |
       O OH

(v)

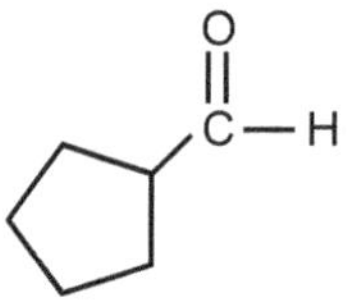

(vi)

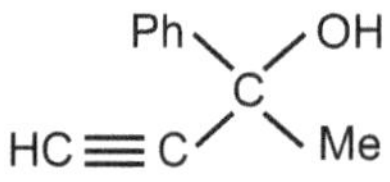

(vii) CH_3— C≡C — CH_2CH_3

(viii) Ph — C — OH with Me and Me groups

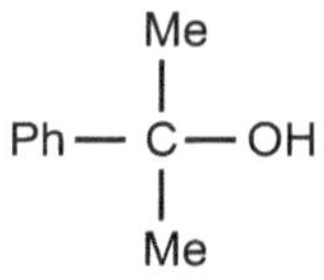

(ix) Ph — $CH(COOEt)_2$

(x)

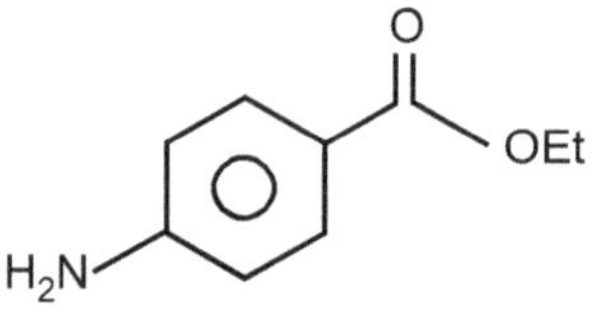

(xi)

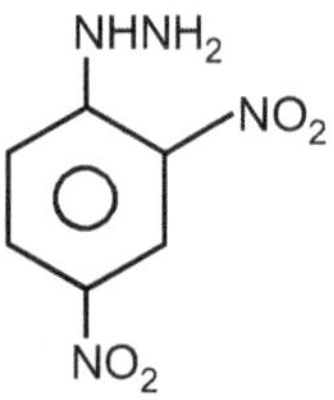

(xii)

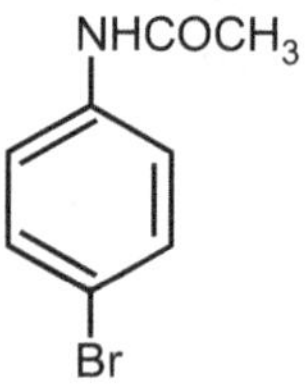

(xiii)

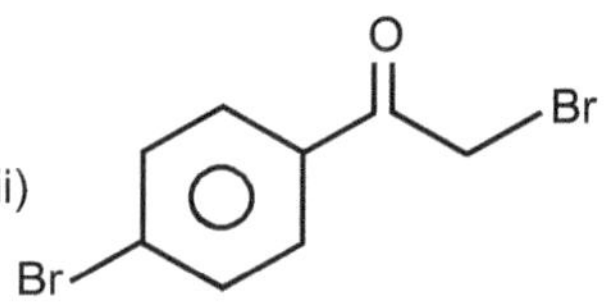

(xiv)

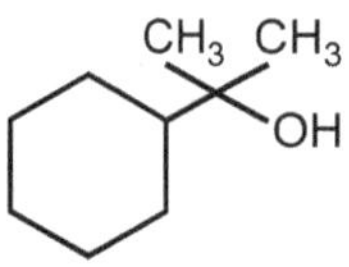

(xv)

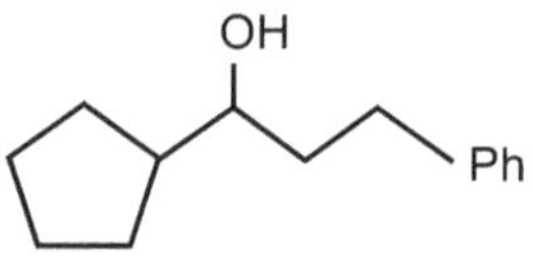

5. **Multiple Choice Questions (MCQs):**

(i)   The first organic compound synthesized in the laboratory was ....

   (a) Formaldehyde   **(b) Urea**

   (c) Ammonia   (d) Methane

(ii) The imaginary fragment produced by a disconnection is ....

   (a) Synthetic equivalent   (b) Cation

   (c) Synthon   (d) Anion

(iii) A ketone is protected during synthesis by converting it to ....

   (a) Alcohol   **(b) Ketal**

   (c) Acid   (d) Acetal

(iv) The compound to be synthesized is ....

   (a) Synthon   (b) Synthetic equivalent

   (c) FGI   (d) Target molecule

(v)   The best method to synthesize aromatic ketones is ....

   (a) Friedel Craft's acylation   (b) Friedel Craft's alkylation

   (c) Wittig reaction   (d) Aldol condensation

(vi) Preparation of cyclohexene from butadiene and ethylene is ....

   (a) Dehydration reaction   (b) Wittig reaction

   (c) Diels-Alder reaction   (d) Grignard reaction

(vii) An α, β-unsaturated aldehyde can be prepared by ....

   (a) Dehydration   **(b) Dehydration of aldol**

   (c) Oxidation   (d) Dehydrogenation

(viii) Synthetic equivalent of an alkyl anion is a ....

   (a) Grignard reagent   (b) Wittig reagent

   (c) Tollen's reagent   (d) Nessler's reagent

(ix) Synthetic equivalent of hydride anion is ....

   (a) Wittig reagent   (b) Grignard reagent

   (c) Sodium borohydride   (d) Alkyl lithium

(x)   The reaction of an ester with excess of Grignard reagent will lead to ....

   (a) Primary alcohol   (b) Secondary alcohol

   (c) Tertiary alcohol   (d) Ketone

■■■

Chapter 3...

Rearrangement Reactions

Contents ...

3.1 Introduction

- The migration of an atom or group from one position to another within the same molecule is known as molecular rearrangement. The rearrangement involves migration of an atom or group of atoms to an adjacent atom (1,2-shift), or in some cases migration is over longer distances.

$$\begin{array}{ccc} M & & M \\ | & \xrightarrow{\ 1,\,2\text{ - shift}\ } & | \\ A-B & & A-B \end{array}$$

where,

A = Migration origin

B = Migration terminus

M = Migrating group

- The atom from which migration begins is known as the migration origin and the atom to which migration group moves is called migration terminus.

- In rearrangement reaction, migrating group shift with its lone pair of electrons called as nucleophilic (anionotropic) rearrangement and migrating group shift without electron pair is called electrophilic (cationotropic) rearrangement. In the rearrangement, if the migration of group is with one electron then it is called free radical rearrangement.

- The most common migrating atoms are carbon, hydrogen or heteroatom. The nucleophilic 1,2-shifts are more common in rearrangement reactions. The rearrangement reaction involves two possible modes of reaction as shown below.

$$
\text{(I)} \quad \overset{\displaystyle R}{\underset{\displaystyle |}{A}} - B \text{ and } \overset{\displaystyle R'}{\underset{\displaystyle |}{A}} - C \rightarrow \overset{\displaystyle R}{\underset{\displaystyle |}{A}} - B \text{ and } \overset{\displaystyle R'}{\underset{\displaystyle |}{A}} - C \text{ with } \overset{\displaystyle R'}{\underset{\displaystyle |}{A}} - B \text{ and } \overset{\displaystyle R}{\underset{\displaystyle |}{A}} - C
$$

Intermolecular rearrangement

$$
\text{(II)} \quad \overset{\displaystyle R}{\underset{\displaystyle |}{A}} - B \text{ and } \overset{\displaystyle R'}{\underset{\displaystyle |}{A}} - C \rightarrow \overset{\displaystyle R}{\underset{\displaystyle |}{A}} - B \text{ and } \overset{\displaystyle R'}{\underset{\displaystyle |}{A}} - C
$$

Intramolecular rearrangement

- 'I' type of rearrangements are called as intermolecular rearrangement in which the group R is completely detached from group A and may end up on the B atom or C atom of another molecule. In 'II' type of rearrangement, R going from A to B in the same molecule is called intramolecular rearrangement.

3.2 Mechanism of Rearrangement Reaction of Carbocation Intermediate

- In this type of reaction the migrating group carries the electron pair with it, the migration terminus B must be an electron deficient atom with only six electrons in its outer shell. The first step is the formation of a carbocation intermediate. Carbocation can be formed from alcohol (the acid treatment of an alcohol to give carbocation from an intermediate oxonium ion), alkyl halide (reaction with $AgNO_3$) and alkene (electrophilic addition to C=C).

Carbocation intermediate

3.3 Rearrangements Involving Carbocation Intermediate

- The skeletal rearrangement of carbocation which involves migration of β-alkyl, aryl or σ-bond is called Wagner-Meerwein rearrangement. In most of the carbocation rearrangement reactions, migration of a atom or group occurs due to the formation of more stable carbocation from less stable carbocation. Neopentyl alcohol on treatment with HCl gives the rearranged product 2-chloro-2-methyl butane.

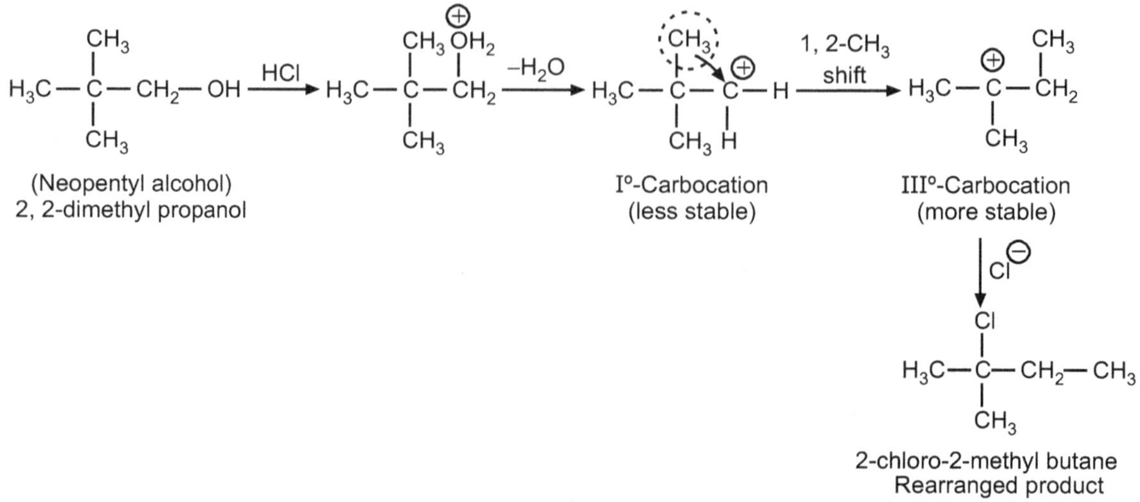

(Neopentyl alcohol)
2, 2-dimethyl propanol

I°-Carbocation
(less stable)

III°-Carbocation
(more stable)

2-chloro-2-methyl butane
Rearranged product

- This rearrangement occurs via carbocation intermediate and involves migration of alkyl group with its lone pair of electrons to an electron deficient carbon atom. It forms more stable carbocation which finally react with nucleophile to give rearranged product.

- In another case, the addition of HCl to 3,3-dimethyl-1-butene forms 3-chloro-2,2-dimethyl butane (an expected product) and 2-chloro-2,3-dimethyl butane (rearrangement product). The rearranged product is the major product.

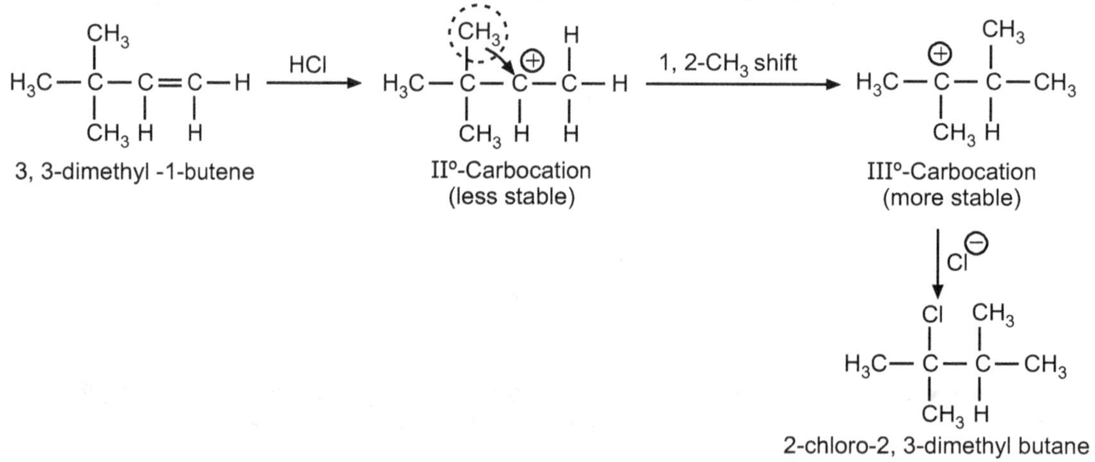

3, 3-dimethyl -1-butene

II°-Carbocation
(less stable)

III°-Carbocation
(more stable)

2-chloro-2, 3-dimethyl butane

- The order of stability of carbocations is $III^{o} > II^{o} > I^{o} > \overset{\oplus}{C}H_3$

- The carbocations rearrange only if they become more stable as a result of rearrangement.

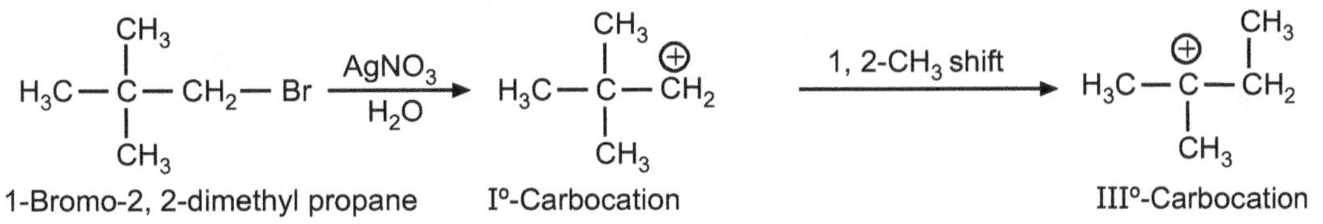

AgNO3
H2O
1, 2-CH3 shift
1-Bromo-2, 2-dimethyl propane
I°-Carbocation
III°-Carbocation

1,2-H shift
1,2 – CH3 shift
1,2 – H shift
III°-Carbocation more stable
II°-Carbocation
II°-Carbocation
III°-Carbocation

3.4 Pinacol Rearrangement

- When vicinal diol is treated with a catalytic amount of acid, it can rearrange to give an aldehyde or ketone by migration of an alkyl or aryl group which is called as Pinacol Rearrangement. The pinacol - pinacolone rearrangement reaction or 1,2- migration can be viewed as a special case of the Wagner–Meerwein rearrangement.

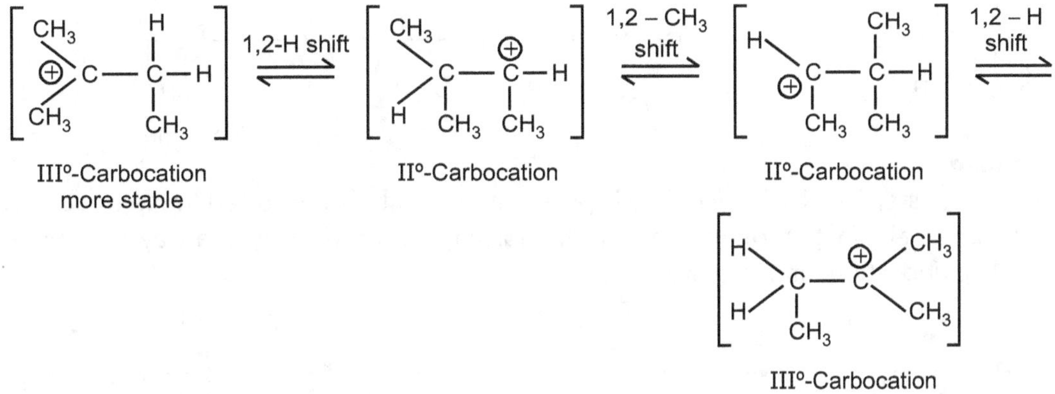

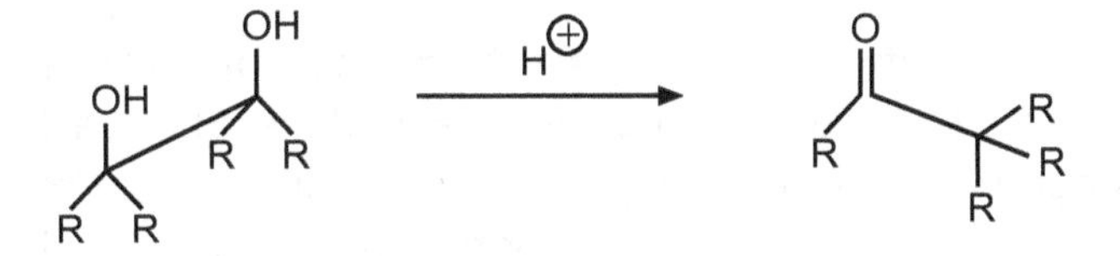

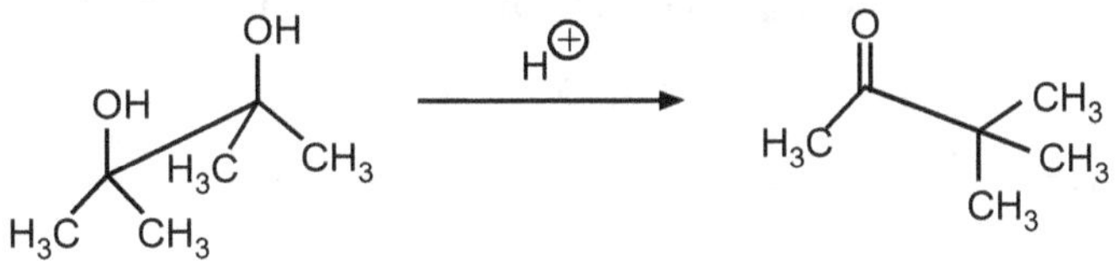

- When $Me_2COHCOHMe_2$ (pinacol) on treatment with acid gives $Me_2COH\overset{\oplus}{C}Me_2$ which on 1, 2-migration of Me to yield Me_3CCOCH_3 is called as pinacolone.

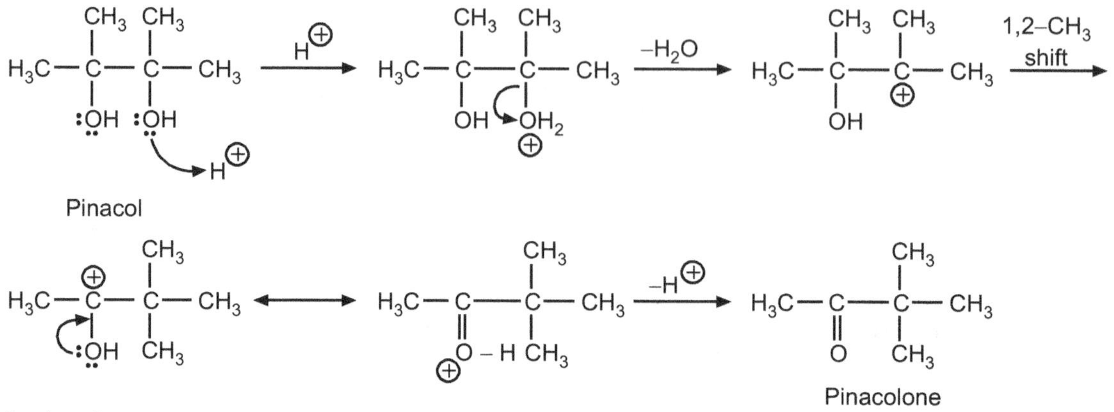

Pinacol

Pinacolone

Mechanism:

- In the first step one hydroxy group is protonated, and thus converted into a good leaving group. The elimination of water from the molecule proceeds in such a way that the more stable carbocation intermediate is formed.

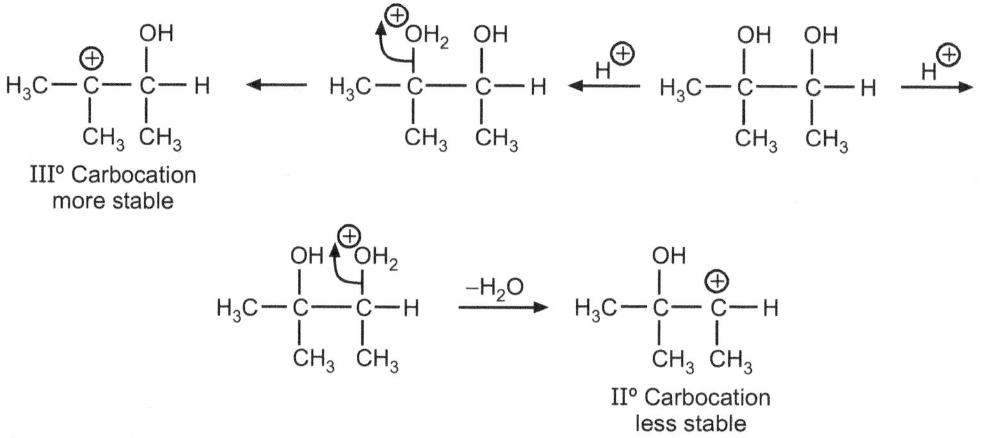

III° Carbocation
more stable

II° Carbocation
less stable

- In the second step, 1,2-shift of a R group to the more stable (III°) carbocation takes place to give a more stable hydroxyl carbocation intermediate. The reaction is intramolecular; the migrating group R is never completely released from the substrate. The driving force is the formation of the more stable rearranged carbocation, which is stabilized by the hydroxy group. In the third step, loss of a proton yields the carbonyl compound.

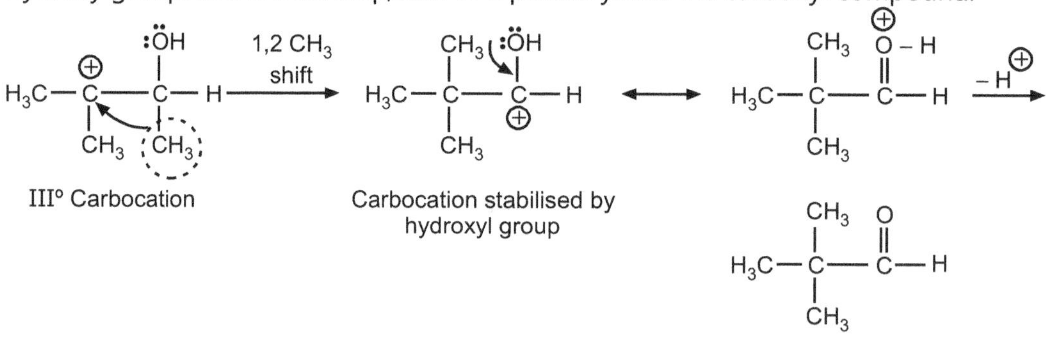

III° Carbocation

Carbocation stabilised by
hydroxyl group

- Reaction with an unsymmetrical diol as starting material may give rise to formation of a mixture of products. Mixtures are product formed, may depend on the reaction conditions, which group preferentially migrates as well as on the nature of the substrate. The order of migration is $R_3C > R_2CH > RCH_2 > CH_3 > H$.

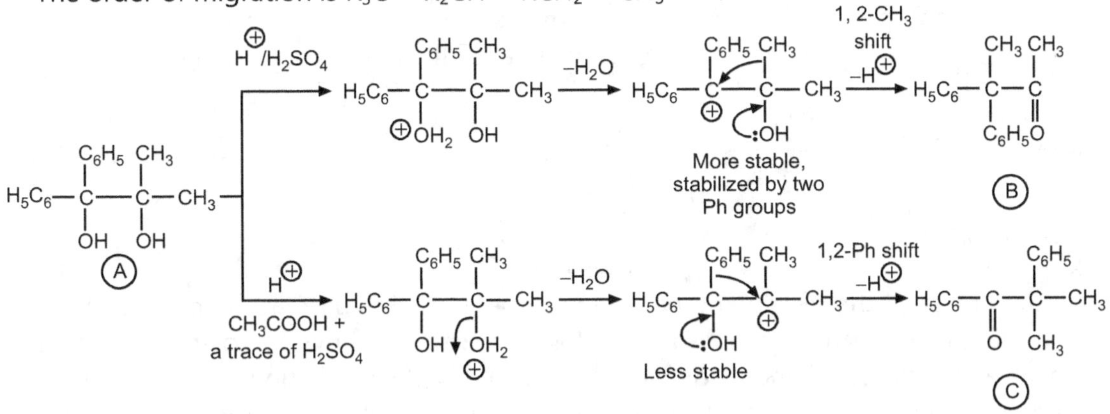

- The action of cold, conc. H_2SO_4 on A produces mainly the ketone B (-CH_3 migration), while treatment of A with acetic acid containing a trace of H_2SO_4 gives mostly C (phenyl migration). If one R is hydrogen, aldehydes can be produced as well as ketones. Generally, aldehyde formation is favored by the use of mild conditions (lower temperatures, weaker acids),

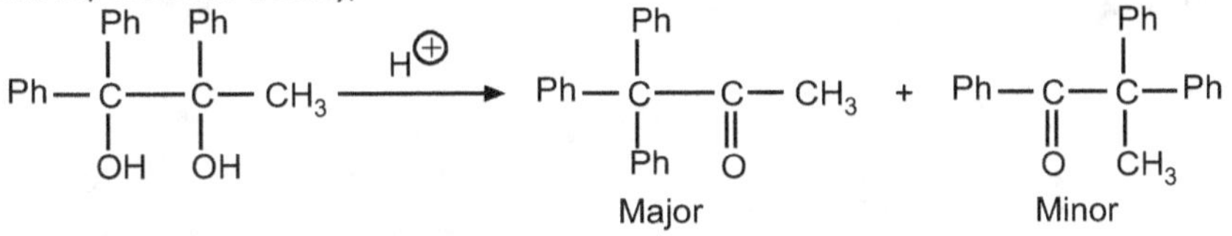

Examples of Pinacol Rearrangement:

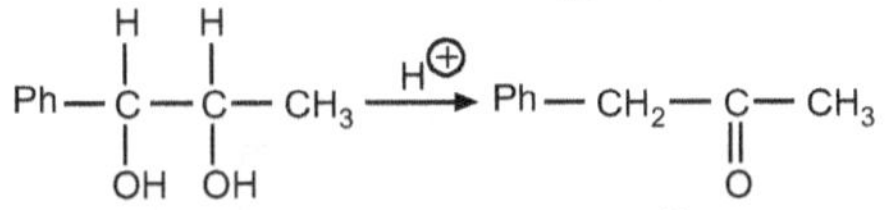

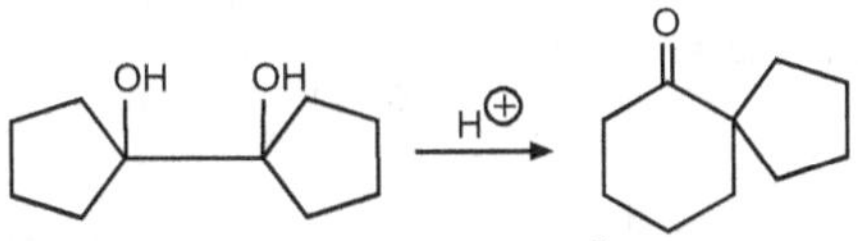

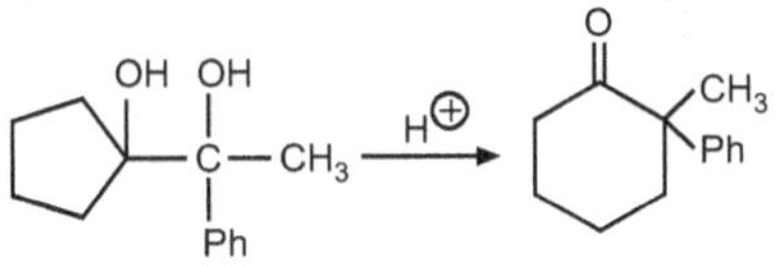

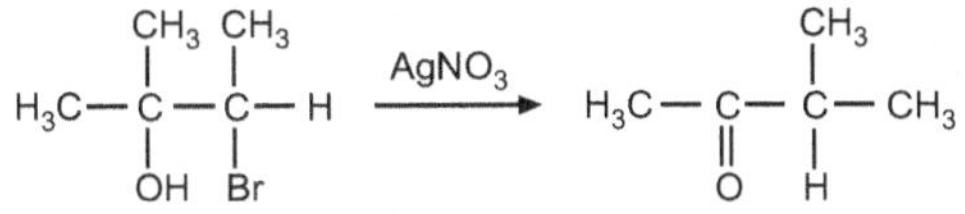

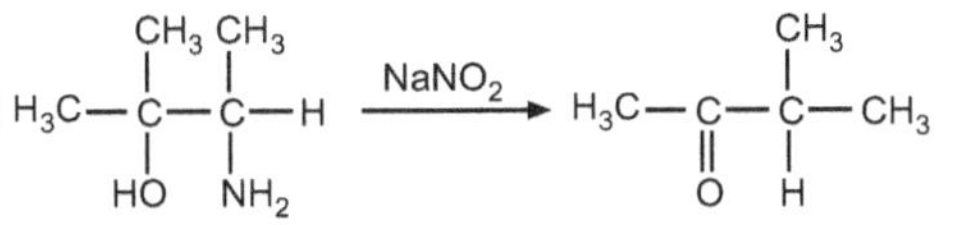

3.5 Favorskii Rearrangement

- α-Halo ketones (chloro, bromo, or iodo) possessing at least one α-hydrogen when treated with a base (NaOH or NaOEt or NaNH$_2$), can undergo a rearrangement reaction via a cyclopropanone intermediate to give a carboxylic acid or an ester or amide, depending on the base used. This reaction is called the *Favorskii rearrangement.*

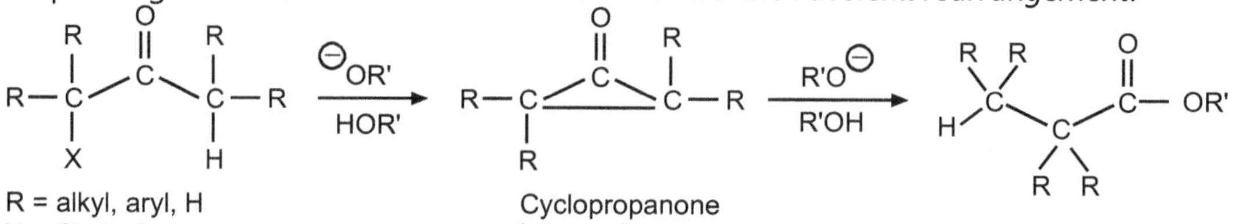

R = alkyl, aryl, H
X = Cl, Br, I

Cyclopropanone
intermediate

- In the first step, the α-halo ketone is deprotonated by the base at the α'-carbon to give the carbanion, which undergoes a ring-closure reaction by an intramolecular substitution to give the cyclopropanone derivative. The nucleophilic addition of the base to the cyclopropanone intermediate leads to the ring opening. With a symmetrically substituted cyclopropanone, cleavage of either C$_\alpha$-CO bond leads to the same product. With unsymmetrical cyclopropanone, that bond is broken preferentially which leads to thermodynamically more stable carbanion. The carbanion intermediate is protonated to give the final product.

Reaction mechanism:

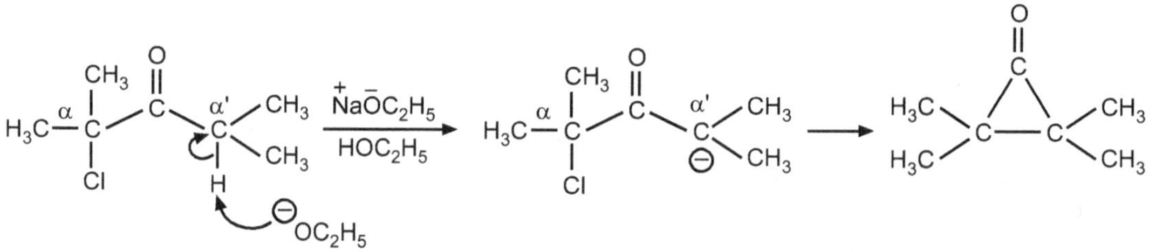

Protons α' to ketone is acidic and sodium ethoxide is strong base that easily abstract the proton to form carbanion as nucleophile

Cl is a leaving group Carbanion attack on the α' carbon atom and substitution reaction takes place to give cyclopropanone

Cyclopropanones are particularly susceptible to nucleophilic addition due to ring strain

- Addition elimination reaction at the carbonyl and cyclopropanone ring opening takes place to generate a stabilised enolate product.

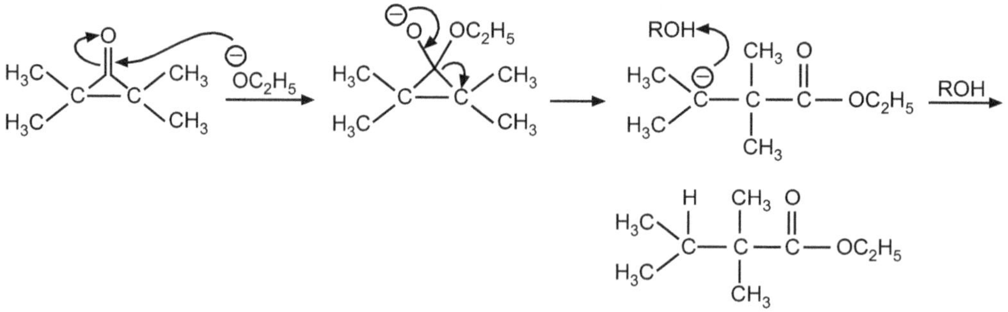

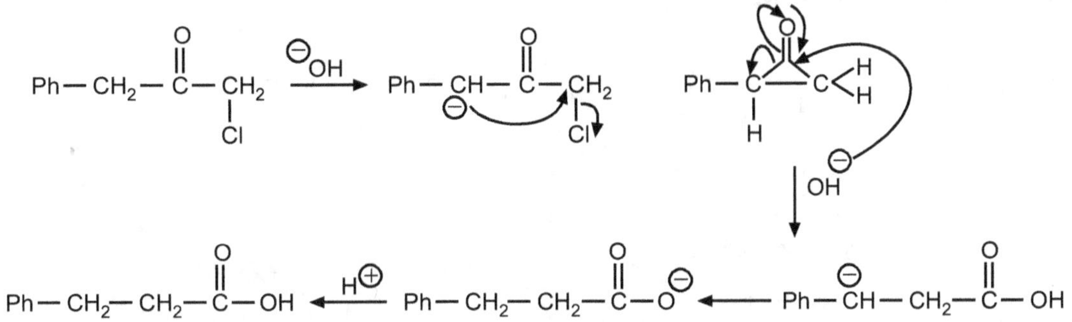

- Cyclic α-halo ketones on treatment with base give ring contraction as shown in the following reaction.

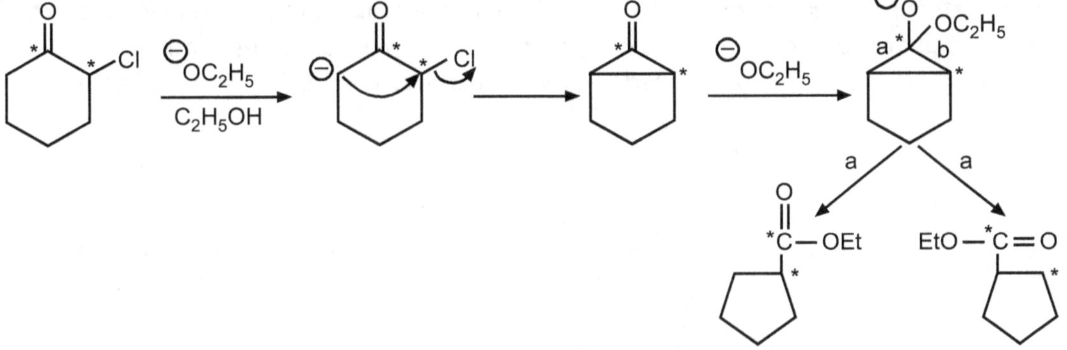

- The two important variations of Favorskii rearrangement are:

1. When β-halo ketones are treated with base, in presence of nucleophile the reaction is called Homo-Favorskii rearrangement. This reaction takes place via a cyclobutanone intermediate.

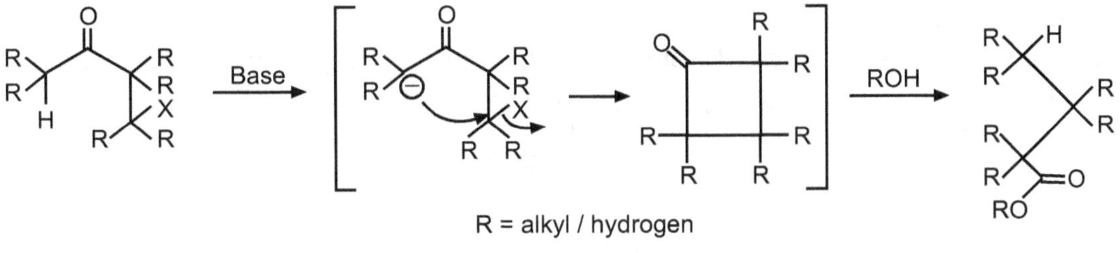

R = alkyl / hydrogen

2. If α-haloketone does not have any enolizable hydrogen then the reaction is called as Quasi-Favorskii rearrangement.

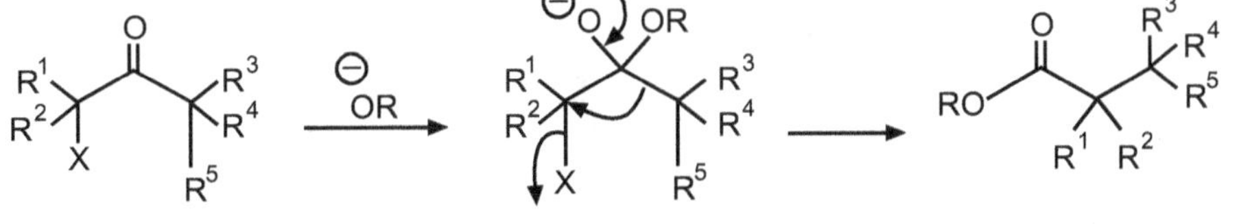

Examples of Favorskii rearrangement:

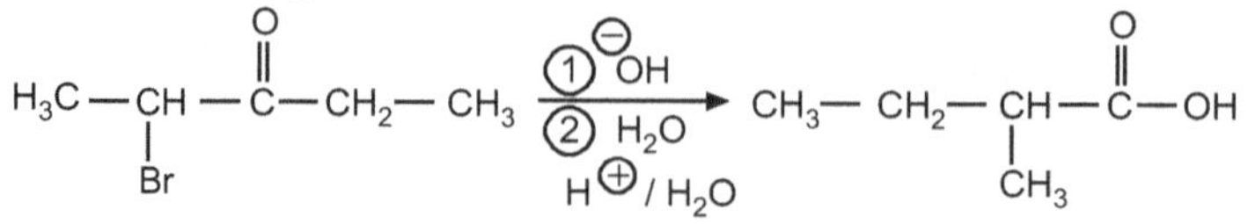

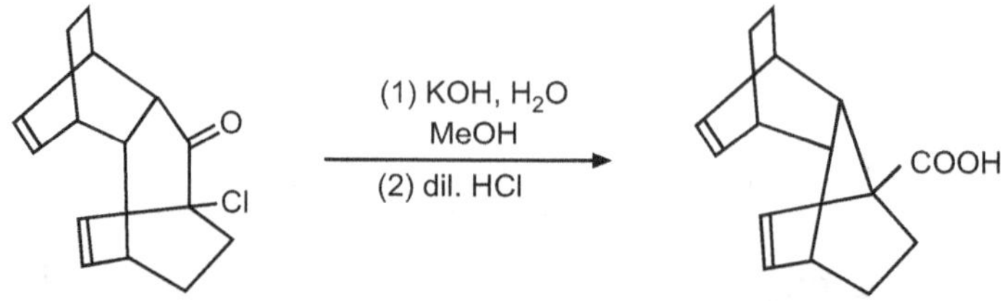

3.6 The Curtius Rearrangement

- The Curtius rearrangement involves the thermal decomposition of an acyl azide to yield an isocyanate by loss of N_2. Isocyanate on hydrolysis gives amine. The Curtius rearrangement can thus be applied to convert carboxylic acids into primary amines.

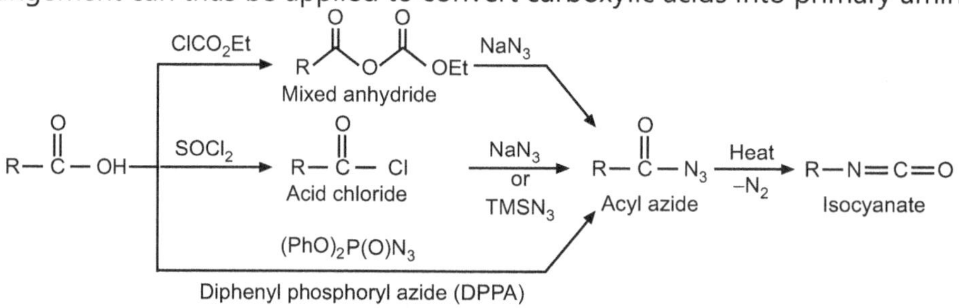

Diphenyl phosphoryl azide (DPPA)

- This reaction can be applied to almost any carboxylic acids such as aliphatic, aromatic, alicyclic, heterocyclic, unsaturated, and containing many functional groups. The required acyl azide can be prepared from the corresponding acyl chloride and azide ion (e.g. with sodium azide) or alternatively from an acyl hydrazine by treatment with nitrous acid or from mixed anhydride.

- Acyl azide can be synthesized from carboxylic acid by using diphenyl phosphoryl azide (DPPA).

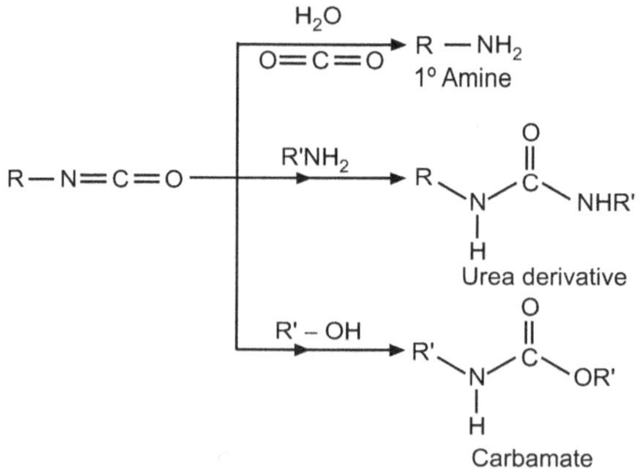

- Loss of N_2 and migration of the group R is likely to be a concerted process, since evidence for a free acyl nitrene RCON in the thermal reaction has not been found.

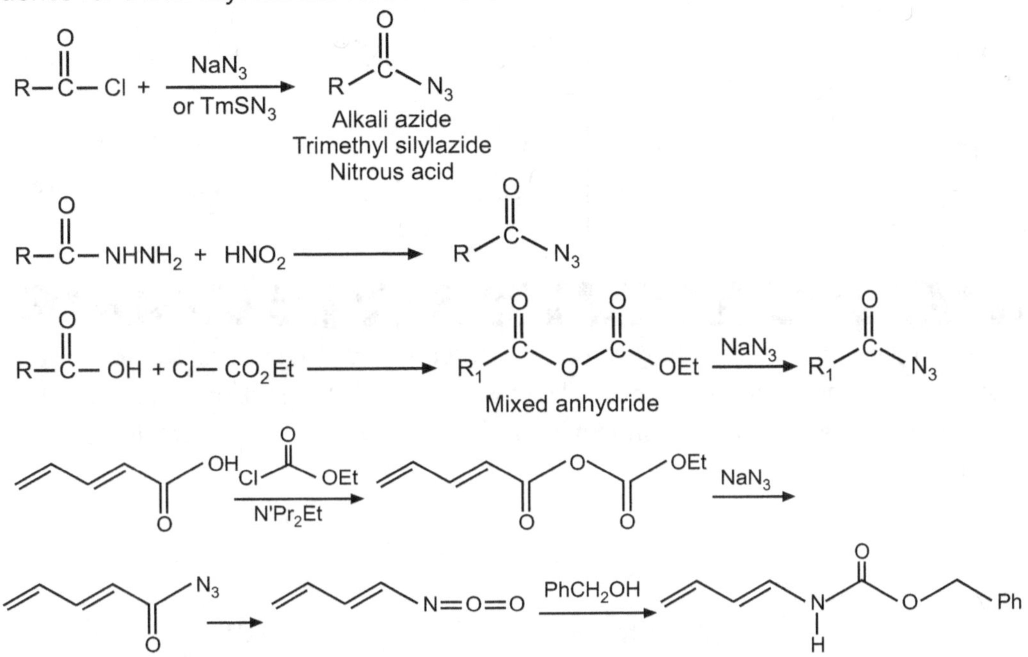

Alkali azide
Trimethyl silylazide
Nitrous acid

Mixed anhydride

- The Curtius rearrangement is catalyzed by Lewis or protic acids, but good yields of product are often obtained also without a catalyst. Isocyanates are highly reactive and they immediately react with water and form amine. When alcohol is used as a solvent, the isocyanate reacts with alcohol to form carbamate. From reaction in an inert solvent (e.g. benzene, chloroform) in the absence of water, the isocyanate can be isolated.

The examples of Curtius rearrangement are:

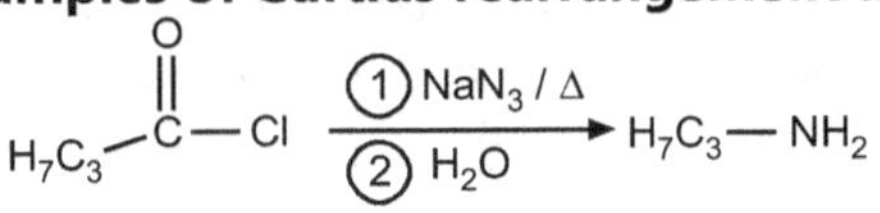

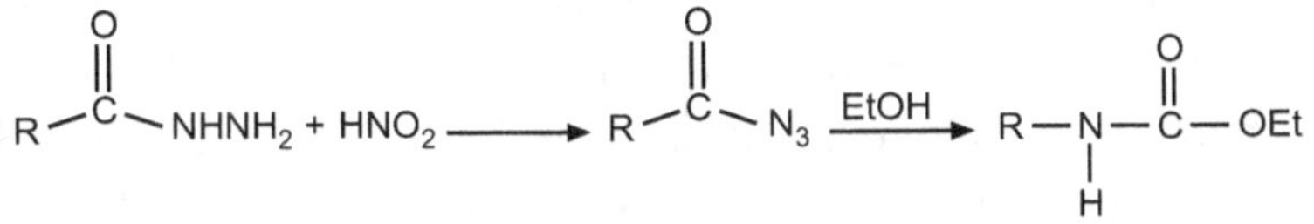

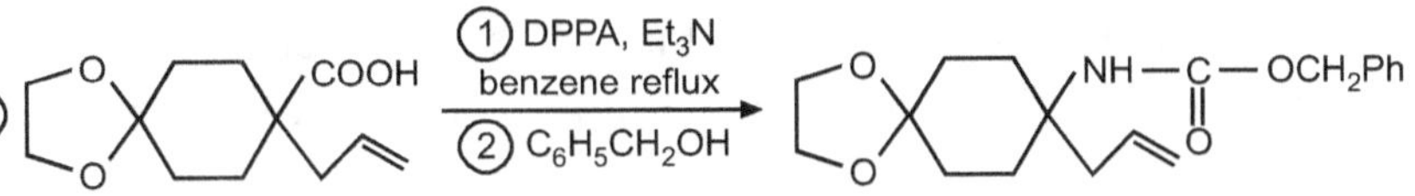

- DPPA is prepared from the corresponding acyl chloride and azide ion (e.g. with sodium azide) or alternatively from an acylhydrazine by treatment with nitrous acid.

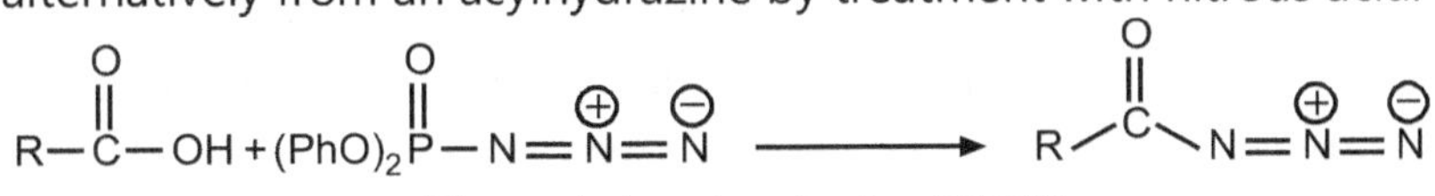

Diphenyl phosphoryl azide (DPPA)

The example of Curtius rearrangement is:

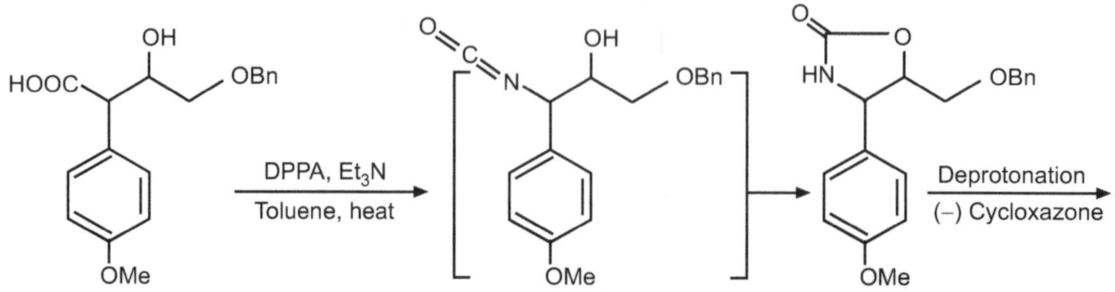

3.7 Beckmann Rearrangement

- Rearrangement of oximes to give N-substituted carboxylic amides, the rearrangement of ketoxime under the influence of acidic reagents to yield N-substituted carboxylic amides, is called the *Beckmann rearrangement*. Aldoximes often are less reactive and they form nitrile.

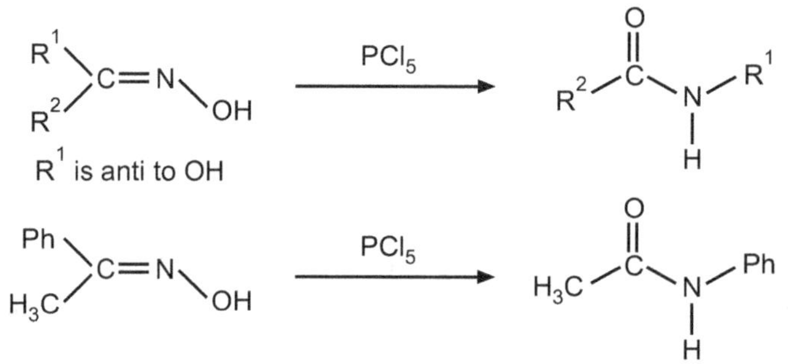

- Upon treatment with a protic acid, the hydroxy group of the oxime is protonated to give an oxonium derivative which can easily lose a water molecule. The anti group migration of the substituent R (together with the bonding electrons) and loss of water proceed simultaneously. The cationic species thus formed reacts with water to give the iminol which tautomerizes to a more stable amide tautomer, the N-substituted carboxylic amide. As reagents are concentrated sulfuric acid, hydrochloric acid, liquid sulfur dioxide, thionyl chloride, phosphorus pentachloride, zinc oxide and even silica gel MoO_3 on silica gel, $RuCl_3$, $Y(OTf)_3$, $HCl–HOAc-Ac_2O$, $POCl_3$, $BiCl_3$, heat with $FeCl_3$, and polyphosphoric acid can be used for *Beckmann rearrangement*. Reagents like phosphorus pentachloride (as well as thionyl chloride and others) first convert the hydroxy group of the oxime into a good leaving group.

- The reaction with oximes of cyclic ketones leads to ring enlargement and form lactam by ring enlargement. This particular reaction is performed on an industrial scale; ε-caprolactam is used as monomer for polymerization to a polyamide for the production of synthetic fibres.

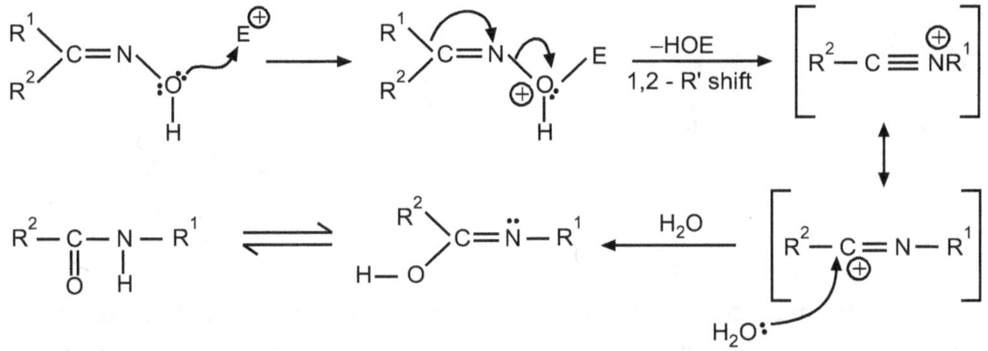

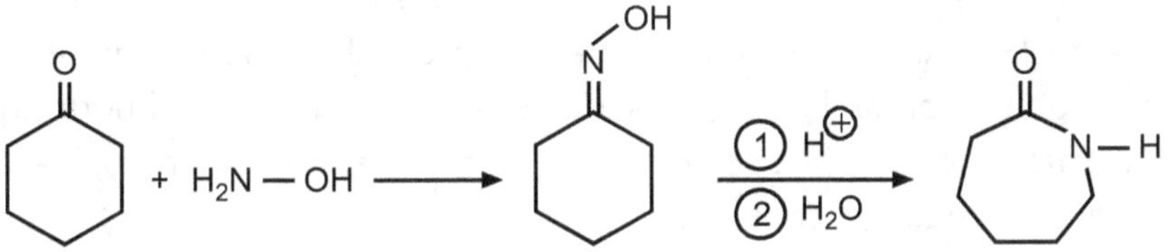

- **Example of Beckmann rearrangement:**

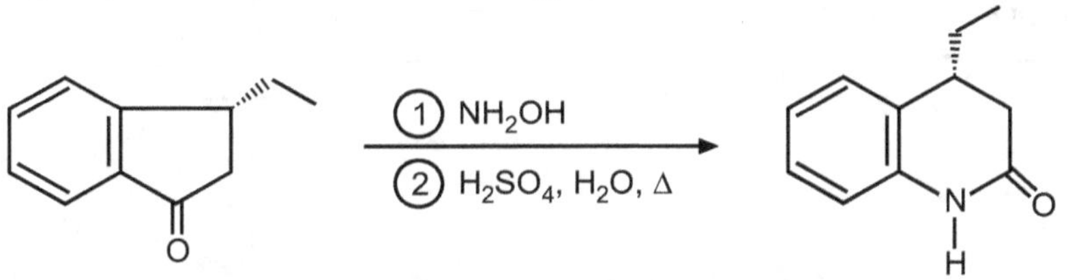

3.8 Baeyer–Villiger Oxidation

- The treatment of ketones with peroxy acids or with hydrogen peroxyde, in the presence of acid catalysts, a formal insertion of oxygen followed by migration of alkyl or aryl group can take place to yield a carboxylic ester. This reaction is called the Baeyer–Villiger rearrangement.

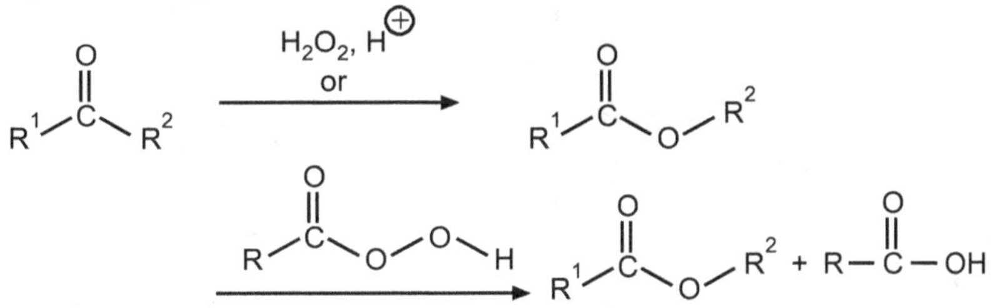

- In a first step, the carbonyl group is taking the proton from acid and protonated to form carbocation intermediate. In the second step, the peracid adds to the carbocation to form *Criegee intermediate*. In the third step, migration of alkyl or aryl takes place with elimination of carboxylic acid.

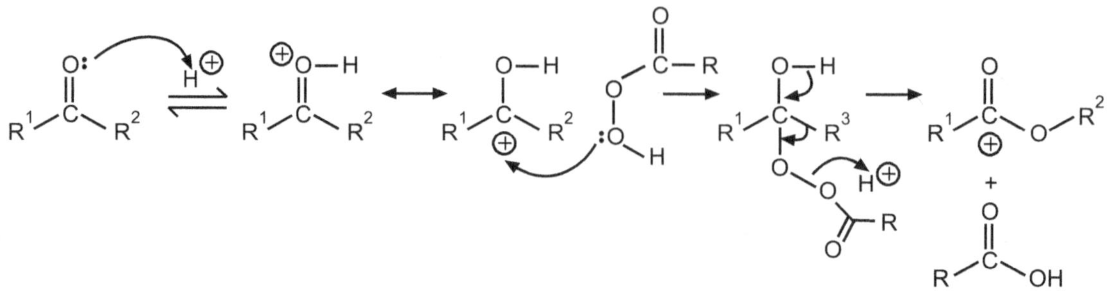

- The ease of migration of substituents R_1, R_2 depends on their ability to stabilize a positive charge in the transition state. For unsymmetrical ketones the approximate order of migration is $R_3C > R_2CH > Ar > RCH_2 > CH_3$. The CH_3 group has a low migrating ability, and the migrating ability of aryl groups is decreased by electron-withdrawing and increased by electron-donating substituents. The Baeyer–Villiger oxidation of unsymmetrical ketones is regioselective.

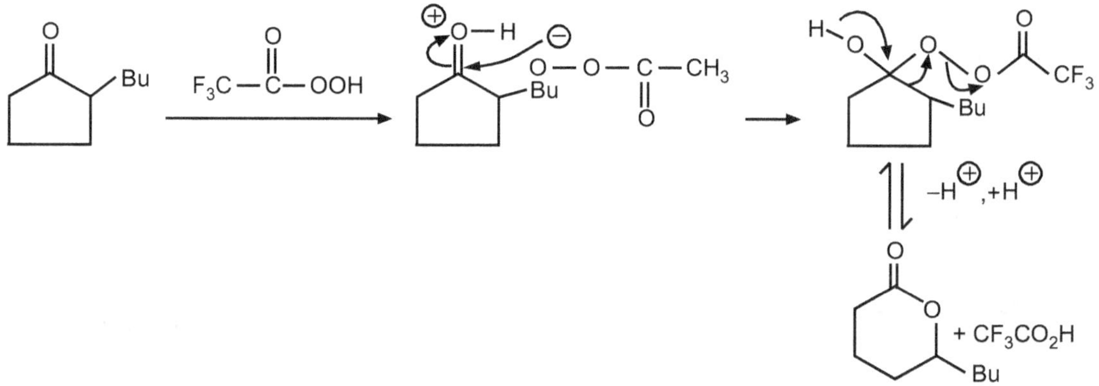

- Cyclic ketones react through ring expansion to yield lactones (cyclic esters). Hydrogen peroxide has been used to convert cyclic ketones to lactones using a catalytic amount of $MeReO_3$.

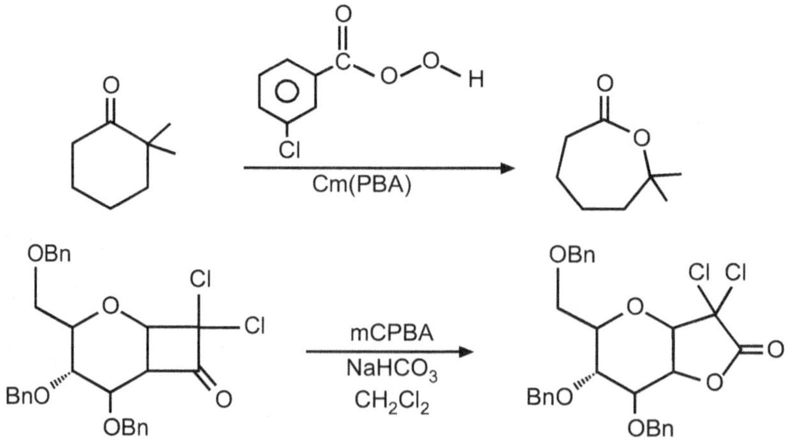

- **Examples of Baeyer–Villiger Oxidation:**

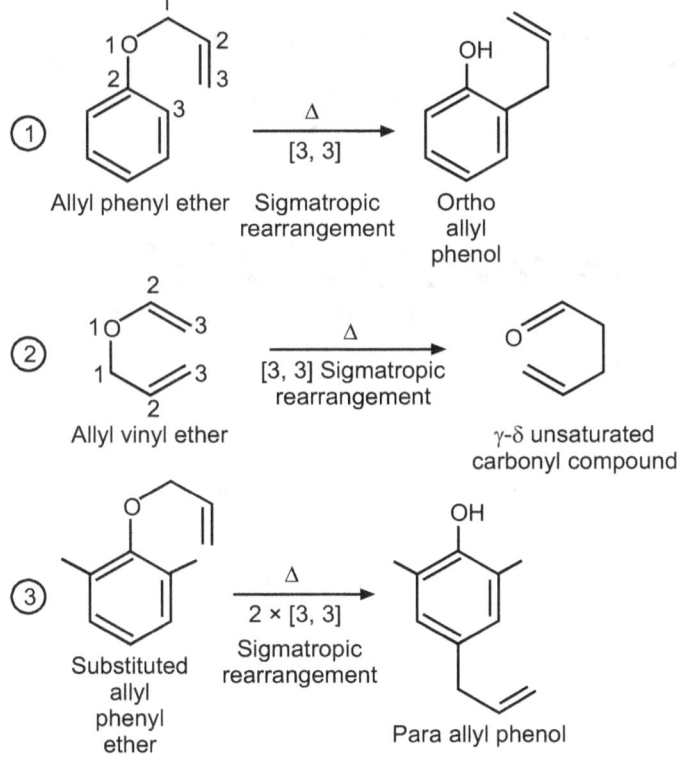

3.9 The Claisen Rearrangement

- Allylic aryl ethers, when heated, rearrange to *ortho*-allylphenols, this reaction is called the Claisen rearrangement. If both *ortho* positions are filled, the allylic group migrates to the para position (para-Claisen rearrangement).

- The Claisen rearrangement reaction is a concerted pericyclic [3,3] sigmatropic rearrangement reaction. A carbon–oxygen bond is cleaved and a carbon–carbon bond is formed followed by tautomerization to the stable aromatic allyl phenol.

- Allylic ethers of enols (allylic vinylic ethers) also undergo the Claisen rearrangement.

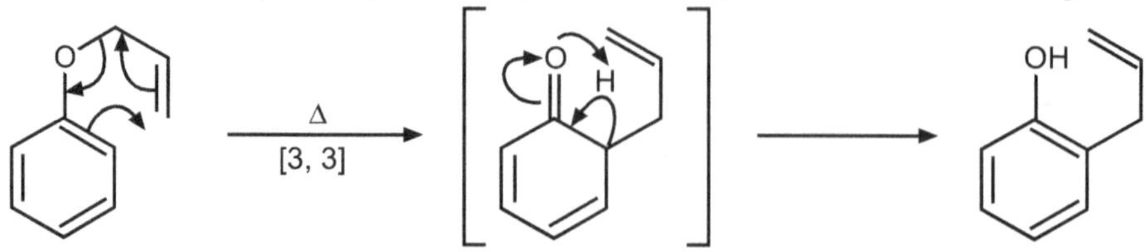

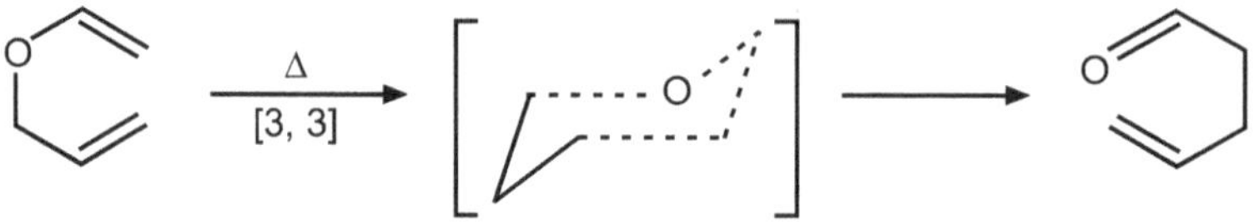

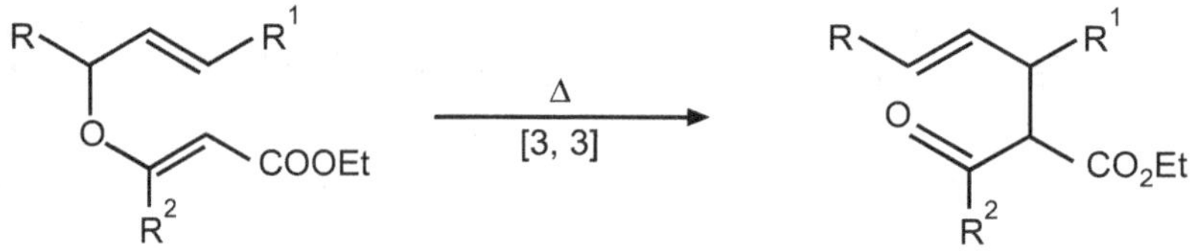

- In the ortho migration, the allylic group always undergoes an allylic shift. Whereas in the para-Claisen rearrangement there is never an allylic shift. The allylic group is found exactly as it was in the original ether.

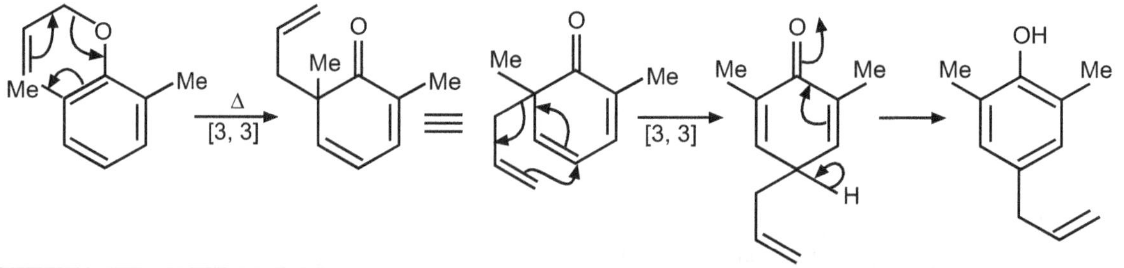

Exercises

1. Define rearrangement reactions. Explain different types of rearrangement reactions.
2. Explain the formation and stability of:
   (i) Carbocation
   (ii) Carbanion
3. Explain with suitable example 'Stability of carbocation plays important role in the rearrangement reaction'.
4. Explain the reaction and mechanism of pinacol-pinacolone rearrangement with suitable example.
5. Explain the reaction and mechanism of Favorskii rearrangement with suitable example.
6. Explain the reaction and mechanism of Curtius rearrangement with suitable example.

7. Explain which intermediate is involved in Curtius rearrangement.

8. Explain the reaction and mechanism of Beckmann rearrangement with suitable example.

9. Explain, Aldoxime on Beckmann rearrangement gives nitrile.

10. Explain the stereochemistry involved in Beckmann rearrangement.

11. Explain the reaction and mechanism of Baeyer-Villiger rearrangement with suitable example.

12. With the help of suitable example explain migrating aptitude of migrating group in Baeyer-Villiger rearrangement.

13. Explain the reaction and mechanism of Claisen rearrangement with suitable example.

14. Write short notes on:

   (a) Rearrangement reactions

   (b) Stability and formation of carbanion

   (c) Stability and formation of carbocation

   (d) Pinacol rearrangement

   (e) Favorskii rearrangement

   (f) Homo-Favorskii and Quasi-Favorskii rearrangement

   (g) Beckmann rearrangement

   (h) Curtius rearrangement

   (i) Baeyer-Villiger rearrangement

   (j) Claisen rearrangement

15. Predict the products:

(i)
OH OH
1. $H^{\oplus}$
2. $NaBH_4$, $HgSO_4$
?

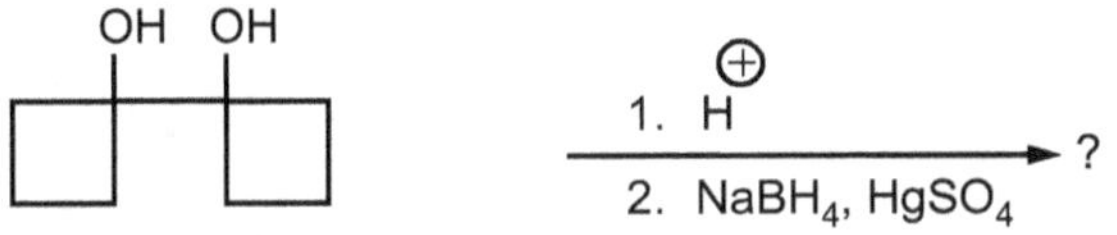

(ii)
N—OH
PPA
?

(iii)
Br
O
NaOEt
?

(iv)
O
Cl
1. NaOH, H_2O
2. $H_3O^{\oplus}$
?

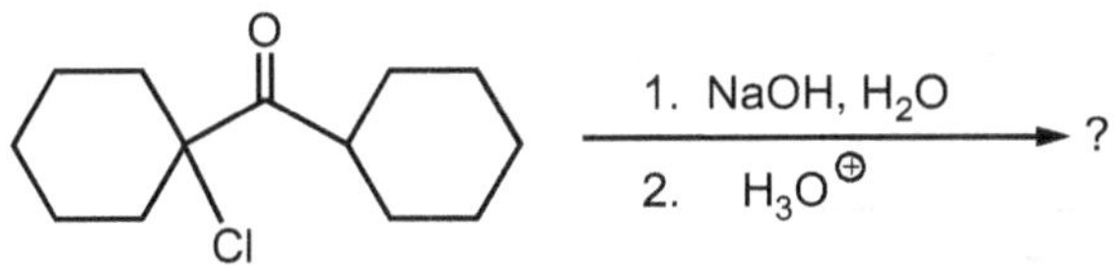

(v)

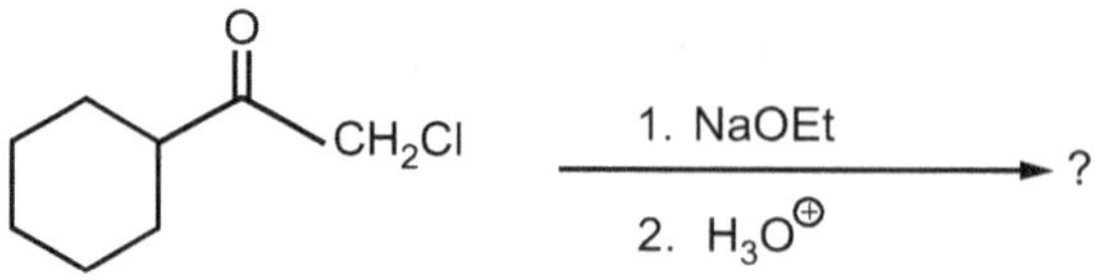

$\xrightarrow[\text{2. } H_3O^{\oplus}]{\text{1. NaOEt}}$?

(vi)

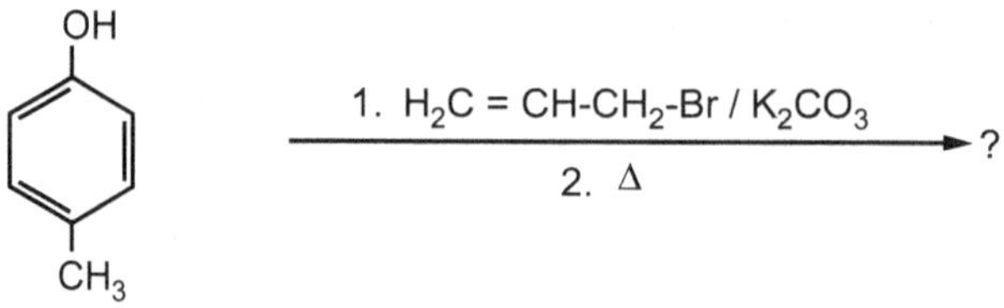

$\xrightarrow[\text{2. } \Delta]{\text{1. } H_2C = CH\text{-}CH_2\text{-}Br / K_2CO_3}$?

(vii)

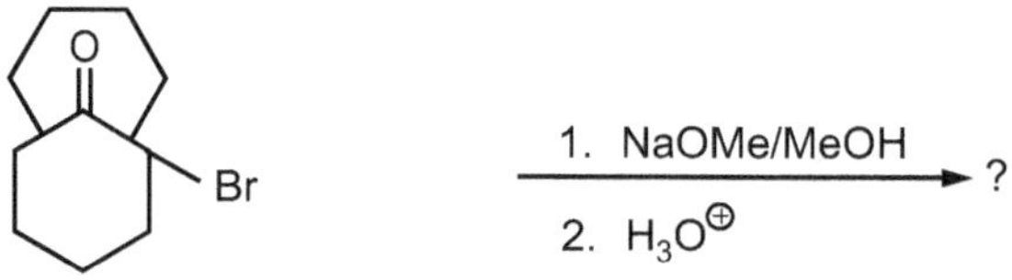

$\xrightarrow[\text{2. } H_3O^{\oplus}]{\text{1. NaOMe/MeOH}}$?

(viii)

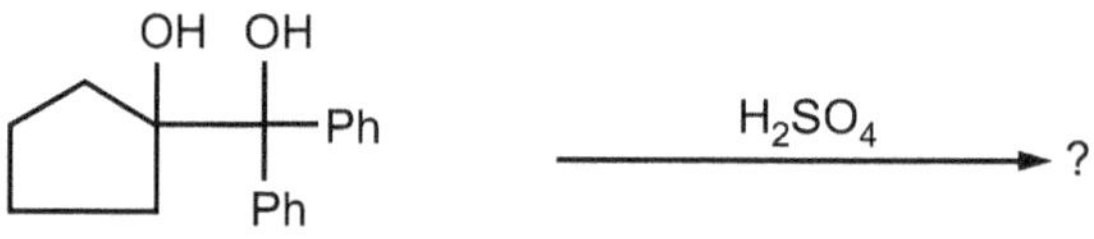

$\xrightarrow{H_2SO_4}$?

(ix)

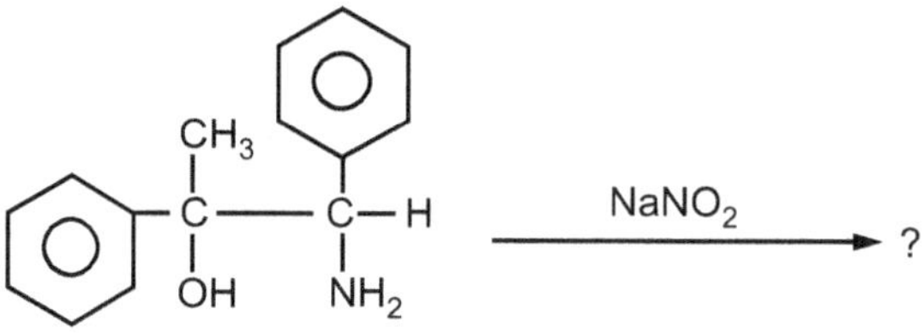

$\xrightarrow{NaNO_2}$?

(x)

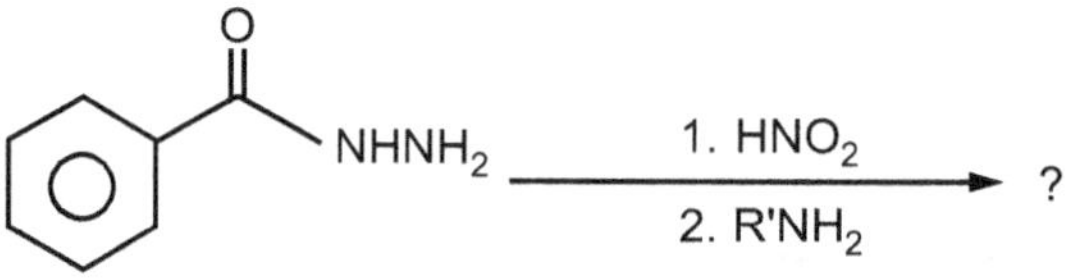

$\xrightarrow[\text{2. R'NH}_2]{\text{1. HNO}_2}$?

(xi)

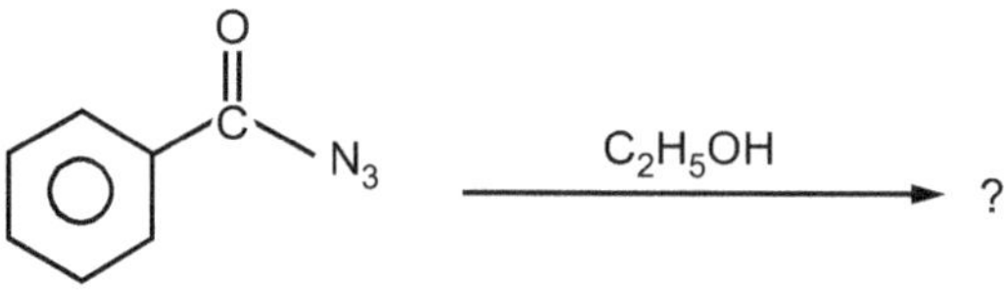

$\xrightarrow{C_2H_5OH}$?

(xii) 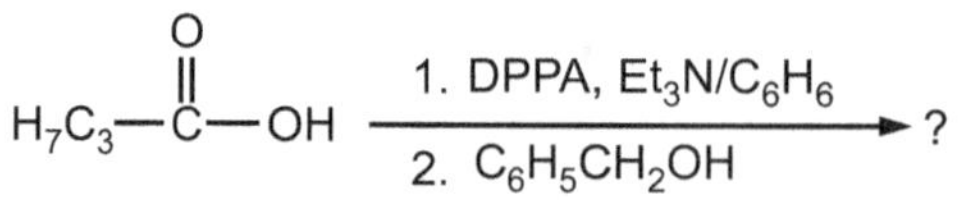 $H_7C_3-\overset{\overset{\displaystyle O}{\|}}{C}-OH$ $\xrightarrow[\text{2. } C_6H_5CH_2OH]{\text{1. DPPA, Et}_3\text{N/C}_6\text{H}_6}$?

16. Explain the mechanism of following reactions:

(i)

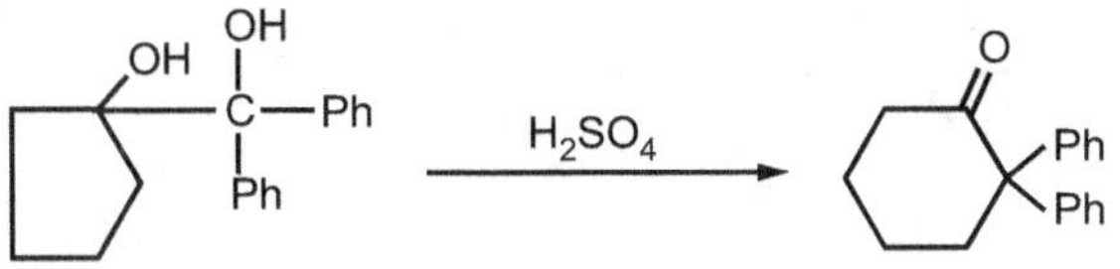

(ii)

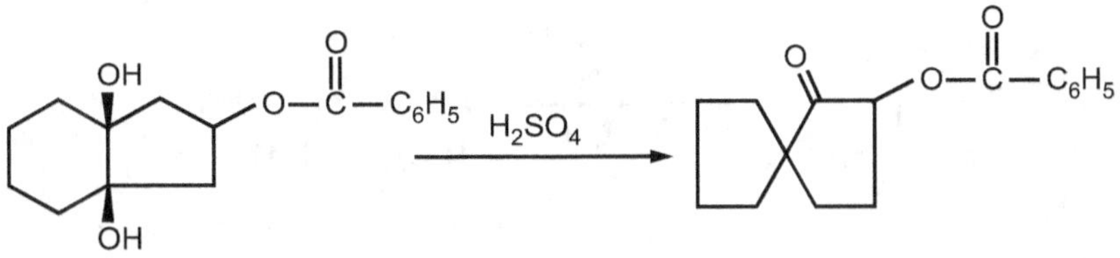

(iii) $(H_3C)_2CHCH-\overset{\overset{\displaystyle O}{\|}}{C}-CH(CH_3)_2$ $\xrightarrow{\ominus OCH_3}$ $[(CH_3)_2CH]_2CHCO_2CH_3$

with Br below the CHCH

(iv)

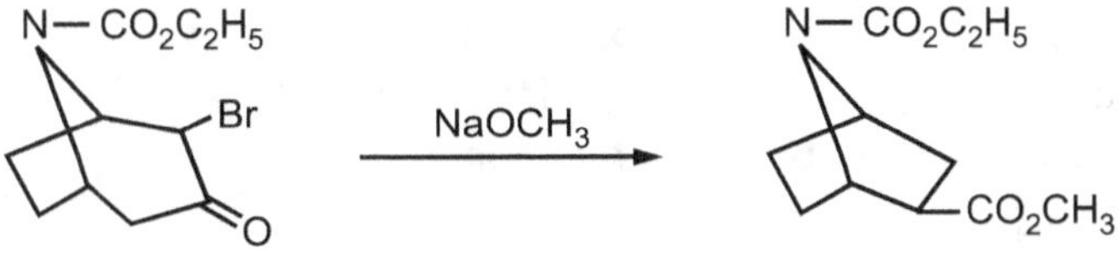

NaOCH$_3$

(v)

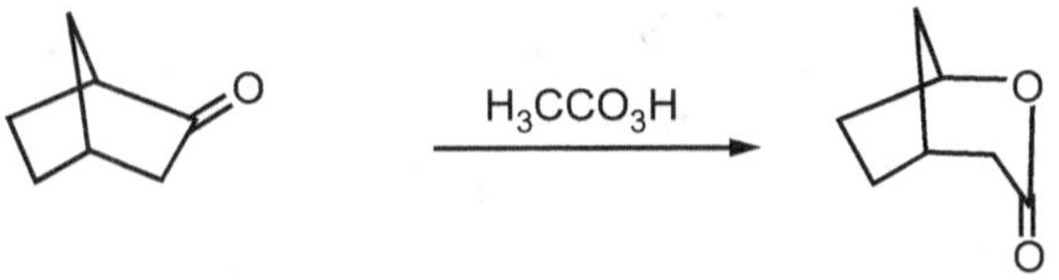

H$_3$CCO$_3$H

(vi)

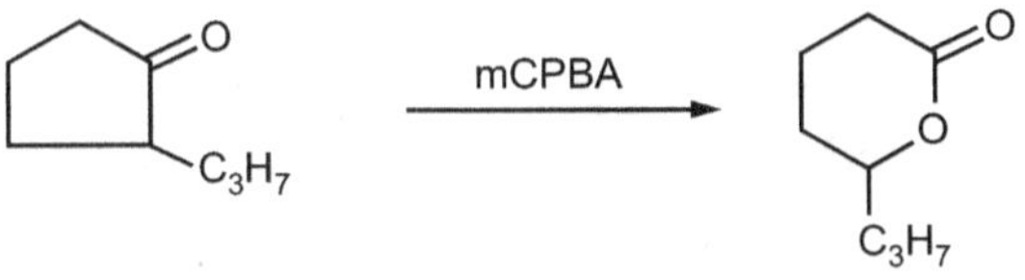

mCPBA

(vii)

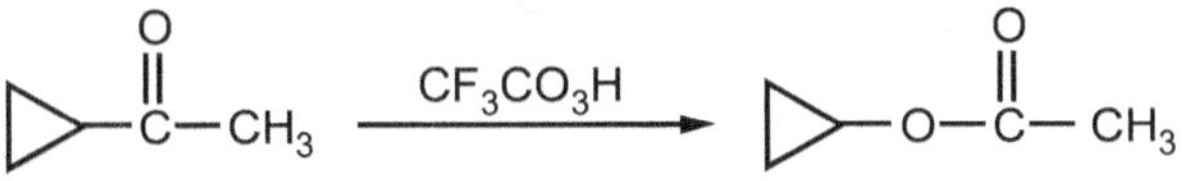

CF$_3$CO$_3$H

(viii)

1. SOCl$_2$
2. NaN$_3$
3. C$_2$H$_5$NH$_2$

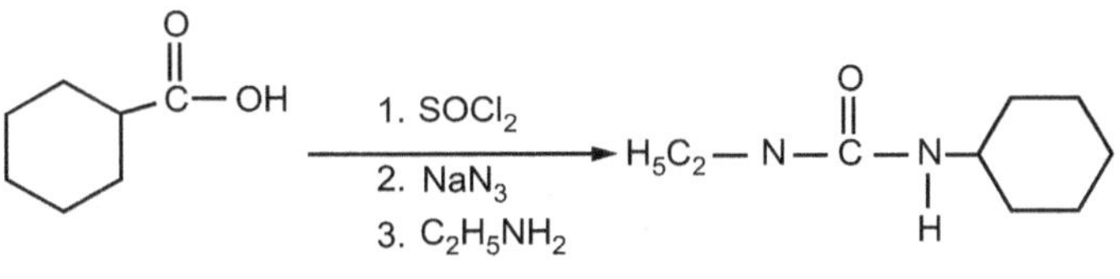

(ix) 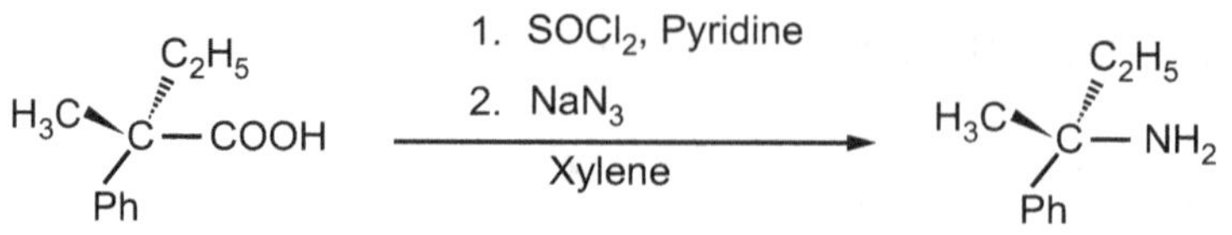
$$H_3C - \underset{\underset{Ph}{|}}{\overset{C_2H_5}{\overset{|}{C}}} - COOH$$

1. SOCl₂, Pyridine
2. NaN₃
Xylene

$$H_3C - \underset{\underset{Ph}{|}}{\overset{C_2H_5}{\overset{|}{C}}} - NH_2$$

(x)

HO_2C (thiophene ring) R

1. $(PhO)_2\overset{O}{\overset{||}{P}}N_3$
   Et₃N
2. tBuOH

$(H_3C)_3CO_2CNH$ (thiophene ring) R

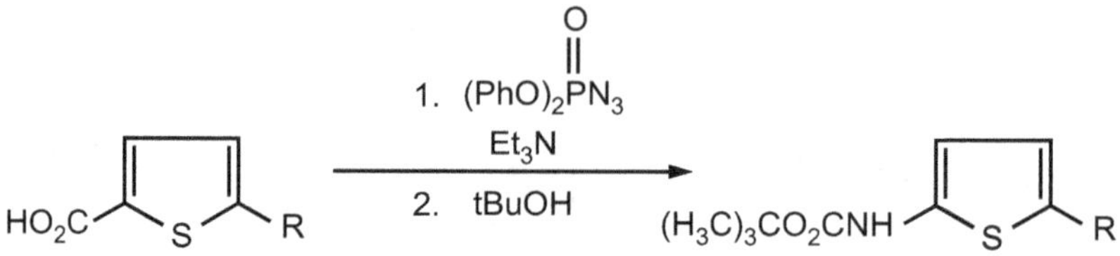

17. Multiple Choice Questions:

(i) Arrange the following carbocations by increasing order of stability.

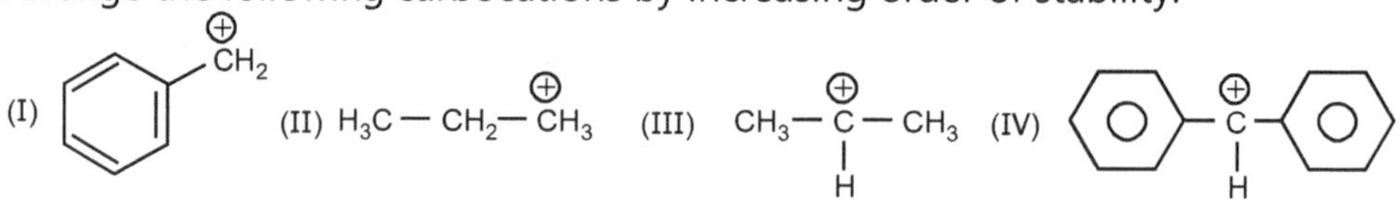

(I) (benzyl cation with $\overset{\oplus}{C}H_2$)

(II) $H_3C - CH_2 - \overset{\oplus}{C}H_3$

(III) $CH_3 - \underset{\underset{H}{|}}{\overset{\oplus}{C}} - CH_3$

(IV) (diphenyl cation)

(a) I < IV < II < III

(b) II < III < I < IV

(c) IV < I < III < I

(d) II < I < III < IV

(ii) The product formed in the following reaction is

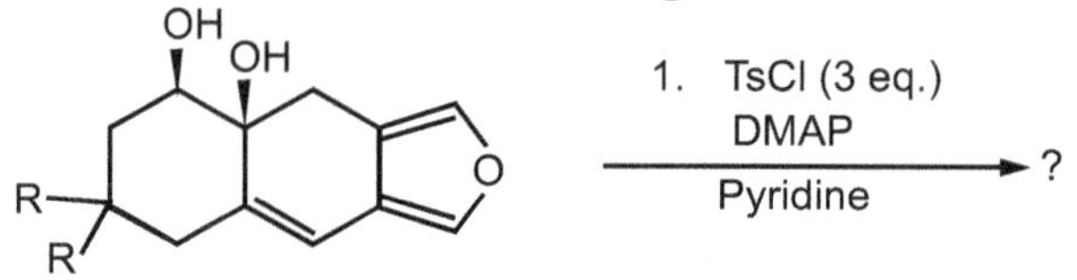

(starting material with OH, OH groups, R, R')

1. TsCl (3 eq.)
   DMAP
   Pyridine

→ ?

(a) 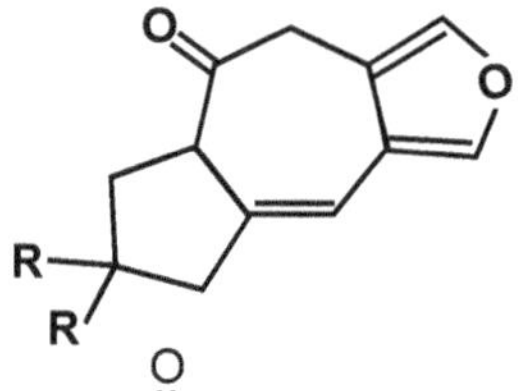 (structure)

(b) 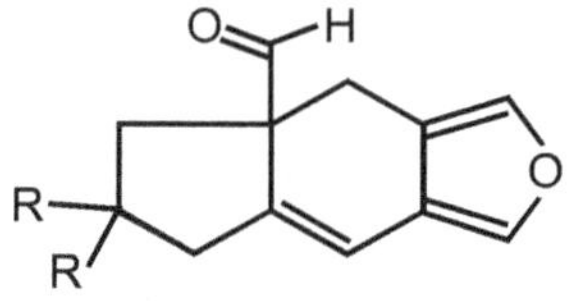 (structure)

(c) 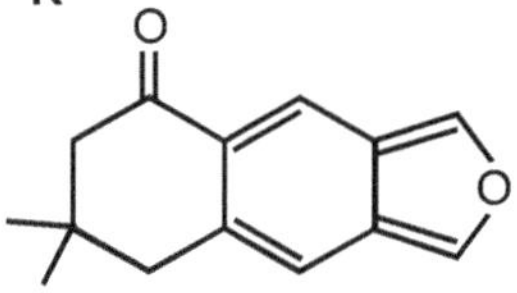 (structure)

(d) 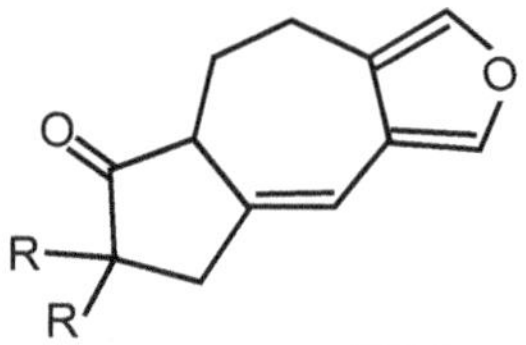 (structure)

(iii) The starting reagent required for the synthesis of (cyclopentane with C(=O)OMe) is

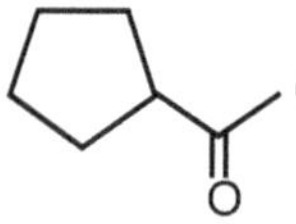

(a) 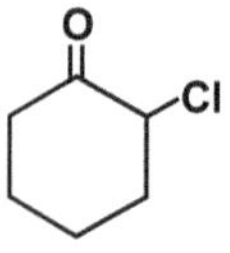 (cyclohexanone with Cl)

(b) 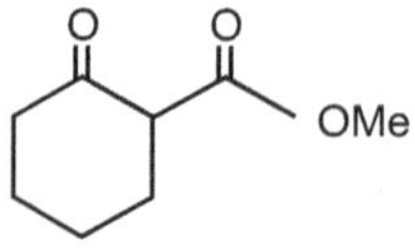 (cyclohexanone with OMe ester)

(c) 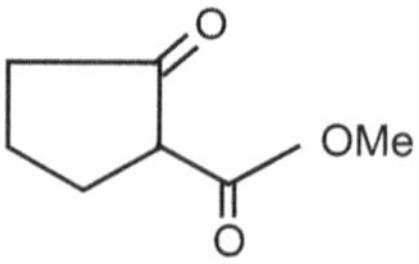 (cyclopentane with OMe ester)

(d) 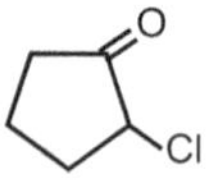 (cyclopentanone with Cl)

(iv) The product formed in the following reaction is

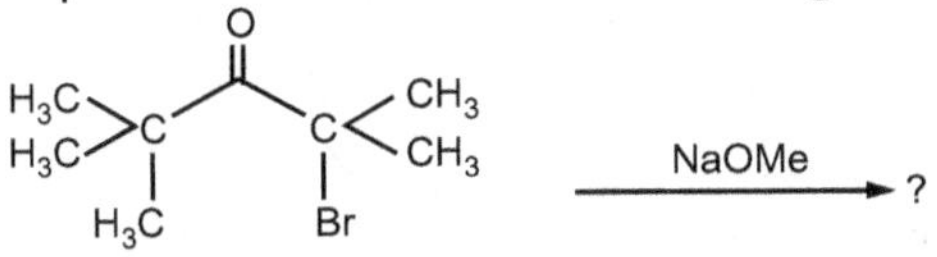

$$\underset{\substack{H_3C}}{\overset{H_3C}{>}}\!C(CH_3)\!-\!\underset{O}{\overset{\|}{C}}\!-\!\underset{Br}{\overset{}{C}}(CH_3)(CH_3) \xrightarrow{\ \text{NaOMe}\ } \ ?$$

(a) $H_3C,\ H_3C{>}C(CH_3)\!-\!C(CH_3)(CH_3)\!-\!C(=O)\!-\!OMe$

(b) $H_3C,\ H_3C{>}C(CH_3)\!-\!\underset{O}{\overset{\|}{C}}\!-\!C(CH_3)(CH_3)(OMe)$

(c) $H_3C\!-\!\underset{O}{\overset{\|}{C}}\!-\!C(H_3C)(CH_3)\!-\!C(CH_3)(OMe)(CH_3)$

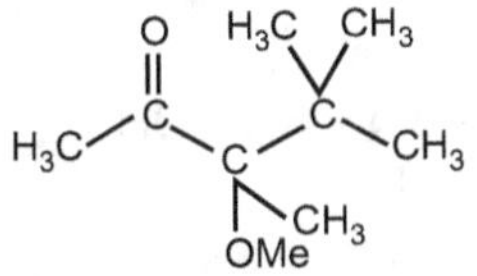

(d) 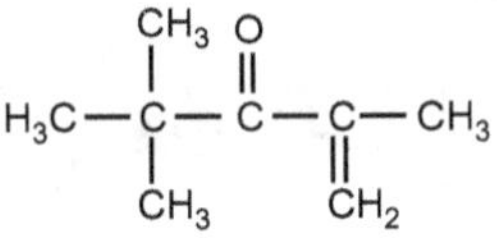 $H_3C\!-\!\underset{CH_3}{\overset{CH_3}{C}}\!-\!\underset{O}{\overset{\|}{C}}\!-\!\underset{CH_2}{\overset{}{C}}\!-\!CH_3$

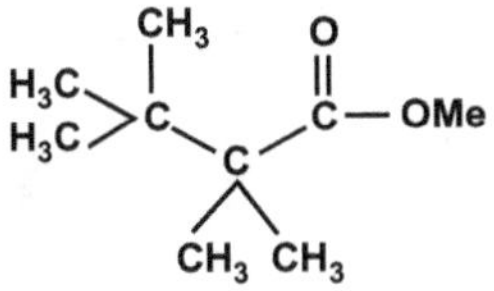

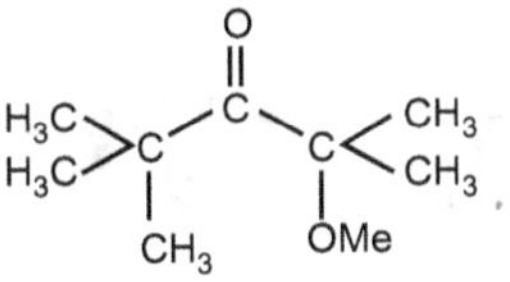

(v) The product formed in the following reaction is

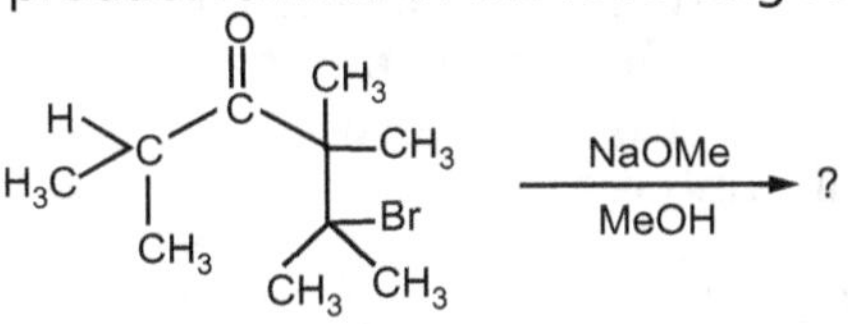

$$\underset{CH_3}{\overset{H}{\underset{|}{C}}}(H_3C)\!-\!\underset{O}{\overset{\|}{C}}\!-\!C(CH_3)(CH_3)(Br)(CH_3)(CH_3) \xrightarrow[\text{MeOH}]{\ \text{NaOMe}\ } \ ?$$

(a) $H_3C,\ H_3C\!>\!C\!-\!C(CH_3)(CH_3)\!-\!C(H_3C)(H_3C)(=O)(OMe)$

(b) (cyclobutanone structure with CH₃ groups)

(c) $MeO\!-\!\underset{O}{\overset{\|}{C}}\!-\!C(CH_3)(CH_3)\!-\!C(H_3C)(CH_3)(CH_3)$

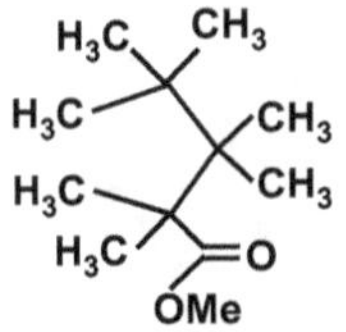

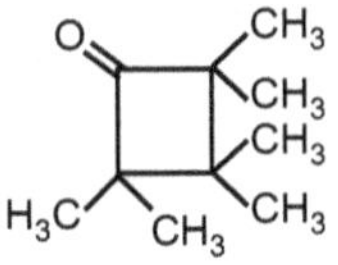

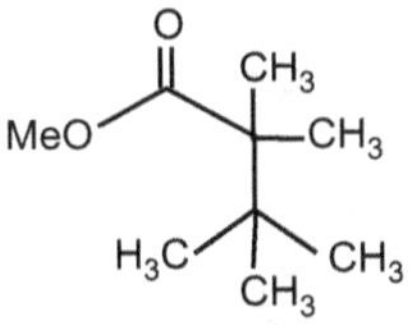

(d) 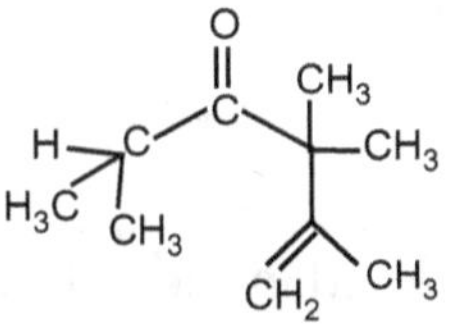 $\underset{H_3C}{\overset{H}{C}}\!-\!\underset{O}{\overset{\|}{C}}\!-\!C(CH_3)(CH_3)\!=\!C(CH_2)(CH_3)$

(vi) The product formed in the following reaction is

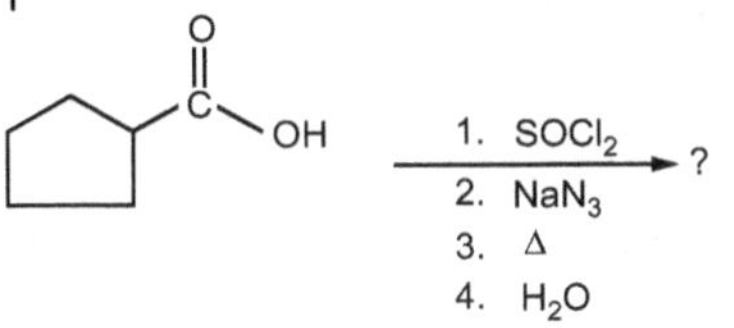

cyclopentane-C(=O)-OH $\xrightarrow[\substack{\text{2. NaN}_3 \\ \text{3. }\Delta \\ \text{4. H}_2O}]{\text{1. SOCl}_2}\ ?$

(a) cyclohexane–NH₂

(b) cyclopentane–NH₂

(c) cyclopentane–NH–C(=O)–OH

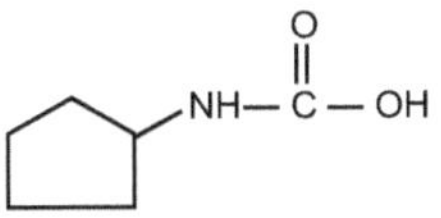

(d) 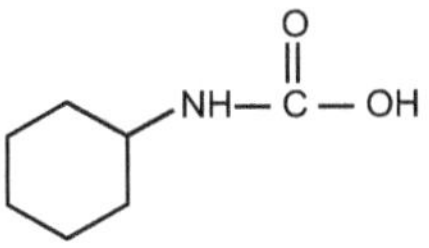 cyclohexane–NH–C(=O)–OH

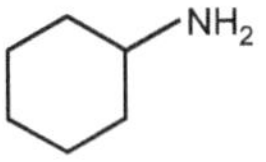

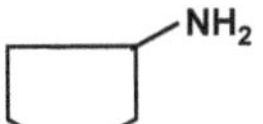

(vii) $H_7C_3 - \overset{\overset{\displaystyle O}{\|}}{C} - OH$ $\xrightarrow[\text{(2) } C_3H_7OH]{\text{(1) } (PhO)_2\overset{\overset{\displaystyle O}{\|}}{P}N_3}$?

(a) $H_7C_3 - \underset{\underset{\displaystyle H}{|}}{N} - \overset{\overset{\displaystyle O}{\|}}{C} - OC_3H_7$ (b) $H_7C_3 - NH_2$

(c) $H_7C_3 - \underset{\underset{\displaystyle H}{|}}{N} - C_3H_7$ (d) $H_7C_3 - \underset{\underset{\displaystyle H}{|}}{N} - \overset{\overset{\displaystyle O}{\|}}{C} - OH$

(viii) The intermediate formed in the Curtius rearrangement is
   (a) Cyanate   **(b) Isocyanate**
   (c) Thioisocyanate   (d) Carbocation

(ix) The product formed in the following reaction is

1. NH_2OH, $H^{\oplus}$
2. BsCl, Et_3N, DMAP → ?

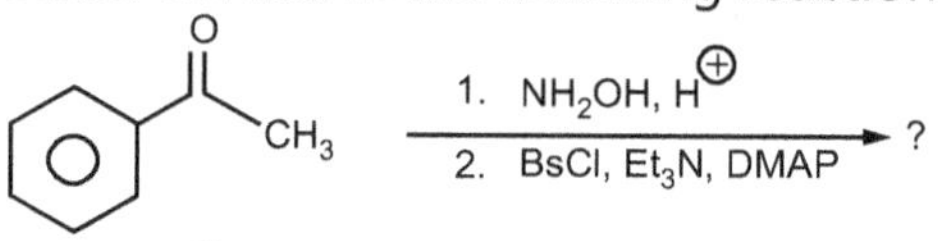

(a) 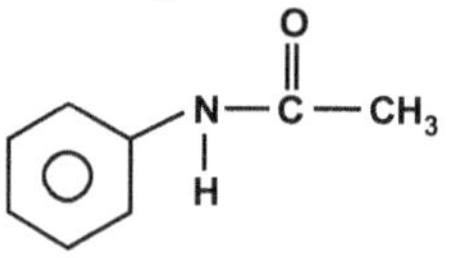   (b)

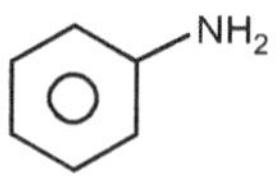

(c) 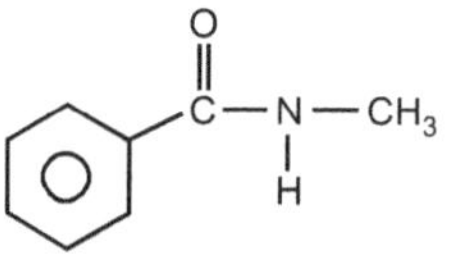   (d)

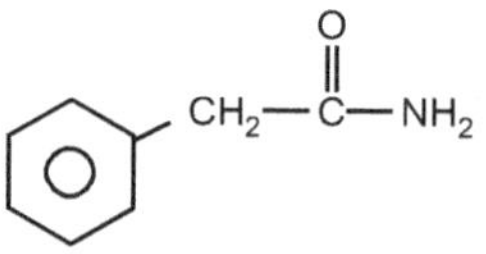

(x) The product formed in the following reaction is

1. $HONH_2HCl$, KOH(aq.)
   MeOH, Reflux
2. MSCl, Et_3N DCM, $-25°C$ → ?

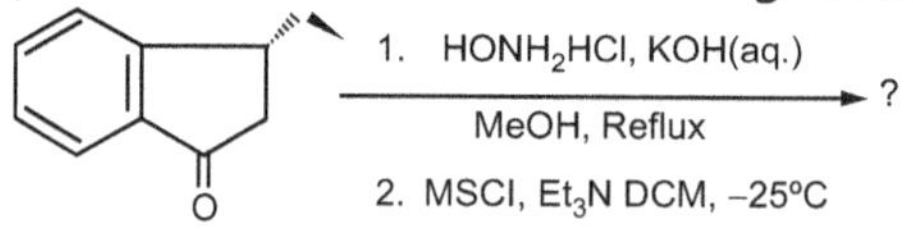

(a) 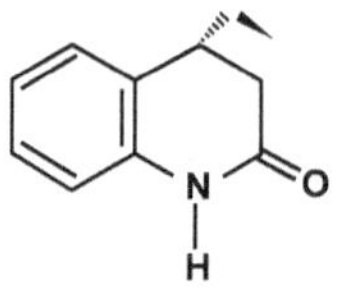   (b)

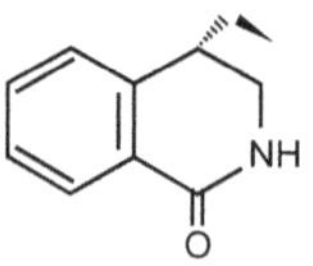

(c) 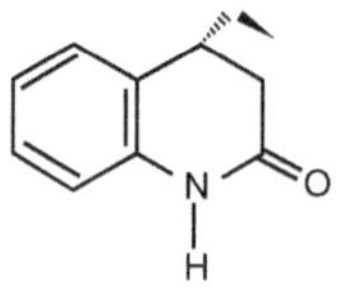   (d)

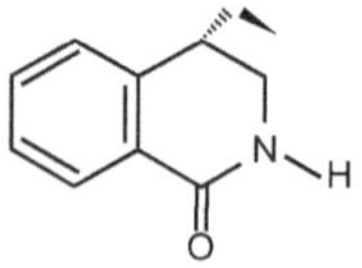

(xi) The product formed in the following reaction is:

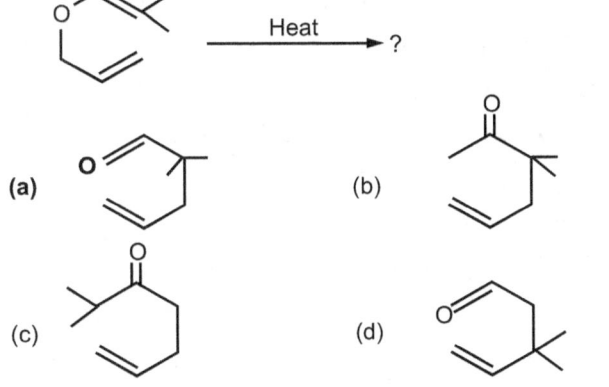

(xii) The product formed in the following reaction is

Chapter 4...

Spectroscopic Methods in Structure Determination of Organic Compounds

Contents ...

4.1 Introduction

- "How can I determine the structure of the molecule?" This question is asked by the synthetic chemist after completing any chemical reaction. It is also foremost in the mind of natural product chemist extracting molecules from plants or animals in hopes of developing new medicinal materials, and the forensic chemist isolating drugs or toxins from a suspect or victim, and the environmental chemist examining the effects of materials present in soil, bodies of water, or the atmosphere, and the archeological chemist tracing dietary information from the food residues in the pottery, and the biological chemist examining enzymatic mechanisms in the body. The quest for structural information on solids, liquids, or gases, on crystalline, powdered, or glassy materials, on mixtures or pure compounds is a continuing challenge to chemist of every type.

- X-ray, neutron or electron diffraction methods offer the ideal solution to many structural problems by providing data that often may lead to a complete structure. However, these methods have practical problems. Equipments for neutron or electron diffraction are not available. X-ray diffraction is restricted to crystalline solids. Crystallographic methods cannot be applied to mixtures. None of these techniques, therefore, can provide quick structural information which is often needed.

- Various forms of spectroscopy can provide a wide array of structural information in the most rapid fashion possible, for all phases of matter, and on mixtures as well as on pure compounds. The equipments are easily available and the amount of sample required is also very less. The samples, in many techniques, are recoverable upto the extent of 100%. The process of structural elucidation by spectroscopic methods is deductive. One or more spectroscopic experiments are carried out, and structural conclusions are reached by analyzing the resulting data. This chapter deals with the three most common and useful forms of organic structural spectroscopy. But before going into the details, we begin with the study of certain properties of light.

4.1.1 Meaning of Spectroscopy?

*   Light is composed of different components, when it is passed through a medium these components can be separated. Such a separation of components constitutes the formation of a spectrum; the study of the interaction of these components of light with the matter is known as *spectroscopy*. The spectra thus produced provide important means of identifying materials and of studying atomic and molecular structures.

4.1.2 Nature of Electromagnetic Radiations

*   Propagation of energy through space is characterized by both electrical and magnetic properties, and so the phenomenon is referred to as *electromagnetic radiation* or *light*. Such radiation has wave properties, in that its magnitude fluctuates sinusoidally over a time (Refer Fig. 4.1) as it moves through the space to produce the electrical and magnetic fields which are mutually perpendicular to each other. Let us examine some parameters of waves.

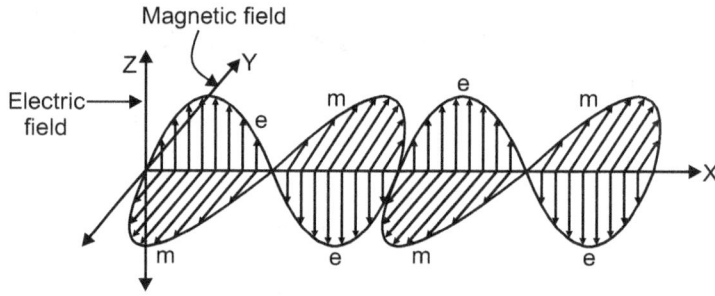

Fig. 4.1

(i)   Wavelength (λ): The length of one full cycle is called as the *wavelength (λ)*, for example, the distance from crest to crest or trough to trough in the following diagram (Refer Fig. 4.2).

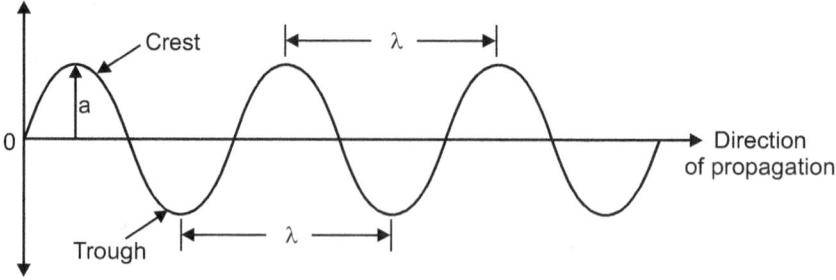

Fig. 4.2

(ii) Amplitude (a): The maximum displacement of the wave from the axis is called as the amplitude of the radiation.

(iii) Frequency (ν): The number of full cycle fluctuations that occur in one second is called the frequency.

(iv) Energy of radiation (E): Energy of radiation is given by the equation:

$$E = h\nu \quad (E \propto \nu) \qquad \qquad ...(4.1)$$

where, $\qquad \qquad$ h = Planck's constant and

$\qquad \qquad \qquad$ ν = frequency of radiation.

However, we know that c = νλ, where c = velocity of radiation (light).

∴ $\qquad \qquad$ ν = c/λ $\qquad$ Substituting this in equation (4.1), we get

$$E = h \times c/\lambda \qquad \qquad ...(4.2)$$

but h × c is constant,

thus $\qquad \qquad$ $E \propto 1/\lambda$ $\qquad \qquad \qquad ...(4.3)$

This shows that **energy of radiation** is *inversely proportional* to its **wavelength**.

Since energy is directly proportional to frequency (E ∝ ν) but inversely proportional to wavelength (E ∝ 1/λ), frequency of radiation and wavelength are inversely related to each other.

$$E \propto \nu \propto 1/\lambda \qquad \qquad ...(4.4)$$

(v) Wave number ($\bar{\nu}$): Number of waves per unit length is called as wave number.

$$\bar{\nu} = 1/\lambda$$

(vi) Units of measurement for wave parameters:

(a) Wavelength is measured in number of units depending on the type of radiation studied.

$$1 \text{ angstrom (A°)} = 10^{-8}\text{cm} = 10^{-10} \text{ m}$$
$$1 \text{ nanometer (nm)} = 10^{-7}\text{cm} = 10^{-9} \text{ m}$$
$$1 \text{ micron (μ)} = 10^{-4}\text{cm} = 10^{-6} \text{ m}$$

For UV and visible radiations, the A° or nm units are used, while for IR the micron (μ) is more convenient unit of measurement.

(b) Frequency is measured in either hertz or cycles per second (cps).

$$1 \text{ hertz} = 1 \text{ cycle per second (cps)}$$
$$1 \text{ kilohertz (kHz)} = 10^3 \text{ hertz}$$
$$1 \text{ megahertz (MHz)} = 10^6 \text{ hertz}$$

(c) Wave number is measured in terms of waves/cm = cm^{-1}

(d) Energy is measured in ergs or joules.

$$10^{-7} \text{ ergs} = 1 \text{ joule}$$

4.1.3 Types of Electromagnetic Radiations

- The electromagnetic radiation is classified on the basis of their wavelength (or energy) into different categories.

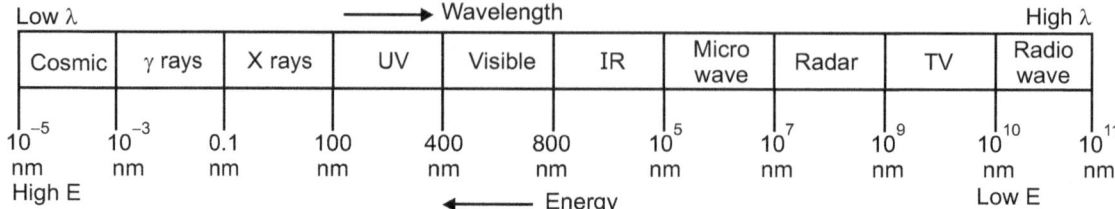

Fig. 4.3: Types of radiations

- As seen in Fig. 4.3, wavelength increases from left to right, whereas frequency and energy increase from right to left. Because there is a sequence of related phenomenon that differ in wavelength, the whole series is called the *electromagnetic spectrum*. Cosmic, gamma, and X-rays have the shortest wavelengths, and radiofrequency waves have the longest wavelength. The region of 400-800 nm is called as visible region as the human eye recognizes the colours of radiations in this region.

4.1.4 Interaction of Radiation with Matter

- When radiation (light) interacts with the matter, it is either reflected, refracted, or diffracted. Organic spectroscopy is essentially the study of how and which radiations are absorbed by organic molecules. By knowing the kind of radiation absorbed we can often find out about the shape, size, atomic arrangement etc. of a molecule.

- As a result of absorption of energy, molecule undergoes excitation i.e., it is raised to higher energy state. The types of excitations produced depend on the energy of the radiation employed.

   (a) **Rotational excitations:** If microwaves are used ($\lambda = 10^5$ to 10^7nm) molecules undergo rotational excitations.

   (b) **Vibrational excitations:** If infrared radiations (800 nm to 10^5 nm) are used they bring about vibrational excitations. As energy of IR radiation is higher than microwaves, it also brings about rotational excitations along with vibrational excitations.

   (c) **Electronic excitations:** If radiations from the visible and UV region (100 nm to 800 nm) are used, it brings about electronic excitations from bonding molecular orbitals to anti-bonding molecular orbitals. As energy of these radiations is higher than the microwave and infrared radiations, it brings about rotational and vibrational excitations along with electronic excitation.

To sum up the interaction of radiations and the excitations they cause, we have:

Microwaves   rotational excitations
Infra red   rotational + vibrational excitations
Visible and UV   rotational + vibrational + electronic excitations

(d) **Molecular energy levels:** The absorption of energy leads to different kinds of excitation of rotational, vibrational and electronic energy levels in a molecule. These energy levels of the molecules are known as molecular energy levels. Each electronic level of excitation consists of a number of vibrational levels and each vibrational level consists of number of rotational levels. These are shown in Fig. 4.4.

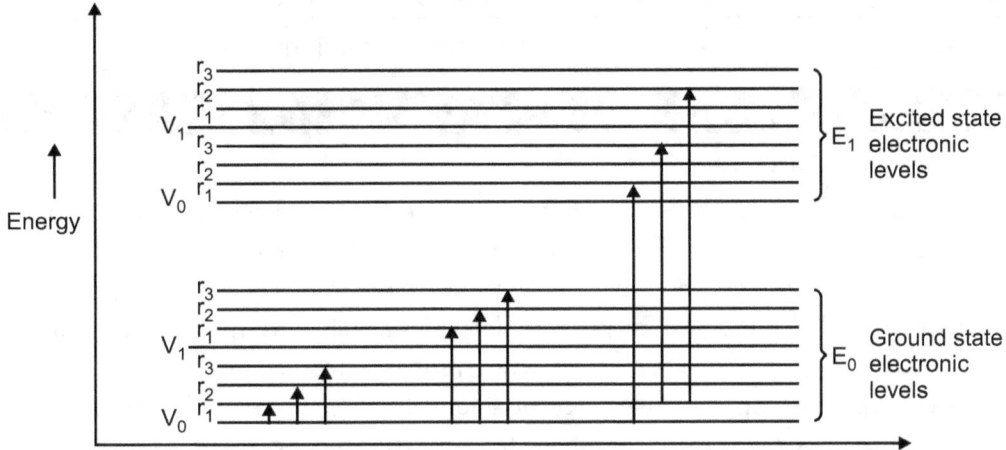

Fig. 4.4

It is clear that when electronic excitation occurs, it is accompanied by vibrational as well as rotational excitations. Whenever there is a vibrational excitation it is accompanied by rotational excitation. Thus, rotational excitations are only pure excitations. The energy separations between the different energy levels depend on the structure of the molecule, i.e., the type and number of atoms, type of bonds etc. present in the molecule.

4.1.5 Types of Spectroscopy and Advantages of Spectroscopic Methods

- In spectroscopic methods, UV, visible, infrared, microwave and radio waves are generally employed. Electronic, vibrational and NMR spectroscopies involve absorption of electromagnetic energy, respectively from the UV/visible, infrared and radiofrequency regions of the electromagnetic spectrum. Each absorption spectroscopy promotes normal or ground state molecules into higher energy or excited states. For **NMR**, only the *spin state of the nucleus* is changed. **Infrared** absorption gives rise to well defined *molecular vibrations*, and **ultraviolet-visible** absorption results in excited *electronic states*. The energy absorbed (ΔE) is roughly 10^{-6} kcal/mol for nuclear spin excitation,

10 kcal/mol for vibrational excitation, and 100 kcal/mol for electronic excitation. Each of these spectroscopies has its preferred units of wavelength, frequency, and energy developed historically according to custom.

Type of spectroscopy	Radiation used	Nature of excitation
U.V. and Visible	U.V. and Visible (100 kcal/mole)	Electronic excitation accompanied by vibrational and rotational excitations
Infra red	Infra red (10 kcal/mole)	Vibrational excitation accompanied by rotational excitation
Micro wave		Rotational excitations
Radio wave		Nuclear excitations

4.2 Ultra Violet Spectroscopy

4.2.1 Introduction

- Electronic absorption spectroscopy measures the energy and probability of promoting a molecule from its ground state electronic state to an electronically excited state. Excitation involves moving an electron from an occupied molecular orbital to an higher, unoccupied orbital. Since an organic molecule typically has numerous occupied and unoccupied molecular orbitals, many different electronic excitations are possible. UV–visible spectroscopy is used to qualitatively detect certain functional groups, according to the position and intensity of the absorption band.

- UV and visible spectroscopy provide us information about the structure of the molecule that contains double bond or triple bond or conjugated bond. This spectroscopy can distinguish between conjugated and isolated dienes, between dienes and trienes, between carbonyl group and α, β-unsaturated system. It also distinguishes the cis-trans isomers.

4.2.2 Nature of U.V.

- The ultra-violet radiation is that part of the electromagnetic radiation which bridges the gap between the longest wavelength X-rays and the shortest wavelength visible light. The UV region, which extends from 40 to 4000 A°, is divided into *near* (2000-4000 A°) and *far* (40-2000 A°) ultra violet regions. Vacuum apparatus is used to study far UV radiation as it is absorbed by air because of moisture, oxygen, nitrogen and carbon dioxide. Therefore this region is also called *vacuum region*. Furthermore glass absorbs radiations of wavelength less than 3000 A° and therefore quartz optics and quartz sample holders are used in the instruments. Consequently this region (2000 to 3000 A°) is referred as *quartz region*.

4.2.3 Beer-Lambert's Law

- The amount of energy absorbed by the molecules is governed by the famous Beer-Lambert's law: *The fraction of incident radiation absorbed is proportional to the number of absorbing molecules in its path.* If the radiation passes through a solution, the amount of light energy absorbed or transmitted is an exponential function of the molecular concentration of the solute and also a function of the length of the path of the radiation through the sample. Thus, Beer-Lambert's law is represented as

$$I = I_o \times 10^{-\varepsilon Cl}$$

or $\qquad -\log I/I_o = \varepsilon Cl$

i.e., $\qquad \log I_o / I = \varepsilon Cl$

where
$\qquad I_o$ = intensity of *incident* radiant energy
$\qquad I$ = intensity of *transmitted* radiant energy
$\qquad C$ = molar concentration of the solute
$\qquad l$ = internal length of the cell in centimeters

- The ratio I/I_o is known as *transmittance T,* and the logarithm of the inverse ratio I_o/I is known as the absorbance A. Therefore,

$$-\log I/I_o = -\log T = \varepsilon Cl$$

i.e., $\qquad \log I_o / I = A = \varepsilon Cl$

Thus, $\qquad A = -\log T = \varepsilon Cl$

or $\qquad \varepsilon = A/Cl$

where ε is the *molar extinction coefficient or molar absorptivity* of the substance whose light absorption is under consideration. This value is constant for the given sample under the given set of conditions. Its value depends on the solvent used for sample preparation. ε is numerically equal to the absorbance of a solution of unit molar concentration (C = 1) in a cell of unit length (l = 1). The units of ε are thus litres mole^{-1} cm^{-1}.

4.2.4 Absorption of UV Radiation by Organic Molecules

- When UV and visible radiations are absorbed by the organic molecules, it brings about electronic excitations. The process of electronic excitation is accompanied by large number of vibrational and rotational changes (Refer Fig. 4.4). As it is difficult to resolve these spectral bands which get mixed together, the UV spectrum is relatively broad. The total energy required for excitation of a molecule from ground state to excited state is given by the equation

$$E = E_{electronic} + E_{vibrational} + E_{rotational}$$

4.2.5 Classification of Electronic Excitations

- The absorption of the electromagnetic radiation of the wavelength 200-750 nm can cause excitation of electrons from occupied bonding molecular orbital (lower energy) to unoccupied molecular orbital (higher energy). This excitation is called electronic excitation.

- There are three kinds of electrons which are present in the organic molecules namely, σ-electrons present in covalent bond, π-electrons present in π-bond, and n-bonding electrons present as unshared electrons. σ and π orbitals have corresponding higher energy anti-bonding molecular orbitals (σ*, π*) bonds but there is no higher energy anti-bonding molecular orbital for non-bonding electrons. The absorption of the electromagnetic radiation by the organic molecule in the UV and visible region involves promotion of the electrons in the ground state (σ, π, n) to higher state (σ*, π*) (Refer Fig. 4.5). The wavelength of absorption depends on the energy difference (ΔE) between bonding and anti-bonding orbitals. The relative energies for transitions are in the following order:

$$\sigma \rightarrow \sigma^* \; > \; n \rightarrow \sigma^* \; > \; \pi \rightarrow \pi^* \; > \; n \rightarrow \pi^*$$

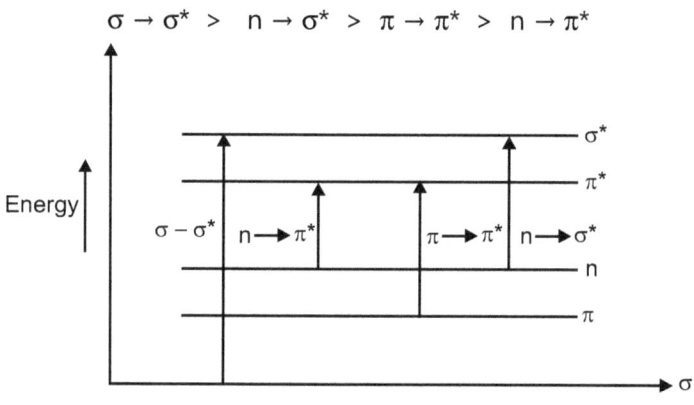

Fig. 4.5

- Electronic transitions commonly observed in the readily accessible UV and visible region have been grouped into four main classes:

  1. **σ-σ* Transition:** This type of transition takes place from σ-orbital to anti-bonding σ* and requires high energy that takes place at very short wavelength (150 nm). Saturated hydrocarbons contain only strong bounded σ electrons and their excitation to anti-bonding σ* requires relatively large energies corresponding to the absorption in the far UV region. Thus, paraffins are used as solvent in UV spectroscopy as their absorptions are not recorded in the UV spectrum.

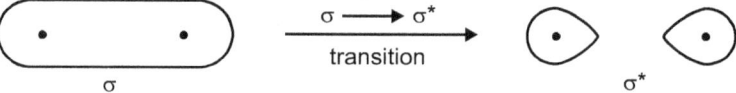

Fig. 4.6

  2. **π-π* Transition:** This type of transition takes place from bonding π-orbital to anti-bonding π* orbitals. Alkenes, alkynes, nitriles and aromatic compounds having double or triple bonds undergo this transition. Although ethylene does not absorb above 185 nm, conjugated π-electron systems are generally of lower energy and absorb above 200 nm.

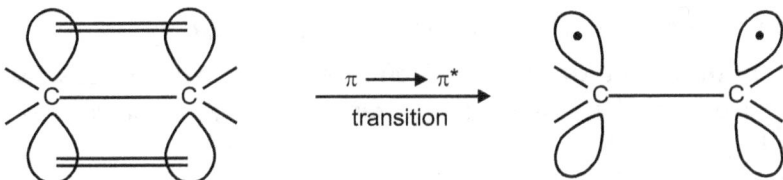

Fig. 4.7

3. **n-π* Transition:** These transitions involve the excitation of an electron in a non-bonding atomic orbital, such as unshared electrons on O, N, S or halogen atom, to an anti-bonding π* orbital associated with an unsaturated centre in the molecule. The transitions occur with compounds that possess double bond involving hetero atoms, for example, C=O, C=S, N=O. The n-π* requires minimum energy and shows absorption towards longer wavelength (250-300 nm).

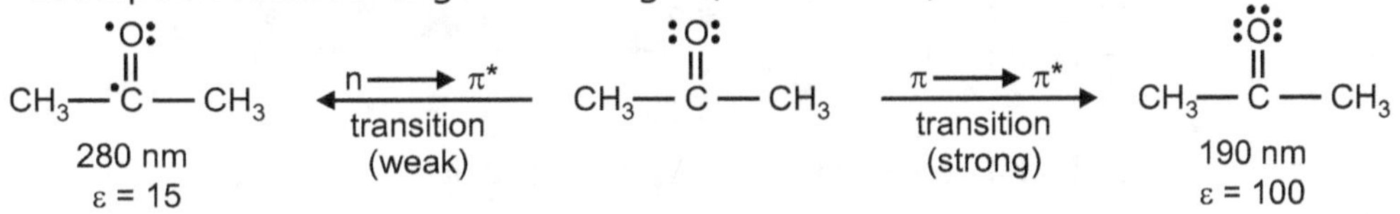

$$CH_3-\overset{\overset{\displaystyle \cdot O:}{\|}}{C}-CH_3 \quad \xleftarrow[\substack{\text{transition} \\ \text{(weak)}}]{n \longrightarrow \pi^*} \quad CH_3-\overset{\overset{\displaystyle :O:}{\|}}{C}-CH_3 \quad \xrightarrow[\substack{\text{transition} \\ \text{(strong)}}]{\pi \longrightarrow \pi^*} \quad CH_3-\overset{\overset{\displaystyle :\ddot{O}:}{\|}}{C}-CH_3$$

280 nm   190 nm
ε = 15   ε = 100

Fig. 4.8

4. **n-σ* Transition:** These transitions are less important than the above two classes, it involves excitation of an electron from a non-bonding orbital to an anti-bonding σ* orbital. Since n electrons do not form bonds, there are no anti-bonding orbitals associated with them. Alcohols, amines, alkyl halides, thiols undergo this type of transition. These transitions are less energetic and hence occur at longer wavelengths. The ε values for these transitions are very small and hence absorption is very weak.

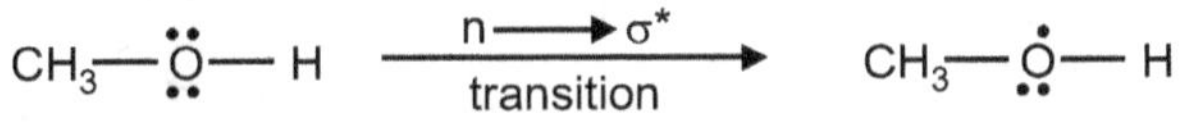

$$CH_3-\overset{\cdot\cdot}{\underset{\cdot\cdot}{O}}-H \quad \xrightarrow[\text{transition}]{n \longrightarrow \sigma^*} \quad CH_3-\overset{\cdot\cdot}{\underset{\cdot\cdot}{O}}-H$$

Fig. 4.9

Significance of ε (Molar absorptivity):

- The ε value indicates the probability of the excitation of electrons, higher ε values indicate the probability of excitation of electrons is high. All n-π* excitations take place at higher wavelength but has lower ε value; on the other hand, π-π* transition requires lower wavelength but their ε value is high. The ε values are affected by the nature of the solvent, polar solvent increases ε value for π-π* transition whereas non-polar solvents increase ε value for n-π* transition.

Excitation	In hexane (non-polar)		In water (polar)	
	λ_{max}	ε	λ_{max}	ε
n - π*	230 nm	12600	243 nm	10000
π - π*	329 nm	41	305 nm	60

4.2.6 Terms Used in Ultra Violet Spectroscopy

1. **Chromophore (Colour bearer):** Groups that are capable of absorbing UV radiations and give rise to electronic transitions are known as chromophores. e.g. $-NO_2$, $-N=O$, $-N=N-$, $C=O$, $-C\equiv N$, $C=C$, $C=S$ etc.

2. **Auxochrome (Colour increaser):** Group which itself does not absorb radiation in near UV region, but when attached to a chromophore, shift the absorption to longer wavelength. e.g. $-OH$, $-OCH_3$, $-NH_2$, $-NR_2$, etc.

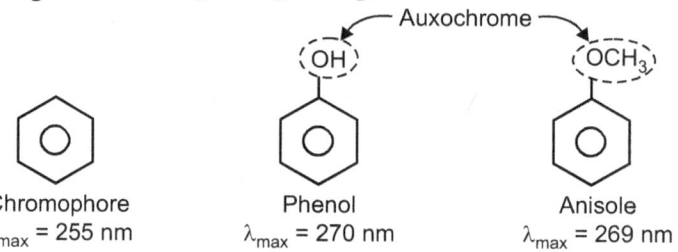

Chromophore   Phenol   Anisole
λ_{max} = 255 nm λ_{max} = 270 nm λ_{max} = 269 nm

Fig. 4.10

3. **Bathochromic shift (Red shift):** Absorption to a longer wavelength is known as bathochromic shift or red shift. e.g. p-nitro phenol shows red shift in alkaline medium. This is due to the electron donating resonance effect of negatively charged oxygen is more than due to the lone pair on oxygen.

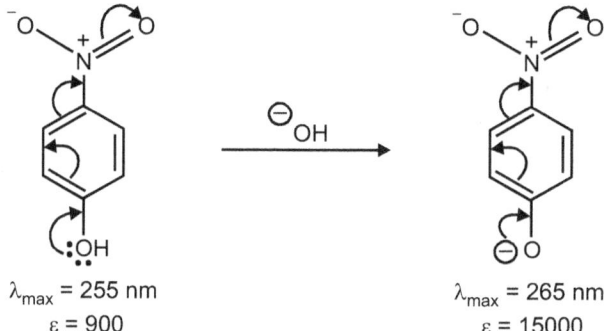

λ_{max} = 255 nm λ_{max} = 265 nm
ε = 900 ε = 15000

Fig. 4.11

4. **Hypsochromic shift (Blue shift):** Absorption to a shorter wavelength is called hypsochromic shift or blue shift. e.g. Aniline shows blue shift in acidic medium. In acidic medium unshared pair of electron on nitrogen of aniline is not available for delocalization as it gets protonated.

λ_{max} = 230 nm λ_{max} = 203 nm

Fig. 4.12

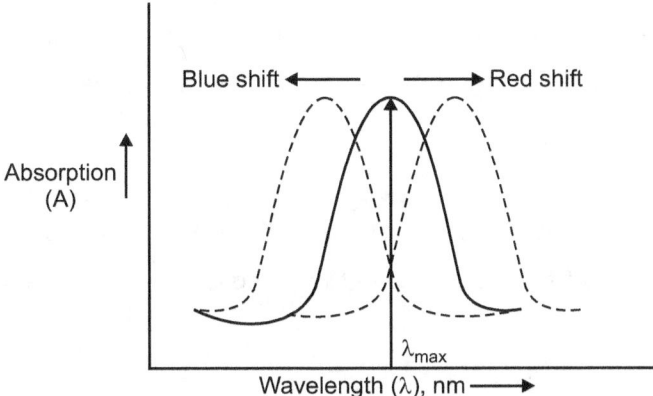

Fig. 4.13

5. **Hyperchromic shift:** When the intensity of absorption increases (ε value increases), it is known as hyperchromic shift.

6. **Hypochromic shift:** When the intensity of absorption decreases (ε value decreases), it is known as hypochromic shift.

4.2.7 Effect of Conjugation on the Position of UV Band

[A] Dienes:

- In simple olefin like ethylene the π - π^* electronic transition takes place in 165-200 nm region, but when the molecule has more than one double bond the π - π^* transition depends on the position of the double bonds.

   (i)   If the two double bonds are isolated by the presence of at least three single bonds, the π - π^* transition is still approximately the same (165-200 nm).

$$CH_2 = CH_2$$

Ethylene	1, 5 - Hexadiene	1, 4 - Cyclohexadiene	Cyclohexene
λ_{max} = 165 nm	λ_{max} = 165 nm	λ_{max} = 168 nm	λ_{max} = 168 nm

   (ii) On the other hand if the two double bonds are in conjugation, the absorption takes place at the longer wavelength. This bathochromic shift suggests that conjugation decreases the energy required for the excitation of electrons. This can be explained by the *molecular orbital theory.*

1, 3 - Butadiene
λ_{max} = 220 nm

- In case of ethylene the frequency of absorption for π - π^* transition depends on the difference in the energy between the π_1 and π_2^* levels. Let the difference in the energies be ΔE_1. Thus,

$$\Delta E_1 = E\pi_2^* - E\pi_1 \qquad \text{... (i)}$$

- In case of 1, 3-butadiene the easiest for π-π^* transition involves excitation of electrons from π_2 to π_3^* level. Let the difference in the energy between the π_2 and π_3^* levels be ΔE_2. Thus,

$$\Delta E_2 = E\pi_3^* - E\pi_2 \qquad \text{... (ii)}$$

- As E_2 for 1, 3-butadiene is less than E_1 for ethylene, it indicates the conjugation decreases the energy required for excitation and hence absorption occurs at longer wavelength.

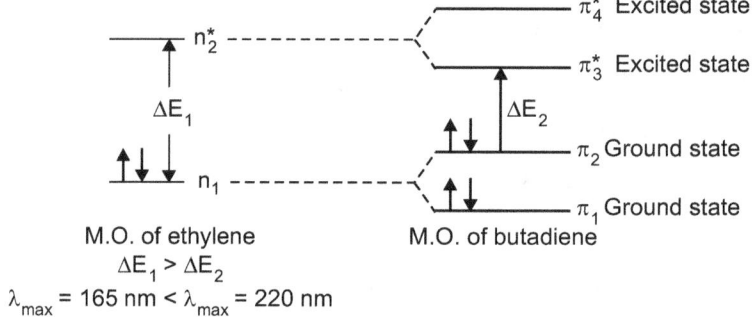

Fig. 4.14: Effect of conjugation

- In 1,3-butadiene π-π^* transition occurs at 220 nm in a non-polar solvent and further increase in conjugation shifts to longer wavelength (about 40 nm for each additional double bond). For example, 1, 2, 3-hexatriene absorbs at 256 nm whereas α-carotene, which has 10 conjugated double bonds absorbs radiation in the visible region at 445 nm.

[B] Enones:

- When C=C bond is in conjugation with a carbonyl group, such compounds are called enones. In crotonaldehyde the double bond chromophore is conjugated with the carbonyl group. We have seen that isolated C=C bond absorbs at 165-200 nm, whereas isolated C=O bond absorbs at about 290 nm. When these two chromophores are in conjugation as in crotonaldehyde or any typical α, β-unsaturated carbonyl compound, the situation is similar to that of 1,3-butadiene. Fig. 4.15 illustrates the energy difference of the isolated C=C double bond, isolated C=O bond and enone.

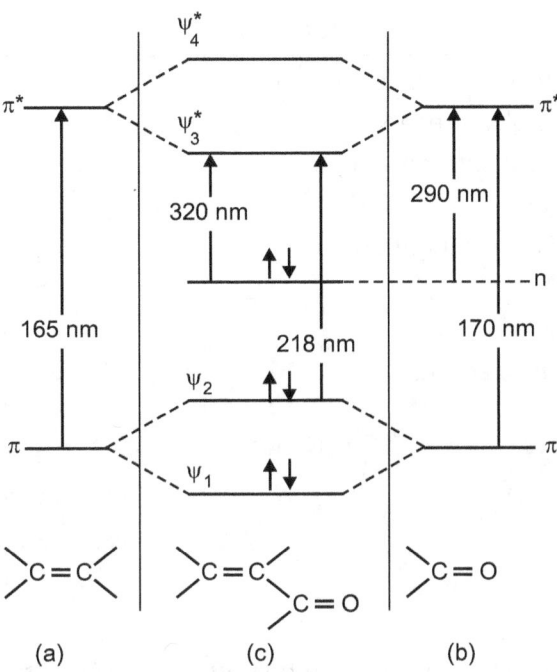

Fig. 4.15: Energy level diagram of (a) an isolated C = C chromophore,
(b) an isolated C = O chromophore, (c) an enone

- For conjugated enone, less energy is required because the transition takes place from n level to the lowest unoccupied ψ_3^* level. Therefore, n–ψ_3^* transition in crotonaldehyde occurs at the longer wavelength (320 nm) as compared to π–π^* in acetaldehyde (293 nm). Fig. 4.15 also shows that ψ_2 – ψ_3^* transition requires less energy than that needed for the isolated C=O bond.

- Thus conjugation decreases the energy for excitation and hence increases the wavelength of absorption in the U.V. region.

4.2.8 Calculation of λ_{max} by Woodward and Fieser Rule

- Extensive correlation between UV spectrum and the structures of the organic compounds lead to simple empirical rule to calculate the wavelength maxima (λ_{max}). These rules are known as Woodward and Fieser rules and deal with the dienes and unsaturated conjugated carbonyl compounds. The general approach to calculate the λ_{max} is to begin with the absorption wavelength for the parent chromophore and add a value of each substituent attached to the chromophore system.

    [A] **Diene system:** Table 4.1 shows the Woodward and Fieser rules for calculating λ_{max} of substituted dienes.

Table 4.1

(i)	Basic λ_{max} for an unsubstituted, conjugated acyclic or heteroannular diene		214 nm
(ii)	Basic λ_{max} for an unsubstituted, conjugated homoannular diene		253 nm
(iii)	Extra double bonds in conjugation for each C=C	add	30 nm
(iv)	Exocyclic double bond	add	5 nm
(v)	Substitutions on vinyl carbons		
	(a) H, O-acyl	add	0 nm
	(b) Alkyl (–R)	add	5 nm
	(c) Halogen (–Cl, –Br)	add	5 nm
	(d) –OH or –OR	add	6 nm
	(e) –SR	add	30 nm
	(f) –NR$_2$	add	60 nm

- The following Table 4.2 illustrates how to recognize various types of dienes, conjugations and double bonds:

Table 4.2

A linear conjugation or acyclic conjugated diene	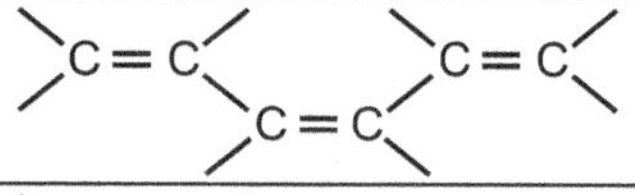
A cross conjugation	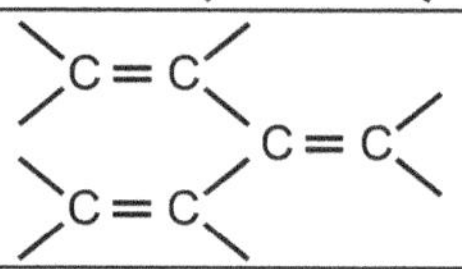
A cyclic diene (two double bonds in conjugation in the same ring)	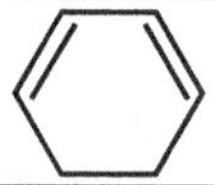
A semicyclic diene (one of the double bond is in the ring while the other is outside the ring; when only one of the two sp^2 hybridized carbons of a double bond is a part of the ring under consideration such a double bond is called an exocyclic double bond)	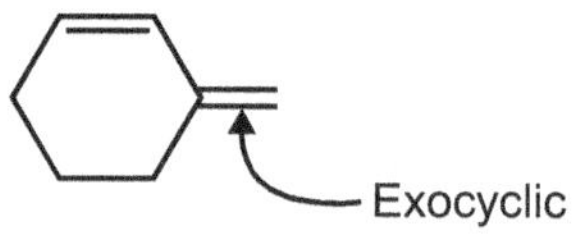 Exocyclic
A homoannular diene (both double bonds are in the same ring)	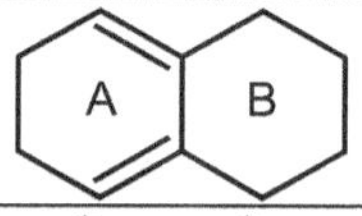
A heteroannular diene (two double bonds are conjugated but present in two different rings; both double bonds are exocyclic to each ring)	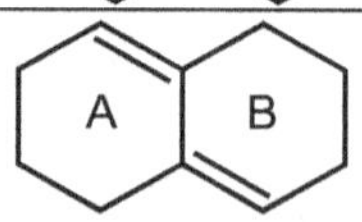

Some illustrative examples are shown below, how to apply these rules:

1.	
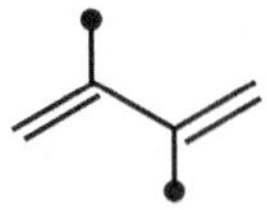 2, 3 - Dimethyl-1, 3 - butadiene	Base value = 214 nm 2 alkyl substituents = 10 nm λ_{max} (cal.) = 224 nm λ_{max} (obs.) = 225 nm
2. 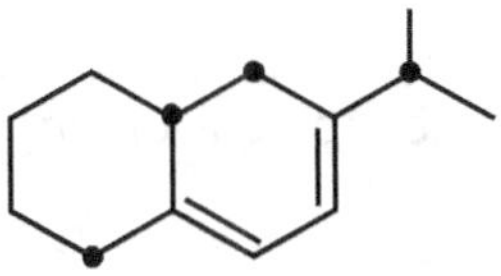	Base value = 253 nm 4 alkyl substituents = 20 nm 1 exocyclic double bond = 5 nm λ_{max} (cal.) = 278 nm λ_{max} (obs.) = 275 nm
3. 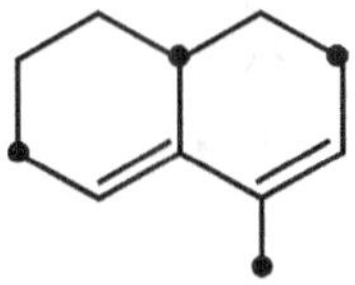	Base value = 214 nm 4 alkyl substituents = 20 nm 1 exocyclic double bond = 5 nm λ_{max} (cal.) = 239 nm λ_{max} (obs.) = 238 nm
4. 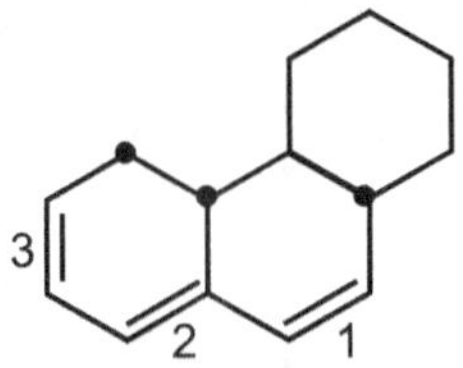	Base value = 253 nm extra double bond = 30 nm 3 alkyl substituents = 15 nm 1 exocyclic double bond = 5 nm λ_{max} (cal.) = 303 nm λ_{max} (obs.) = 302 nm
5. 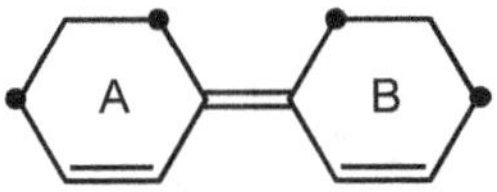	Base value = 214 nm extended conjugation = 30 nm 2 exocyclic double bonds = 10 nm 4 alkyl substituents = 20 nm λ_{max} (cal.) = 274 nm λ_{max} (obs.) = 274 nm

6.

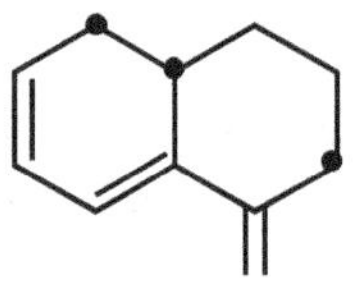	Base value $=$ 253 nm 1 extra double bond $=$ 30 nm 2 exocyclic double bonds $=$ 10 nm <u>3 alkyl substituents $=$ 15 nm</u> λ_{max} (cal.) $=$ 308 nm λ_{max} (obs.) $=$ 306 nm

[B] Enone system: Table 4.3 shows the Woodward and Fieser rules for calculating λ_{max} of enone derivatives.

Table 4.3

(i)	Parent enone (acyclic or rings larger than 5 members)			215 nm
(ii)	Five membered cyclic enone			202 nm
(iii)	Aldehydes			207 nm
(iv)	Extended conjugation for each C=C		add	30 nm
(v)	Homoannular component		add	39 nm
(vi)	Exocyclic double bond		add	5 nm
(vii)	Substituents			
	(a) H		add	0 nm
	(b) Alkyl (-R)	α	add	10 nm
		β	add	12 nm
		γ and higher	add	18 nm
	(c) – Cl	α	add	15 nm
		β	add	12 nm
	(d) – OH	α	add	35 nm
		β	add	30 nm
		γ	add	50 nm
	(e) – OR	α	add	35 nm
		β	add	30 nm
		γ	add	17 nm
		δ	add	31 nm
	(f) – SR	β	add	85 nm
	(g) – NR$_2$	β	add	95 nm
	(h) – OCOR	α, β, γ	add	6 nm
	(i) – Br	α	add	25 nm
		β	add	30 nm

Some illustrative examples are shown below, how to apply these rules:

1. 	Base value = 215 nm α-alkyl group = 10 mm 2 β-alkyl groups = 24 nm λ_{max} (cal.) = 249 nm λ_{max} (obs.) = 249 nm
2. 	Base value = 202 nm 1 extra double bond = 30 nm Homoannular component = 39 mm 1 δ-alkyl group = 18 nm λ_{max} (cal.) = 289 nm λ_{max} (obs.) = 290 nm
3. 	Base value = 215 nm 2 extra double bonds = 60 nm 1 homoannular component = 39 nm 1 exocyclic double bond = 15 nm 1 β-substituent = 12 nm 1 higher substituent = 18 nm λ_{max} (cal.) = 349 nm λ_{max} (obs.) = 350 nm
4. 	Base value = 202 nm 2 exocyclic double bonds = 10 nm 2β alkyl substituents = 24 nm 1 α alkyl substituent = 10 nm λ_{max} (cal.) = 246 nm λ_{max} (obs.) = 245 nm
5. 	Base value = 215 nm 1α substituent = 10 nm 2β substituents = 24 nm λ_{max} (cal.) = 249 nm λ_{max} (obs.) = 250 nm

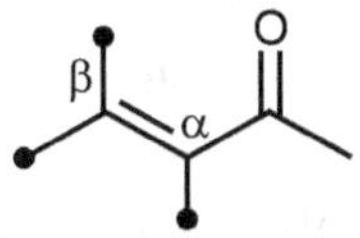

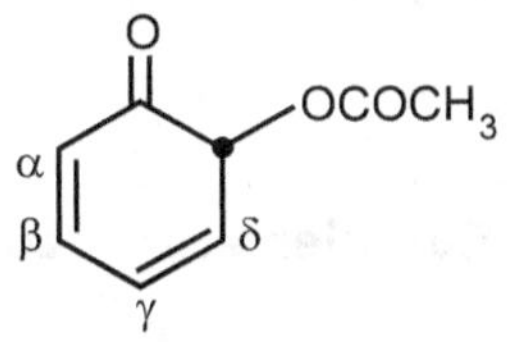

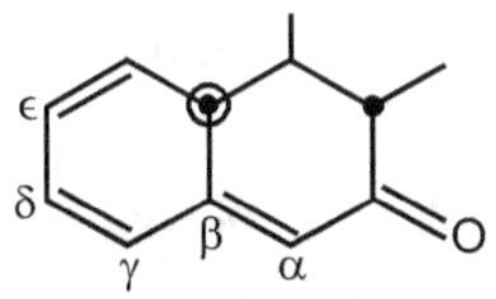

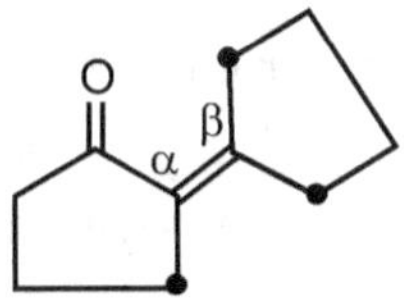

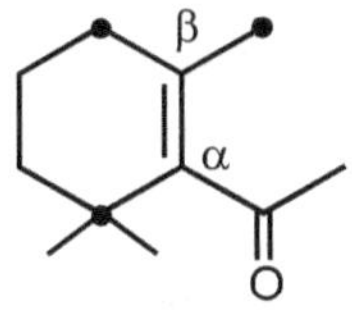

4.2.9 Colour and Visible Spectrum

• The human eye responds in the visible region (400 to 800 nm). When the light falls on a substance, it either absorbs all the radiation and appears black, or totally reflects and appears white. However, if the substance absorbs partly and reflects partly it appears to be coloured. For example, when substance absorbs radiations with wavelength 400 nm, which corresponds to blue colour, it appears yellow to the human eye which is its *complementary colour*. Hence blue and yellow colours are complementary colours. Table 4.4 gives the relation between the light absorbed and complementary colour that is observed.

Table 4.4

Wavelength (nm)	Colour absorbed	Complementary colour (visible)
400-435	Violet	Yellow
435-480	Blue	Yellow
480-490	Green-blue	Orange
490-500	Blue-green	Red
500-560	Green	Purple
560-580	Yellow-green	Violet
580-595	Yellow	Blue
595-605	Orange	Green-blue
605-750	Red	Blue-green

4.2.10 Applications of UV Spectroscopy

(a) **Determination of structure:** UV spectroscopy is one of the methods of studying the structure of organic compound, and useful in determining the presence or absence of chromophore. In fact UV spectroscopy is often employed to confirm conclusions drawn by other methods. The steps are as follows:

(i) Determination of various elements and functional groups present in the molecule.

(ii) Using the rules, calculation of λ_{max} for expected chromophore and comparison with the experimental values obtained for the unknown.

(iii) Comparison of the spectrum of the unknown with those for model compounds or similar compounds listed in the literature.

(b) **Determination of stereochemistry (cis and trans):** A *trans* isomer has a greater λ_{max} and ε_{max} value than the corresponding *cis* isomer. Thus UV spectrum is useful to distinguish between *cis* and *trans* isomer.

For example, Ph–CO–CH–CH–Ph, the trans isomer absorbs radiation at 250 nm
$$\underset{O}{\diagup \diagdown}$$

(ε_{max} = 16,800), whereas the cis isomer absorbs radiation at 248 nm (ε_{max} = 12,900).

The cis isomer absorbs at shorter wavelength because (i) steric hindrance due to close proximity of the two cis substituents which disturbs the planarity of the molecule thereby inhibiting resonance and (ii) the length of the chromophore decreases.

Compound	Cis isomer	Trans isomer
Stilbene (Ph – CH = CH – Ph)	278 nm, ε = 9,350	294 nm, ε = 24,000
Cinnamic acid (Ph – CH = CH – COOH)	268 nm, ε = 10,700	272 nm, ε = 15,900
Azobenzene (Ph – N = N – Ph)	285 nm, ε = 9,100	319 nm, ε = 2,200

4.3 Infra Red Spectroscopy

4.3.1 Introduction

- IR spectrum of an organic molecule reveals a good deal of information about the *functional groups* present in it. We know that the energy of a molecule can be resolved into at least four components, (i) translational, (ii) rotational, (iii) vibrational and (iv) electronic. IR radiations have longer wavelength which are capable of affecting both the vibrational and rotational energy levels in the molecule.

4.3.2 Principle of I.R. Spectroscopy

- A molecule is not a rigid assemblage of atoms. The atoms and the molecule itself continuously rotate, vibrate and move from one point to other. Even at $0°K$ when the kinetic energy of the entire molecule is zero, the atomic nuclei vibrate about the bond which connects them. The atoms in the molecule vibrate in many different ways and each vibration requires different energy i.e., molecule has number of vibrational energy levels each of which is quantized. If a molecule absorbs the I.R. radiation it gets excited to higher vibrational energy level. The type of I.R. wavelength absorbed by the molecule depends on the type of atoms and the chemical bonds in the molecule. In the IR spectrum the position of the peak is specified in terms of frequency (ν), or the

  wavelength (λ) or the wave number ($\bar{\nu}$) of the IR radiation absorbed. Frequency (ν) is expressed in Hz. Wavelength (λ) is expressed in μ (micron or micrometer).

  $1\ \mu = 10^{-6}$ m = 10^{-4} cm. Wave number ($\bar{\nu}$) is expressed as number of waves in one cm. Therefore $\nu = 1/\lambda$. Thus wavelength of 4 μm corresponds to wave number of 2500 cm^{-1}.
  $$\nu = 1/\lambda\ =\ 1/4 \times 10^{-4}\,cm = 10,000/4 = 2500\ cm^{-1}$$

- Wave number is more convenient unit in I.R. spectroscopy. Energy of radiation is inversely proportional to the wavelength but directly proportional to the wave numbers.

4.3.3 Fundamental Modes of Vibrations

- We know that chemical bonds are not rigid but elastic. A molecule can be said to resemble a system of balls of varying masses, corresponding to the atoms of the molecule, and springs of varying strengths, corresponding to the chemical bond in the molecule. A molecule is constantly vibrating: its bonds stretch, contract or bend with respect to each other. The numbers of different ways in which a molecule can vibrate are known as *fundamental modes of vibration*. This number depends on the total number of atoms present in the molecule and the geometry of the molecule. The fundamental modes of vibrations are calculated as follows:

  (i) For linear molecule, containing N atoms, there are **3N-5** possible fundamental modes of vibrations.

  (ii) For non-linear molecule, containing N atoms, there are **3N-6** possible fundamental modes of vibrations.

- Table 4.5 shows fundamental modes of vibrations for different molecules.

Table 4.5

Molecules	Atoms 'N'	Geometry of the molecule	Fundamental modes of vibrations
NO	2	Linear (3N-5)	1
CO_2	3	Linear (3N-5)	4
H_2O	3	Non-linear (3N-6)	3
NH_3	4	Non-linear (3N-6)	6
CH_4	5	Non-linear (3N-6)	9
C_6H_6	12	Non-linear (3N-6)	30

4.3.4 Types of Vibrations

- There are two types of vibrations in the molecule: (a) stretching vibrations and (b) bending vibrations.

  (a) Stretching vibrations: These are characterized by the change of internuclear distance. Thus the distance between two atoms increases or decreases, but atoms remain in the same bond axis. These modes of vibrations are further classified as: (i) symmetrical stretching and (ii) unsymmetrical stretching (Refer Fig. 4.16)

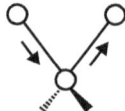

Symmetrical stretching   Unsymmetrical stretching

Fig. 4.16: Stretching vibrations

(b) Bending vibrations: These are characterized by the change in the angle between two covalent bonds, due to change in the position of the atoms with respect to the original bond axis. These modes are further divided into: (i) Scissoring, (ii) Rocking, (iii) Wagging and (iv) Twisting (Refer Fig. 4.17). The scissoring and rocking vibrations occur in the plane while the wagging and the twisting vibrations occur out of plane.

Bending vibrations require less energy than stretching vibrations.

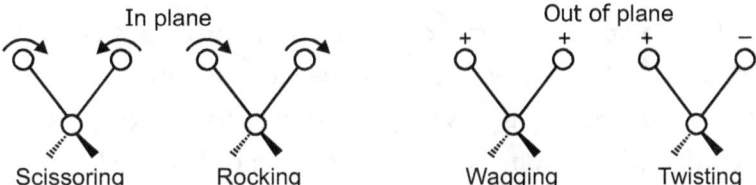

Fig. 4.17: Bending vibrations

4.3.5 Conditions for Absorption of I.R. Radiations

- Even the molecule can vibrate in number of ways, each and every vibration does not absorb I.R. frequency. The absorption of I.R. radiation takes place only if the following two conditions are met:

(i) When the frequency of the vibration of a bond and frequency of I.R. radiation used for excitation match perfectly, then only IR energy is absorbed.

(ii) Only those vibrations which result in the change in the dipole moment of the molecule, absorb IR radiations. Such vibrations are said to be IR active. Symmetrical stretching of C≡C in acetylene or O=C=O in carbon dioxide does not result in change in dipole moment and hence does not absorb in the IR region. Such vibrations are called as IR inactive.

4.3.6 Vibration of Diatomic Molecules

- Frequency and amplitude are the characteristics of vibrational motion. The vibration frequency is given by Hooke's law. The vibrational frequency of a bond may be related to the masses of vibrating atoms and the force constant (f) of the vibrating bond by the equation given below. Consider two balls connected by a spring in which the force constant is the restoring force provided by the spring.

$$\text{Vibrational frequency } \nu = \frac{1}{2\pi c}\sqrt{\frac{f}{\mu}} \qquad \qquad \dots (4.1)$$

where
ν = vibrational frequency in cm^{-1}

c = velocity of light

f = force constant of bond (dynes/cm) proportional to bond energy.

μ = reduced mass of atoms.

i.e., $\mu = \dfrac{m_a \times m_b}{m_a + m_b}$ ... (4.2)

where m_a = mass of atom 'a' and m_b = mass of atom 'b'.

- Equation (4.1) is used to calculate the vibrational frequency of a diatomic molecule. It is clear from the equation that

  (a) Frequency of vibration is directly proportional to force constant (f) i.e., bond energy. Thus stronger bonds will have higher frequency of vibration.

  (b) Frequency of vibration is inversely proportional to reduced masses of the atoms. Thus when one of the atoms in the covalent bond is H which has the lowest atomic weight (O–H, N–H, C–H) the reduced mass becomes small and hence stretching frequency becomes high. Therefore O–H, N–H, C–H bonds have high stretching frequencies (in the range 3000-3600 cm^{-1}).

For O–H $\mu = \dfrac{16 \times 1}{16 + 1} = 0.94$

For N-H $\mu = \dfrac{14 \times 1}{14 + 1} = 0.93$

For C–H $\mu = \dfrac{12 \times 1}{12 + 1} = 0.92$

whereas for C-C $\mu = \dfrac{12 \times 12}{12 + 12} = 6.0$

- **Relation between force constant, frequency and bond length:** As the bond order increases, the force constant increases i.e., bond energy increases and hence frequency increases while bond length decreases.

Bond	Bond length	Force constant	Frequency
C – C	1.54 A°	5×10^5 dynes/cm	~ 1100 cm^{-1}
C = C	1.34 A°	10×10^5 dynes/cm	~ 1650 cm^{-1}
C $\equiv$ C	1.20 A°	15×10^5 dynes/cm	~ 2200 cm^{-1}

- **Thus the bond between heavier atoms vibrates at lower frequency and stronger bond between atoms vibrate at higher frequency.**

4.3.7 Parts of I.R. Spectrum

- The IR region (4000 to 667 cm^{-1}) is divided into three regions from the point of view of interpreting the IR spectrum. (Refer Fig. 4.18)

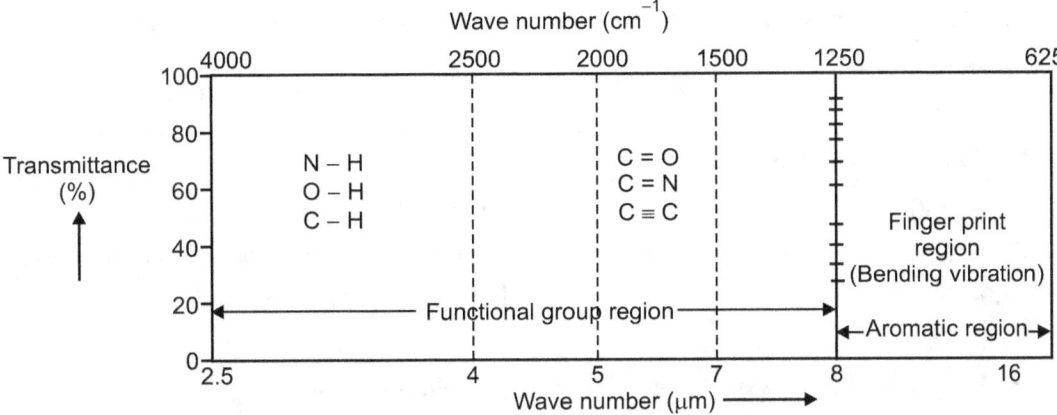

Fig. 4.18: Regions of Infra red spectrum

(a) **Functional group region:** The region between 4000 to 1300 cm^{-1} is very useful for the organic chemist as the absorption bands due to vibrations of functional group such as –O–H, –N–H, –C–H, –S–H in the range 3700-2500 cm^{-1} appear in this region.

The absorption band in the region 2500-2000 cm^{-1} is due to the presence of triple bonds, as in the case of C≡C and C≡N, and is known as triple bond region.

The important IR band in the region 1800-1680 cm^{-1} is due to carbonyl group of acid, acid halide, ester, anhydride, ketone, aldehyde or amide. Thus, these functional groups are easily identified from the absorption bands in IR.

The IR bands appearing in the region from 1680-1620 cm^{-1} are due to C=C stretching frequency in alkenes while from 1600-1500 cm^{-1} are due to C=C stretching frequencies in aromatic compounds.

(b) **Finger print region:** The IR region between 1300-900 cm^{-1} is known as finger print region. This part of the spectrum is very complex and arises due to skeletal stretching and vibrations. This region is not useful for interpretation but is helpful for a comparison. If the finger print region of two molecules is identical then the two molecules are identical.

(c) **Aromatic region:** The region below 900 cm^{-1} is known as aromatic region. The bands that occur in this region are due to bending vibrations of C–H bond in the aromatic molecule. This region also helps in predicting the substitution pattern in the aromatic ring.

Table 4.6: Characteristic absorption frequencies of some functional groups

Frequency range in cm^{-1}	Bond	Type of compound
[A] Bonds to hydrogen atoms		
3600-3650	–O–H (free)	Alcohols, Phenols
3200-3500	–O–H (bonded)	Hydrogen bonded alcohols and phenols
3450-3600	Sharp	Intramolecular 'H' bond
3200-3550	Broad	Intramolecular 'H' bond
2500-3200	Very broad	Chelated 'H' bond
3300-3350	–N–H	Amines, Amides
3200-3310	≡C–H	Acetylenic
3000-3100	=C–H	Ethylenic and aromatic
2850-2950	–C–H	Saturated hydrocarbons
2700-2900	–CO–H	Aldehydes
2550-2900	–S–H	Thiols
2500-3600	–COO–H	Carboxylic acid (very broad)
[B] Triple bond region		
2240-2260	–C≡N	Nitriles (non-conjugated)
2215-2240	–C≡N	Nitriles (conjugated)
2100-2140	–C≡CH	Alkynes (terminal)
2200-2260	–C≡C–	Alkynes (non-terminal)
[C] Double bond region		
1740-1850	R–CO–O–CO–R	Anhydrides
1770-1815	R–CO–X	Acyl halides
1730-1750	R–CO–OR	Esters
1730-1740	R–CO–H	Aldehydes
1705-1720	R–CO–R	Ketones
1700-1725	R–CO–OH	Acids
1680-1700	R–CO–NH–	Amides
1620-1680	–C=C–	Alkenes
1590-1690	–C=N–	Imines, Oximes
1500-1600	–C=C–	Aromatic
1370-1540	–NO$_2$	Nitro group

[D] Single bond region		
1000-1300	–C–O–	Alcohol, Phenol, Ester, Ether etc.
1100-1120	–C–C–	Saturated alkanes
500-750	–C–X	Alkyl halides
[E] C–H bending vibrations (aromatic region)		
690-710 and 730-770	=C–H	Mono substituted benzene
735-770	=C–H (o)	Ortho di substituted benzene
750-810	=C–H (m)	Meta di substituted benzene
790-850	=C–H (p)	Para di substituted benzene
[F] C–H bending vibrations (alkenes)		
980-960	RHC=CHR	1,2-di substituted C–H bond (trans)
730-675	RHC=CHR	1,2-di substituted C–H bond (cis)
840-800	$RHC=CR_2$	1,1,2-tri substituted alkene
890	$R_2C=CH_2$	1,1-di substituted alkene
990 and 910	$RHC=CH_2$	Mono substituted alkene

4.3.8 Characteristics of I.R. Absorption of Some Functional Groups

(a) **Hydrocarbons:** IR spectrum of hydrocarbons show characteristic absorption bands due to C–C and C–H bond stretching.

    (i) **Alkanes:** The C-C bond stretching frequency in alkanes is very weak and appears in the region 1200-800 cm^{-1}. These peaks are not very useful for identification as these absorption peaks are seen for almost all organic compounds.

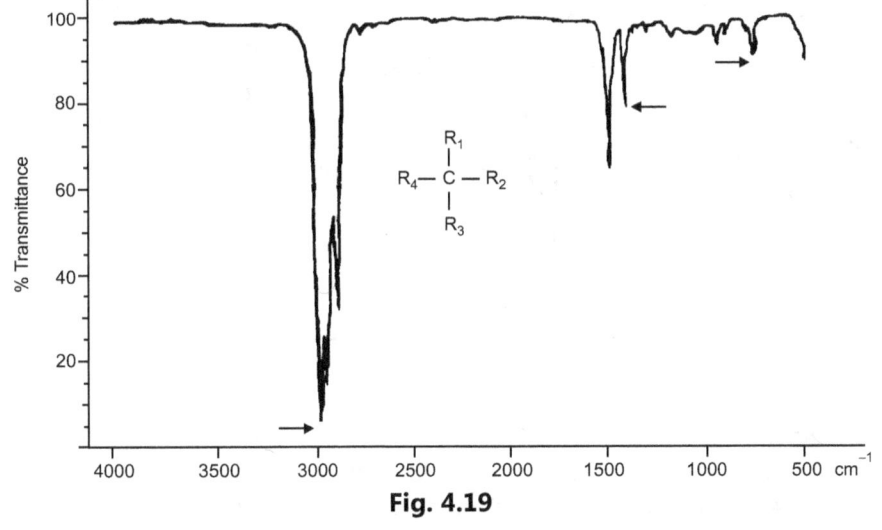

Fig. 4.19

(ii) **Alkenes:** The un-conjugated C=C bond stretching frequency appears near 1640 cm^{-1}. The di-substituted *trans* double bond absorbs at 1670 cm^{-1} [Refer Fig. 4.20 (a)], while the *cis* C=C bond absorbs at 1650 cm^{-1} [Refer Fig. 4.20 (b)]. However the C=C absorption is not observed for symmetrical alkenes.

Trans-alkene

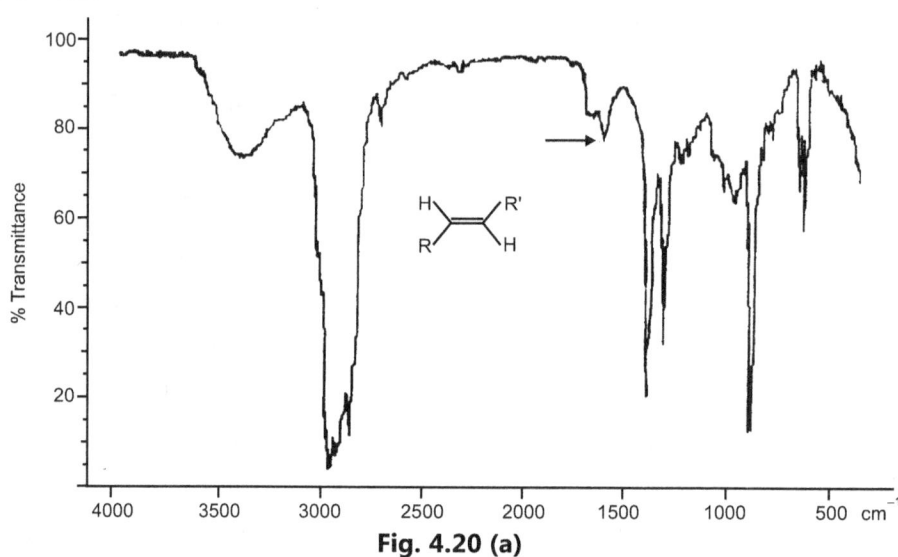

Fig. 4.20 (a)

Cis-alkene

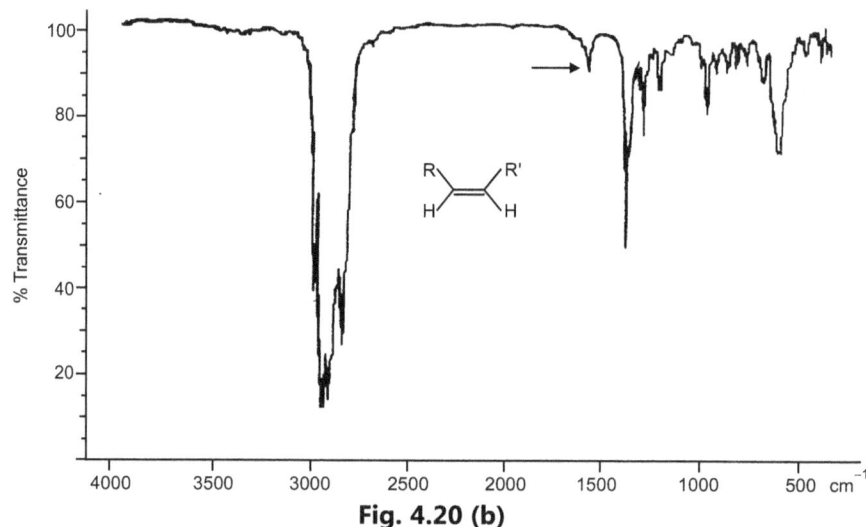

Fig. 4.20 (b)

(iii) **Alkynes:** The C≡C stretching occurs in the region 2100-2260 cm^{-1}. The terminal acetylenic C≡C stretching absorption at 2100-2140 cm^{-1} [Fig. 4.21 (a)], while the internal C≡C triple bond appears at higher frequency

(2190-2260 cm^{-1}) [Fig. 4.21 (b)]. If the alkyne is symmetrical it does not show any absorption band as the dipole moment does not change during stretching of C≡C bond.

The ≡C–H stretching occurs in the range 3270-3300 cm^{-1}, while the ≡C–H bending vibration appears in the range 610-700 cm^{-1}.

Terminal alkyne: 3340 – 3270 cm^{-1} (s) 2140 –2100 cm^{-1} (w)

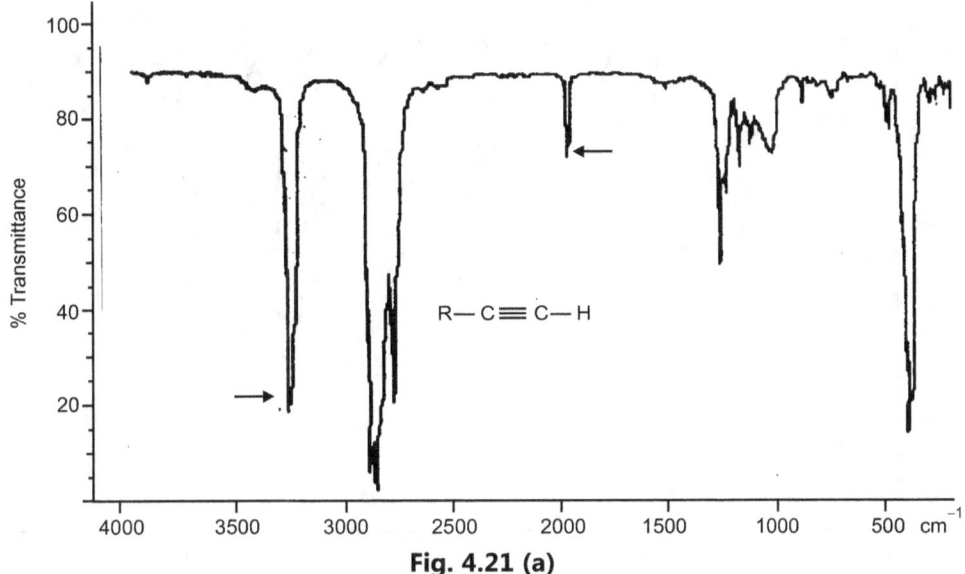

Fig. 4.21 (a)

Internal alkyne: 2260 – 2190 cm^{-1} (w)

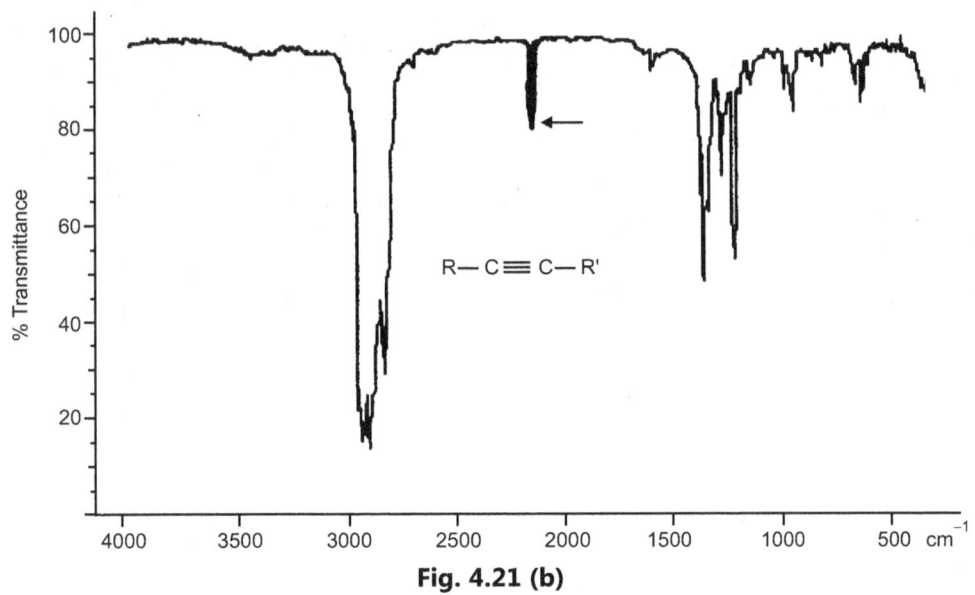

Fig. 4.21 (b)

(iv) Aromatic: The characteristic C=C bond stretching frequency of aromatic compounds appears in the range 1500-1600 cm^{-1}. The =C–H stretching occurs in the range 3000-3100 cm^{-1}, while the =C–H bending occurs in the range 675-710 cm^{-1}. Three to four bonds in the region 1500-1600 cm^{-1} are characteristic of aromatic compound.

Monosubstituted aromatic: 700 cm^{-1} (s)

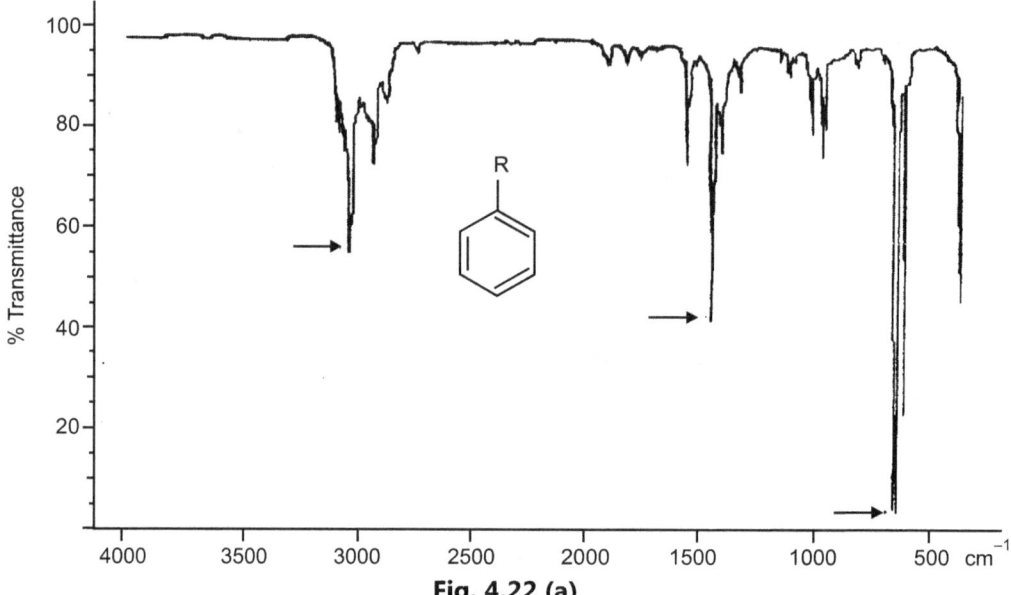

Fig. 4.22 (a)

Ortho disubstituted aromatic: 750 cm^{-1} (s)

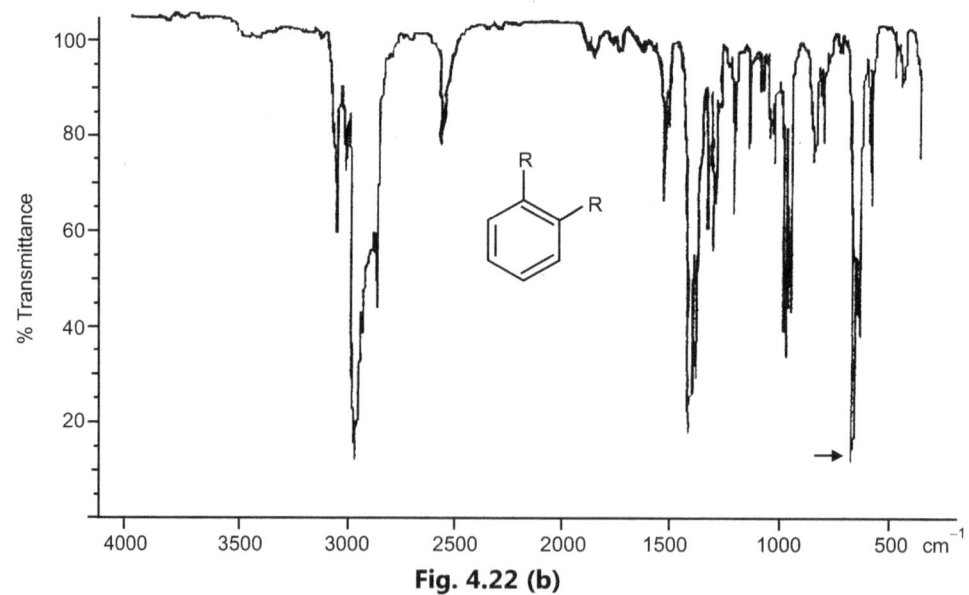

Fig. 4.22 (b)

Meta-disubstituted aromatic: 725-680 cm^{-1} (m)

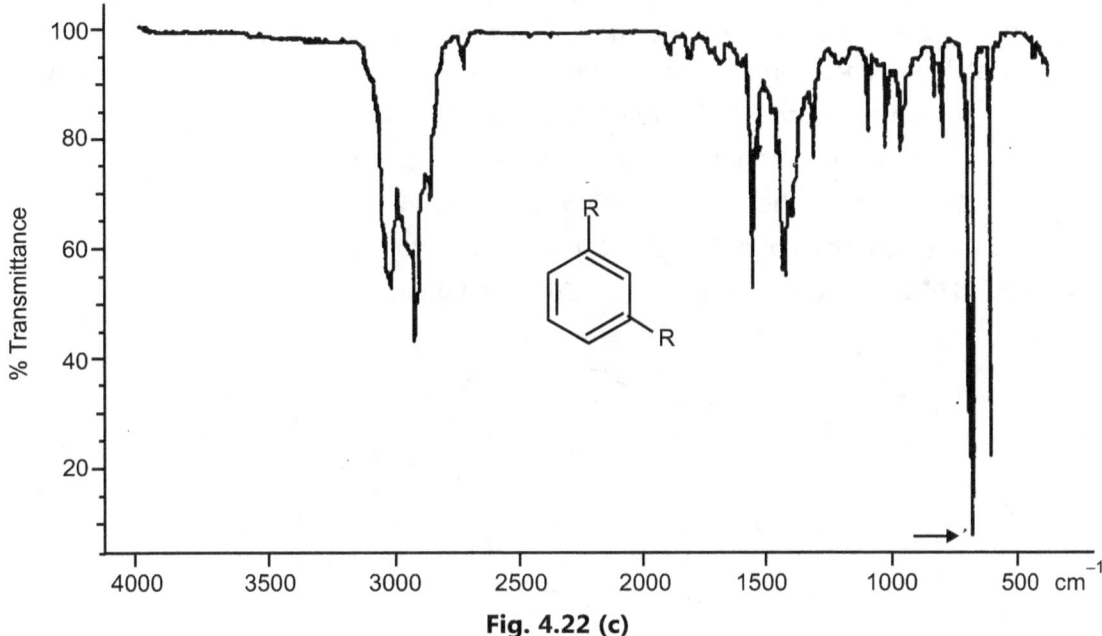

Fig. 4.22 (c)

Para-disubstituted aromatic: 830 – 800 cm^{-1}

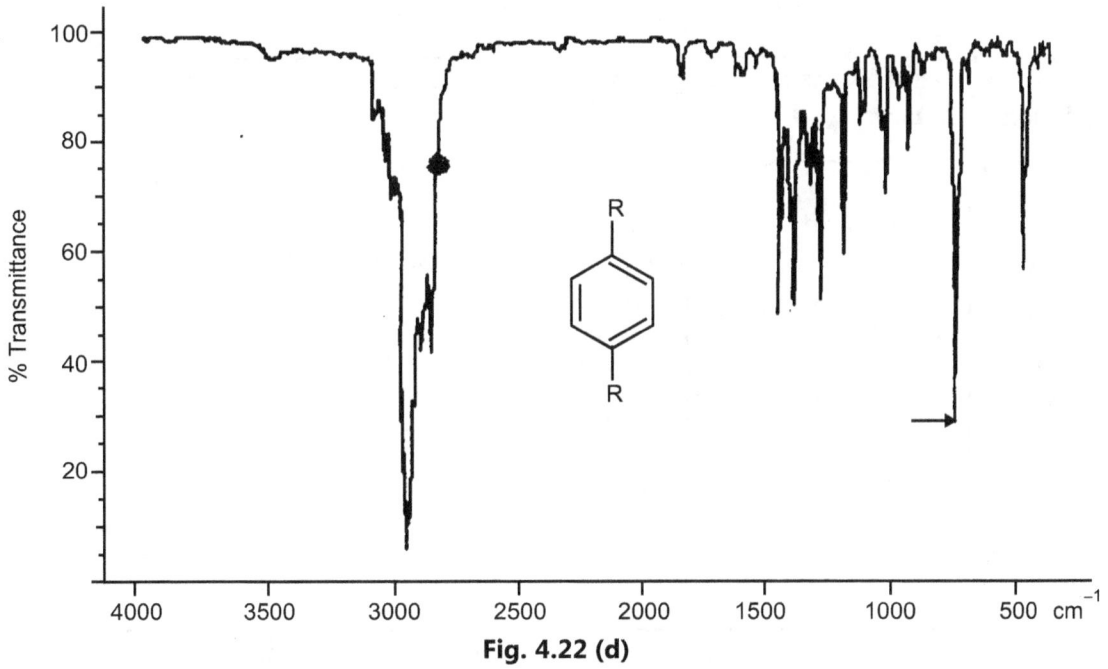

Fig. 4.22 (d)

(b) Alcohol and Ethers: IR spectrum of alcohols and phenols show strong and broad absorption bands in the range 3200-3600 cm^{-1} due to O–H stretching. Another strong band due to C–O stretching appears in the region 1000-1200 cm^{-1}. The exact stretching depends on the type of the alcohol.

Primary alcohol C–O stretching about 1050 cm^{-1}

Secondary alcohol C–O stretching about 1100 cm^{-1}

Tertiary alcohol C–O stretching about 1150 cm^{-1}

Aromatic alcohol C–O stretching about 1230 cm^{-1}

Alcohol: 1050 – 1230 cm^{-1} (s)   **3200 – 3600 cm^{-1} (s)**

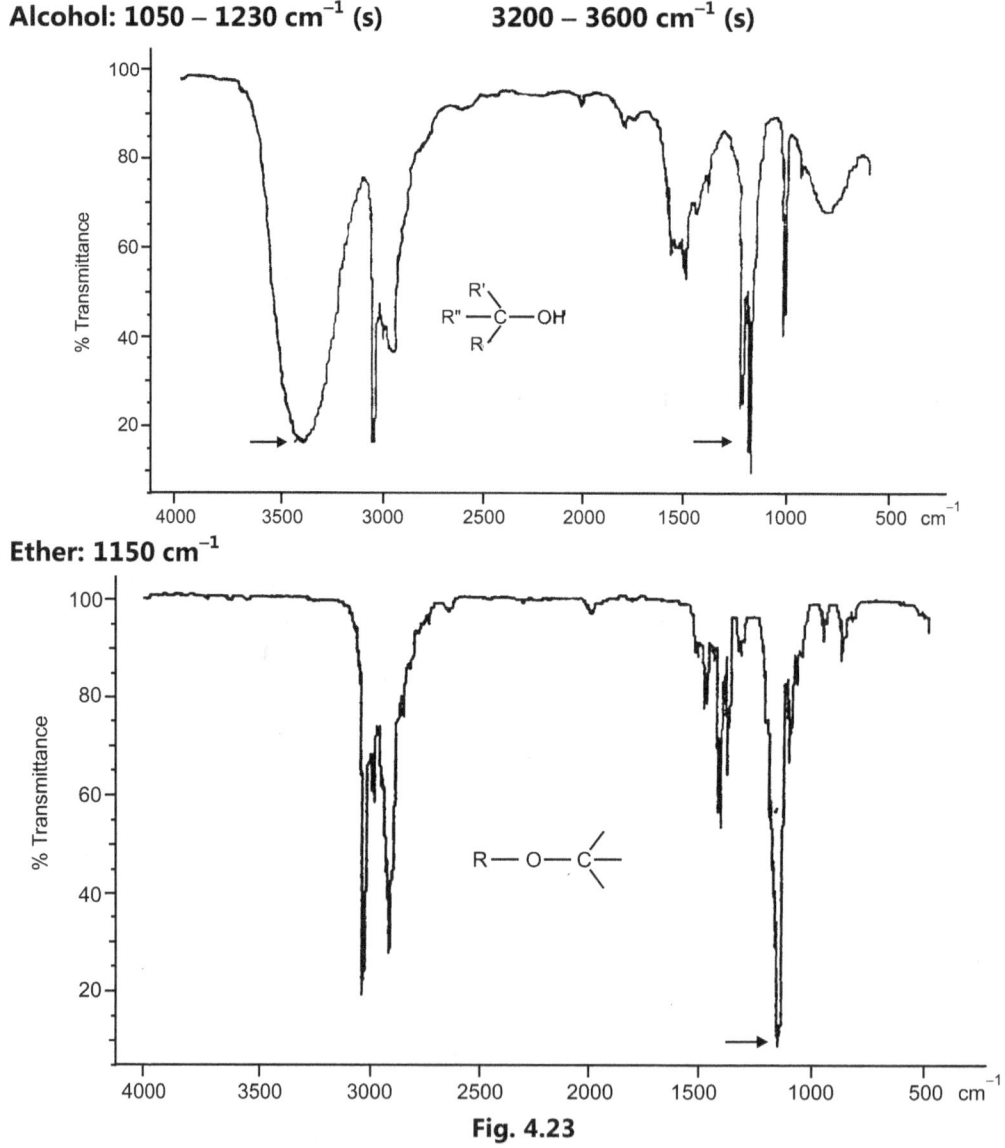

Ether: 1150 cm^{-1}

Fig. 4.23

(c) **Alkyl halides:** The halogenated hydrocarbons show strong absorption due to C–X stretching. Aliphatic C–Cl absorption is observed between 800-600 cm^{-1}. CCl$_4$ shows an intense peak at 795 cm^{-1}. Brominated compounds absorb in the range 600-500 cm^{-1}, while iodo compounds in the region 550-500 cm^{-1}.

Alkyl fluoride: 1000 – 1400 cm^{-1} (s)

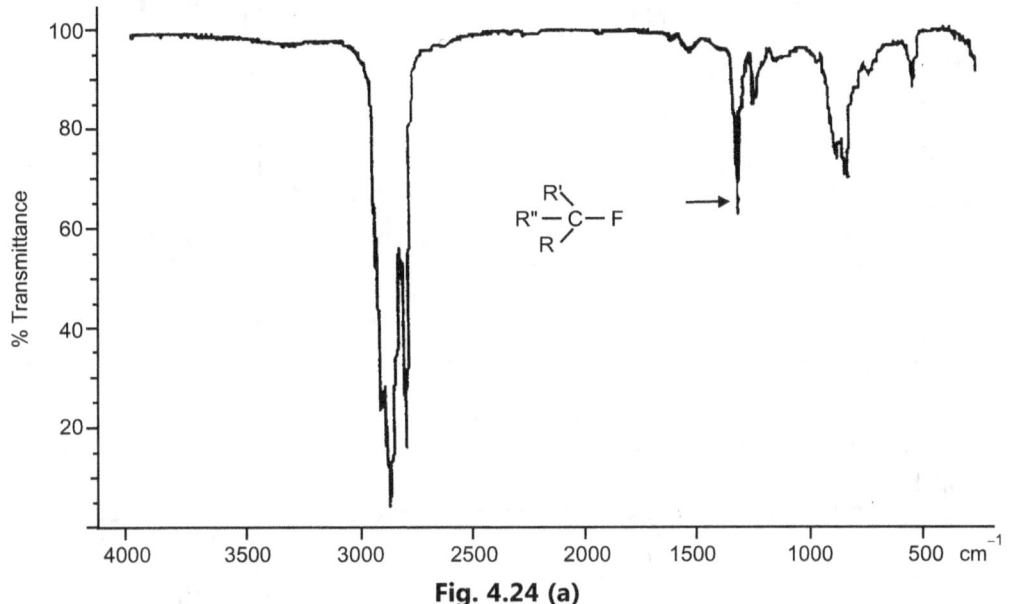

Fig. 4.24 (a)

Alkyl chloride: 800 – 600 cm^{-1} (s)

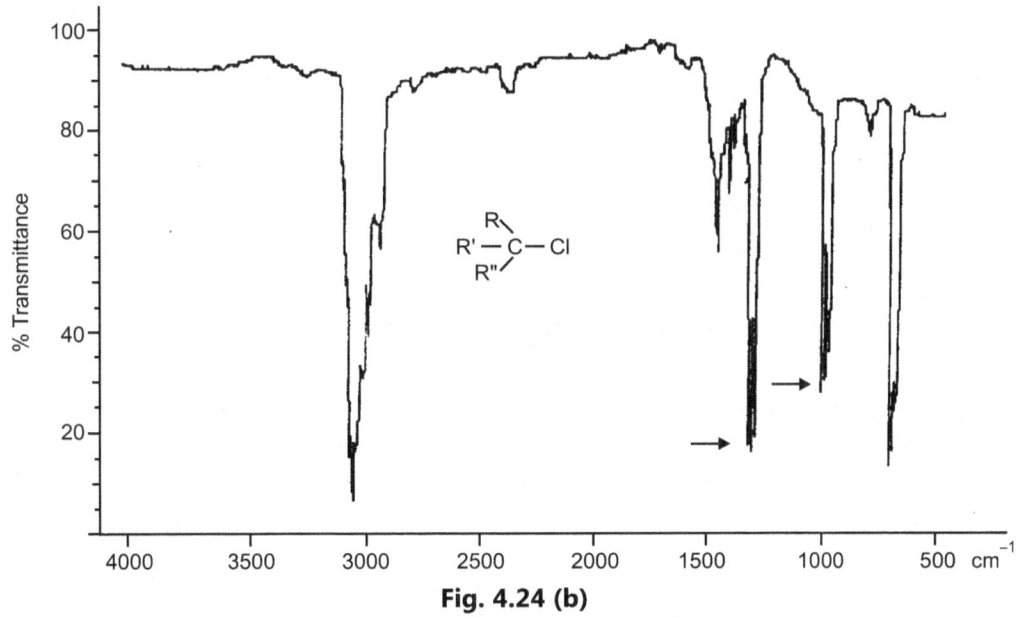

Fig. 4.24 (b)

Alkyl bromide: 500 – 600 cm^{-1} (s)

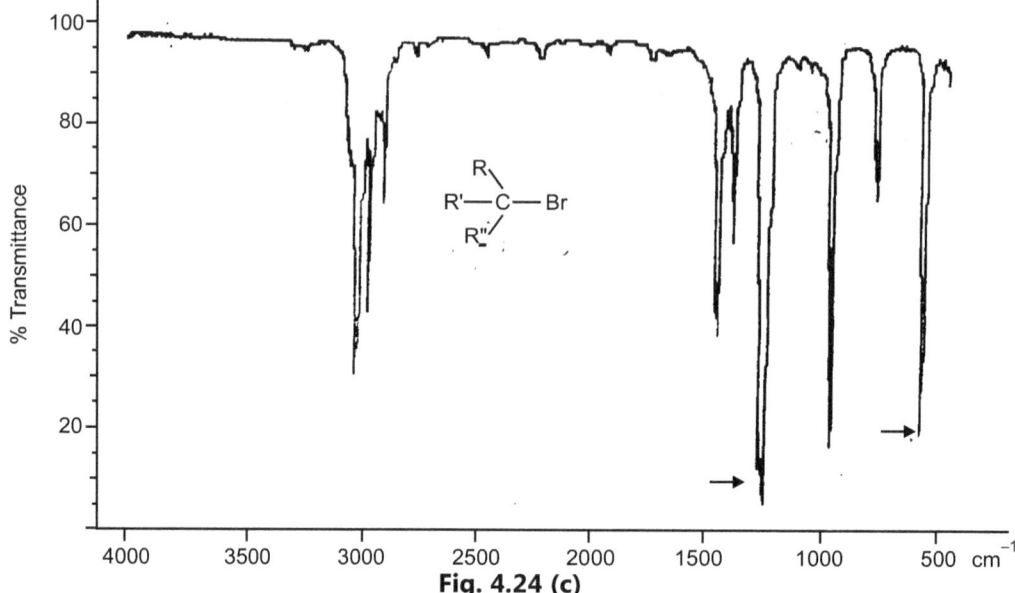

Fig. 4.24 (c)

Alkyl iodide: 500 – 550 cm^{-1} (w)

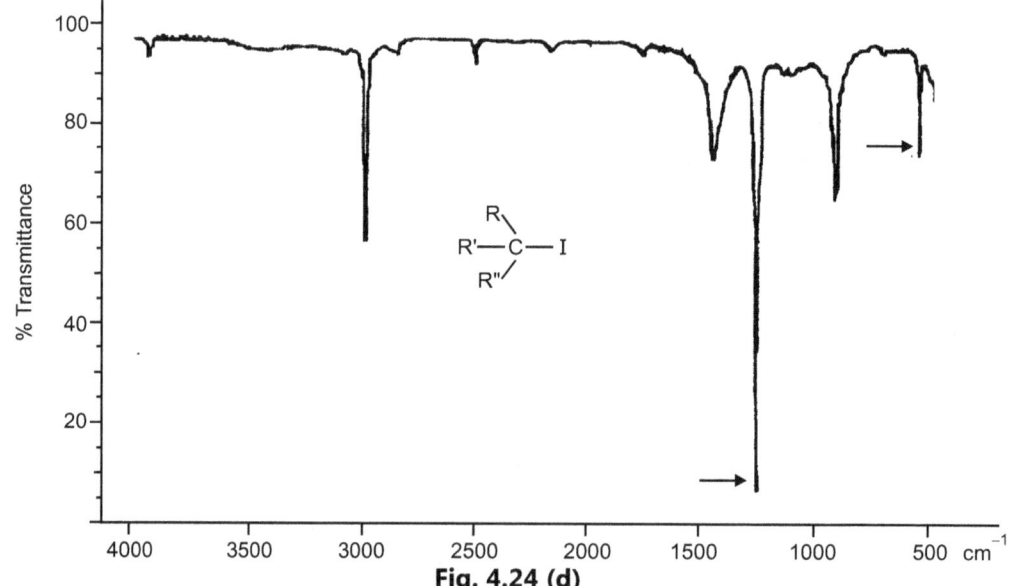

Fig. 4.24 (d)

A strong CH$_2$ wagging band is observed for CH$_2$-X in the region 1150-1300 cm^{-1}. Chlorobenzene absorbs in the range 1089-1096 cm^{-1}.

R⫫F
1400 – 1000

R⫫Cl
800 – 600

R⫫Br
600 – 500

R⫫I
500 – 550

1089 – 1096

(d) Carbonyl compounds: Aldehydes, ketones, acids, esters, lactones, anhydrides, amides and lactams show a strong absorption frequency in the region 1540-1740 cm^{-1}. This absorption peak is very strong in intensity and usually is not interfered by any other absorption peak and hence easy to recognize.

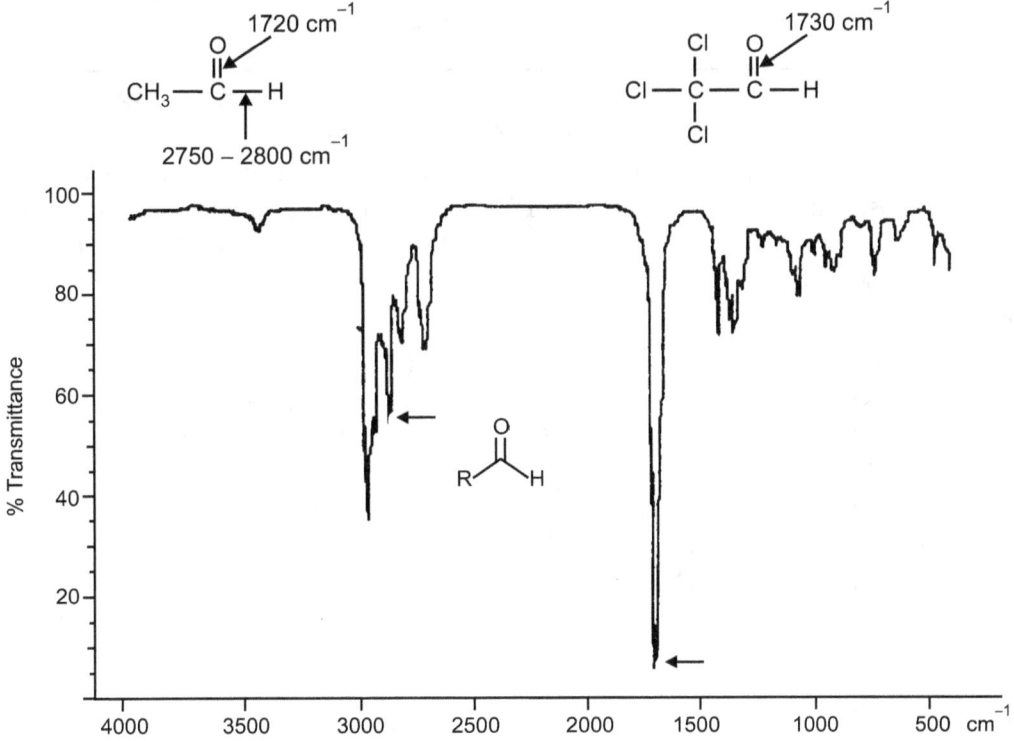

(i) Aldehydes: The C=O stretching frequency of aldehydes is observed near 1720-1740 cm^{-1}. The absorption frequency is affected by inductive, resonance and steric effects discussed in the next section. Aldehydes also show two characteristic C–H peaks near 2700-2850 cm^{-1}, these are absent in other C=O containing functional groups.

Fig. 4.25: I.R. Spectrum of aldehyde

(ii) Ketones: A very important peak in all ketones is the strong C=O stretching at about 1710-1715 cm^{-1}. This absorption frequency is affected by inductive, resonance and steric effects.

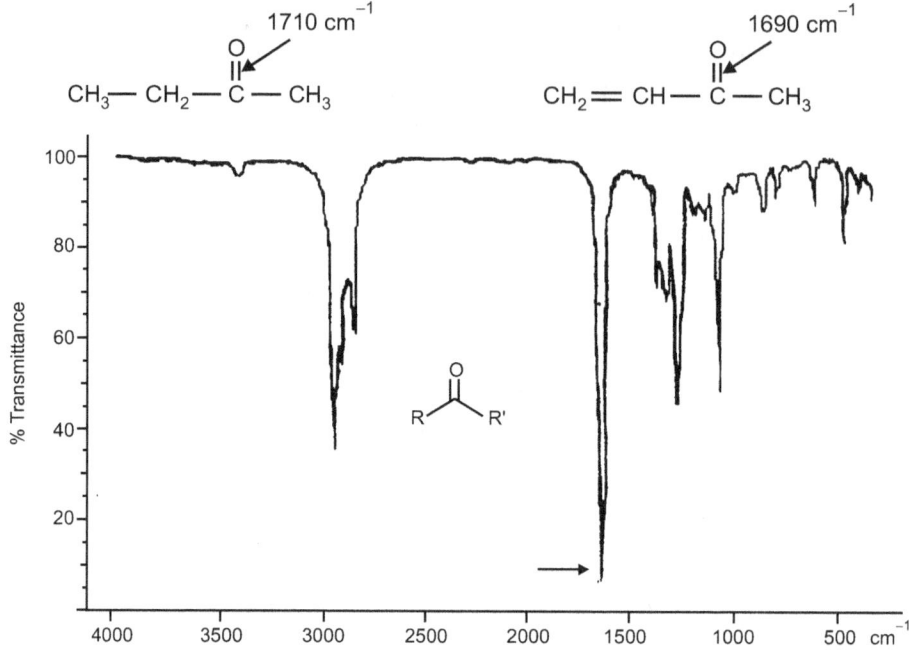

Fig. 4.26: I.R. Spectrum of ketone

(iii) Acids and esters: Carboxylic acids and esters also show carbonyl stretching absorption band in the range 1730-1750 cm^{-1}. In addition, acids show a broad O–H stretching near 3300 cm^{-1}, while esters show the C–O stretching near 1100-1300 cm^{-1}.

Acid:

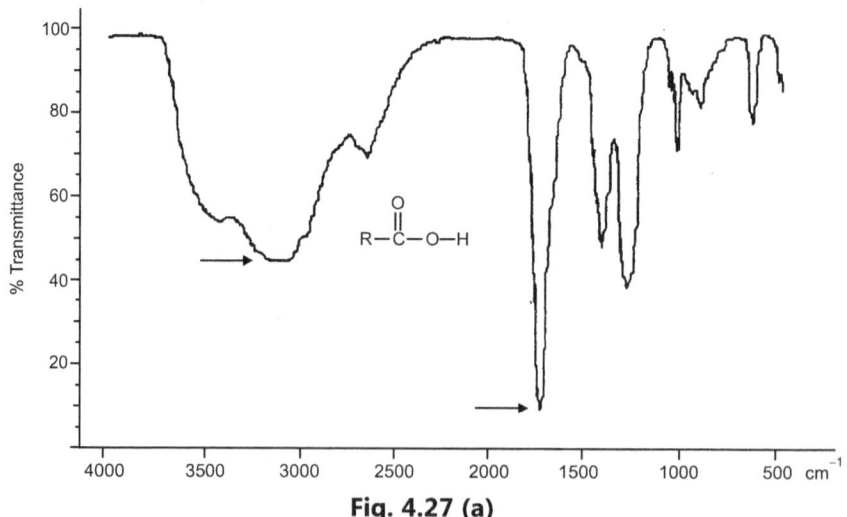

Fig. 4.27 (a)

Acid chloride:

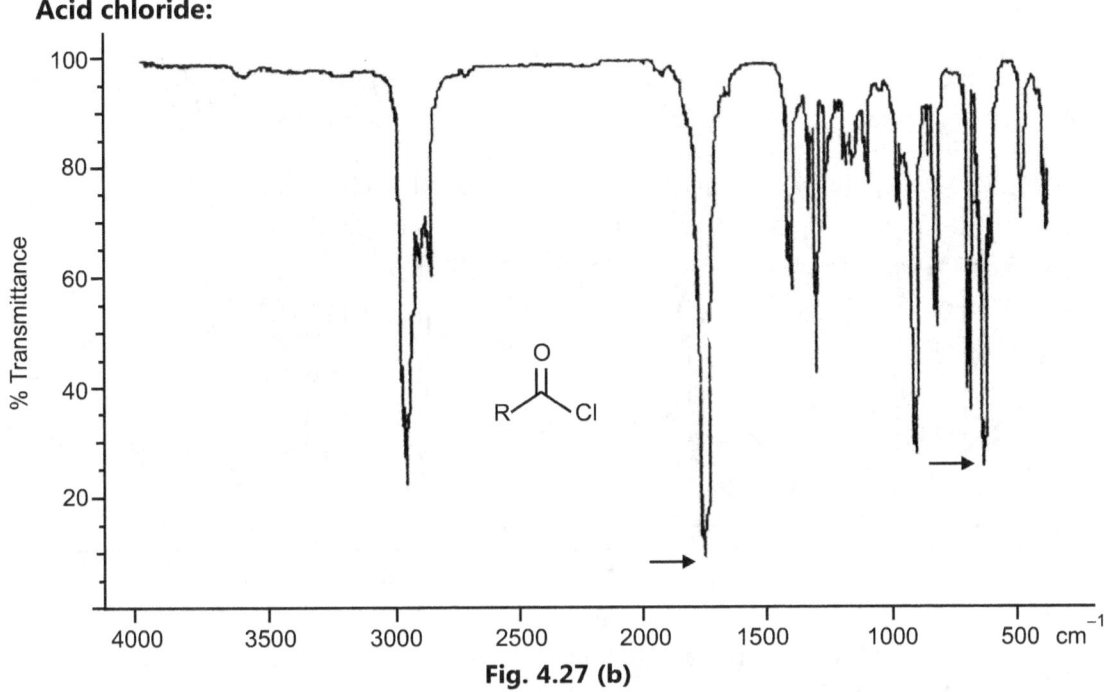

Fig. 4.27 (b)

Anhydride:

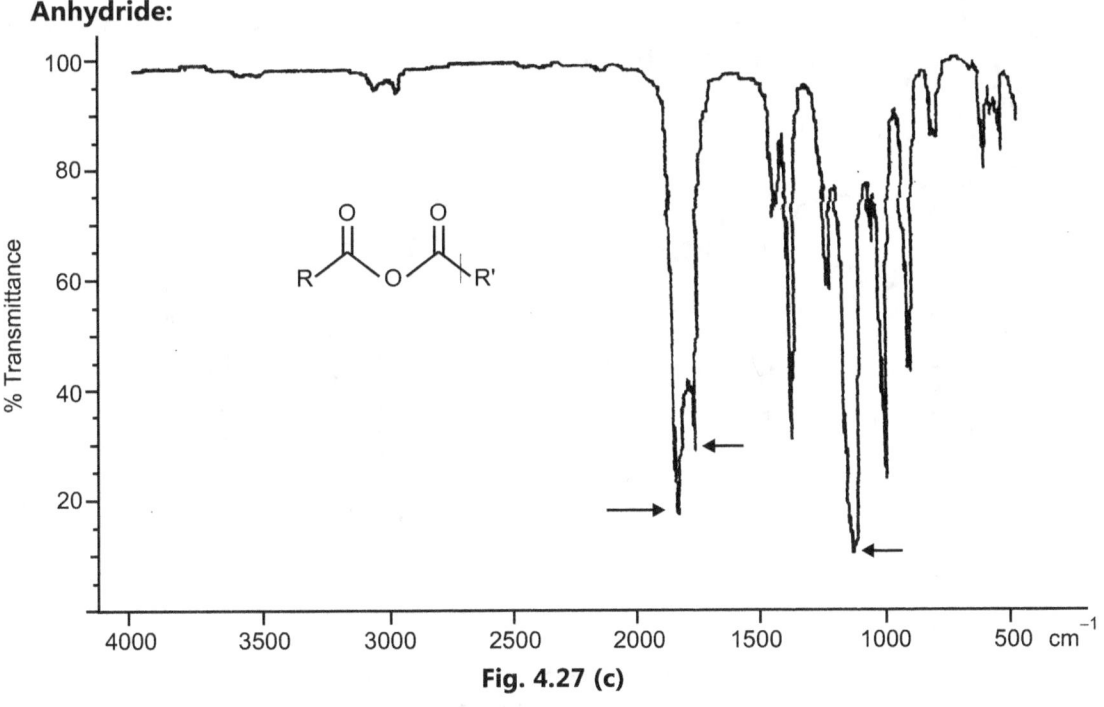

Fig. 4.27 (c)

Ester:

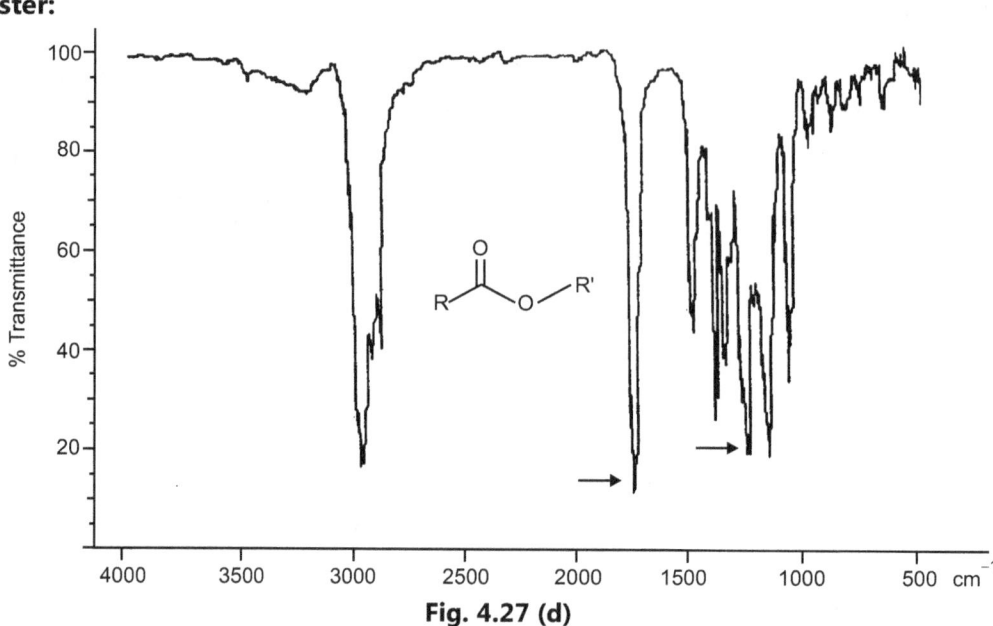

Fig. 4.27 (d)

(iv) Amines and amides: Aliphatic amine absorbs at 3200-3500 cm^{-1} due to N-H stretching, while the aromatic primary amine at slightly higher frequency. The primary amine shows two bands while secondary amine shows only one band and no peak for tertiary amine in the range 3200-3500 cm^{-1}. The N-H bending (scissoring) is observed in the range 1510-1650 cm^{-1}. .

Amine:

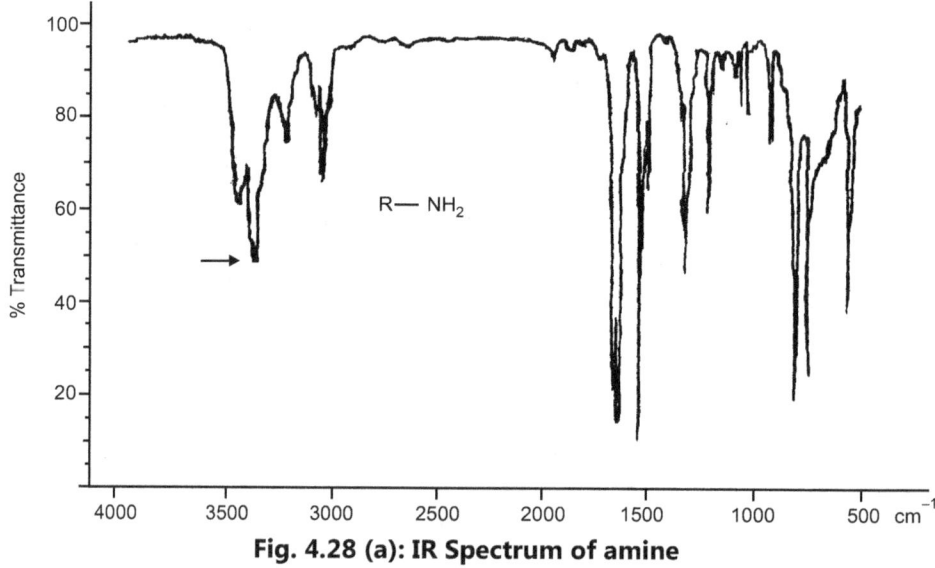

Fig. 4.28 (a): IR Spectrum of amine

Amide:

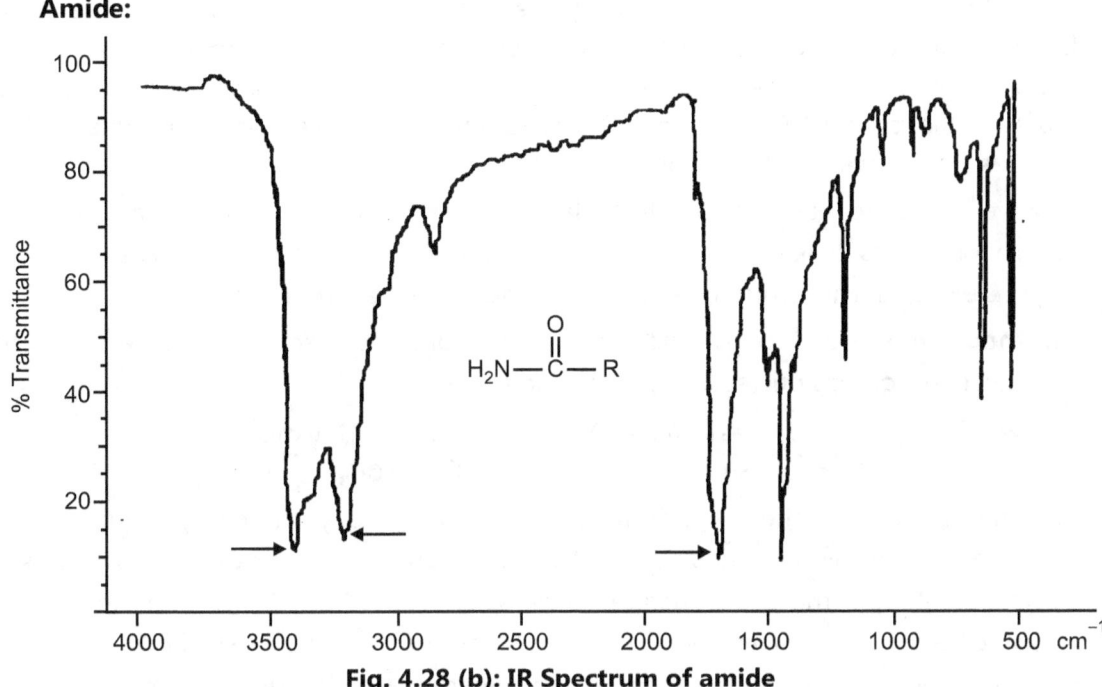

Fig. 4.28 (b): IR Spectrum of amide

In addition C-N stretching band is observed in the range 1030-1230 cm^{-1} for the aliphatic amines. The C-N stretching for the aromatic amine occurs at slightly higher frequency (1260-1340 cm^{-1}) because of the force constant of C-N bond is increased by the resonance with the ring.

(e) Aromatic compounds: The most prominent and most informative band in the IR spectra of aromatic compounds occurs in the low frequency region (675-900 cm^{-1}). These bands appear as a result of out of plane bending of the ring C–H bonds. In plane bending band appears in the 1000-1300 cm^{-1} region. The C=C bond stretching appears in the region 1500-1600 cm^{-1}. The C–H bending vibrations of aromatic compounds are influenced by the substitution pattern of the ring (Refer Fig. 4.22 a – d).

(i)	Mono substituted benzene	690-710 cm^{-1} and 730-770 cm^{-1}
(ii)	Ortho di-substituted benzene	735 -770 cm^{-1}
(iii)	Meta di-substituted benzene	750 -810 cm^{-1}
(iv)	Para di-substituted benzene	851-790 cm^{-1}

4.3.9 Factors Affecting I.R. Frequencies

- According to Hook's law the frequency of absorption depends on (i) bond strength and (ii) the reduced mass of the atoms forming the bond. Thus any factors that increase the bond strength will increase the stretching frequency of the bond and if the mass of the atoms forming the bond is increased, the reduced mass increases, and the stretching frequency will decrease. For a functional group the type of bond and atoms are fixed, therefore, the stretching frequency should remain fixed. Thus, carbonyl groups of ketones absorb in the range 1710-1715 cm^{-1}. IR spectrum therefore is very useful for determining the presence of functional group in a molecule.

- However, there are many other factors which influence and thus modify the frequency of absorption and its peak position in the spectrum. There are mainly four factors which are responsible for the absorption frequencies of the functional groups in the molecule:

(a) Inductive effect: Groups which are electron donating effects (+I) when attached to functional groups decrease the stretching frequency.

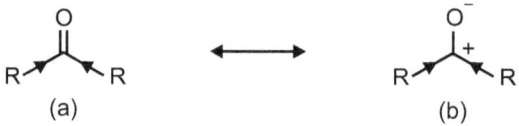

The additional +I effect in acetone decreases the carbonyl stretching frequency. The +I effect actually decreases the double bond character of the carbonyl bond. This is apparent from the two structures shown below in which the second structure is stabilized by the +I effect of the methyl group, thus increases the single bond character of C=O bond. As single bond energies are less than the double bond energy, according to Hook's law, the +I effect decreases the frequency.

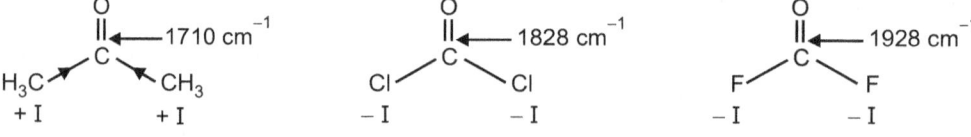

In aldehydes there is only one R group, i.e., more double bond character and hence higher frequency.

Ketones carbonyl stretching will always appear at lower frequency than aldehydes.

On these lines the groups which are electron withdrawing (-I) increase the double bond character of the carbonyl group and hence increase the stretching frequency.

Strong –I effect of three fluorine atoms increase the carbonyl frequency.

(b) Resonance effect: When the carbonyl group is conjugated to a carbon-carbon double bond, there is electron donating resonance effect, which decreases the double bond character of the carbonyl group, this decreases the stretching frequency of the carbonyl group.

Electron donating (+R) groups decrease the stretching frequency and electron withdrawing (-R) groups increase the stretching frequency of the carbonyl group.

Following examples show the conjugation effect on the carbonyl stretching frequencies:

Aldehydes and Ketones: When the number of conjugated double bond increases, the effect is the lowering of stretching frequency.

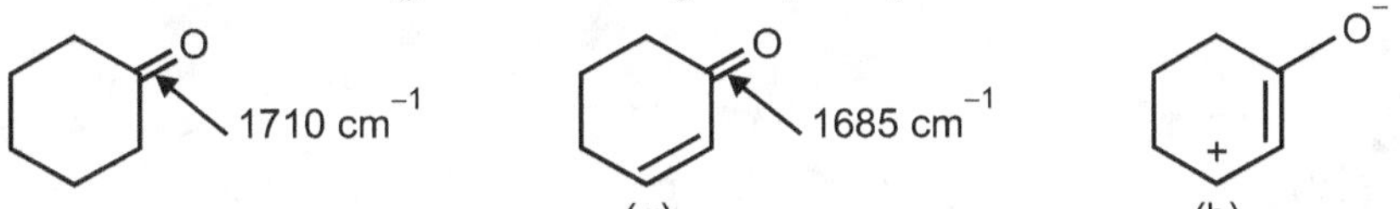

(a)   (b)

Aromatic ketones and aldehydes also show similar effect with much lower values than normal values.

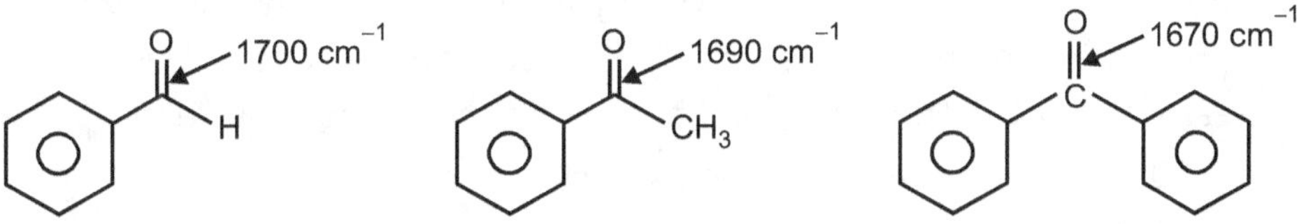

Acids: The lone pair of oxygen is conjugated to the carbonyl and exert a +R effect which decreases carbonyl stretching but also exerts –I effect which increases the C=O stretching frequency. As a result of these two opposing effects, the C=O absorption appears around 1720 cm^{-1}.

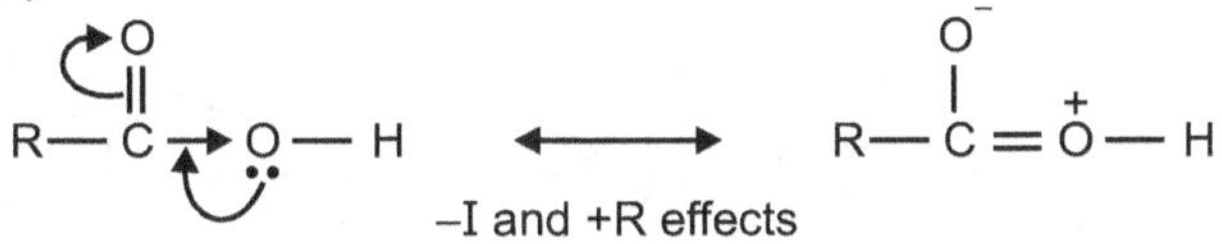

–I and +R effects

The conjugation to carbonyl group will decrease the stretching frequency as expected.

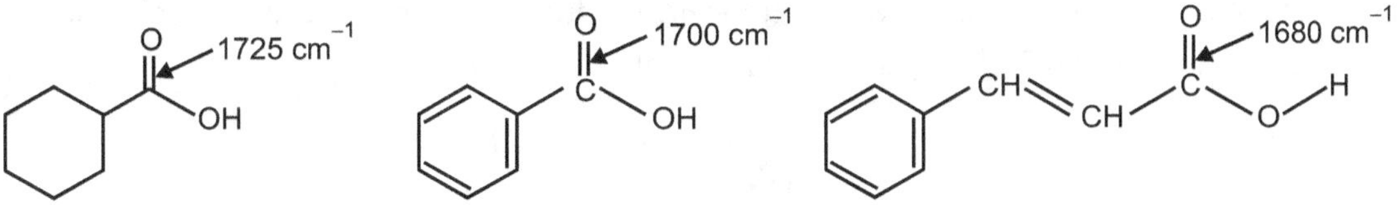

Esters: In esters also there are two effects +R and –I of the oxygen atom operating simultaneously as a result of these the carbonyl stretching appears at 1740 cm^{-1}.

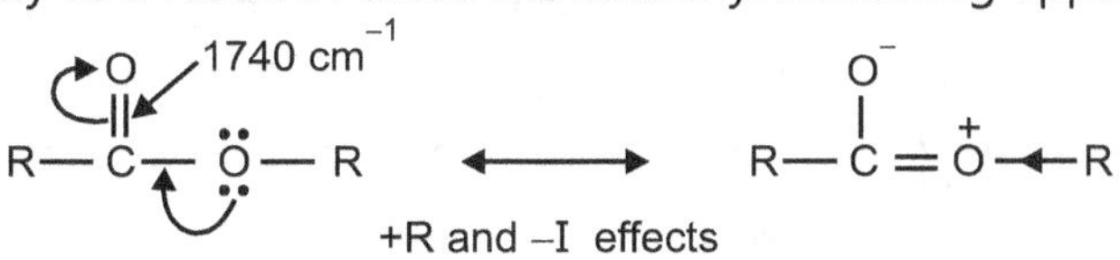

+R and –I effects

Acid halides: In case of acid halides the –I effect exceeds far more than their +R effect and as a result the carbonyl stretching of acid halides absorbs at very high values: Acid fluorides at highest value of 1850 cm^{-1}.

$$-I >> +R \qquad\qquad\qquad\qquad -I >> +R$$

Amides: In case of amides, the electron donating resonance effect of nitrogen far exceed than its –I effect. Therefore the carbonyl frequency decreases considerably and have the lowest value (1690 cm^{-1}) as compared to all other carbonyl groups.

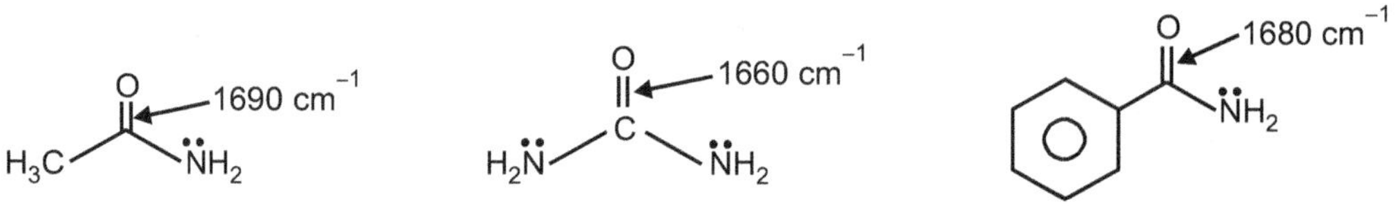

(c) **Hydrogen bonding:** Carboxylic acids, alcohols, phenols, amines and amides show strong hydrogen bonding effect. The hydrogen bonding weakens the C=O bond, lowering the carbonyl as well as O–H stretching frequency. Hydrogen bonding increases the O–H bond length and hence its bond strength decreases.

    O–H   H-bonded stretching 2700-2500 cm^{-1}

    O–H   free or no H-bonding 3500 cm^{-1}

Intramolecular H-bonding shows greater effect of –C=O and O–H stretching than intermolecular H-bonding.

Intermolecular H - bonding

Intramolecular H-bonding

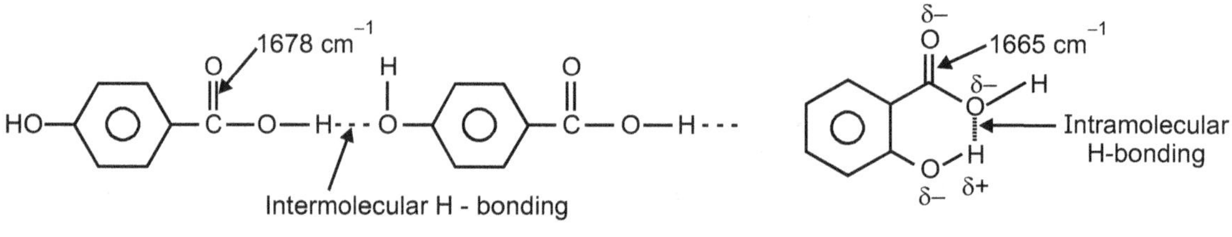

Carboxylic acid exists in the dimeric form due to strong hydrogen bonding thus lowering the C=O absorption frequency at 1721 cm^{-1}.

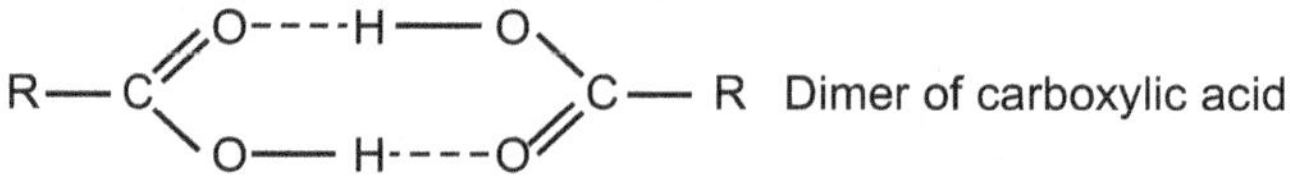

R—C ... C—R Dimer of carboxylic acid

Alcohols and phenols also show H-bonding effects similar to acids. H-bonded alcoholic O–H stretching peak appears in the range 3200-3500 cm^{-1}. Primary, secondary amines and amides also show H-bonding effects.

Effects of dilution: When IR spectrum of acid, amide, amine or alcohol is recorded with dilute solution (in aprotic solvents), the intermolecular H-bonding effect decreases due to intervening solvent molecules. As a result, the O–H stretching frequency shift to higher value and C=O stretching in case of acid or amide, also shifts to higher value.

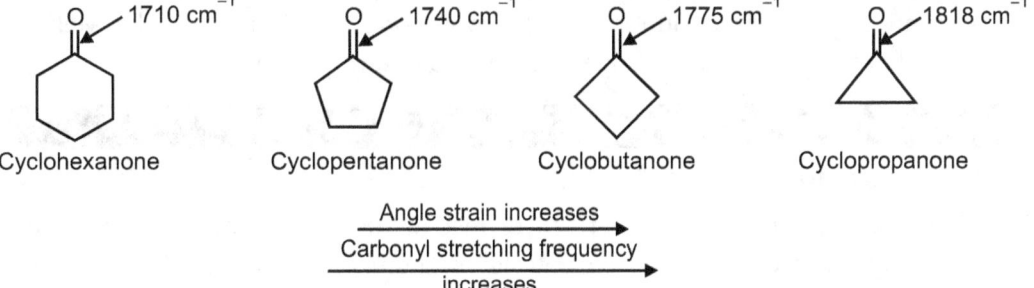

However if H-bonding is intramolecular, the effect of dilution is not observed.

(d) **Steric effects:** Steric effects also modify the stretching frequencies. Consider the carbonyl frequencies of the following cyclic ketones, as the ring size decreases the angle strain in the ring increases, this increases the carbonyl stretching frequencies.

O $1710\ cm^{-1}$	O $1740\ cm^{-1}$	O $1775\ cm^{-1}$	O $1818\ cm^{-1}$
Cyclohexanone	Cyclopentanone	Cyclobutanone	Cyclopropanone

Angle strain increases

Carbonyl stretching frequency increases

4.3.10 Applications of I.R. Spectroscopy

(a) **Determination of structure:** The observation of the IR peaks in functional group region helps to detect the functional groups. If the peaks are shifted to higher or lower frequencies indicate that factors like inductive effect, resonance or steric effects are operative. The finger print region is characteristic of the molecule. No two molecules can have identical finger print region. Thus comparison of the finger print region helps to establish the identity of the molecule. The aromatic region gives the idea of the substitution pattern in the aromatic ring.

(b) **Study of chemical reaction:** IR spectroscopy is useful in following the progress of chemical reaction. It also helps to study the kinetics of the reaction. Most chemical reactions involve changes in the functional groups. Thus when a functional group undergoes change during the reaction, it is identified by the disappearance of the peak and/or observation of a new peak due to the corresponding change in the functional group. This is explained by the following examples:

(c) Hydrogen bonding: IR spectroscopy is also useful in distinguishing intermolecular from intramolecular H-bonding. Intermolecular and free O–H groups appear at higher frequency (3600-3650 cm^{-1}) whereas 'H' bonded appears at lower frequency (3200-3500 cm^{-1}). When the IR spectrum of the H-bonded molecule remains unchanged even after dilution the hydrogen bonding is intramolecular while if shifts to higher frequency the hydrogen bonding is intermolecular.

4.4 NMR (or PMR) Spectroscopy

4.4.1 Introduction

- The phenomenon of nuclear magnetic resonance (NMR) spectroscopy was first observed in 1946 and then routinely used by petroleum chemists. With the advancement in the instrumentation it has become the most powerful tool of the organic chemist for structure elucidation. In NMR spectroscopy we study the interaction of the magnetic component of the electromagnetic radiation with certain nuclei. The nucleus of the atom is exposed to very long but low energy radio waves (λ=1000-10000 cm). The nuclear magnetic resonance spectroscopy is mainly studied for the nucleus of hydrogen and therefore termed as Proton Magnetic Resonance (PMR). With the availability of instruments with high field strength, other nuclei are also studied like carbon, nitrogen, fluorine, phosphorus, silicon etc. In this section we will be dealing with PMR.

4.4.2 Principles of NMR Spectroscopy

- The NMR spectroscopy deals with the nucleus of the atoms that possess a magnetic moment. The nucleus being positively charged and spin about its axis generates a magnetic field directed along the axis of spin. Thus, the nucleus behaves as a tiny bar magnet.

- **Magnetic Properties of Nuclei:** Nuclei of certain isotopes possess a mechanical spin or angular momentum. The total angular momentum depends on the nuclear spin or spin number **I**, which may have values of 0, 1/2, 1, 3/2, ... (The individual protons and neutrons have spin quantum numbers +1/2 and -1/2. Therefore depending on the number of nucleons {protons and neutrons}, nuclei have a spin quantum number I). The spin quantum number 'I' is characteristic of the nucleus. All nucleus that have spin quantum number 'I' greater than zero, are magnetic in nature. The numerical value of the spin number I is related to the mass number and the atomic number as follows:

Mass number	Atomic number	Spin number, I	Examples
Odd	even or odd	1/2, 3/2, 5/2, ...	$^1H_1$, $^{13}C_6$, $^{19}F_9$, $^{31}P_{15}$, ...
Even	even	0	$^8Be_4$, $^{12}C_6$, $^{16}O_8$, ...
Even	odd	1, 2, 3, ...	$^2D_1$, $^{14}N_7$, ...

- **Nuclear excitation-Generation of nuclear energy levels:** Since electrical charge is associated with an atomic nucleus, the spinning nucleus gives rise to a magnetic field whose axis is coincident with the axis of its spin. Thus the nucleus behaves as a tiny bar magnet. When such nucleus is placed in an external magnetic field, it is found that the magnetic dipole assumes only discrete set of orientations. The system is said to be quantized. The magnetic nucleus can assume any one of the $(2I + 1)$ orientations with respect to the direction of the applied magnetic field. Thus a proton ($I = 1/2$) assumes any of the two possible orientations that corresponds to energy levels of $\pm \mu B_o$, in an applied magnetic field, where B_o is the strength of the external magnetic field and μ is the magnetic moment of the nucleus. The transition of the nuclei from one orientation to the other can be affected by the absorption or emission of the discrete amount of energy such that $E = h\nu = 2\mu B_o$, where ν is the frequency of electromagnetic radiation absorbed or emitted. For protons in a magnetic field of 1.4 Tesla, the frequency of such energy is in the radio frequency region- about 60 MHz.

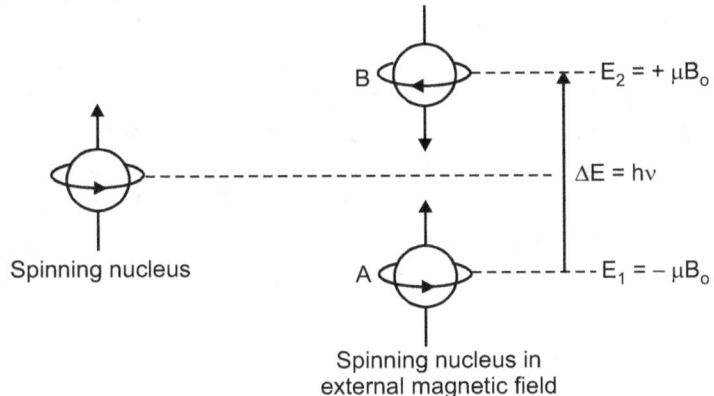

Spinning nucleus

Spinning nucleus in external magnetic field

Fig. 4.29: Orientation of H. nucleus in external magnetic field

- **Precessional motion:** Unless the axis of the nuclear magnet is oriented exactly parallel or anti-parallel with the direction of the applied magnetic field, there will be a certain force by the external field to so orient it. But because the nucleus is spinning the effect is that its rotational axis draws out a circle perpendicular to the applied field (Refer Fig. 4.30). This motion is called precession (an example is the gyroscopic motion of the spinning top). The precessional frequency of the nucleus depends upon the strength of the applied magnetic field and the nature of the nucleus.

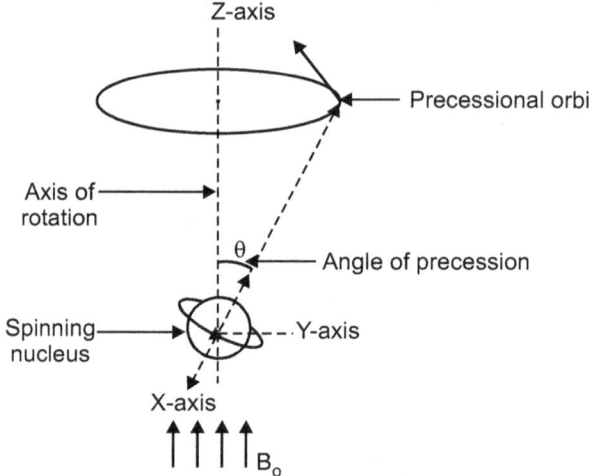

Fig. 4.30: Precessional motion of nucleus in applied magnetic field

- *When the precessional frequency of the spinning nucleus is exactly equal to the frequency of electromagnetic radiation necessary to induce a transition from one nuclear spin state to another, they are said to be in resonance.* This phenomenon is known as nuclear magnetic resonance (NMR).

- The theory of electromagnetic radiation indicates that the probability of an upward transition by absorption of energy from the magnetic field is exactly equal to the probability of the downward transition by a process stimulated by the field. Thus if the two possible spin states in a collection of the nuclei were populated equally, the probability of an upward transition (absorption) would exactly equal to that of the downward transition (emission), and there would be no observable nuclear resonance effect. Under ordinary conditions, however, there is a slight excess of nuclei in the lower spin state (lower energy orientation); they take up a Boltzmann distribution (under ordinary conditions the Boltzmann factor is about 0.001%). It is this very small finite excess of nuclei in the lower energy state that gives rise to the net absorption of energy in the radio frequency region.

4.4.3 NMR Instrumentation

- The NMR instrument (Refer Fig. 4.31) used for recording the spectrum consists of the following parts:

  (i)   a powerful electromagnet

  (ii) a sweep generator

(iii)   a radiofrequency oscillator

(iv)   a radio frequency detector

(v)   recorder.

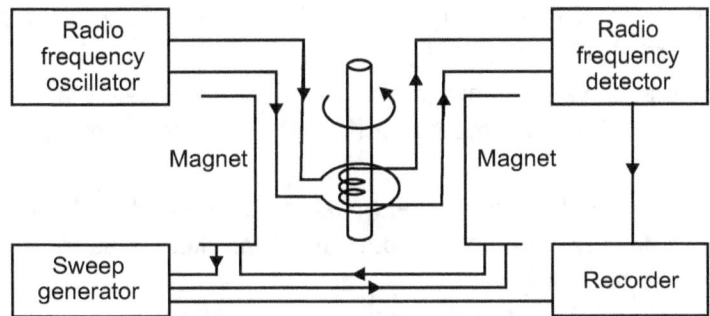

Fig. 4.31: Schematic diagram of NMR instrument

(i)   **Magnet:** A powerful magnet producing a very strong homogeneous field of the order of 1.4 Tesla or more. With instruments working on higher fields, superconducting magnets are used. Homogeneous field is required otherwise nuclei in the different part of the sample will experience different magnetic field. In order to maintain the homogeneity the sample tube containing the compound is rotated at 30 Hz.

(ii)   **Sweep generator:** It is used to supply DC voltage to produce the electromagnet.

(iii)   **Radiofrequency oscillator:** It provides the necessary radio frequency to bring about the transition of nuclei from the lower energy spin state to the higher energy spin state.

(iv)   **Radiofrequency detector:** The detector is placed orthogonal to both the direction of the applied magnetic field and the radio frequency oscillator. It records the radio frequency absorbed by the nucleus during excitation.

(v)   **Recorder:** The signal detected by the detector is amplified and then send to the recorder. The recorder records the signal in the form of graph, absorbance vs magnetic field/radio frequency.

4.4.4 Recording NMR Spectrum

- The sample is prepared by dissolving it in a suitable solvent. The solvent used for recording NMR spectrum should not have protons of their own as their signal may interfere with the proton signals of the compound under study. Thus usually CCl_4 (with no protons) or deuterated solvents ($CdCl_3$, DMSO-d_6, Acetone-d_6, pyridine-d_5, dioxane-d_8, ...) are used.

- The NMR spectrum can be recorded by **continuous wave** (CW) or by **pulse technique (FT).**

- In the continuous wave technique the spectrum can be recorded in two ways:
  (i) By keeping the magnetic field constant and varying the radiofrequency (**frequency sweep**) from lower to higher value. Different protons absorb at different frequencies.
  (ii) By keeping the frequency constant and varying the field (**field sweep**). Different protons absorb at different fields.

- Practically it is easier to vary the magnetic field more accurately than the radio frequency and hence most of the instruments work with fixed radio frequency and changing magnetic field.

- In the pulse technique the magnetic field is kept constant while a radio frequency pulse which is modulated, with the help of modulator, is applied so as to bring all the protons into resonance simultaneously.

- There are many advantages of pulse NMR as the time required to record a spectrum is much less as compared to CW technique. The FT (pulse) NMR technique is useful for the nuclei with low natural abundance (^{13}C, ^{15}N, etc.).

4.4.5 Number of NMR Signals

- If all protons in a given molecule absorb at same field, they would produce only one signal. However, protons in different chemical environment absorbs at different magnetic fields. Thus the number of signals is equal to the number of types of protons. Chemically equivalent protons absorb at the same field and produce one signal, but chemically non-equivalent protons absorb at different magnetic field and produce different signals. In methane as all the four protons are chemically equivalent, it produces only one signal. In ethyl chloride, there are two types of chemically equivalent protons, three protons of methyl group and two protons of methylene group, therefore two signals appear in the NMR spectrum (Refer Fig. 4.32). The following examples show the types of protons and corresponding NMR signals:

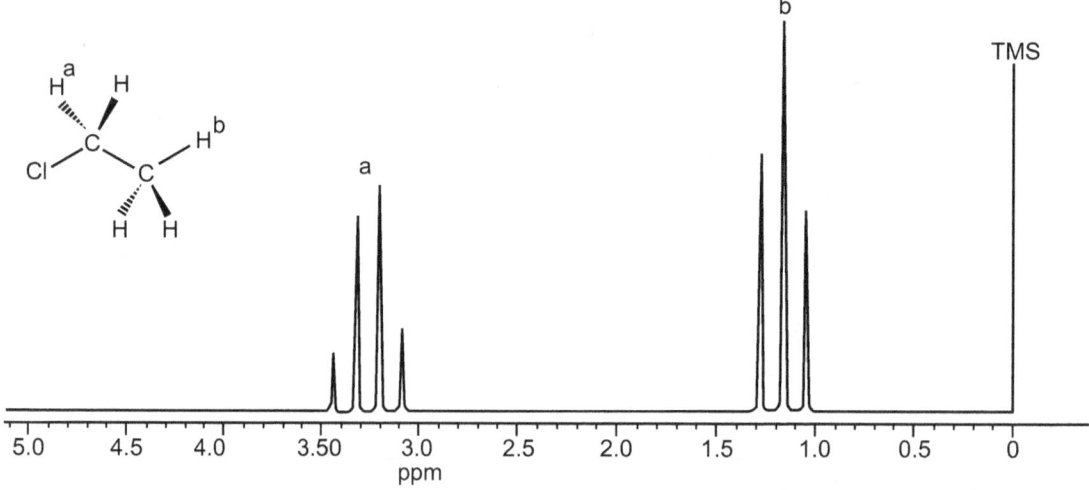

Fig. 4.32: NMR Spectrum of ethyl chloride

Structure	No. of type of protons	No. of signals
CH_3-CH_3	1	1
CH_3-CH_2-Br	2	2
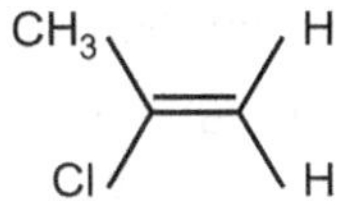	3	3
$CH_3-\overset{O}{\overset{\Vert}{C}}-H$	2	2
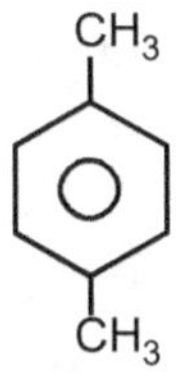	2	2
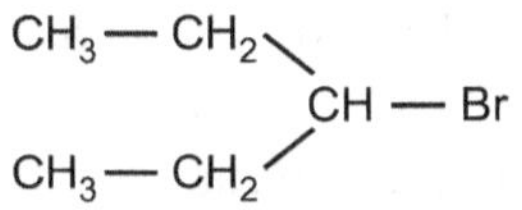	3	3

- So far we have considered only the nucleus of hydrogen atom i.e., proton. However, such nacked proton does not exist. The proton is always associated with its electrons involved in the covalent bond formation with the other atoms like C, N, O, etc. The proton therefore is always surrounded by bonding pair of electrons. When an external magnetic field is applied the circulating bonding electron pair produces its own magnetic field known as diamagnetic field or induced magnetic field (Refer Fig. 4.33).

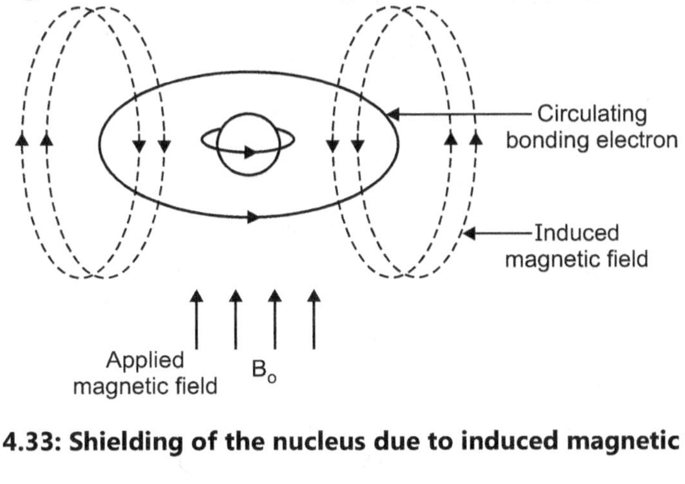

Fig. 4.33: Shielding of the nucleus due to induced magnetic field

4.4.6 Position of NMR Signal: The Chemical Shift

- If the resonance frequencies of all the protons were the same, the NMR would be of little use as one would observe only one peak for the compound, regardless of the number or the nature of protons present. As the NMR frequencies are dependent on the molecular environment of the nucleus, different protons will absorb at different frequencies. The surrounding *electrons* shield the nucleus, so the effective magnetic field experienced by the nucleus is not the same as the applied magnetic field. The electrons have charge and also spins and circulate around the nucleus generating its own magnetic field, this induced field is in the opposite direction of the applied field. Therefore the effective magnetic field experienced by the nucleus is changed by this small local field such that $B_{effec} = B_o - \sigma B_o$ where σB_o is the induced magnetic field owing to circulation of electrons. This phenomenon is known as *shielding*. Protons in different environment in the molecule are shielded to different extent by the circulation of electrons, hence their precessional frequencies are different, and they absorb different radiofrequency.

- It is difficult to determine the exact position of absorption with accuracy because the strength of the applied field cannot be determined to the required degree of accuracy (one part in 10^8). However, *relative* proton frequencies can readily be determined with an accuracy of about ± 1 Hz. The separation of resonance frequencies of nuclei in different environments from some arbitrary chosen standard is termed as *chemical shift*.

Choice of standard/reference:

- Tetramethyl silane (TMS) is found to fulfill all the necessary criteria for a good reference:

  (i)   It gives one sharp signal for the four identical methyl groups (12 protons).

  (ii) The TMS signal appears at high field, therefore, does not overlap with the signals for most of the organic compounds.

  (iii) TMS is inert and low boiling liquid and which can be removed easily so that the compound can be recovered after recording the NMR spectrum.

$$CH_3$$
$$|$$
$$H_3C - Si - CH_3$$
$$|$$
$$CH_3$$

Tetramethylsilane (TMS)

- The radio-frequency which the TMS protons absorb is taken as zero. The position of the peaks due to sample protons is then measured with respect to the TMS protons. The separation between the peak position of the sample proton with respect to TMS proton is known as *chemical shift*, and is calculated as follows:

$$\text{Chemical shift} = \delta = \frac{\text{Frequency of sample (Hz)} - \text{Frequency of TMS (Hz)} \times 10^6}{\text{Frequency of the instrument (MHz)}}$$

- The chemical shift is dimensionless and is expressed as parts per million (ppm). Thus chemical shift for TMS is 0 ppm. In the above equation the denominator i.e., frequency of the instrument is included to make the δ values independent of the NMR used. If NMR spectrum is recorded on different instruments with different magnetic fields, the δ value does not change. e.g., On a 60 MHz instrument the chloroform peak appears at 437 Hz, but on 100 MHz the peak appears at 728 Hz downfield with respect to TMS signal. When chemical shift δ value is calculated we find that the δ value is same for both the instruments, thus δ value is independent of the instrument used.

(a) with 60 MHz

$$\delta = \nu_{sample} - \nu_{TMS}/\nu_{instrument} \times 100$$
$$= \frac{437\ Hz - 0\ Hz}{60 \times 10^6\ Hz} \times 10^6$$
$$= 7.28\ ppm$$

(b) with 100 MHz

$$\delta = \nu_{sample} - \nu_{TMS}/\nu_{instrument} \times 100$$
$$= \frac{728\ Hz - 0\ Hz}{100 \times 10^6\ Hz} \times 10^6$$
$$= 7.28\ ppm$$

- If instrument is changed, the relative peak position is changed but δ values are not changed.

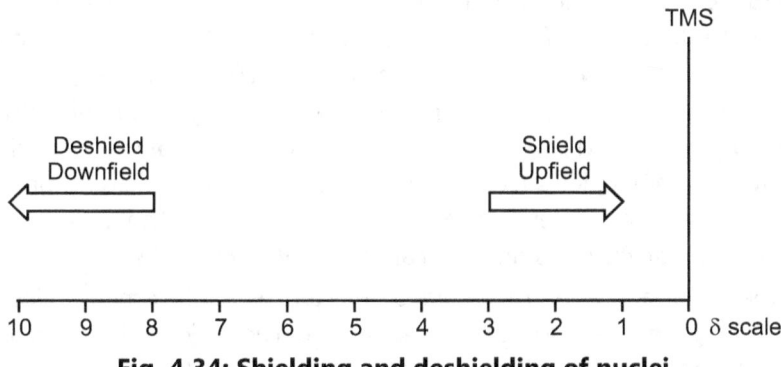

Fig. 4.34: Shielding and deshielding of nuclei

- Fig. 4.34 shows that δ values increase from right to left, whereas magnetic field increases from left to right.

(a) The shielded protons appear at higher fields (upfield), they have lower δ values.

(b) The deshielded protons appear at lower fields (downfield), they have higher δ values.

- **Thus as shielding increases, δ value decreases and as deshielding increases, δ value increases.**

4.4.7 Factors Affecting Chemical Shifts

- The chemical shift of the protons depends on the chemical environment around the protons. As the protons experience different chemical environment they are shielded or deshielded to different extent and thus appears at different δ values. The extent of shielding or deshielding of the protons is predominantly affected by the following factors:

  (a) Electronegativity: The electronegative atom if attached would pull the electrons in the covalent bond towards itself, thus, decreases the electron density around the protons. This results in the deshielding of the proton. In the following example we notice that as the electronegativity of the atom increases, the methyl protons get more deshielded and thus appear at downfield region.

  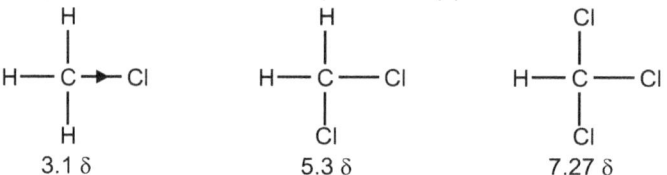

  $$CH_3 \rightarrow F \qquad CH_3 \rightarrow Cl \qquad CH_3 \rightarrow Br \qquad CH_3 \rightarrow I$$

  $$4.3\ \delta \qquad\qquad 3.1 \qquad\qquad 2.7 \qquad\qquad 2.2$$

  Similarly, when the number of electronegative atoms increases the deshielding increases. Thus, methyl chloride protons appear at 3.1 δ, methylene chloride protons appear at 5.3 δ, while the chloroform protons appear at 7.27 δ.

  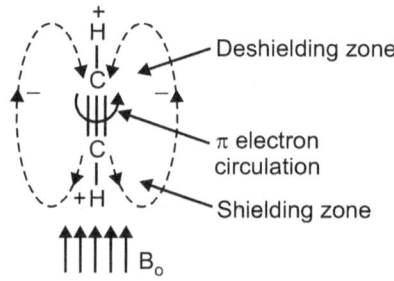

  3.1 δ 5.3 δ 7.27 δ

  (b) Anisotropy: Another factor which has a bearing effect on the chemical shift is the anisotropic effect. This effect originates as a result from the electronic circulations within the molecules when they are specifically *oriented* with respect to the magnetic field. These electronic circulations produce a secondary magnetic field that is parallel to the applied magnetic field frequently shielding the neighbouring nucleus. In relatively rigid molecules such currents can either cause shielding or deshielding of a proton. These effects depend on the *orientation* of the proton relative to the induced magnetic currents and are called *anisotropic effects*.

  When the linear acetylene molecule is oriented parallel to the applied field, it results in the diamagnetic shielding of the proton. The electronic circulation within the cylindrical sheath of π electron cloud induces a diamagnetic shielding at the acetylenic proton.

The proton of an aldehyde group absorbs at much lower field 9-10 δ. This is predicted on the grounds of anisotropic effect. When the carbonyl group is oriented such that the plane of the trigonal carbon atom is perpendicular to the applied field, diamagnetic circulations of π electrons in the group produce an anisotropic effect at the proton that results in its deshielding.

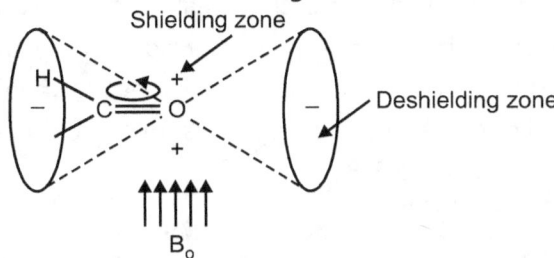

Alkane and alkene protons differ in absorption position by about 4 ppm. This difference is accounted on the basis of the diamagnetic deshielding. The carbon-carbon double bond orients such that the plane of the C=C bond is perpendicular to the applied field, diamagnetic circulations of the π electrons cause deshielding of the protons.

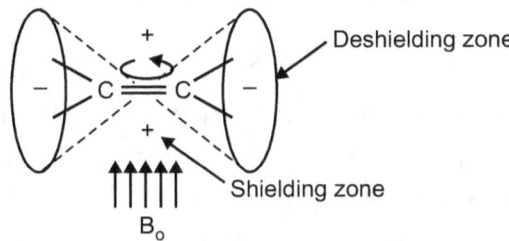

Aromatic nuclei contain large closed loops of π electrons in which strong diamagnetic currents are induced by the magnetic field. This effect results in a *paramagnetic shielding* at the aromatic proton as shown below. This is called *ring current*. Any group that is sterically held above or below the plane of the aromatic nucleus will be *shielded* because of the ring current.

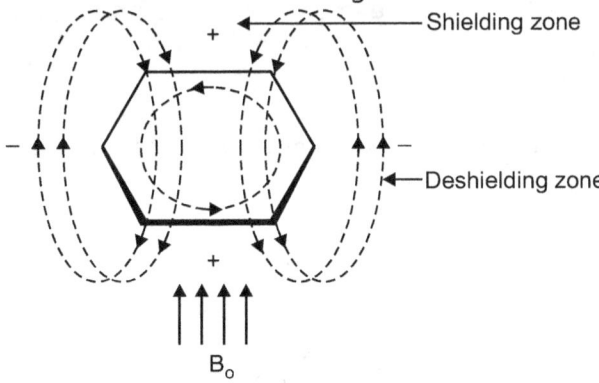

4.4.8 Area under the Peak: Proton Ratio

- It is observed that area under the peak is directly proportional to the number of protons which produces that peak. This area is measured electronically by the instrument. It draws an integration line across each peak (Refer Fig. 4.35). The height of the integration line is directly proportional to the area under that peak and is directly proportional to the number of protons responsible for that peak. Consider the following NMR spectrum of toluene, we observe two signals in the ratio 5: 3. The downfield signal is due to five aromatic protons while the high field signal is due to three methyl protons. The integration line is also in the ratio 5: 3.

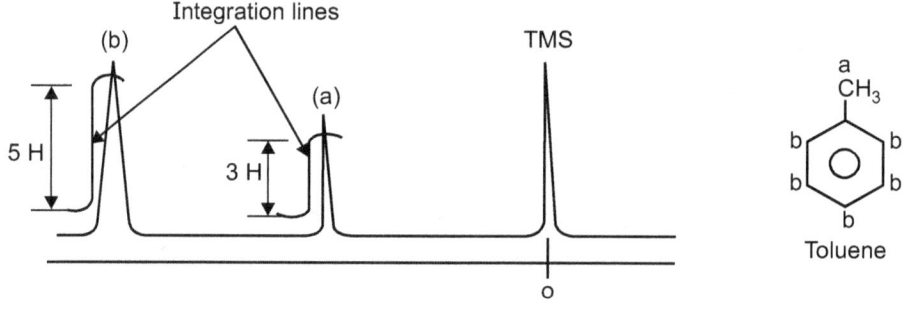

Fig. 4.35

4.4.9 Splitting of NMR Peaks: Spin-spin Coupling

- The NMR spectrum of ethyl chloride shows two signals (Refer Fig. 4.32), one appearing as quartet at 3.4 δ and the other signal appearing as triplet at 1.8 δ. This separation of NMR signal into number of peaks is known as splitting of NMR signal. Recall that the magnetic nuclei such as protons, orient their spins with or against an applied magnetic field. These orientations influence the spin states of the nearest bonding electron which, in turn, affect the spin of the other bonding electrons and so on through to the next proton. Thus information concerning their spin states is transmitted to one another by neighbouring nuclei by means of the intervening bonding electrons. The effect is known as *spin-spin splitting*.

One neighbouring interacting nuclei:

- Consider two protons 'a' and 'b' on adjacent carbon atoms interacting with each other in an organic compound.

(a) Deshielding of H_a due to H_b

(b) Shielding of H_a due to H_b

- When placed in an external magnetic field, each of the two nuclei can assume the two orientations either +1/2 (↓ spin) or -1/2 (↑ spin) (Refer Fig. 4.36). If H_a has ↑ spin, the bonding electron (H_a-C_1 bond) having ↓ spin tend to remain near H_a. The statistical probability of the other electron with ↑ spin being nearer to the C_1 is thus greater. The second electron of the C_1 atom (C_1-C_2 bond) will have the same spin ↑ (according to Hund's rule), while the electron of the C_2 have ↓ spin. Further the second electron of C_2 will have the same spin ↓, which in turn orients the electron of H_b in the ↑ spin state that causes the spin of the H_b ↓. This polarization of bonding electrons caused by the spin orientation of the H_a thus affects the energy required for a magnetic transition of H_b (because the pairing of the neighbouring magnets lowers the potential energy of the system). As there are many H_a and H_b in the sample molecule, the H_b proton peak in the spectrum splits into a doublet.

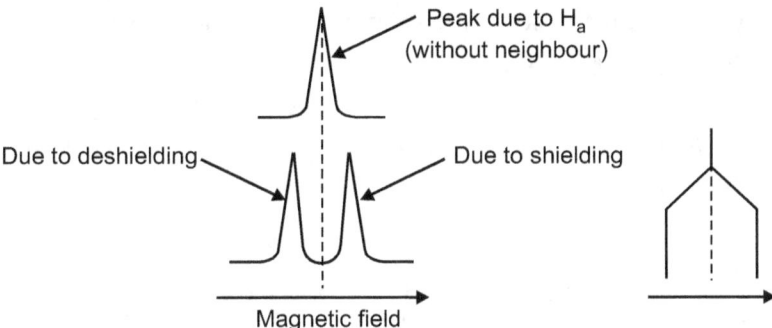

Fig. 4.36

- Another explanation for this phenomenon is that the magnetic moment resulting from (–1/2) or (+1/2) orientation of H_a nucleus either reinforces or diminishes the applied magnetic field. The H_b proton in close proximity thus experiences either increased or diminished magnetic field and the H_b proton peak consequently appears as doublet in the spectrum.

Peak due to H_a
(without neighbour)

Due to deshielding

Due to shielding

Magnetic field

Proton with one neighbouring proton producing doublet

- Thus when there is one neighbouring proton H_b it couples with the given proton H_a in two ways one leading to shielding and other leading to deshielding. The signal due to H_a is split into two peaks- doublet with intensity 1: 1. One peak of the doublet is at slightly higher field and the other at lower field. The average of these two is same as that of the unsplit signal. Just as coupling of H_b with H_a splits the signal due to H_a into a doublet, the signal due to H_b will also be split by the H_a proton into a doublet.

Two neighbouring interacting nuclei:

- Consider the proton H_a in the molecule which has two neighbouring protons H_b and H_b'.

  The spin state of H_a can couple with H_b and H_b' in three ways as shown below. (Fig. 4.37).

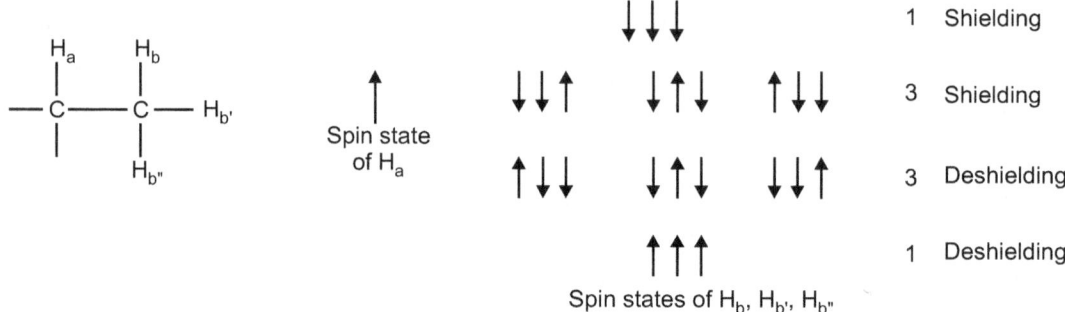

Fig. 4.37

1. Both H_b and H_b' have parallel spin with H_a. This will lead to deshielding of H_a and the peak will shift downfield.
2. Both H_b and H_b' have anti-parallel spin with H_a. This will lead to shielding of H_a and the peak will shift upfield.
3. H_b have parallel spin with H_a and H_b' have antiparallel spin with H_a or vice versa. This will lead to deshielding of H_a and the peak will shift downfield. The net effect is there will be neither shielding nor deshielding of H_a, which will appear at the same position as that of unsplit signal.

   In this way, the H_a proton split into a triplet with the signal intensity $1 : 2 : 1$.

Three neighbouring interacting nuclei:

- Consider the proton H_a in the molecule which has three neighbouring protons H_b, H_b' and H_b''. The spin state of H_a can couple with H_b, H_b' and H_b'' in four ways as shown below. (Refer Fig. 4.38)

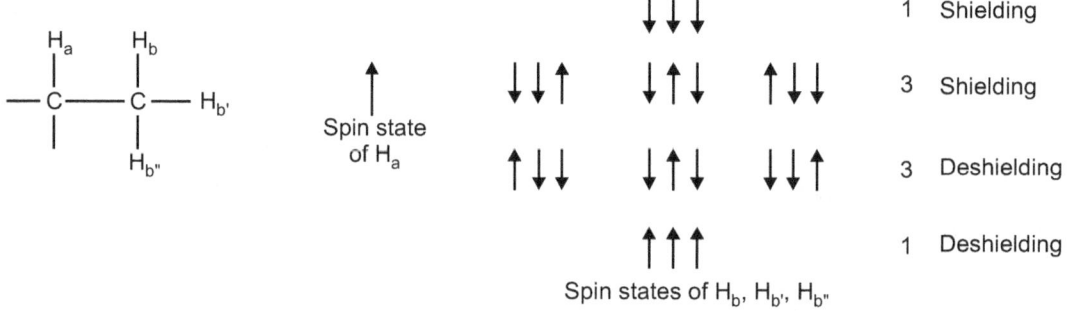

Fig. 4.38

1. H_b, H_b' and H_b'' have parallel spin with H_a. This will lead to deshielding of H_a and the peak will shift downfield.

2. H_b, $H_{b'}$ and $H_{b''}$ have anti-parallel spin with H_a. This will lead to shielding of H_a and the peak will shift upfield.

3. Two of the three protons (H_b, $H_{b'}$ or $H_{b''}$) have parallel spin but one of them is antiparallel with H_a. There are three such possibilities and will lead to net deshielding of H_a and the peak will shift downfield.

4. Two of the three protons (H_b, $H_{b'}$ or $H_{b''}$) have anti-parallel spin but one of them has parallel spin with H_a. There are three such possibilities and will lead to net shielding of H_a and the peak will shift upfield.

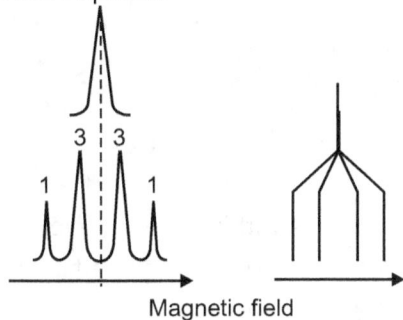

Magnetic field

In this way, the H_a proton split into a quartet with the signal intensity 1: 3: 3: 1.

*   In general, the **multiplicity of the peak depends on the number of neighbouring protons.** In general the multiplicity of the signal is given by the formula (2nI + 1), where n = number of neighbouring nucleus and I = spin number of the nucleus. For protons this general formula reduces to (n + 1) as I = 1/2 for protons. The relationship between the number of neighbouring protons and the multiplicity of the signal and relative intensities of the peaks in the multiplet is shown in the following table.

Table 4.7

No. of neighbouring protons (n)	Peak multiplicity (n + 1)	Relative intensities
0	Singlet	1
1	Doublet	1 :1
2	Triplet	1 :2 :1
3	Quartet	1 :3 :3 :1
4	Quintet	1 :4 :6 :4 :1
5	Sextet	1 :5: 10 :10 :5 :1
6	Septet	1 :6 :15 :20 :15 :6 :1

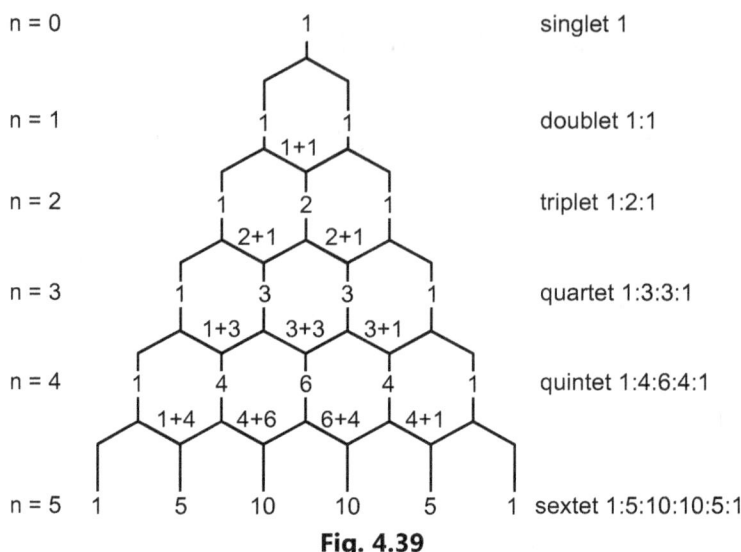

Fig. 4.39

- The relative intensities of the peaks within the multiplet can be found out using Pascal's triangle (Refer Fig. 4.39) or by taking the coefficient of the terms in $(r + 1)^n$, where n = number of neighbouring protons.

n = 1	$(r + 1)^1 = r + 1$	=	1: 1
n = 2	$(r + 1)^2 = r^2 + 2r + 1$	=	1: 2: 1
n = 3	$(r + 1)^3 = r^3 + 3r^2 + 3r + 1$	=	1: 3: 3: 1

- Thus, multiplicity of peaks is very useful in elucidating the structure of the molecule as it provides the number of neighbouring protons. i.e., if the signal is split into a triplet there should be two neighbouring protons. Similarly if the signal is singlet there is no neighbouring proton.

Types of coupling:

   (a) Vicinal (three bond) coupling: The protons on adjacent carbon atoms show a three bond coupling.

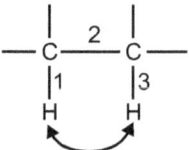

   (b) Geminal (two bond) coupling: The protons on the same carbon atom but are in different chemical environment (diastereotopic protons) show two bond coupling.

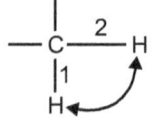

(c) **Long range (four or more bond) coupling:** When the protons are placed four or more bond away from each other they show long range coupling. This type of coupling however is generally weak.

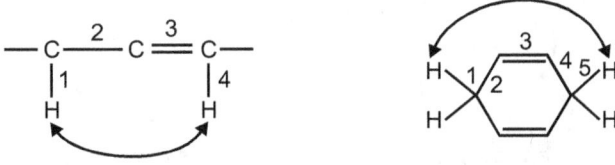

| 4-bond coupling | 5-bond coupling |

Rules of spin-spin coupling: The spin-spin coupling is governed by the following rules:

(a) Coupling is observed between non-equivalent or chemically different protons. **Equivalent protons do couple but their coupling is not observed in the spectrum.**

(b) The multiplicity of the signal is given by the formula $2nI + 1$, where n = total number of neighbouring protons and I = spin number of proton.

(c) The relative intensity of the peaks within a multiplet is given by the value of the coefficients of the binomial expansion $(r + 1)^n$.

(d) Protons which are insulated by hetero atoms like O, S, N do not couple except under exceptional conditions. Thus in ethyl alcohol the methylene protons do not show coupling with hydroxy proton under ordinary conditions.

(e) Mutually coupled protons have the same coupling constant value.

• **Coupling constant:** It is defined as the **measure of the strength of interaction between the sets of protons.** The separation between the peaks within a multiplet is known as coupling constant (J) and is measured in Hz. **The value of the coupling constant is independent of the field strength.** Thus a doublet with J = 7 Hz on a 60 MHz instrument will show same J value of 7 Hz on a 100 MHz instrument. In the NMR spectrum of ethyl chloride shown below (Refer Fig. 4.40), the methyl protons appear as triplet as they couple with two neighbouring methylene protons and the methylene protons in turn appear as quartet because of three methyl protons. We observe that the triplet for the methyl proton has a coupling constant value, J = 7 Hz and the quartet for the methylene proton also with J = 7 Hz. **Thus mutually coupled protons have the same coupling constant value.**

$$Cl—CH_2—CH_3 \qquad J_{ab} = 7 \text{ Hz}$$
$$b a$$

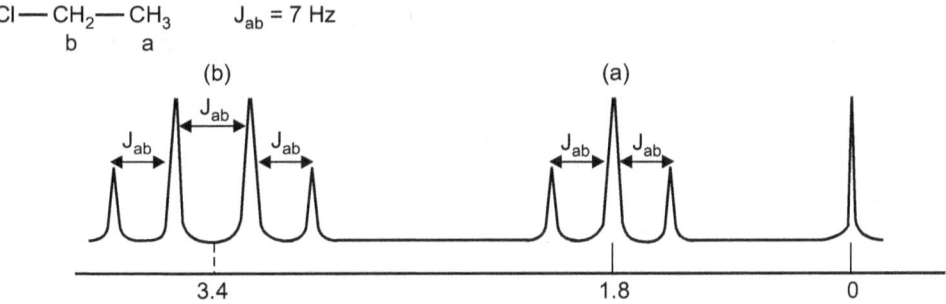

Fig. 4.40: NMR of ethyl chloride showing coupling constant

- Coupling constant values are also many times useful in predicting the stereochemistry of the protons. e.g. Cis coupled protons has J = 10 Hz while the trans coupled protons has J = 16 Hz.

Trans coupling   Cis coupling

4.4.10 Applications of NMR in Organic Chemistry

- NMR spectrum is more informative as compared to the UV or IR spectrum. It provides valuable information and helps to deduce the structure of an unknown organic compound.
  1. It provides information about the number of types of protons in the molecule.
  2. The integration of the signals gives the number of each type of protons.
  3. The chemical shift value of the signals provides the information of the chemical environment of the proton.
  4. The multiplicity of the signal tells us the number of neighbouring protons.
  5. The NMR spectrum gives idea about the exchangeable protons if present in the molecule i.e. O–H, N–H or S–H.
  6. The coupling constant values are helpful in deciding the stereochemistry of the protons in the molecule.

4.4.11 Important Regions of PMR Spectrum

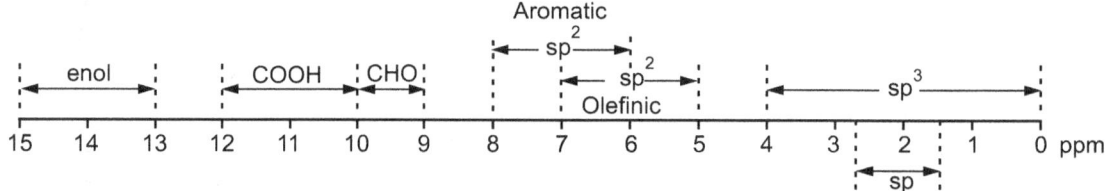

Fig. 4.41

- Some representative 'H chemical shift values for various types of protone (w.r.t. TMs as internal reference).

CH – $\underline{CH_3}$ 0.9   O – C – $\underline{CH_3}$ 1.4   C = C – $\underline{CH_3}$ 1.6

Ph – $\underline{CH_3}$ 2.3   O = C – $\underline{CH_3}$ 2.9   N – CH_3 2.3

S – $\underline{CH_3}$ 2.1   O $\underline{CH_3}$ 3.3   – $\underline{H}$ 0.7

$\diagdown$C – $\underline{CH_2}$ 4.6 $\diagdown$C – $\underline{CH_2}$ 5.3 $\diagdown$C – $\underline{CH}$ 5.1 – 5.3

(exocyclic)   (open chain)

Ar – $\underline{H}$ 6 - 8   O = C – $\underline{H}$ 9 - 10   O = C – $\underline{OH}$ 10 - 12

O – C – C = $\underline{CH}$ 6.8   O – C –$\underline{CH}$= C 5.7   Ph – C ≡ $\underline{CH}$ 2.9

4.59

- Applications of PMR to distinguish pair of organic compounds:

(a)

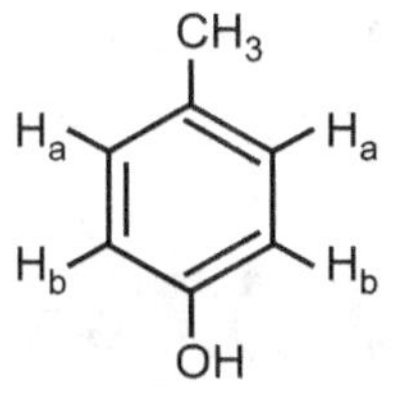

       I 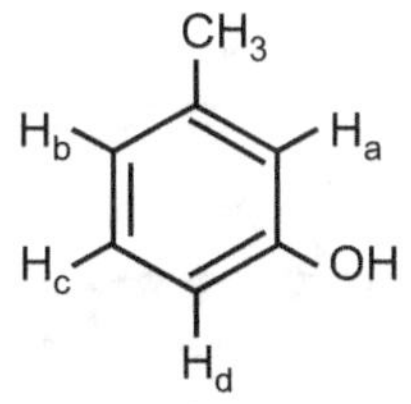   II

The p-disubstituted compound (I) shows two sets of chemically equivalent aromatic protons (one pair ortho to CH_3 and the other pair ortho to OH) and therefore two signals in PMR, while the m-substituted compound (II) has four aromatic protons all of them have different chemical environment and thus show four signals in its PMR spectrum.

(b)

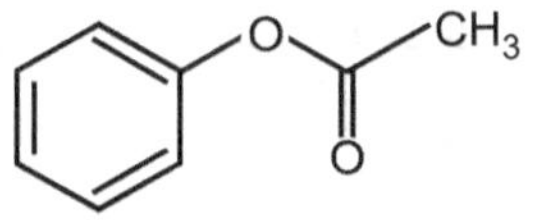

       I 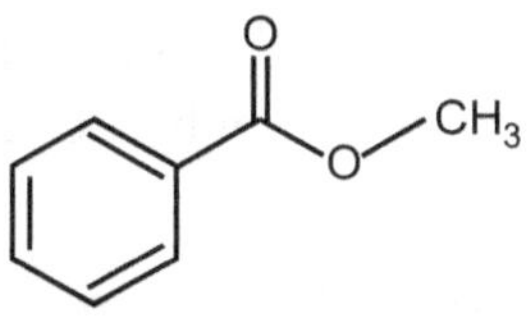   II

In compound (I) the methyl group is attached to C = O, therefore the methyl protons resonate at 2.3 δ while in compound (II) the methyl group is attached directly to oxygen, therefore the methyl protons are more deshielded and resonate at 3.8 δ.

(c)

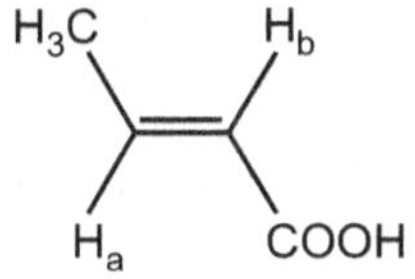

       I 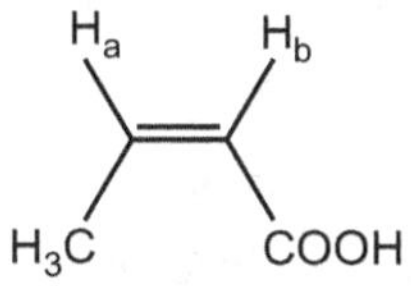   II

Compound (I) has trans-configuration and therefore the olefinic protons show higher coupling value ($^3J_{ab}$ = 16 Hz), while compound (II) has cis-configuration and the olefinic protons show lower coupling constant value ($^3J_{ab}$ = 10 Hz).

(d)

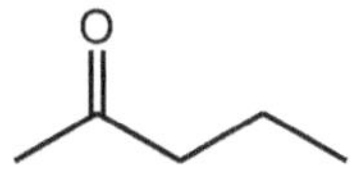

       I 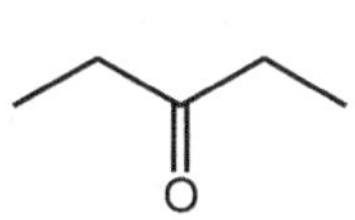   II

Compound (I) has four sets of protons (CH_3 attached to C = O, CH_2 attached to C = O, CH_2 flanked by CH_2 and CH_3 and CH_3 attached to CH_2) and therefore shows four signals while compound (II) has only two sets of protons (both CH_3 groups are chemically equivalent and so are both CH_2 groups) and therefore show only two signals in its PMR spectrum.

4.5 Spectroscopic Problems based on UV, IR and NMR

4.5.1 Introduction

- We have seen that none of the spectroscopic techniques discussed earlier is in itself sufficient to elucidate the structure of the organic compound. The UV spectrum gives information about the conjugation in the molecule, while the IR predicts the presence or absence of functional groups. The PMR gives the information about the number and nature of the protons present in the molecule. However, the information obtained from all the spectroscopic techniques when put together can be of great help in elucidating the structure. Before solving the spectroscopic problems from the given data, it is necessary to calculate the index of hydrogen deficiency or sites of unsaturation or double bond equivalent.

4.5.2 Sites of Unsaturation

- The number of sites of unsaturation (total number of rings and double bonds) or the index of hydrogen deficiency (IHD) or double bond equivalent (DBE) can be calculated by any of the following two methods:

  Method 1: For a molecule $C_wH_xN_yO_z$, the sites of unsaturation is given by the formula

  $$\text{S.U. or IHD or DBE} = \tfrac{1}{2}(2w - x + y + 2)$$

- For example, for the molecule $C_7H_{14}O$, the total number of rings and double bonds (IHD or S.U.) is $= \tfrac{1}{2}(2 \times 7 - 14 + 2) = 1$.

  Method 2: This is the most widely used method. According to this method, following changes are made in the molecular formula

  (a) Each 'O'/ 'S' atom is neglected.

  (b) Each 'N' atom is replaced by 'CH'.

  (c) Each 'halogen atom' is replaced by 'H'.

  Then using the formula C_nH_{2n+2} rule the hydrogen deficiency is calculated.

  For example, the molecule with formula $C_9H_{14}O$,

  (a) Neglecting the oxygen atom the formula becomes C_9H_{14}.

  (b) The given compound should have 20 hydrogens (according to C_nH_{2n+2} rule).

  (c) As there are 6 hydrogen atoms less, the given compound must contain 3 sites of unsaturation.

For molecular formula $C_3H_3Cl_3$,

(a) Replace 3 Cl atoms with 3 H atoms, the formula becomes C_3H_6.

(b) The given compound should have 8 hydrogens (according to C_nH_{2n+2} rule).

(c) As there are 2 hydrogen atoms less, the given compound must contain 1 site of unsaturation.

4.5.3 Nature of Site of Unsaturation

The unsaturation site in the organic molecule may be of the following type:

(a) Each double bond C=C, C=S, C=N, C=O, corresponds to one site of unsaturation.

(b) Each triple bond C≡C, C≡N, corresponds to two sites of unsaturation.

(c) Each ring corresponds to one site of unsaturation.

(d) Each benzene ring corresponds to four sites of unsaturation (3 due to three double bonds and 1 due to the ring).

4.5.4 Solved Problems on Joint Applications of UV, IR and PMR

Example 1: Molecular formula: C_3H_6O

I.R.: 2720, 1720 cm^{-1}

PMR: 9.5 (t, 1H); 2.5 (quintet, 2H); 1.2 (t, 3H)

Solution:

(i) Sites of unsaturation:

(a) Neglecting the oxygen atom, we get C_3H_6.

(b) The given compound must have 8 hydrogen atoms (according to C_nH_{2n+2} rule).

(c) As there are 2 hydrogen atoms less, the given compound must contain 1 site of unsaturation.

(ii) The IR spectrum shows peak at 2720 cm^{-1} is due to presence of aldehyde (C–H stretching), along with 1720 cm^{-1} (C=O stretching) which confirms the presence of CHO group, accounts for one site of unsaturation.

(iii) The PMR spectrum shows quintet at 2.5 δ for two protons indicate the presence of CH_2 group attached to CHO group on one side and a CH_3 on the other side. The triplet at 1.2 δ for three protons confirms the presence of CH_3-CH_2 group. Considering the evidences gathered from the given data following structure is assigned to the given organic compound.

$$CH_3 - CH_2 - \overset{\overset{\textstyle O}{\|}}{C} - H$$

Propanal

Example 2: Molecular formula: $C_4H_7BrO_2$

I.R.: 3300, 1725, 600 cm^{-1}

PMR: 11.2 (s, 1H); 4.3 (t, 1H); 2.2 (quintet, 2H); 1.1 (t, 3H)

Solution:

(i)   Sites of unsaturation:

   (a)   Neglecting the oxygen atom and replacing Br with 'H' we get C_4H_8.

   (b)   The given compound must have 10 hydrogen atoms (according to C_nH_{2n+2} rule).

   (c)   As there are 2 hydrogen atoms less, the given compound must contain 1 site of unsaturation.

(ii) The IR spectrum shows peak at 3300 cm^{-1} is due to presence of hydroxyl (O–H stretching), along with 1725 cm^{-1} (C=O stretching) which confirms the presence of COOH group, accounts for one site of unsaturation. The peak at 600 cm^{-1} indicates the C-Br stretching.

(iii) The PMR spectrum shows quintet at 2.2 δ for two protons indicate the presence of CH_2 group attached to four neighbouring protons, possibly one CH_3 group on one side and a CH on the other side. The triplet at 1.1 δ for three protons confirms the presence of CH_3-CH_2 group. 4.3 triplet for one proton indicates presence of CH group that it is attached to electronegative atom possibly a COOH and Br group as well as CH_2 group (signal shows a triplet). Considering the evidences gathered from the given data following structure is assigned to the given organic compound.

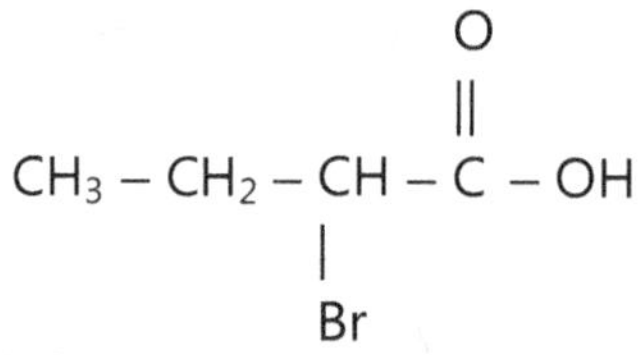

$$
\begin{array}{c}
\text{O} \\
\parallel \\
CH_3 - CH_2 - CH - C - OH \\
\mid \\
Br
\end{array}
$$

Example 3: Molecular formula: C_9H_{12}

I.R.: 3100, 1510, 1620 cm^{-1}

PMR: 7.2 (s, 3H); 2.4 (s, 9H)

Solution:

(i)   Sites of unsaturation:

   (a)   The given compound must have 20 hydrogen atoms (according to C_nH_{2n+2} rule).

   (b)   As there are 8 hydrogen atoms less, the given compound must contain 4 sites of unsaturation.

(ii) The peaks at 1510 and 1620 cm^{-1} are due to C=C stretching (aromatic) frequency. The 3100 cm^{-1} is due to C–H stretching.

(iii) The PMR spectrum shows singlet at 2.4 δ for nine protons indicate the presence of three CH_3 group. The singlet at 7.2 indicates three identical aromatic protons. i.e., 1,3,5-trisubstituted benzene, which accounts for four sites of unsaturation. Therefore, the three meta substituents may be three CH_3 groups. Considering the evidences gathered from the given data following structure is assigned to the given organic compound.

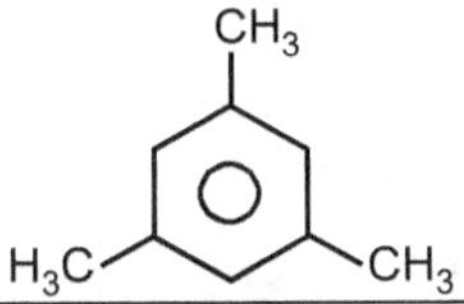

Example 4: Molecular formula: $C_9H_{10}O$, UV: 265 λ_{max}

I.R.: 1690, 1500, 1600, 700, 750 cm^{-1}

PMR: 7.2 (s, 5H); 2.5 (q, 2H); 1.1 (t, 3H)

Solution:

(i)   Sites of unsaturation:

   (a)   Neglecting the oxygen atom, we get C_9H_{10}.

   (b)   The given compound must have 20 hydrogen atoms (according to C_nH_{2n+2} rule).

   (c)   As there are 10 hydrogen atoms less, the given compound must contain 5 sites of unsaturation.

(ii) The UV shows λ_{max} at 265 indicates presence of benzene ring.

(iii) The IR spectrum shows peak at 1690 cm^{-1} is due to presence of carbonyl group (C=O stretching) in conjugation, which accounts for one site of unsaturation. The peaks at 1510 and 1620 cm^{-1} are due to C=C stretching (aromatic) frequency. Peaks at 750 and 700 cm^{-1} indicate that the benzene ring may be monosubstituted.

(iv) The PMR spectrum shows quartet at 2.4 δ for two protons indicate the presence of CH_2 group attached to electron withdrawing group (C=O) on one side and also adjacent to CH_3 group. Therefore the partial structure could be $-CO-CH_2-CH_3$. The triplet at 1.1 δ for three protons confirms that the methyl group is adjacent to methylene group. The singlet at 7.2 δ for five protons indicates aromatic protons. i.e., monosubstituted benzene, which accounts for four sites of unsaturation. Considering the evidences gathered from the given data following structure is assigned to the given organic compound.

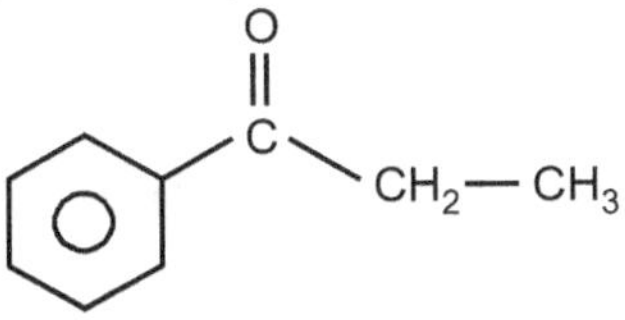

Example 5: Molecular formula: C_7H_8O

    I.R.: 3500, 3030, 1600, 1500, 1100 cm^{-1}

    PMR: 7.2 (s, 5H); 4.4 (s, 2H); 3.7 (s, 1H)

Solution:

(i)   Sites of unsaturation:

     (a) Neglecting the oxygen atom, we get C_7H_8.

     (b) The given compound must have 16 hydrogen atoms (according to C_nH_{2n+2} rule).

     (c) As there are 8 hydrogen atoms less, the given compound must contain 4 sites of unsaturation.

(ii) The IR spectrum shows peak at 3500 cm^{-1} is due to presence of hydroxyl group (O–H stretching). The peaks at 1500 and 1600 cm^{-1} are due to C=C stretching (aromatic) frequency. The peak at 1100 cm^{-1} indicates the presence of C–O bond.

(iii) The PMR spectrum shows singlet at 7.2 δ for five aromatic protons indicating monosubstituted benzene ring, which accounts for four sites of unsaturation. The peak at 4.4 δ for two protons indicate that it must be attached to an electronegative atom i.e., with 'O' atom. Therefore, the substituent may be CH$_2$-OH group. Considering the evidences gathered from the given data following structure is assigned to the given organic compound.

Example 6: Molecular formula: C_8H_7N

    I.R.: 2220, 1510, 1620 cm^{-1}

    PMR: 7.2 (d, 2H); 2.4 (s, 3H); 7.5 (d, 2H)

Solution:

(i)   Sites of unsaturation:

     (a) The given compound contains one nitrogen atom, by replacing it by 'CH', we get C_9H_8.

     (b) The given compound must have 20 hydrogen atoms (according to C_nH_{2n+2} rule).

     (c) As there are 12 hydrogen atoms less, the given compound must contain 6 sites of unsaturation.

(ii) The IR spectrum shows peak at 2250 cm^{-1} is due to presence of nitrile group (C≡N stretching), which accounts for two sites of unsaturation. The peaks at 1510 and 1620 cm^{-1} are due to C=C stretching (aromatic) frequency.

(iii) The PMR spectrum shows singlet at 2.4 δ for three protons indicate the presence of CH_3 group. The doublet at 7.2 and 7.5 δ indicates two different types of aromatic protons. i.e., p-Disubstituted benzene, which accounts for four sites of unsaturation. Therefore, the two para substituents may be C≡N and CH_3 groups. Considering the evidences gathered from the given data following structure is assigned to the given organic compound.

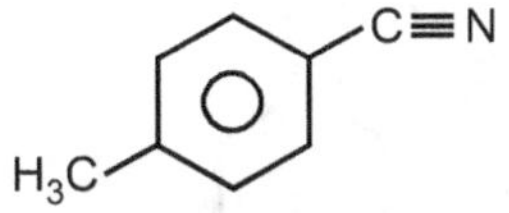

Exercises

Introduction to Spectroscopy

1. Define the terms:
   (a) Frequency
   (b) Wavelength
   (c) Amplitude
   (d) Wave number

2. What is electromagnetic radiation? Classify the electromagnetic radiation on the basis of wavelength.

3. What are the different excitations possible when molecule absorbs the energy? Illustrate using the molecular orbital diagram.

4. Numerical problems:
   (i) If wavelength of radiation is 4.3×10^{-11} sec, find its frequency in hertz.
   (ii) If wavelength of radiation is 6.28×10^{-11} sec, find its wavelength in cm, nm, A° and μ units.
   (iii) Calculate the energies for the following wavelengths of radiation.
      (a) 740 cm
      (b) 38 nm
      (c) 4.23 μ
   (iv) A radiation has wavelength of 254 nm. Calculate
      (a) wavelength in cm
      (b) frequency in Hz
      (c) energy in ergs
      (d) wave number in kaysers

Ultra Violet Spectroscopy

1. Explain the following terms:
   (a) Chromophore
   (b) Auxochrome
   (c) Red shift
   (d) Blue shift

2. Distinguish the following pairs by UV spectroscopy:
   (a) Aniline and nitrobenzene
   (b) Aniline in neutral and acidic medium
   (c) Phenol in neutral and basic medium
   (d) Cis and trans stilbene

3. Define Beer-Lambert's law. Explain the significance of molar absorptivity.

4. Explain the term 'electronic excitation'. What are the four types of electronic excitations?

5. How does conjugation affect the position of UV bands? Explain this effect in enone system with the help of energy level diagram.

6. Calculate λ_{max} using Woodward and Fieser rule, for each of the following molecules:

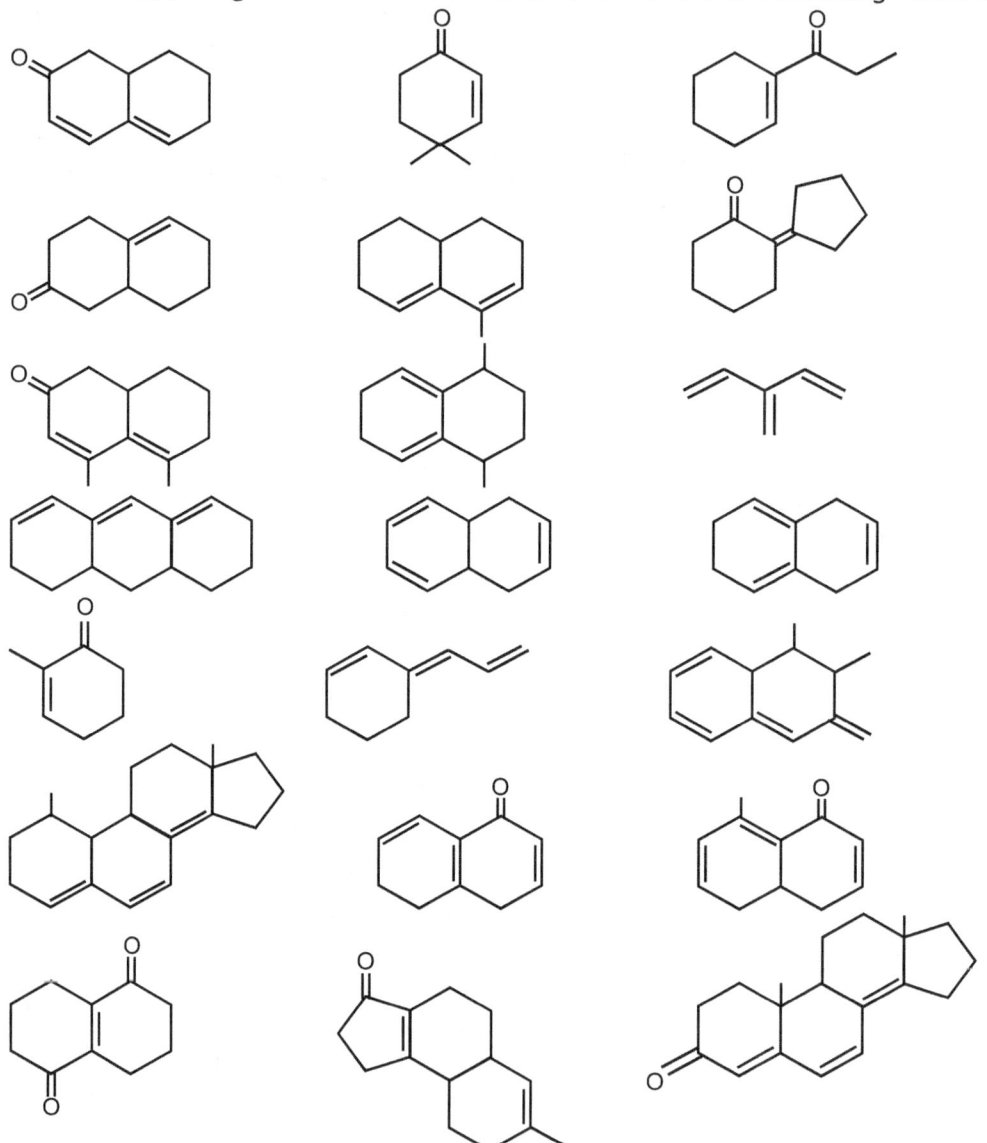

7. Explain the following:
   (a) UV spectroscopy helps in differentiating the cis and trans isomers.
   (b) p-nitro phenol turns yellow to red in alkaline medium.

(c)   1,3-butadiene absorbs at longer wavelength than 1,4-butadiene.

(d)   Benzene shows absorption in UV region while n-hexane is transparent.

(e)   Ethanol can be used as solvent for UV but acetone cannot be used.

8.   Write notes on:

(a)   Applications of UV spectroscopy

(b)   Beer-Lambert's law

(c)   Colour and visible spectrum

Infra-Red Spectroscopy

1.   What are different types of vibrations? How are fundamental modes of vibrations calculated for linear and non-linear molecules?

2.   Calculate the fundamental modes of vibrations for the following molecules:

(a)   Carbon monoxide   (b)   Ethane

(c)   Nitrous oxide   (d)   Ammonia

(e)   Benzene   (f)   Methane

3.   Differentiate the following pairs by using IR spectroscopy:

(a) $CH_3-CH_2-C{\equiv}N$ and $CH_3-CH_2-C{\equiv}CH$

(b)   Acetone   and   Acetaldehyde

(c)   Cis 2-butadiene   and   trans 2-butadiene

(d)   o-Xylene   and   p-Xylene

(e)   Acetamide   and   Ethanamine

(f)   Methyl iodide   and   Methyl fluoride

(g)   Butanoic acid   and   Methyl ethanoate

(h)   Phenol   and   Anisole

4.   Explain the following:

(a)   Peaks due to stretching and bending vibrations appear at different frequencies.

(b)   Benzaldehyde absorbs at 1710 cm^{-1} while salicyldehyde absorbs at 1695 cm^{-1}.

(c)   Phenyl acetate absorbs at 1770 cm^{-1} while methyl benzoate absorbs at 1725 cm^{-1}.

(d)   Cyclohexanone absorbs at 1710 cm^{-1} while cyclobutanone absorbs at 1775 cm^{-1}.

(e)   IR spectrum of carboxylic acids when recorded in dilute aprotic solvent show the O-H stretching frequency at 3550 cm^{-1}.

(f)   Cyclohexanone can be distinguished from cyclohexenone by IR spectroscopy.

5.   How will you follow the following sequence of reaction by IR spectroscopy?

(a)

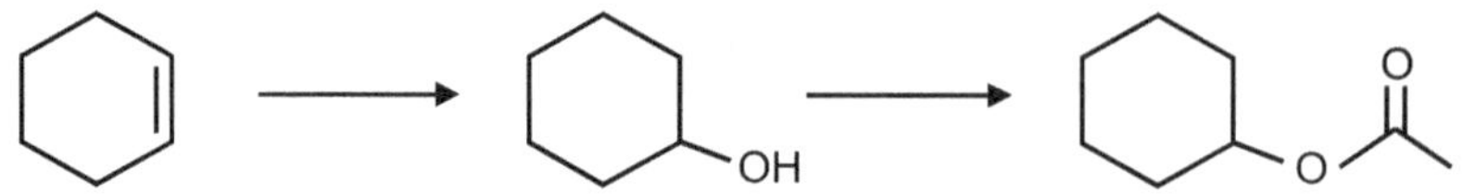

(b)

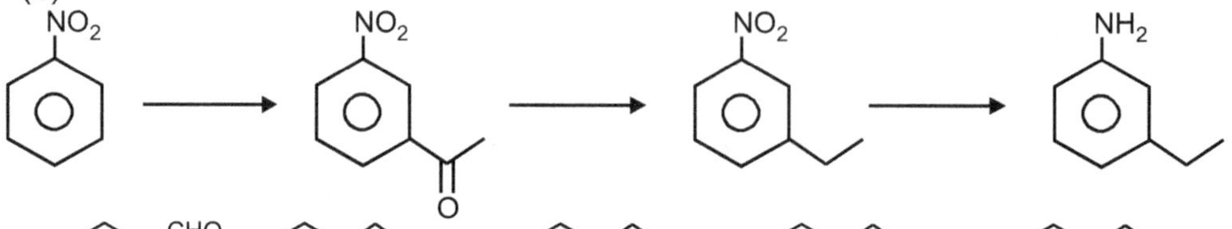

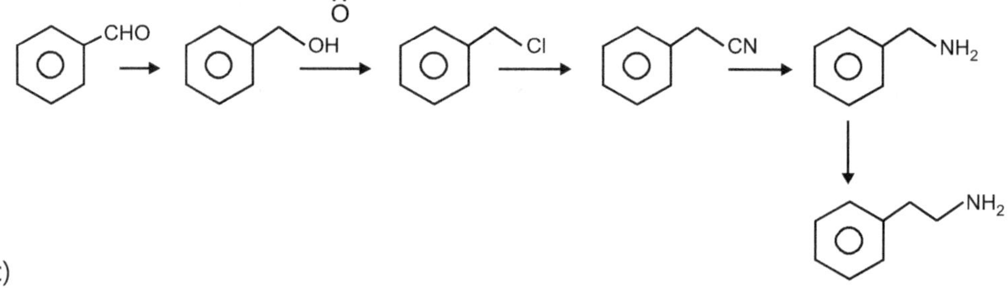

(c)
(d)

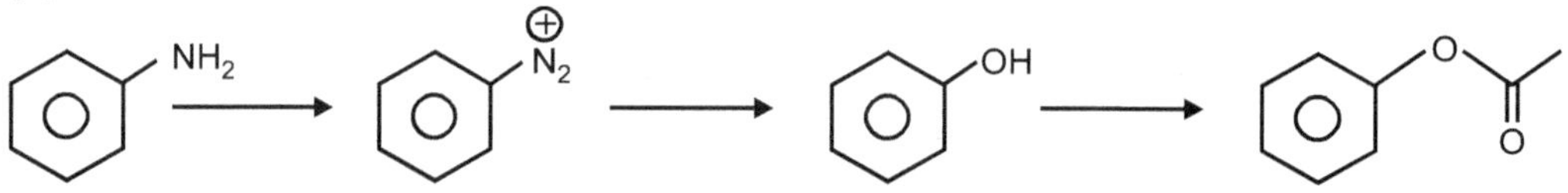

(e)

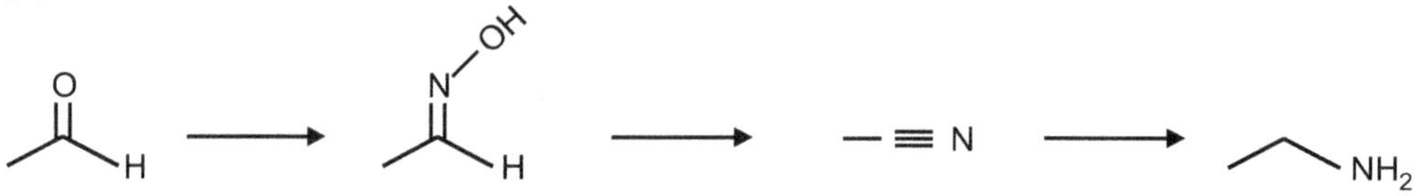

(f)

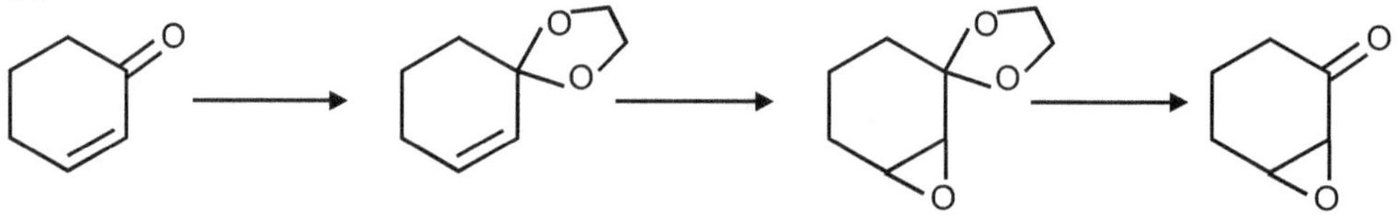

(g)

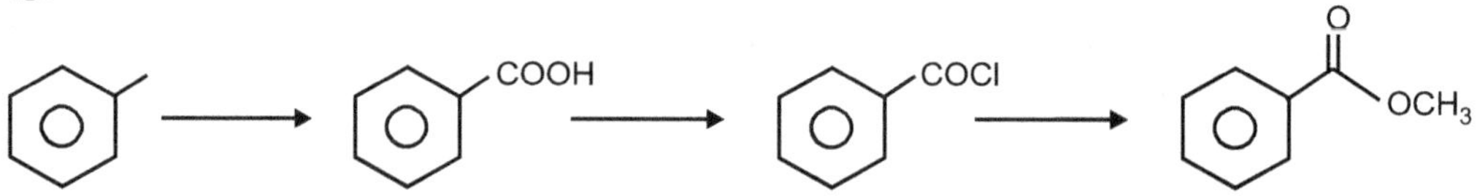

(h)

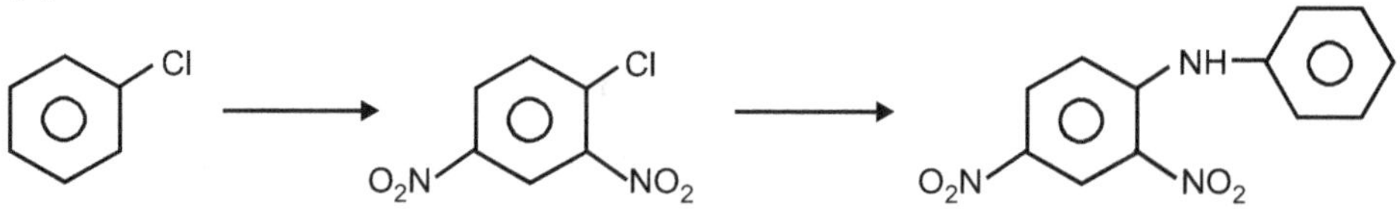

6.   Suggest the probable structure for the following compounds:

(a) C_3H_4 3300 cm^{-1} (b) C_3H_6 3350, 1620, 990, 910 cm^{-1}

(c) C_3H_6O 1620, 990, 910 cm^{-1} (d) C_4H_6 3300, 2100 cm^{-1}

(e) C_4H_6 1620, 990, 910 cm^{-1} (f) C_3H_5N 2200 cm^{-1}

(g) C_5H_8O 1780 cm^{-1} (h) $C_6H_{10}O$ 1720, 1620 cm^{-1}

(i) $C_6H_{10}O$ 2720, 1700 cm^{-1} (j) $C_6H_{10}O$ 1690 cm^{-1}

(k) C_7H_6O 3400, 2750, 2250, 1700, 1450-1600 cm^{-1}

(l) C_3H_7NO 3400-3200, 3100, 2900, 1650, 1550 cm^{-1}

(m) C_7H_5OCl 3400-3200, 3100, 2900, 2200, 1780, 1600-1450 cm^{-1}

(n) $C_5H_8O_2$ 3110, 2980-2920, 1748, 1667, 1250-1200, 1027, 868 cm^{-1}

7.   Write short notes on:

(a) Applications of IR spectroscopy

(b) Types of vibrations

Nuclear Magnetic Resonance Spectroscopy

1.   Which type of nuclei are NMR active? What is the relation of spin number I with atomic mass number and atomic weight?

2.   Explain the various parts of NMR instrument with the help of labelled block diagram.

3.   Explain shielding and deshielding of protons.

4.   What is chemical shift? What are the factors affecting the chemical shift of protons?

5.   Explain spin-spin coupling. Explain why $-CH_3$ group show a triplet while $-CH_2$ group show a quartet in ethyl chloride.

6.   Write notes on:

(a) Chemical shift

(b) Spin-spin coupling

(c) Coupling constant

(d) Anisotropy effect

(e) Vicinal coupling

(f) Geminal coupling

7.   Why TMS is used as a internal standard in PMR?

8.   Deuterated solvents are used to record PMR spectrum. Explain.

9.   How many peaks do you expect in the PMR spectrum for the following compounds?

(a) Acetone   (b) Methyl iodide

(c) Methyl acetate   (d) 1-chloro-2-bromoethane

(e) p-cresol   (f) dibromomethane

10. How will you differentiate the following pairs by PMR spectroscopy?

    (a)   o-dichlorobenzene   and   p-dichlorobenzene

    (b)   2-methyl-1-propene   and   1-butene

    (c)   1,1,1-trichloroethane   and   1,1,2-trichloroethane

    (d)   Acetone   and   Propanal

    (e)   Diethyl ether   and   Ethyl propyl ether

    (f)   1-butyne   and   2-butyne

11. Deduce the structure of the following compounds. All PMR spectra are recorded on 60 MHz instrument with TMS as a internal standard.

    (i)   MF: C_3H_6O 1.2 (t, 7Hz, 3H); 2.5(quintet, 7Hz, 2H); 9.7(d, 7Hz, 1H)

    (ii)   MF: C_3H_5ON 3.5 (s, 3H); 4.22(s, 2H)   IR: 2250 cm^{-1}

    (iii) MF: $C_5H_{10}O$ 1.1 (d, 7Hz, 6H); 2.1(s, 3H); 2.5(septet, 7Hz, 1H)

    (iv) MF: $C_8H_{10}O$ 1.3 (d, 7Hz, 3H); 1.6(bs, 1H); 4.2(q, 7Hz, 1H); 7.4(s, 5H)

    (v)   MF: C_9H_{12} 2.2 (s, 9H); 6.7(s, 3H)   IR: 1550, 1600, 2950, 3030 cm^{-1}

    (vi) MF: $C_4H_5O_2N$ 3.5 (s, 2H); 3.8(s, 3H)   IR: 2250, 1750 cm^{-1}

    (vii) MF: C_3H_6O 1.2(t, 7Hz, 3H); 2.5(quintet, 7Hz, 2H); 9.7(d, 7Hz, 1H)

12. Deduce the structures of following compounds. All PMR spectra are taken in $CdCl_3$ at 60 Hz.

    1.   MF $C_5H_{10}O$

        0.95 δ(t, J = 7.2, 6H); 2.3 δ, (q, J = 7.2, 4H)

    2.   MF C_9H_{12}

        1.25 δ(d, 7.2 Hz, 18 mm); 2.41 δ (Septet, 7.2 Hz, 3 mm); 7.25 δ(s, 15 mm)

    3.   MF $C_8H_8O_3$

        4.1 δ(s, 7.5 mm); 6.2 δ(broad singlet, exchangeable with D_2O, 2.5 mm) 6.8 – 7.5 δ (broad singlet, 7.5 mm); 9.78 δ (singlet, 2.5 mm)

    4.   MF $C_8H_{11}NO$

        3.6 δ (d, I = 7 Hz, 8 mm); 3.4 δ (s, 4 mm, exchangeable with D_2O) 3.8 δ (s, 8 mm, exchangeable with D_2O); 4.5 δ (t, J = 7.0 Hz, 4 mm) 7.2 δ (s, 20 mm)

    5.   MF C_4H_8O

        1.2 δ (d, J = 7 Hz, 15 mm); 2.2 δ (s, 15 mm) 4.1 δ (s, 5 mm, exchangeable with D_2O); 4.3 δ (q, J = 7 Hz, 5 mm)

    6.   MF $C_6H_{12}O$

        1.2 δ (quintet, J = 6.5 Hz, 12 mm); 1.4 δ (quintet, J = 6.5, 7.0 Hz, 12 mm) 1.6 δ (quartet, J = 7.0 Hz, 6.0 Hz, 12 mm); 3.1 δ (s, 6 mm) 3.6 δ (quintet, J = 6.0 Hz, 6 mm)

7. MF $C_7H_7NO_2$

    2.4 δ (s, 9 mm); 6.8 – 7.9 δ (broad single, 12 mm)

8. MF C_7H_9NO

    3.0 δ(s, 7.5 mm), 3.5 δ(s, 5 mm); 6.3 – 6.5 δ(s, 10 mm)

9. MF $C_4H_{11}N$

    1.0 δ (s, 1 H, D_2O exchangeable); 1.2 δ (t, 6H); 2.5 δ(q, 4H)

10. MF C_7H_8O

    3.9 δ (s, 9 mm); 7.03 δ (s, 15 mm)

11. MF C_9H_8O

    6.62 δ (d, J = 7.8 Hz, 16.3 Hz, 3 mm); 7.41 δ(d, J = 16 Hz, 3 mm)

    7.40 δ (m, 15 mm); 9.66 δ (d, J = 7.41 Hz, 3 mm)

12. MF C_8H_8O

    2.47 δ s, 3 H; 7.4 – 8.2 δ 'bs' 5H

13. MF $C_4H_8O_2$

    1.23 δ 't', J = 7.1 Hz, 3 H); 1.97 δ s, 3 H; 4.06 δ (q, J = 7.1 Hz, 2 H)

14. MF $C_4H_6O_3$

    2.18 δ 's' 6H

15. MF C_2H_5NO

    2.00 δ 's' 3 H; 6.15 δ 'bs' 2 H

16. MF C_8H_9NO

    2.09 δ 's' 3 H; 3.09 δ 'bs' 1H; 7.27 δ - 7.75 δ 'bs' 5H

17. MF C_7H_9N

    2.16 δ 's' 3H; 3.24 δ 's' 2H; 6.3 - 6.8 δ, 'bs' 4H

18. MF C_8H_{10}

    0.90 δ (t, J = 9Hz, 3H); 2.61 δ (q, J = 9Hz, 2H); 7.12 δ 's' 5H

19. MF C_9H_{10}

    2.11 δ 's' 3 H; 5.05 δ 'd' 1 H, J = 0.8 Hz;

    5.34 δ 'd' 1 H, J = 0.8Hz; 7.34 δ, 'bs' 5H

20. MF C_8H_6

    2.98 δ 's' 1 H; 7.4 δ 'bs' 5H

21. MF $C_2H_3Cl_3$

    3.95 δ 'd' 2H; 5.77 't' 1H

22. MF C_2H_5I

    1.8 δ, t, 3H, J = 6Hz; 3.2 δ, q, 2H, J = 6Hz

Ans.

(1) $CH_3-CH_2-\overset{\overset{\displaystyle O}{\|\|}}{C}-CH_2-CH_3$	(2) a benzene ring with $-\overset{\overset{\displaystyle CH_3}{\|}}{\underset{\underset{\displaystyle CH_3}{\|}}{C}}-H$	(3) a benzene ring with OCH_3 and $-\overset{\overset{\displaystyle O}{\|\|}}{C}-H$ and $O-H$
(4) a benzene ring with $\overset{\displaystyle OH}{|}CH-CH_2-NH_2$	(5) $H_3C-\overset{\overset{\displaystyle OH}{\|}}{CH}-\overset{\overset{\displaystyle O}{\|\|}}{C}-CH_3$	(6) a cyclohexane ring with $-OH$
(7) a benzene ring with CH_3 and NO_2	(8) a benzene ring with $O-CH_3$ and NH_2	(9) $H_3C-H_2C-NH-CH_2-CH_3$
(10) a benzene ring with OCH_3	(11) a benzene ring with $\overset{\displaystyle H}{\diagup}C=C\overset{\displaystyle CHO}{\diagdown}{\diagdown H}$	(12) a benzene ring with $-\overset{\overset{\displaystyle O}{\|\|}}{C}-CH_3$
(13) $CH_3-\overset{\overset{\displaystyle O}{\|\|}}{C}-O-CH_2-CH_3$	(14) $O=C\overset{\diagup O-CH_3}{\diagdown O-CH_3}$	(15) $CH_3-\overset{\overset{\displaystyle O}{\|\|}}{C}-NH_2$
(16) a benzene ring with $NH-\overset{\overset{\displaystyle O}{\|\|}}{C}-CH_3$	(17) a benzene ring with CH_3 and NH_2	(18) a benzene ring with CH_2-CH_3
(19) a benzene ring with $\overset{\displaystyle CH_3}{\diagdown}C=C\overset{\diagup H}{\diagdown H}$	(20) a benzene ring with $-C\equiv C-H$	(21) $Cl-CH_2-\overset{\overset{\displaystyle Cl}{\|}}{\underset{\underset{\displaystyle Cl}{\|}}{C}}$
(22) CH_3-CH_2-I		

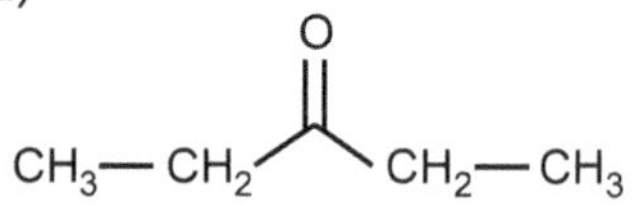

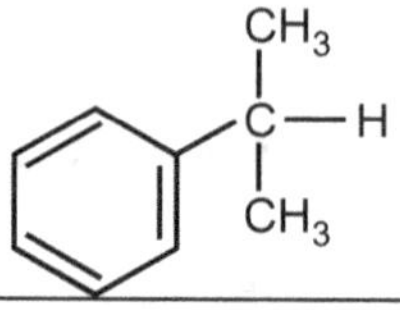

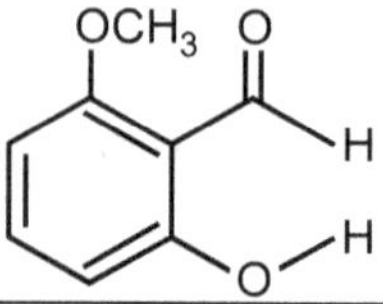

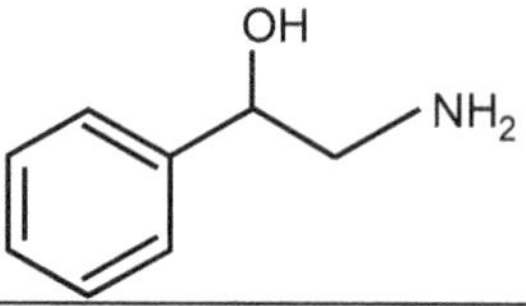

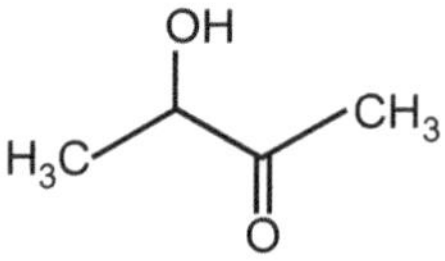

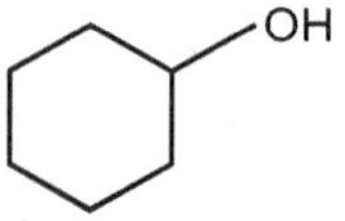

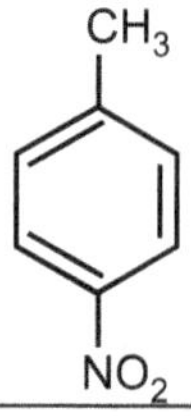

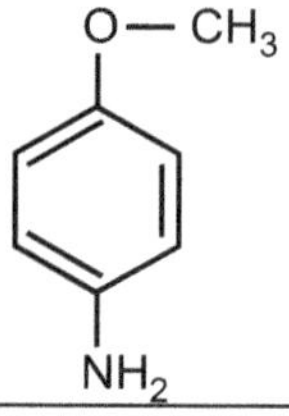

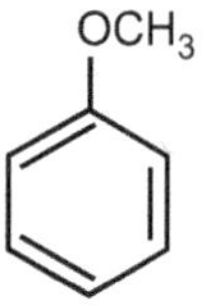

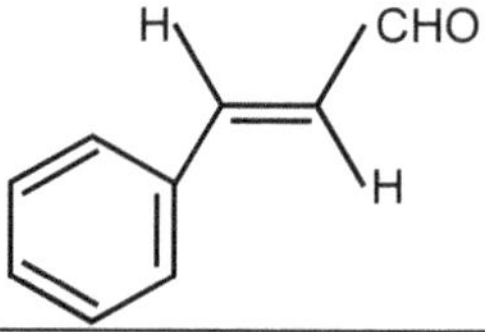

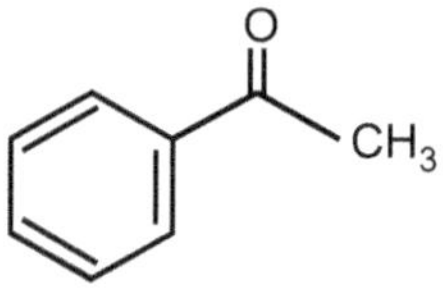

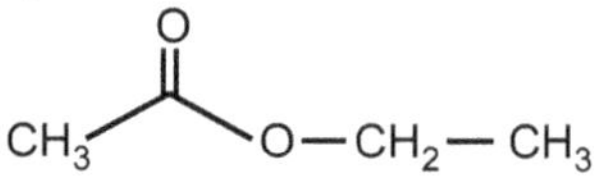

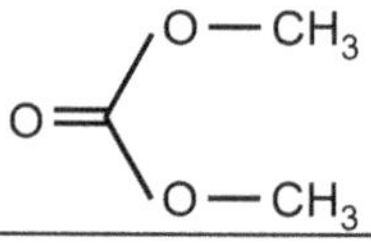

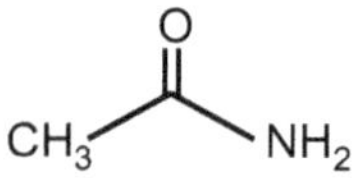

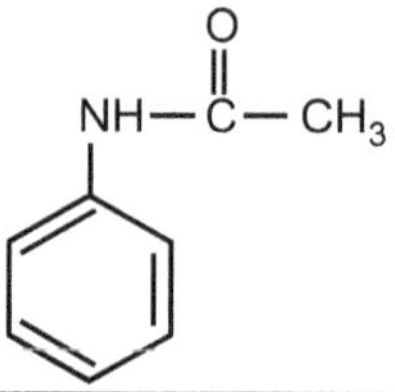

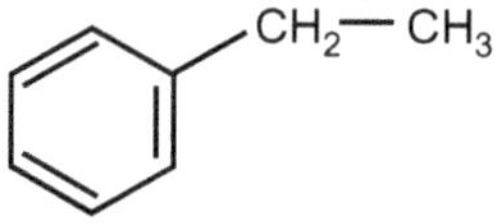

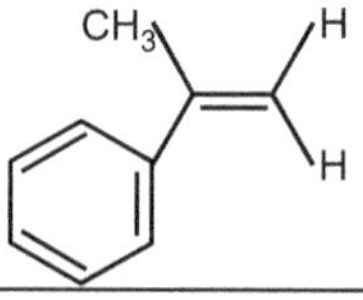

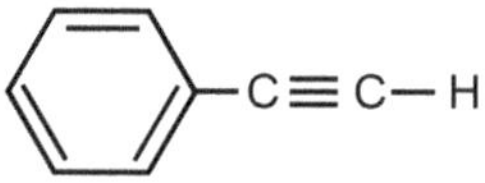

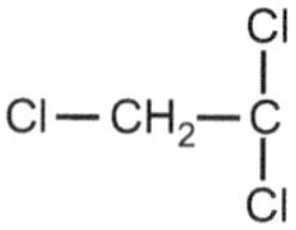

Spectroscopic Problems based on UV, IR and NMR

Problem 1:

Derive structure of the compound using following spectral data:

1. MF   : C_3H_6O
    UV   : No λ_{max} above 210 nm
    IR   : $2941 - 2857$ (m) cm^{-1}
          1458 cm^{-1} (m)
    NMR   : 4.75 δ (+, J = 7.1 Hz, 29.4 mm)
          2.75 δ (quintet, J = 7.1 Hz, 14.6 mm)

Ans.

2. MF   : C_4H_7N
    UV   : No λ_{max} above 200 nm
    IR   : $2941 - 2857$ cm^{-1} (m)
          2273 cm^{-1} (m)
          1460 cm^{-1} (m)
    NMR   : 2.72 δ (septet, 4.2 mm, J = 6.7 Hz)
          1.33 δ (d, 25.9 mm, J = 6.7 Hz)

Ans.

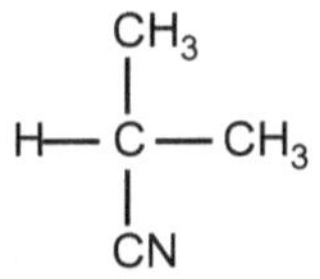

$$\begin{array}{c} CH_3 \\ | \\ H\!-\!C\!-\!CH_3 \\ | \\ CN \end{array}$$

3. MF   : C_3H_5ON
    UV   : No λ_{max} above 210 nm
    IR   : $2941 - 2857$ cm^{-1} (m)
          2247 cm^{-1} (m)
          1460 cm^{-1} (m)
    NMR   : 4.22 δ (s, 16.8 mm)
          3.49 δ (23.9 mm)

Ans. $\begin{array}{c} H_2C - OCH_3 \\ | \\ CN \end{array}$

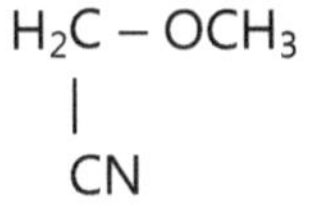

4. MF   : C_4H_8O
    UV   : λ_{max} = 274 nm, ε = 17
    IR   : $2941 - 2857$ cm^{-1} (m)
          1715 cm^{-1} (m)
          1460 cm^{-1} (m)
    NMR   : 2.42 δ (q, J = 7.3 Hz, 12 mm)
          2.12 (s, 17.6 mm)
          1.17 (t, J = 7.3 Hz, 18.2 mm)

Ans.

$$CH_3 - \overset{\displaystyle O}{\overset{\displaystyle \|}{C}} - CH_2 - CH_3$$

5. MF   : C_3H_7ON
    UV   : λ_{max} = 219 nm, ε = 60 (water)
    IR   : 3413 cm^{-1} (m)
            3236 cm^{-1} (m)
            3030 – 2899 (m) cm^{-1}
            1667 cm^{-1} (s)
            1634 cm^{-1} (s)
            1460 cm^{-1} (m)
    NMR : 6.5 δ (very broad singlet 13.0 mm)
            2.25 δ (q, J = 7.5 Hz, 12.8 mm)
            1.10 δ (t, J = 7.5 Hz, 19.7 mm)

Ans.

$$H_2N - \overset{\displaystyle O}{\overset{\displaystyle \|}{C}} - CH_2 - CH_3$$

6. MF   : $C_4H_8O_2$
    UV   : λ_{max} = 206 Nm, ε = 50
    IR   : 3049 – 2924 cm^{-1} (m)
            1736 cm^{-1} (s)
            1445 cm^{-1} (m)
    NMR : 8.07 δ (s, 5.9 nm)
            4.12 δ (t, J = 7 Hz, 12.2 mm)
            1.67 δ (sextet, J = 7.0 Hz, 11.6 mm)
            0.95 δ (t, J = 7.0 Hz, 18.6 mm)

Ans. 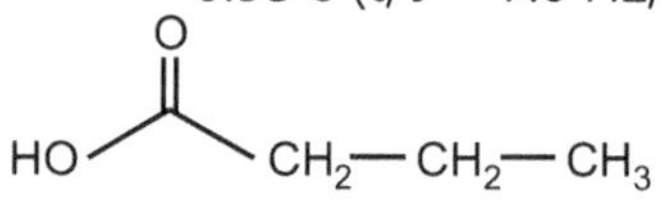 $HO - \overset{\displaystyle O}{\overset{\displaystyle \|}{C}} - CH_2 - CH_2 - CH_3$

7. MF   : $C_4H_8O_3$
    UV   : λ_{max} = 203 nm, ε = 40 (water)
    IR   : 3125 – 2857 cm^{-1} (m)
            2695 cm^{-1} (w)
            2625 cm^{-1} (w)
            1718 cm^{-1} (s)
            1449 cm^{-1}
    NMR : 10.95 δ (s, 5.4 mm)
            4.13 (s, 11.0 mm)
            3.66 (q, J = 7.1 Hz, 10.6 mm)
            1.27 (t, J = 7.1 Hz, 16.2 mm)

Ans. 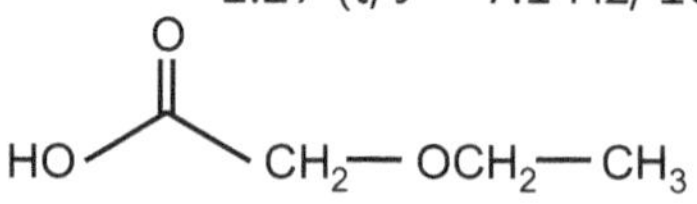 $HO - \overset{\displaystyle O}{\overset{\displaystyle \|}{C}} - CH_2 - OCH_2 - CH_3$

8. MF   : C_7H_8O
    UV   : λ_{max} = 25.5 nm, ε = 2.00 (water)
    IR   : 3401 cm^{-1} (s, b)
             3077 cm^{-1} (w)
             2899 cm^{-1} (m)
             1499 cm^{-1} (w, sh)
             1456 cm^{-1} (m, sh)
    NMR   : 7.26 (s, 24.7 mm)
             4.60 (s, 9.8 mm)
             3.86 (s, 5.2 mm)

Ans.

9. MF   : $C_7H_{12}O$
    UV   : λ_{max} = 210 nm, ε = 50
    IR   : 2941 cm^{-1} (m)
             1810 cm^{-1} (s)
    NMR   : 1.57 δ (s)

Ans.

10. MF   : $C_5H_8O_3$
    UV   : λ_{max} = 270 nm, ε = 25 (water)
    IR   : 3125 – 2857 cm^{-1} (m)
             2710 cm^{-1} (w), 2625 cm^{-1} (w)
             1712 cm^{-1} (s), 1439 cm^{-1} (m)
    NMR   : 10.98 (s, 5 mm)
             3.00 – 2.42 (m, 20.8 mm)
             2.12 (s, 14.8 mm)

Ans.

11. MF   : C_9H_{12}
    UV   : 268 nm, ε = 480
    IR   : 3067 – 2907 (m)
             1608 cm^{-1}, (m, sh)
             1473 cm^{-1}
    NMR   : 6.8 δ (s, 10.4 mm)
             2.26 δ (s, 31.0 mm)

Ans.

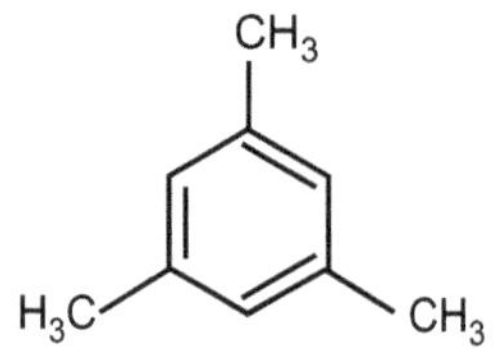

12. MF   : $C_5H_{10}O_4$
    UV   : 215 nm, ε = 70 (methanol)
    IR   : 2941 – 2857 cm^{-1} (m)
            1786 cm^{-1} (s)
            1460 cm^{-1}
    NMR : 4.8 δ (s, 4.3 mm)
            3.8 δ (s, 13.2 mm)
            3.48 δ (s, 25.8 mm)

Ans.

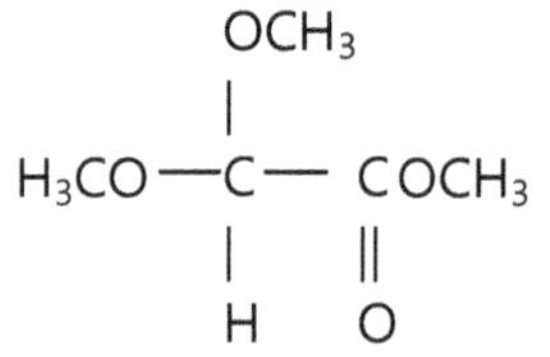

13. MF   : $C_8H_{12}O$
    UV   : λ_{max} = 225 and 311 nm, ε = 9200 and 40
    IR   : 3077 – 2857 cm^{-1} (m)
            1681 (s), 1661 (m)
            1453 cm^{-1} (m)
    NMR : 6.76 (dd, J = 7.9, 16.2 Hz, 3.2 mm)
            6.08 δ (d, J = 16.2 Hz, 3.4 mm)
            2.80 – 2.45 δ (m, 3.5 mm)
            2.24 δ (s, 10.1 mm)
            1.30 – 1.90 δ (m, 26.4 mm)

Ans.

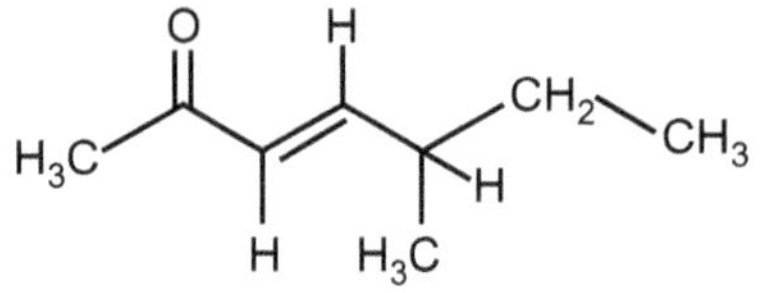

14. MF   : $C_8H_8O_3$
    UV   : λ_{max} = 230, 280, 310 nm, ε = 16000, 10700 and 10600
    IR   : 3497 cm^{-1} (m, b)
            2941 – 2847 cm^{-1} (w)
            2841 cm^{-1} (w), 2755 cm^{-1} (w)
            1686 cm^{-1} (s)
            1605 cm^{-1} (m)
            1575 cm^{-1} (m), 1508 cm^{-1} (m)

NMR   :   9.80 δ (s, 5.1 mm)
           7.50 δ – 6.90 δ (m, 15.5 mm)
           6.50 δ (b, s, 4.9 mm)
           3.9 δ (s, 15.8 mm)

Ans.

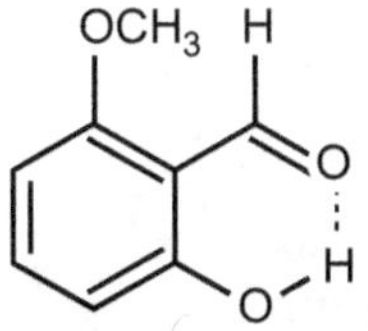

15.   MF   : $C_8H_{14}O_3$
      UV   :   225 nm, ε = 50 (hexene)
      IR   :   3077 – 2857 cm^{-1} (m); 1828 cm^{-1} (s), 1757 cm^{-1} (m); 1456 cm^{-1} (m)
      NMR   :   2.70 δ (septet, J = 6.7 Hz, 6.4 mm); 1.2 δ (doublet, J = 6.7 Hz)

Ans.

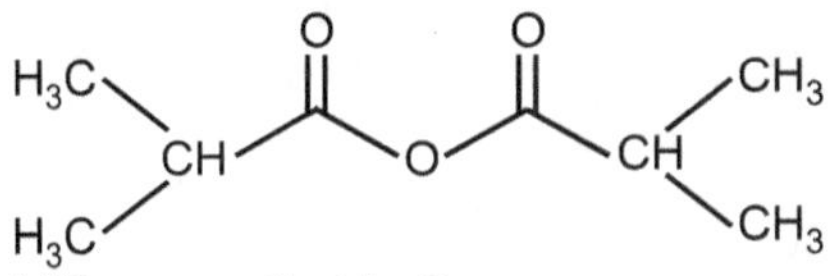

16.   MF   : $C_{10}H_{12}O_2$
      UV   :   220 nm, ε = 1800
      IR   :   3077 cm^{-1} (w); 2976 cm^{-1} (w); 1745 cm^{-1} (s); 1608 cm^{-1} (m),
                1497 cm^{-1} (m); 1456 cm^{-1} (m)
      NMR   :   7.29 (s, 16.5 mm); 4.30 (t, J = 7.3 Hz, 6.2 mm);
                3.00 (t, J = 7.3 Hz, 6.7 mm); 2.12 (s, 10.2 mm)

Ans.

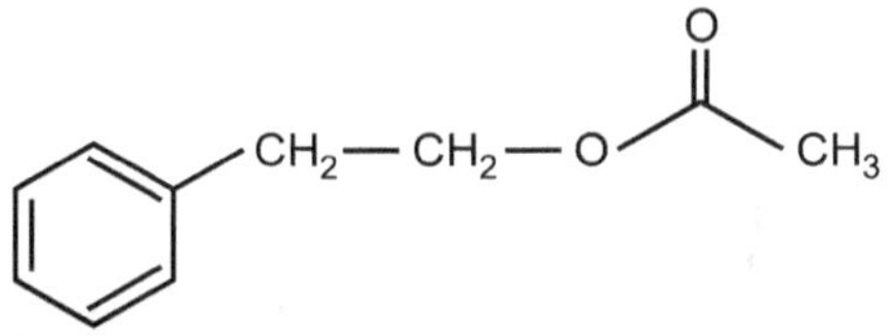

17.   MF   : $C_8H_{14}O_4$
      UV   : λ_{max} = 213 nm, ε = 60
      IR   :   1941 – 2857 cm^{-1} (m); 1745 cm^{-1} (s); 1458 cm^{-1} (m)
      NMR   :   4.14 (q, J = 7.2 Hz, 10.4 mm); 2.60 (s, 10.8 mm);
                1.27 (t, J = 7.2 Hz, 16.0 mm)

Ans.

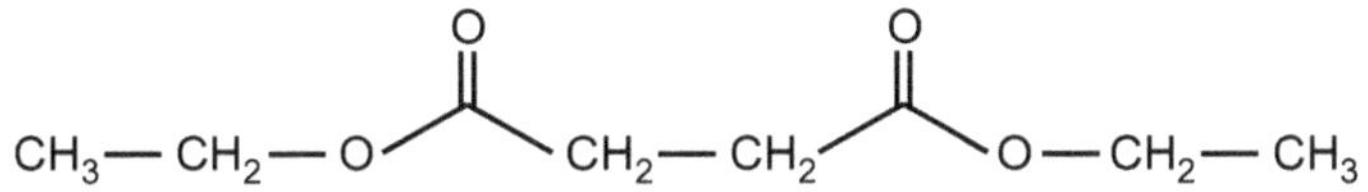

18.   MF   : $C_2H_4Br_2$
      UV   :   No λ_{max} above 210 mm
      IR   :   3058 cm^{-1} (m); 1449 cm^{-1} (m)
      NMR   :   5.89 δ (q, J = 6.0 Hz, 9.8 mm); 2.50 (d, J = 6.0 Hz, 30.3 mm)

Ans.

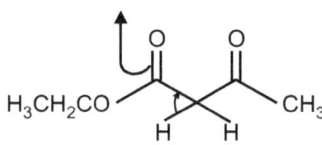

19.   MF   : $C_7H_{10}O_4$
      UV   : λ_{max} = 216 nm, ε = 80
      IR   : 3530 cm^{-1}; 3941 – 2857 cm^{-1}; 1745 cm^{-1} (s); 1681 cm^{-1} (s),
               1634 cm^{-1} (s); 1460 cm^{-1} (m)
      NMR : 6.17 (broad singlet 4.7 mm); 5.53 (d, J = 6.7 Hz, 4.4 mm),
               4.39 (q, J = 7.2 Hz, 9.0 mm); 2.1(s, 14.8 mm);
               1.38 (t, J = 7.2 Hz, 15.1 mm)

Ans.

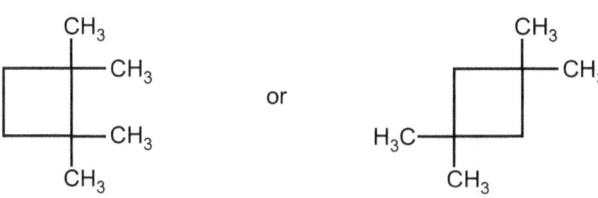

20.   MF   : C_3H_7Cl
      UV   : 204 and 276 nm, ε = 4800 and 20
      IR   : 3030 – 2924 cm^{-1}; 1555 cm^{-1} (m); 1466 cm^{-1} (m)
      NMR : 4.7 δ (septet, J = 6.7 Hz, 6.2 mm); 1.43 δ (d, J = 6.7 Hz, 37.8 mm)

Ans.

CH$_3$
|
H— C —CH$_3$
|
H

21.   MF   : C_8H_{16}
      UV   : No λ_{max} above 200 nm
      IR   : 2924 cm^{-1} (m); 1456 cm^{-1} (m)
      NMR : 1.8 δ (s, 11.9 mm); 1.4 δ (s, 35.7 mm)

Ans.

    CH$_3$ CH$_3$
        —CH$_3$ —CH$_3$
                  or
        —CH$_3$ H$_3$C—
    CH$_3$ CH$_3$

Chapter **5**...

Natural Products

Contents ...

[A] TERPENOIDS

5.1 Introduction

- The terpenoids are a group of compounds which occur mainly in plants; a few terpenoids have been obtained from other sources. Earlier, the term **'Terpene'** (originally named after turpentine, the volatile oil from pine trees used in oil painting) referred to only volatile C_{10} and C_{15} hydrocarbons that were isolated from various parts of plants, even from the wood in some cases. This was then modified and all the naturally occurring hydrocarbons having multiples of five carbon atoms in their structures, as well as their functionally substituted derivatives (such as alcohols, aldehydes etc.) were called **terpenes**. Although, this name is still used, the more general name **'terpenoids'** is many times used. This is because, the suffix 'ene' signifies unsaturated hydrocarbons, and then the name 'terpene' is not proper to include compounds such as, alcohols, aldehydes, ketones etc. Hence the term 'terpenoids' is in current use.

5.1

5.2 Classification of Terpenoids

- Most natural terpenoid hydrocarbons have the molecular formula $(C_5H_8)_n$. These terpenoids are then classified on the basis of number of carbon atoms that they contain. Thus,

Number of carbon atoms	Molecular formula	Class
10	$C_{10}H_{16}$	Monoterpenoids
15	$C_{15}H_{24}$	Sesquiterpenoids
20	$C_{20}H_{32}$	Diterpenoids
25	$C_{25}H_{40}$	Sesterterpenoids
30	$C_{30}H_{48}$	Triterpenoids
40	$C_{40}H_{64}$	Tetraterpenoids (Carotenoids)
More than 40	$(C_5H_8)_n$	Polyterpenoids (Natural rubber)

- The simpler **mono** and **sesqui**-terpenoids are the main constituents of the *essential oils* (because they contain the *essence* i.e. the odour or fragrance of the plant).

- These are the volatile oils obtained from the sap and tissues of certain plants and trees. The essential oils have been used in perfumery for many years. The study of the composition of essential oils ranks as one of the oldest areas of organic chemical research.

- The **di**- and **tri**-terpenoids which are not steam volatile, are obtained from the plant and tree gums and resins.

- The **tetra**-terpenoids form a group of compounds known as the *carotenoids* and usually it is treated as a separate group.

- **Natural rubber** is the most important **poly**-terpenoid.

- Each class of terpenoids is further classified into subgroups *on the basis of number of rings present* in their molecules e.g. Monoterpenoids are classified as acyclic, monocyclic and bicyclic monoterpenoids.

5.3 Isoprene Rule

- Scientist Wallach in 1887 first pointed out that the thermal decomposition of almost all terpenoids give *isoprene* (2-methyl-1, 3-butadiene) C_5H_8 as one of the products.

$$Terpenoids \xrightarrow[\text{decomposition}]{\text{Thermal}} \underset{\textbf{isoprene } (C_5H_8)}{H_2C=\overset{\overset{\displaystyle CH_3}{|}}{C}-CH=CH_2} \equiv$$

- This observation led to the suggestion that the skeleton structures of all naturally occurring terpenoids can be built-up of isoprene units (two or more). This is known as the *'Isoprene rule'*. Thus, any naturally occurring terpenoid should be divisible into isoprene units.

- Further, in 1925, Ingold pointed out that the isoprene units in natural terpenoids were joined in a 'head-to-tail' manner (the head being the branched end of isoprene). This divisibility into isoprene units and their head to tail joining is referred to as 'special isoprene rule'.

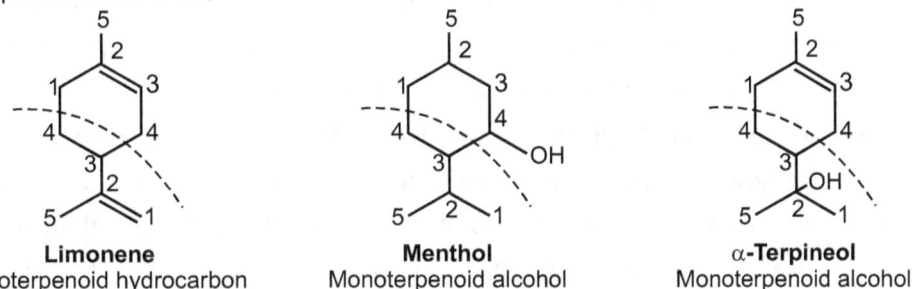

Head-to-tail joining in monoterpenes (acyclic)

- For example, myrcene, an acyclic monoterpenoid hydrocarbon and geraniol, an acyclic terpenoid alcohol.

Myrcene   **Geraniol**

Acyclic sesquiterpene skeleton with three isoprene units joined in a head-to-tail manner   e.g.   **Farnesol**, a sesquiterpene alcohol

- Monocyclic, monoterpenoids contain a six membered ring and these are also divisible into isoprene units. Thus,

Limonene   **Menthol** α-**Terpineol**
Monoterpenoid hydrocarbon   Monoterpenoid alcohol   Monoterpenoid alcohol

- However, it should be noted, that this rule which has proved very useful, can only be used as a guiding principle and not as a fixed rule. This is because several exceptions are observed e.g. carotenoids are joined tail-to-tail at their centre; squalene, a triterpenoid is formed by joining of two C_{15} units in a tail-to-tail manner.

- Since, terpenoids are formed by combination of isoprene units, they are also referred to as *isoprenoid compounds* or simply 'isoprenoids'.

5.4 Isolation from Natural Sources (Plants)

- Essential oils are first extracted from plants and then individual terpenoids are separated from these essential oils by using techniques like fractional distillation, column chromatography etc. Plants containing essential oils usually have the greatest concentration at some particular time. e.g. jasmine at sunset.

- In general, there are four methods for extraction of oils from plants. These are (i) expression, (ii) steam distillation, (iii) extraction by means of volatile solvents and (iv) adsorption in purified fats (enfleurage):

  (i)   Expression: The plant material is crushed and juice is filtered to remove large particles. The juice is centrifuged when major part of the essential oil is obtained in the centrifugate. Some oil is obtained by distillation from the residual material.

  (ii) Steam distillation: This is the most widely used method. The plant material (usually leaves and flowers) is first soaked in water and then subjected to steam distillation. Steam volatile terpenoids are carried along with the steam and are collected in the distillate. This distillate is then extracted with organic solvents like light petrol. The solvent is then removed by distillation under reduced pressure when a mixture of mono- and sesqui-terpenoids is obtained.

  Some terpenoids decompose under the conditions of steam distillation or undergo structural changes. These are then separated by solvent extraction.

  (iii) Solvent extraction: The plant material is extracted with solvents like petroleum ether (40°-60°C) or diethyl ether. Solvent is then removed by distillation. The essential oil obtained by this method has the natural odour. This method is more efficient than steam distillation but more expensive also.

  (iv) Adsorption in purified fats (enfleurage): The fat is warmed to about 50°C and then the flower petals are spread on the surface of the fat. The fat is saturated with essential oils by keeping for several days. This saturated fat is then digested with ethanol when essential oil dissolves in ethanol. Some fat also dissolves in ethanol, which is then removed by cooling to 20°C. Ethanol is removed by distillation and essential oil obtained is subjected to fractional distillation. The terpenoid hydrocarbons distil first, and these are followed by the oxygenated derivatives. Distillation of the residue under reduced pressure gives the sesquiterpenoids.

  Recently, chromatography (in its various forms) has been used both for isolation and separation of terpenoids.

5.5 General Methods for Determination of Structure

1. **Molecular formula:** A pure specimen of the natural product is analysed for detection of elements. Elemental analysis of the sample then estimates the percentage of different elements from which empirical formula is determined. Molecular weight is found out by mass spectrometry and other methods. From empirical formula and molecular weight, molecular formula is determined.

2. **Optical activity:** If the terpenoid is optically active, its specific rotation is measured. Optical activity may be used as a means of distinguishing structures.

3. **Detection of unsaturation:** The presence of double bonds is determined by means of bromine, and the number of double bonds is determined by analysis of the bromide or by quantitative hydrogenation.

$$\underset{\text{alkene}}{\overset{\diagdown}{\underset{\diagup}{C}}=\overset{\diagup}{\underset{\diagdown}{C}}} + Br_2 \xrightarrow{\text{Addition}} \underset{\text{dibromide}}{-\overset{|}{\underset{|}{C}}-\overset{|}{\underset{|}{C}}-}$$
$$\qquad\qquad\qquad\qquad\qquad\qquad\quad Br \quad Br$$

Thus, one molecule of bromine is added for each carbon-carbon double bond. Hydrogen halides and nitrosyl chloride are also used for detecting the presence and position of double bonds.

4. **Nature of oxygen function:** If oxygen is present in the molecule, it may be a hydroxyl, aldehyde, ketone etc. This can be detected by carrying out certain tests as follows:

    (a) **Hydroxyl group (–OH):** The presence of this group may be detected by the action of acetic anhydride, acetyl chloride or benzoyl chloride. If hydroxyl groups are present, then their number can also be estimated.

    $$R - OH + Ac_2O \rightarrow R - OAc + AcOH$$
    $$\text{Acetyl derivative}$$

    Formation of monoacetyl derivative indicates the presence of one –OH group. Dehydration of alcohols using sulphuric acid or phosphoric acid can be useful for distinguishing between primary, secondary and tertiary alcohols. Primary alcohols undergo very slow dehydration as compared to secondary and tertiary alcohols.

    (b) **Carboxyl group (–COOH):** The solubility of the compound in aqueous sodium bicarbonate, sodium carbonate or ammonia indicates the presence of a carboxyl group.

    $$R - COOH + NaHCO_3 \rightarrow R{\cdot}COO^{\ominus} Na^{\oplus} + H_2O + CO_2\uparrow$$

    Titration with a standard alkali solution can indicate number of such groups. Formation of esters also shows the presence of a carboxyl group.

    $$R\ COOH + R'\ OH \xrightarrow{H^+} R - COOR' + H_2O$$

(c) **Carbonyl group** $\left(\diagdown C = O \right)$: This can be either aldehydic or ketonic. It can be detected by formation of an oxime, semicarbazone and phenylhydrazone.

$$\diagdown C = O + H_2NOH \longrightarrow \diagdown C = N - OH + H_2O$$

Hydroxylamine   Oxime

$$\diagdown C = O + H_2N - NHC_6H_5 \longrightarrow \diagdown C = N - NHC_6H_5 + H_2O$$

Phenylhydrazine   Phenylhydrazone

$$\diagdown C = O + H_2N \cdot NH \cdot CONH_2 \longrightarrow \diagdown C = N \cdot NH \cdot CONH_2 + H_2O$$

Semicarbazide   Semicarbazone

Aldehydic group can be distinguished from the ketonic group by *silver mirror test* with *Tollen's reagent.*

$$R - CHO + 2Ag(NH_3)_2^+ + 3\ OH^- \rightarrow 2\ Ag \downarrow + RCOO^- + 4NH_3 + 2H_2O$$

Aldehyde   Colourless solution   Silver mirror

(d) **Methyl ketone group (–COCH₃):** Presence of this group can be detected by *iodoform test*. The ketone is treated with iodine and sodium hydroxide (sodium hypoiodite, NaOI).

$$R - \underset{\underset{O}{\|}}{C} - CH_3 + 3\ NaOI \rightarrow R \cdot COO^{\ominus}\ Na^{\oplus} +\ \ CHI_3\ \ + 2\ NaOH$$

Iodoform

Methyl ketone

A methyl ketone gives a yellow precipitate of iodoform.

5. **Dehydrogenation:** The terpenoid is subjected to dehydrogenation with sulphur, selenium, platinum or palladium and the products obtained are examined. This gives important information about the nature of carbon skeleton and the relative position of substituents on rings. e.g.

Dipentene   **p-Cymene**
Monocyclic monoterpenoid   (methyl and isopropyl groups are in 1, 4 positions)

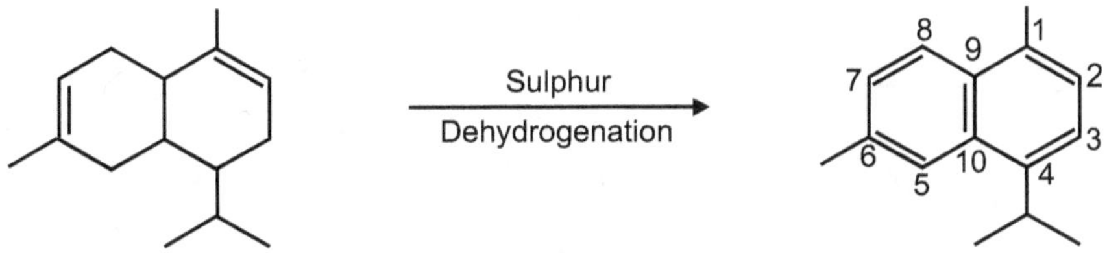

Cadinene
(Bicyclic sesquiterpenoid)

Cadalene
(1, 6-dimethyl-4-isopropylnaphthalene)

6. **Oxidative degradation:** This is the most important tool for elucidating the structure of terpenoids. The reagents used for this purpose are neutral or alkaline $KMnO_4$, chromic acid, ozone, osmium tetroxide (OsO_4), HNO_3, sodium hypobromite (NaOBr), lead tetra-acetate, peroxy acids etc. It is now possible to select a reagent for oxidizing a particular group in the molecule.

   (a) Alkaline $KMnO_4$: This reagent converts alkenes into 1, 2-diols or glycols.

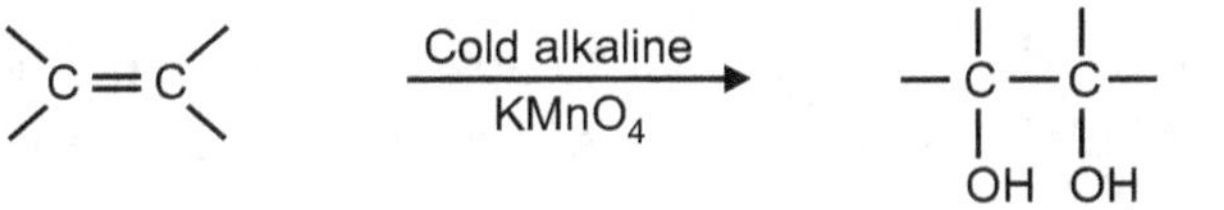

alkene — 1, 2-diol or glycol

e.g. $3\,CH_2 = CH_2 + 2\,KMnO_4 + 4H_2O \rightarrow 3\,\underset{OH}{\underset{|}{CH_2}}-\underset{OH}{\underset{|}{CH_2}} + 2\,MnO_2 + 2\,KOH$

The diols can be further cleaved by reagents like sodium periodate.

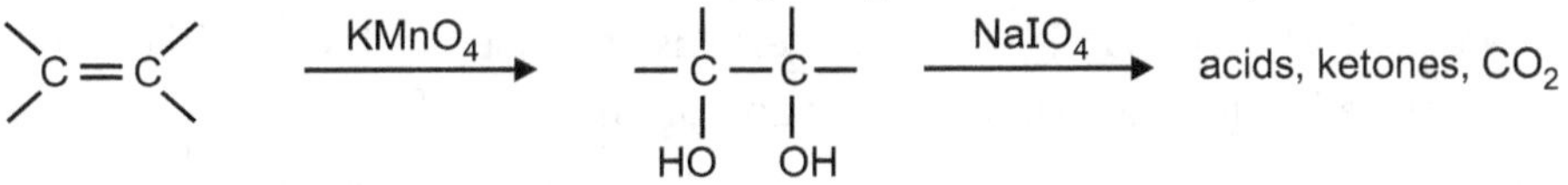

Carboxylic acids are usually obtained instead of aldehydes. A terminal = CH_2 group is oxidized to CO_2. For example,

$$CH_3\,CH = \overset{CH_3}{\overset{|}{C}} - CH_3 \xrightarrow[\text{(ii) } NaIO_4]{\text{(i) } KMnO_4} CH_3\,COOH + O = C\begin{matrix} CH_3 \\ CH_3 \end{matrix}$$

$$CH_3\,CH_2\,CH_2\,CH = CH_2 \xrightarrow[\text{(ii) } NaIO_4]{\text{(i) } KMnO_4} CH_3\,CH_2\,CH_2\,COOH + CO_2\uparrow$$

   (b) Ozone (O_3): This is a very useful reagent for cleavage of double bonds. Addition of ozone to the double bond forms an ozonide, which is then hydrolysed to yield the cleavage products. The products are aldehydes and ketones. Terminal alkenes give formaldehyde as one of the products.

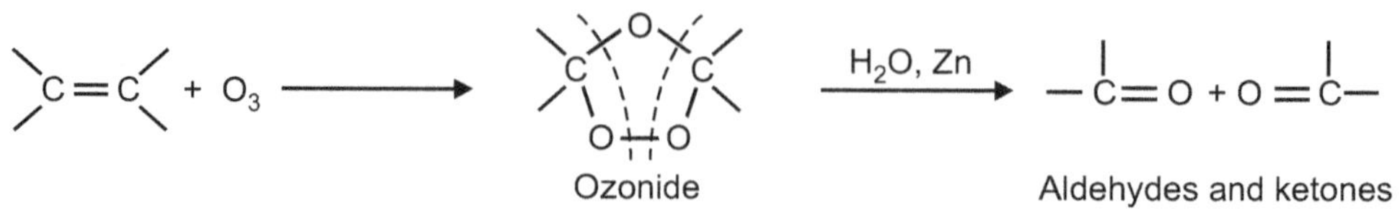

Ozonide   Aldehydes and ketones

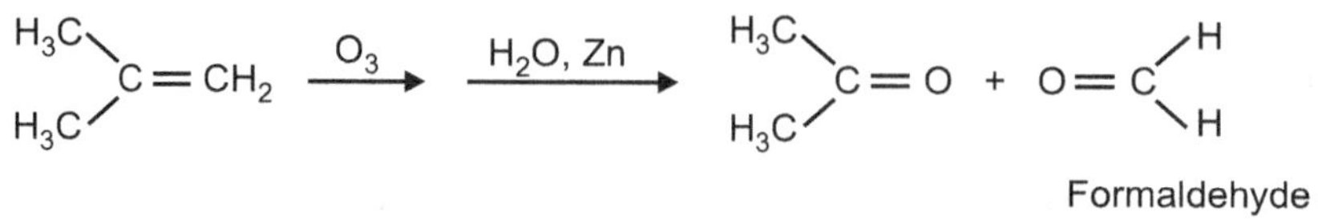

Formaldehyde

(c) Osmium tetroxide (OsO₄):

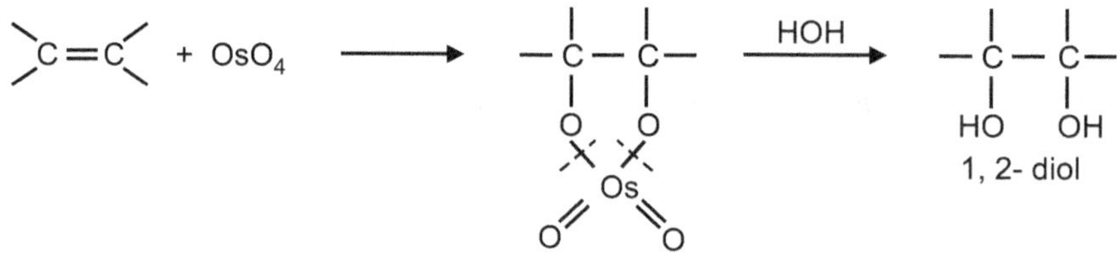

1, 2- diol

Osmium tetroxide is superior to potassium permanganate for selective conversion of olefins to cis-1,2-diols in high yield, but, at the same time it is very toxic and expensive.

In general, *oxidative degradation* has been the most important tool for elucidating the structures of terpenoids.

7. **Spectroscopic methods:** These are the modern methods used for determination of structures of terpenoids.

Ultraviolet (UV) spectroscopy has been extensively used in terpenoid chemistry and its main application is in the detection of conjugation.

Infrared (IR) spectroscopy is also very useful in terpenoid chemistry and is valuable in detecting the presence of a hydroxyl group –OH (~ 3400 cm^{-1}), a carbonyl group $\text{C} = \text{O}$ (~1700-1750 cm^{-1}) and an α, β-unsaturated carbonyl group (~ 1660-1700 cm^{-1}).

Nuclear magnetic resonance (NMR) spectroscopy is used to detect and identify double bonds, to determine the nature of end groups and also the number of rings present and to find the orientation of methyl groups in the molecule. In many cases, definite structures have been assigned on the basis of NMR spectra.

Mass spectrometry (MS) is frequently used as a means for elucidating the structure of terpenoids. It is possible to determine molecular weights, molecular formulae, nature of various functional groups and the relative positions of double bonds.

8. **X-ray analysis:** X-ray analysis is sometimes very useful for elucidating the structure and stereochemistry of terpenoids.

9. **Synthesis:** After arriving at the tentative structure (or structures) from analytical evidence, the final proof of the structure depends on synthesis. The terpenoid is synthesized in the laboratory, starting from known compounds and is compared with the natural compound which finally confirms its structure. Now, by using stereoselective synthesis, it is possible to prepare particular configurational forms of many terpenoids.

5.6 Structure Determination of Citral

- This is the most important member of *acyclic monoterpenoids*. Citral is widely distributed in nature and occurs to the extent of 60-80% in lemon grass oil.

- **Isolation:** It is isolated from lemon grass oil (which is obtained from lemon grass by steam distillation) by formation of sodium bisulphite addition product, which on hydrolysis gives citral.

Physical properties:

1. It is a colourless liquid with b.p. 229°C.

2. It is optically inactive.

3. It has smell of lemons.

Structure:

1. **Molecular formula:** $C_{10}H_{16}O$.

2. **Presence of unsaturation:** Citral readily adds two molecules of bromine and forms a tetrabromo derivative.

$$C_{10}H_{16}O + 2Br_2 \longrightarrow C_{10}H_{16}OBr_4$$

   Citral   Tetrabromo derivative

   Similarly, citral on catalytic hydrogenation forms a tetrahydro derivative.

$$C_{10}H_{16}O \xrightarrow[\text{catalyst}]{H_2} C_{10}H_{20}O$$

   Citral   Tetrahydro derivative

   Both these reactions indicate the presence of *two carbon-carbon double bonds,* $\diagdown C = C \diagup$ in citral.

3. The molecular formula of the parent saturated hydrocarbon of citral becomes $C_{10}H_{22}$, which corresponds to the general formula C_nH_{2n+2} (n = 10). This suggests that citral is an open chain or *acyclic terpenoid*.

4. **Nature of oxygen :** Citral forms an oxime with hydroxylamine and bisulphite addition product with saturated sodium bisulphite ($NaHSO_3$) solution. These reactions indicate that citral contains either an aldehyde or a ketone group.

(a) Citral on reduction with sodium amalgam (Na-Hg) in dil. acid forms a primary alcohol geraniol $C_{10}H_{18}O$.

$$C_{10}H_{16}O \xrightarrow[\text{reduction}]{\text{Na-Hg/HCl}} C_{10}H_{18}O$$

Citral   Geraniol

(b) Citral on oxidation with silver oxide, Ag_2O forms geranic acid $C_{10}H_{16}O_2$ without the loss of carbon atom.

$$C_{10}H_{16}O \xrightarrow[\text{oxidation}]{Ag_2O} C_{10}H_{16}O_2$$

Citral   Geranic acid

Both these reactions indicate the presence of an aldehyde $\left(- C \begin{smallmatrix} H \\ \\ O \end{smallmatrix}\right)$ group in citral.

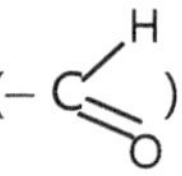

5. The ultra violet (UV) spectrum of citral shows a strong absorption at λ_{max} = 238 nm (ϵ = 13500). This is characteristic of the α, β - unsaturated carbonyl system.

   Hence, citral must be an *α, β-unsaturated aldehyde.*

6. **Nature of carbon skeleton:** On heating with potassium hydrogen sulphate, $KHSO_4$, citral forms p-cymene (1-methyl-4-isopropyl benzene).

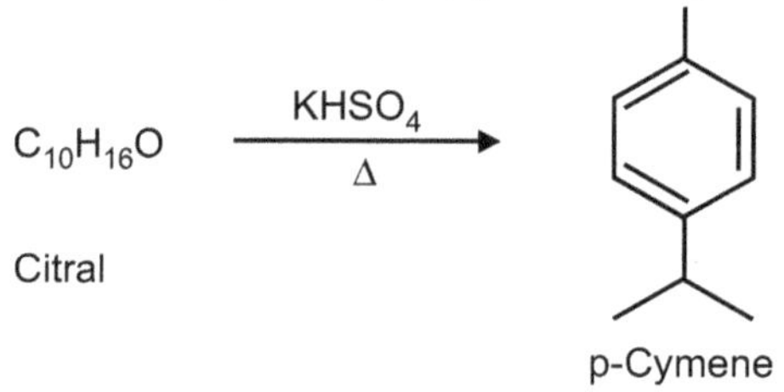

$$C_{10}H_{16}O \xrightarrow[\Delta]{KHSO_4}$$

Citral

p-Cymene

This reaction determines the relative positions of methyl and isopropyl groups in citral.

Since citral is acyclic in nature, carbon skeleton **I** in which two isoprene units are joined in a head-to-tail manner is suggested for citral.

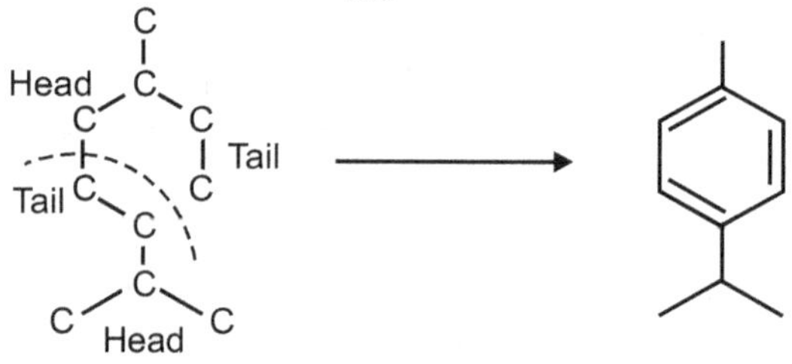

I

7. **Oxidative degradation:**

   (a) Oxidation of citral with alkaline potassium permanganate, followed by chromic acid, gives acetone, oxalic acid and laevulic acid.

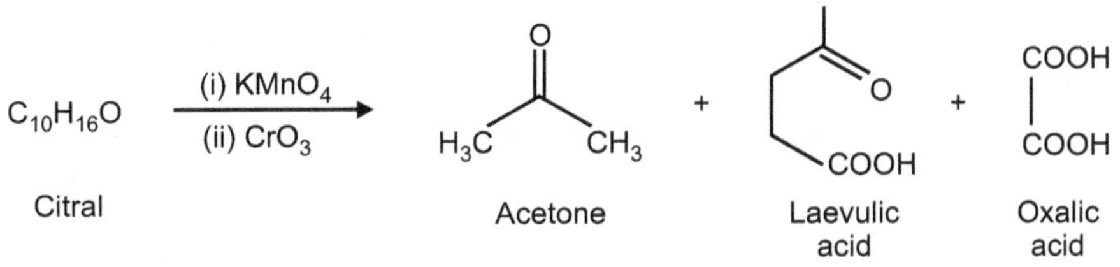

Citral → Acetone + Laevulic acid + Oxalic acid

(i) KMnO$_4$
(ii) CrO$_3$

C$_{10}$H$_{16}$O

(b) Further, *ozonolysis* of citral gives acetone, laevulaldehyde and glyoxal.

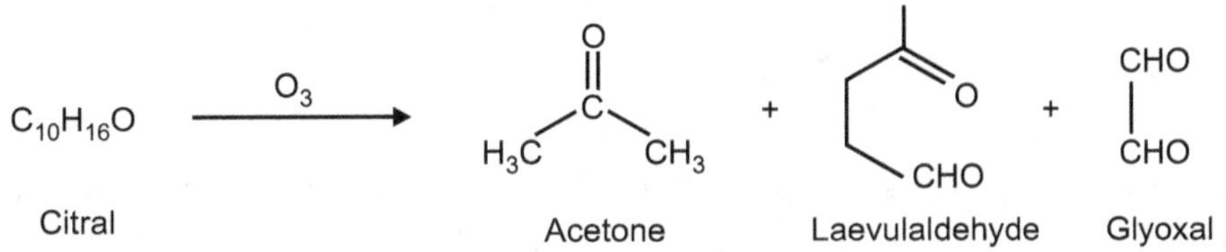

C$_{10}$H$_{16}$O → Acetone + Laevulaldehyde + Glyoxal

Citral

O$_3$

Formation of acetone in both of the above reactions indicates the presence of terminal *isopropylidene* group, Me$_2$C = in citral.

Formation of these oxidation products and products from other reactions can be explained if citral is assumed to have structure **II**.

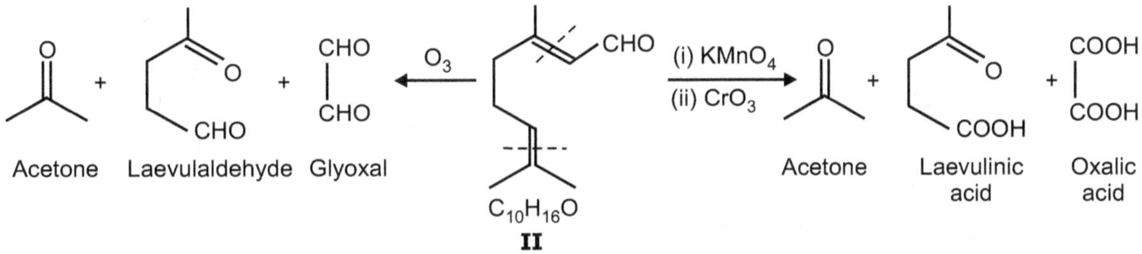

Acetone   Laevulaldehyde   Glyoxal

C$_{10}$H$_{16}$O
II

Acetone   Laevulinic acid   Oxalic acid

8. This structure is supported by the fact that citral gives 6-methylhept-5-en-2-one and acetaldehyde on treatment with aq. K$_2$CO$_3$.

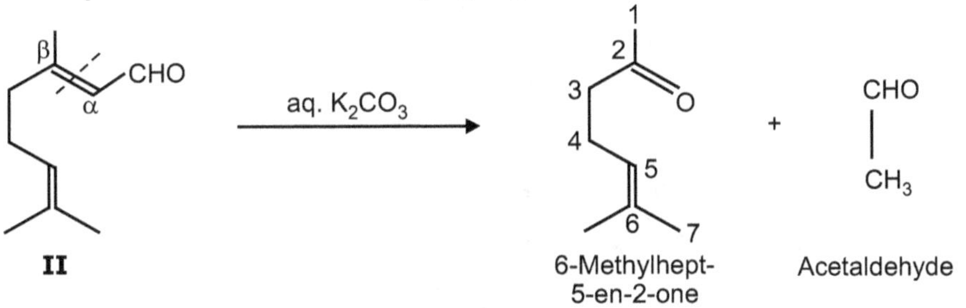

II

aq. K$_2$CO$_3$

6-Methylhept-5-en-2-one   +   Acetaldehyde

Formation of these products is readily explained if we assume that **II** undergoes cleavage at the α, β-double bond. This cleavage is a characteristic reaction of α, β-unsaturated aldehyde compounds.

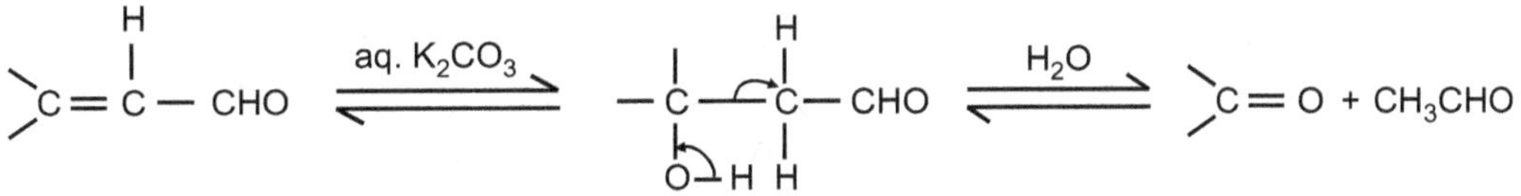

$$C=C-CHO \xrightleftharpoons{aq.\ K_2CO_3} -C-C-CHO \xrightleftharpoons{H_2O} C=O + CH_3CHO$$

Further, methylheptenone itself is also oxidized to acetone and laevulic acid which is in accord with structure **II** of citral.

Thus, the final structure for citral as indicated above, is in fact represented by **II**.

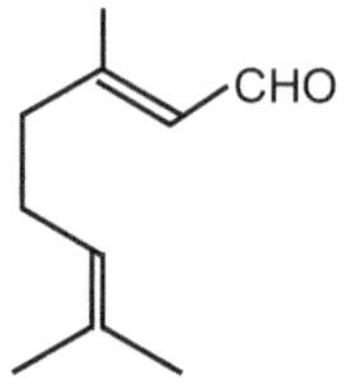

Citral $(C_{10}H_{16}O)$

II

This structure readily explains all the reactions of citral which are considered above. e.g.

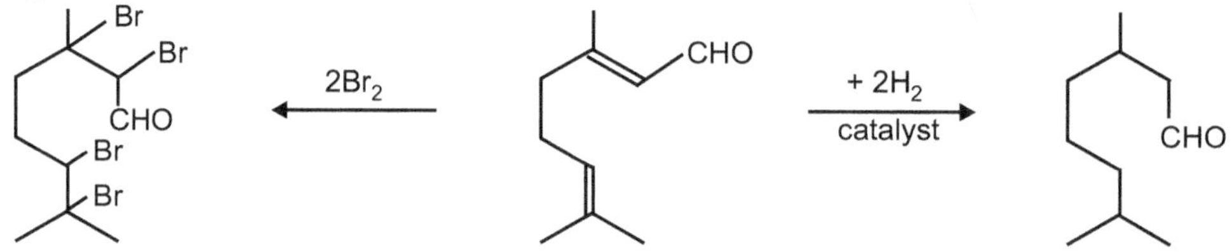

Tetrabromo derivative
$(C_{10}H_{16}OBr_4)$

Citral $(C_{10}H_{16}O)$

Tetrahydro derivative
$(C_{10}H_{20}O)$

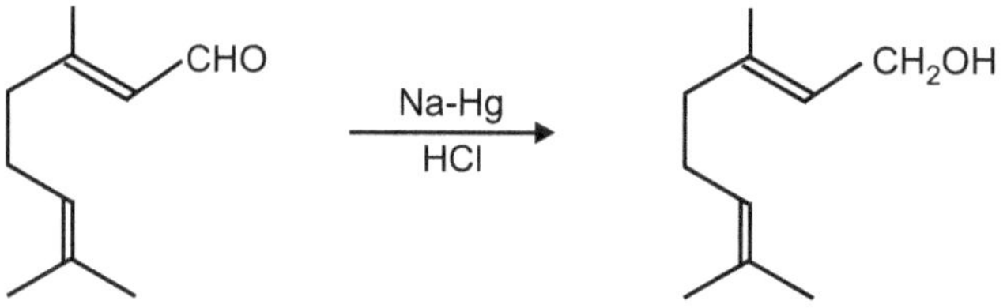

Citral
$(C_{10}H_{16}O)$

Geraniol
$(C_{10}H_{18}O)$

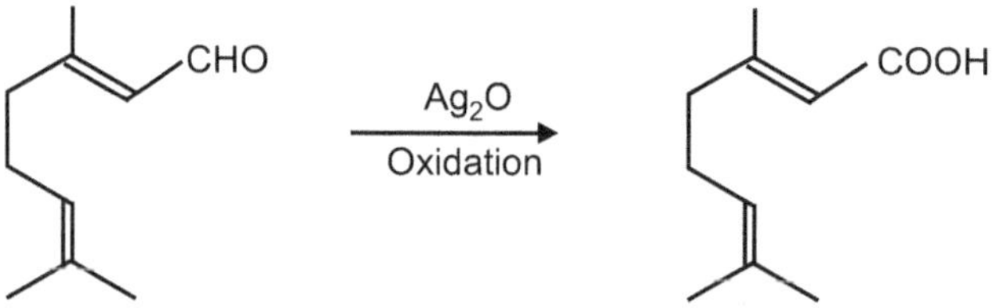

Citral
$(C_{10}H_{16}O)$

Geranic acid
$(C_{10}H_{16}O_2)$

This structure of citral was confirmed by its synthesis.

9. **Synthesis of Citral:** The structure of citral was confirmed by the synthesis of methylheptenone, its conversion into geranic ester (**Barbier and Bouveault, 1896**) and heating a mixture of calcium salts of geranic acid and formic acid (**Tiemann, 1898**) to give citral.

(a) Synthesis of methylheptenone:

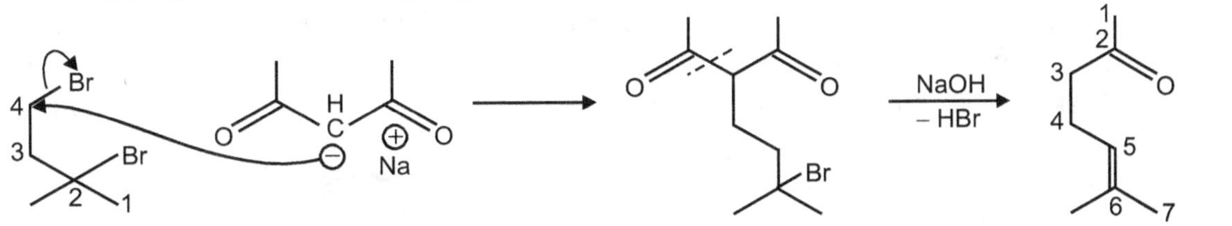

| 2, 4-Dibromo-
2-methyl butane | Sodio acetyl acetone
(from acetyl acetone and base) | Bromodiketone | 6-Methyl-hept-5-en-2-one |

Here, the most acidic proton is that between the two carbonyl groups of acetylacetone. So, it can be easily removed by a base like NaOH to form sodio acetyl acetone. This will react with 2, 4-dibromo-2-methylbutane and the primary bromide will react very much faster than the tertiary bromide as a result of the steric and electronic effects of the two methyl groups. The only product is therefore the bromodiketone. Treatment of this with sodium hydroxide achieves two things. First, hydrogen bromide is eliminated forming thermodynamically most stable trisubstituted double bond. Secondly, the $- COCH_3$ group is removed in a reverse aldol reaction of the diketone. The product of this treatment is therefore, 6-methyl-hept-5-en-2-one.

(b) Conversion of methylheptenone to citral:

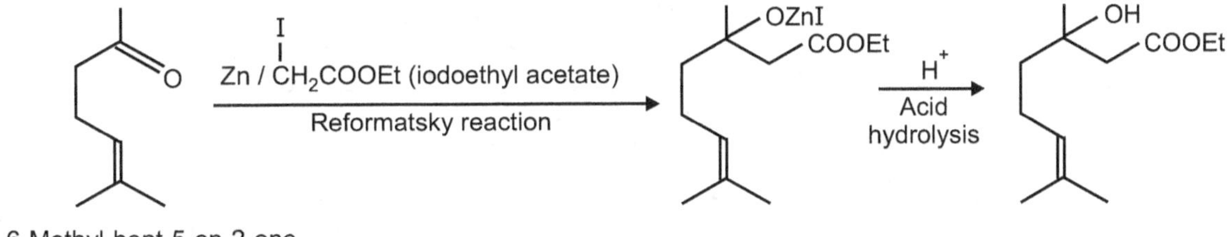

6-Methyl-hept-5-en-2-one

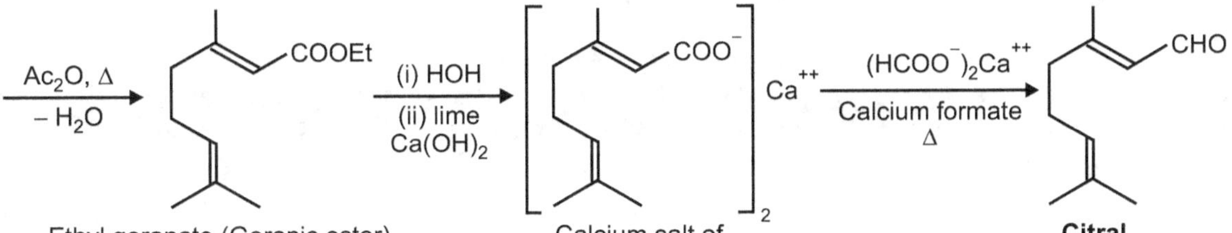

| Ethyl geranate (Geranic ester) | Calcium salt of
geranic acid | Citral |

This synthetic citral was shown to be identical in all respects to the natural citral and thus confirmed its structure elucidation.

10. Stereochemistry of citral: Structural formula of citral on close examination suggests that two geometrical isomers are possible. The aldehyde group is either *trans* or *cis* with respect to the methylene group of the main chain. Both isomers occur in natural citral and their structures are as given below.

Citral-a or Geranial trans - (or E) form	**Citral-b or Neral** cis - (or Z) form

These two forms have slightly different boiling points and form two different semicarbazone derivatives.

The configurations of these two forms have been determined by considering the cyclisation of corresponding alcohols geraniol and nerol. Nerol readily cyclises as compared to geraniol. The two structures of citral are confirmed by examination of their NMR spectra in $CDCl_3$. Thus, δ values of $- CH_2$ and $-CH_3$ are different due to different magnetic shielding effects of the carbonyl double bond in CHO.

| | **Citral-a** | | **Citral-b** |

	CH_2	CH_3
Citral - a	δ 2.24	δ 2.16
Citral - b	δ 2.58	δ 1.98

Natural citral is a 2: 1 mixture of geranial (citral-a) and neral (citral-b).

[B] ALKALOIDS

5.7 Introduction

- The term *alkaloid* means alkali-like i.e. having properties (particularly basic nature) similar to alkalies. Hence, the name *alkaloid* is given to all organic bases isolated from plants and which contain at least one nitrogen atom as part of a heterocyclic ring. This definition covers a wide variety of compounds. In general, alkaloids are very poisonous but if used in very small quantities, they act as medicines. Many such alkaloids are in use from earlier days e.g. morphine was used to get relief from pain, quinine in the treatment of malarial fever, ephedrine as a broncho dialater in the treatment of bronchial asthma etc. Thus, basic properties, complex structures (usually), physiological action and plant origin are the main features of alkaloids.

5.8 General Properties of Alkaloids

(i) The alkaloids are usually colourless, crystalline, non-volatile solids but some alkaloids like coniine and nicotine are liquids and few alkaloids are coloured e.g. berberine is yellow.

(ii) Solid alkaloids are insoluble in water, but are soluble in ethanol, ether, chloroform etc. while liquid alkaloids like coniine and nicotine are soluble in water.

(iii) Most alkaloids have a bitter taste and are optically active (laevorotatory). Optically active alkaloids are very useful for resolving racemic acids.

(iv) The alkaloids contain one or more nitrogen atoms and in the tertiary state nitrogen is usually part of a ring system. Some alkaloids also contain an oxygen atom.

(v) The alkaloids form insoluble precipitates with solutions of phosphotungstic acid, phosphomolybdic acid, picric acid, potassium mercury-iodide etc. Many of these precipitates have definite crystalline shapes and may be useful in identification of alkaloids.

5.9 Extraction and Purification of Alkaloids

- Alkaloids are found in seeds, roots, leaves or bark of the plant and generally occur as salts of various plant acids like acetic, oxalic, citric, malic, tartaric etc. General method for isolation of alkaloids is as follows:

(i) The plant material is dried, then finely powdered and extracted with boiling methanol.

(ii) The solvent is distilled off, and the residue is treated with inorganic acids when the bases are extracted as their water soluble salts.

(iii) The free bases are liberated by the addition of sodium carbonate to aqueous solution of salts and extraction with various solvents like ether, chloroform etc.

(iv) After evaporation of solvent, the residue obtained contains a mixture of alkaloids. This mixture is then separated into individual compounds by using different techniques like preparative thin layer chromatography, column chromatography etc.

5.10 Classification of Alkaloids

- Today, we know thousands of alkaloids which are isolated from plants. But still there is no rational classification of alkaloids because of the diverse nature of carbon skeletons in them. One of the most satisfactory classification is according to the nature of the nucleus (carbon skeleton) present or the nature of the heterocyclic ring system present. Thus, some groups of alkaloids are:

(i)   Phenylethylamine group

(ii)   Pyrrolidine group

(iii)   Pyridine and piperidine groups

(iv)   Pyrrolidine-pyridine group

(v)   Quinoline group

(vi)   Isoquinoline group

(vii)   Phenanthrene group

(viii) Indole group

• Of course, different classifications are possible, e.g. some alkaloids from Isoquinoline group can be separately grouped as Benzylisoquinoline alkaloids because they contain 1-Benzylisoquinoline ring system. Many times, different alkaloids obtained from the same plane have similar chemical structures and are classified according to the source of these alkaloids, e.g. Opium alkaloids, Tobacco alkaloids, Cinchona alkaloids etc.

• There is no systematic nomenclature of alkaloids. Trivial names are used and these end in 'ine' (indicating a base) and usually indicate the source of the alkaloid e.g. Ephedrine from Ephedra species, Atropine from Atropa belladona, Cinchonine from Cinchona tree etc.

5.11 Some Examples of Alkaloids and their Natural Sources

(i) Phenylethylamine group:

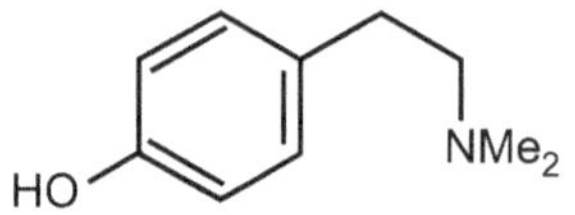

Hordenine
From Hordeum vulgare
(germinating barley)

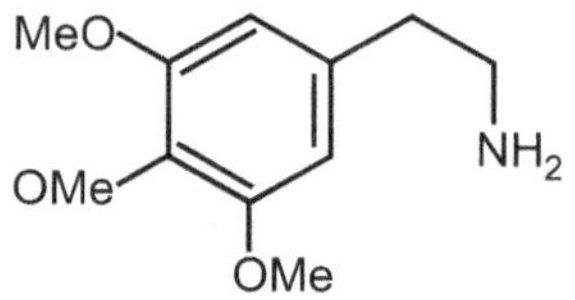

Mescaline
(From mescal buttons)

(ii) Pyrrolidine group:

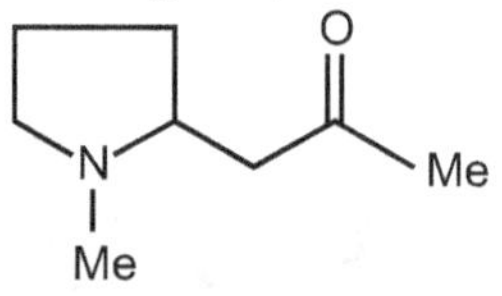

Hygrine
(coca alkaloid)

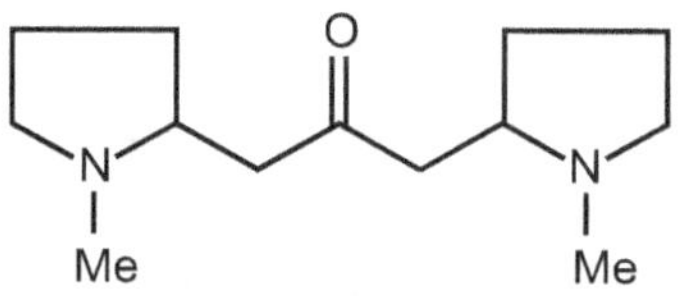

Cuscohygrine
(occurs along with Hygrine)

(iii) Pyridine-Piperidine group:

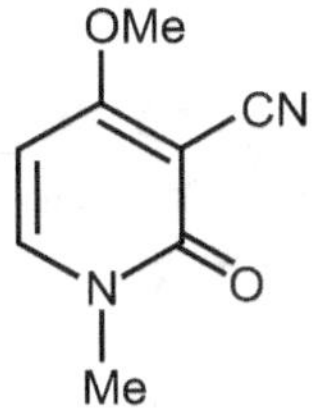

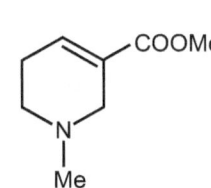

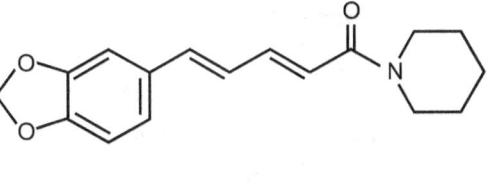

Ricinine
From Ricinus communis L
(castor-oil seed)

Arecoline
From Arecanut
(Betel nut)

Piperine
From Piper nigrum
(Black pepper)

(iv) Pyrrolidine-Pyridine group:

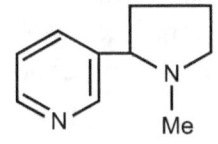

Nicotine
From Nicotiana tabaccum (Tobacco leaves)

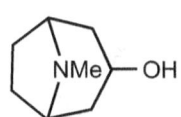

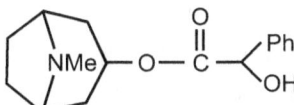

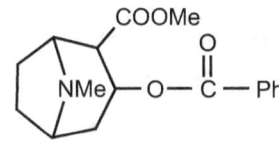

Tropine

Atropine
(From Atropa Belladona)

Cocaine
(From coca leaves)

(v) Quinoline group:

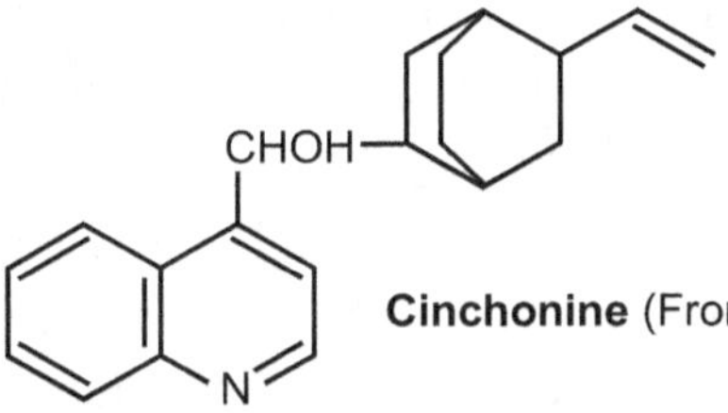

Cinchonine (From Cinchona tree)

(vi) Isoquinoline group:

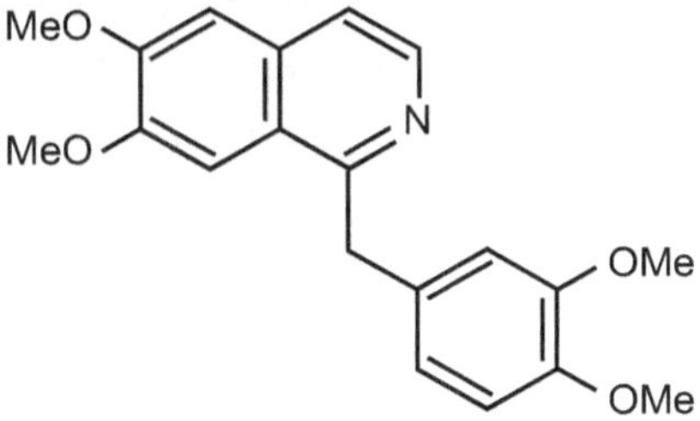

Papaverine
(From Papaver somniferum
(opium poppy)

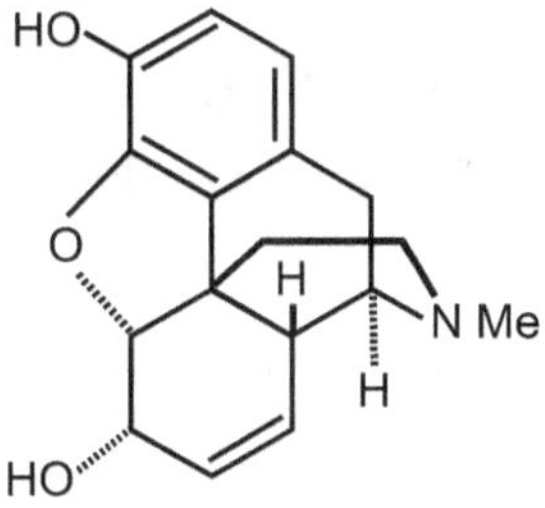

Morphine
(From Papaver somniferum
(opium poppy)

5.12 General Methods for Determination of Structure of Alkaloids

1. **Molecular formula:** A pure specimen of the alkaloid is subjected to qualitative analysis for detection of elements. Alkaloids contain carbon, hydrogen and nitrogen and most alkaloids also contain oxygen. It is then subjected to quantitative analysis to obtain the empirical formula. Determination of molecular weight then leads to molecular formula.

2. **Optical activity:** If the alkaloid is optically active, its specific rotation is measured.

3. **Detection of unsaturation:** The presence of unsaturation in an alkaloid may be determined by addition of bromine or halogen acids (as discussed in terpenoids) or by the ability to be hydroxylated with dilute alkaline permanganate. Reduction by using sodium amalgam, sodium and ethanol, tin and hydrochloric acid, hydriodic acid may also be used to show the presence of unsaturation. Sometimes, reduction may decompose the molecule. Here, mild reducing agents like lithium aluminium hydride ($LiAlH_4$) and sodium borohydride ($NaBH_4$) are more useful.

4. **Nature of oxygen function:**

    (a) Hydroxyl group: The presence of this group may be detected by the action of acetic anhydride, acetyl chloride or benzoyl chloride on the alkaloid (as discussed in terpenoids). If hydroxyl groups are present then their number is also estimated by acetylation etc.

    If hydroxyl group is present then it is to be decided whether the hydroxyl group is alcoholic or phenolic. It is phenolic if the alkaloid is soluble in sodium hydroxide and reprecipitated by carbon dioxide. Colouration with ferric chloride also indicates the presence of phenolic group.

    If the compound does not behave as a phenol, the –OH group may be alcoholic and this may be verified by the action of dehydrating agents. Most alkaloids containing an alcoholic group are readily dehydrated by sulphuric acid or phosphorous pentoxide. Additionally, the behaviour of the compound towards oxidizing agents will also indicate the presence of an alcoholic group.

    (b) Carboxyl group (–COOH): The solubility of the alkaloid in aqueous sodium carbonate or ammonia indicates the presence of a carboxyl group. Formation of esters also shows the presence of a carboxyl group.

    (c) Carbonyl group $\left(\diagup\diagdown C = O \right)$: The presence of a carbonyl group can be detected by formation of an oxime, semicarbazone and phenylhydrazone (as discussed in terpenoids).

    (d) Ester, lactone, amide, lactum: These groups can be detected by hydrolysis of the alkaloid and examination of the products. Thus,

$$R - \overset{\overset{\textstyle O}{\|}}{C} - OR' \quad \xrightarrow[\text{NaOH}]{\Delta} \quad R - \overset{\overset{\textstyle O}{\|}}{C} - \overset{\ominus}{O} \overset{\oplus}{Na} \; + R'OH$$

Ester   Na-salt of acid   Alcohol

$$R - \overset{\overset{\textstyle O}{\|}}{C} - NH_2 \quad \xrightarrow[\text{NaOH}]{\Delta} \quad R - \overset{\overset{\textstyle O}{\|}}{C} - \overset{\ominus}{O} \overset{\oplus}{Na} \; + NH_3\uparrow$$

Amide   Na-salt of acid   Ammonia

$$\underset{\gamma}{R-CH} - \underset{\beta}{CH_2} - \underset{\alpha}{CH_2} \quad \xrightarrow[\text{HOH}]{\Delta} \quad \underset{\gamma}{R-CH} - \underset{\beta}{CH_2} - \underset{\alpha}{CH_2}$$

γ-Lactone γ-Hydroxy acid

(with O—C=O bridge on lactone; OH and COOH on product)

$$\underset{\gamma}{R-CH} - \underset{\beta}{CH_2} - \underset{\alpha}{CH_2} \quad \xrightarrow[\text{HOH}]{\Delta} \quad \underset{\gamma}{R-CH} - \underset{\beta}{CH_2} - \underset{\alpha}{CH_2}$$

γ-Lactum γ-Amino acid

(with HN—C=O bridge on lactam; NH$_2$ and COOH on product)

(e) Methoxy group (–OCH₃): The presence of methoxy groups and their number may be determined by **Zeisel's method**. Here, a known weight of the alkaloid is heated with concentrated hydriodic acid (HI) at its boiling point (126°C) when the methoxy groups are converted to methyl iodide.

$$R - O - CH_3 + HI \xrightarrow{\Delta} R - OH + CH_3I$$

Methyl iodide

The methyl iodide generated is then absorbed by ethanolic silver nitrate when silver iodide precipitates. This silver iodide (AgI) is separated, dried and weighed. From the weight of alkaloid and weight of AgI, number of methoxy groups can be estimated.

$$CH_3I + AgNO_3 \rightarrow AgI\downarrow + CH_3NO_3 \text{ or } CH_3ONO_2$$

Thus,

$$1 \text{ mole of AgI} \equiv 1 \text{ methoxy group } (-OCH_3)$$
$$235 \text{ g} \equiv 31 \text{ g}$$

$\therefore$ Amount of methoxy group $= \dfrac{\text{Wt. of AgI}}{\text{Wt. of substance}} \times \dfrac{31}{235} = \ldots\ldots \text{ g}$

$\therefore$ Number of methoxy groups $= \dfrac{\text{Amount of methoxy group} \times \text{Mol. Wt.}}{31}$

(f) Methylene dioxy group (–O – CH₂ – O–): When the alkaloid is heated with hydrochloric or sulphuric acid, formation of formaldehyde indicates the presence of this group.

$$H_2C \overset{O-}{\underset{O-}{<}} \quad \xrightarrow[H_2SO_4]{2HOH} \quad \left[H_2C \overset{O-H}{\underset{O-H}{<}} \right] \quad \xrightarrow{-H_2O} \quad \overset{O}{\underset{}{\overset{\|}{H-C-H}}}$$

unstable   Formaldehyde

If the amount of formaldehyde formed is measured, then the number of methylene dioxy groups can also be estimated.

5. Nature of Nitrogen:

(a) All alkaloids must contain nitrogen atom and most of the times it is basic in nature. Primary, secondary and tertiary nature of nitrogen may be determined by the general reactions with acetic anhydride, methyl iodide and nitrous acid (HNO_2). The tertiary nitrogen atom forms amine oxide with 30% H_2O_2.

(b) The nature and number of alkyl groups attached to nitrogen can be determined by distillation of an alkaloid with aqueous potassium hydroxide. The formation of methylamine (CH_3NH_2), dimethylamine ($(CH_3)_2NH$) or trimethylamine ($(CH_3)_3N$) indicates respectively the attachment of one, two or three methyl groups to a nitrogen atom. Formation of ammonia, NH_3 shows the presence of an amino group.

(c) N-methyl Group $\left(\overset{}{\underset{}{>}} N-CH_3 \right)$: The presence of N-methyl groups and their number in an alkaloid may also be determined by ***Herzig-Meyer method***. When the alkaloid is heated with hydriodic acid (HI) at 150–300°C under pressure, N-methyl groups are converted into methyl iodide.

$$\overset{}{\underset{}{>}}N-CH_3 + HI \quad \xrightarrow{\Delta} \quad \overset{}{\underset{}{>}}N-H + CH_3I$$

The methyl iodide formed can be reacted with ethanolic silver nitrate when silver iodide precipitates (as in Zeisel's method). From the weight of precipitated silver iodide, number of N-methyl groups can be found out.

(d) The Zerewitinoff active hydrogen determination: An active hydrogen atom is the one joined to oxygen, nitrogen or sulphur when such compounds react with a Grignard reagent, the alkyl group is converted to an alkane. Thus,

$$R.MgX + H_2O \rightarrow RH + Mg(OH)X$$

Methyl magnesium iodide is normally used as the Grignard reagent. The methane which is liberated is measured by volume, one molecule of methane being equivalent to one active hydrogen atom. e.g.

$$RNH_2 + CH_3MgI \rightarrow CH_4\uparrow + RNHMgI$$

$$R_2NH + CH_3MgI \rightarrow CH_4\uparrow + R_2 NMgI$$

Only one hydrogen atom in a primary amine reacts at room temperature. At sufficiently high temperature, the active hydrogen in RNHMgI will react with another molecule of CH_3MgI.

$$RNHMgI + CH_3MgI \rightarrow CH_4\uparrow + RN(MgI)_2$$

(e) **Nature of heterocyclic ring:** Different methods are used for opening of heterocyclic rings with the elimination of nitrogen. From the nature of the carbon skeleton of the saturated hydrocarbon formed, size of the heterocyclic ring can be determined.

(i) **Hofmann's exhaustive methylation:** This method is applicable to heterocyclic rings containing β-hydrogen atoms.

The general procedure involves hydrogenation of heterocyclic ring (if it is unsaturated) and conversion of this compound to the quaternary methyl ammonium hydroxide which is then heated. Here a water molecule is eliminated, a hydrogen atom in the β-position with respect to the nitrogen atom combines with the hydroxyl group and the ring is opened at the nitrogen atom at the same side as the β-hydrogen eliminated. The process is repeated on the product, which results in complete removal of the nitrogen atom from the molecule, leaving an unsaturated hydrocarbon which generally isomerizes to a conjugated diene e.g.

Formation of 1, 3-pentadiene indicates that nitrogen atom must be present in a six membered ring. Similarly, a five membered ring containing nitrogen forms 1, 3-butadiene.

In general, exhaustive methylation involves heating the quaternary hydroxide at about 200°C.

When the base does not contain a β-hydrogen atom, the exhaustive methylation method is not useful. In such cases, **Emde** modification is useful.

(ii)   Emde modification: In this method, the quaternary ammonium halide is reduced with sodium amalgam in aqueous ethanol or with sodium in liquid ammonia or is catalytically hydrogenated.

e.g.

| Isoquinoline | 1, 2, 3, 4 - Tetrahydro isoquinoline | Quaternary ammonium salt with β - H atom |

$$\xrightarrow[\text{+ 4 (H)}]{\text{Na-C}_2\text{H}_5\text{OH}}$$

$$\xrightarrow[\text{(ii) AgOH}]{\text{(i) 2 MeI}}$$

$$\xrightarrow[\text{Hoffmann degradation}]{\Delta, -\text{H}_2\text{O}}$$

Quaternary ammonium iodide with no
β - H atom

$$\xrightarrow{\text{MeI}}$$

$$\xrightarrow[\substack{\text{H}_2\text{O-C}_2\text{H}_5\text{OH} \\ \text{Emde}}]{\text{Na-Hg}}$$

o-Methyl styrene   + Me$_3$N

(iii) Von Braun's method: Secondary cyclic amines:

Piperidine

$$\xrightarrow[\text{NaOH}]{\text{C}_6\text{H}_5\text{COCl}}$$

$$\xrightarrow{\text{PBr}_3\text{-Br}_2}$$

$$\xrightarrow[\substack{\text{under} \\ \text{reduced} \\ \text{pressure}}]{\text{Distillation}}$$

1, 5-Dibromo pentane
+ C$_6$H$_5$CN

Formation of 1, 5-dibromopentane indicates that nitrogen atom is present in a six membered ring.

Tertiary cyclic amines: Here, the reagent used is cyanogen bromide BrCN.

N-methyl piperidine

+ BrCN $\longrightarrow$

$$\xrightarrow[\text{Boil}]{\text{HBr}}$$

$$\xrightarrow[\substack{(-\text{CN} \rightarrow \text{COOH}) \\ \text{(ii) } -\text{CO}_2}]{\text{(i) HOH}}$$

Secondary amine

Repetition of this process can lead to 1,5-dibromopentane. This cyanogen bromide method is often successful with compounds where the Hofmann method fails. Further, where both methods are applicable, ring opening occurs at different points of the ring.

(iv) In many cases, the ring may be opened by heating with hydriodic acid, HI at 300°C. e.g.

Pyridine   n-Pentane

6. **Oxidation:** This is one of the most important methods for determining the structure of alkaloids. By varying the strength of the oxidizing agent, it is possible to obtain a variety of products. Various oxidizing agents like hydrogen peroxide, ozone, alkaline potassium ferricyanide, alkaline potassium permanganate, chromium trioxide in acetic acid, chromium trioxide-sulphuric acid, potassium dichromate – sulphuric acid, conc. nitric acid etc. are used. Studying the nature of the oxidation products formed, greatly helps in elucidating the structure of the alkaloid.

7. **Physical methods:** Along with chemical methods, physical methods like UV, IR, NMR and mass spectroscopy, X-ray analysis are of great importance in structure determination of alkaloids. They give important information about the likely structure, nature of functional groups, stereochemical features, type of the nucleus present – aromatic or heterocyclic, size and structure of side chains which helps in finalizing the structure of the compound.

8. **Synthesis:** The tentative structure (or structures) of the alkaloid suggested by all the chemical and physical methods discussed earlier is further confirmed by synthesis of that compound in the laboratory. Synthesis gives additional evidence for the structure assigned and may also provide a much better way of obtaining a particular alkaloid than from natural sources.

5.13 Structure Determination of Ephedrine

* Ephedrine belongs to phenyl ethyl amine group of alkaloids. Physiological action of many compounds of this group is to increase the blood pressure. Hence, they are often referred to as the *pressor drugs*.

    D(–) Ephedrine occurs in plants of genus *Ephedra*.

* It is one of the most important drugs in Chinese medicine. It can be taken orally and has been used in the treatment of hay fever, bronchial asthma etc. but it increases the blood pressure.

Physical properties:

(i)   It is a solid with m.p. 38.1°C.

(ii)   It is optically active and laevorotatory $[\alpha]_D - 6.3°$.

Structure:

1. **Molecular formula of ephedrine is $C_{10}H_{15}NO$.**

2. **Nature of the carbon skeleton.**

    Ephedrine on oxidation forms benzoic acid.

    $$C_{10}H_{15}NO \xrightarrow{\text{Oxidation}}$$

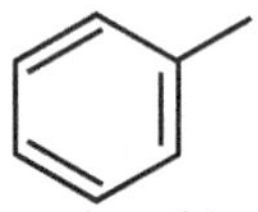

    Ephedrine   Benzoic acid

    Therefore, ephedrine must *contain a* benzene ring with only one side chain.

3. **Nature of nitrogen atom:**

    (a)   When treated with nitrous acid, HNO_2, ephedrine forms a nitroso compound.

    $$C_{10}H_{15}NO + HO - N = O \,(HNO_2) \rightarrow {\Large >}N - N = O \,+\, H_2O$$

    Ephedrine   Nitrous acid   N-nitroso compound

    (b)   Ephedrine consumes two moles of methyl iodide, CH_3I to form a quaternary ammonium iodide.

    $$C_{10}H_{15}NO \xrightarrow{2CH_3I} C_{10}H_{14}ON^{\oplus}(CH_3)_2 \, I^{\ominus} + HI$$

    Ephedrine   Quaternary salt

    Both these reactions indicate that ephedrine is a *secondary amine* i.e. it contains ${\Large >}N - H$ grouping.

    (c)   Ephedrine is heated with hydriodic acid (HI) at 150-300°C under pressure (Herzig-Meyer method) when one mole of CH_3I is formed.

    $$C_{10}H_{15}NO + HI \xrightarrow[\text{Under pressure}]{\Delta} {\Large >}N - H + CH_3I$$

    This suggests that ephedrine contains an ${\Large >}N{-}CH_3$ group, with H below N.

4. **Nature of oxygen atom:**

    Ephedrine on benzoylation forms a dibenzoyl derivative which indicates that oxygen atom is present as hydroxyl group (–OH). This is because formation of dibenzoyl derivative can be explained when one benzoyl group is introduced at

$|$

$- N - H$ group and the other at $-OH$ group.

$$C_{10}H_{13} \begin{Bmatrix} - OH \\ - NH \end{Bmatrix} + 2\ C_6H_5COCl \xrightarrow{\text{NaOH}} C_{10}H_{13} \begin{Bmatrix} - O - CO \cdot C_6H_5 \\ - N - CO \cdot C_6H_5 \end{Bmatrix}$$

Thus, ephedrine contains

(i)   a monosubstituted benzene ring

(ii)   an $- N - CH_3$ group
$\qquad\quad |$
$\qquad\quad$ H

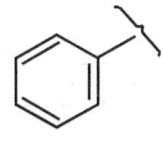

(iii) a hydroxyl group $-OH$

5. **Nature of side chain:** Ephedrine on heating with hydrochloric acid forms methyl amine and propiophenone.

$$C_{10}H_{15}NO \xrightarrow[\Delta]{\text{HCl}} CH_3NH_2 \quad + \quad$$

Ephedrine   Methyl amine   Propiophenone

Formation of these products can be explained if ephedrine has one of the following structures.

(I)   (II)

However, it has been observed that, compounds of structure (II) undergo the *hydramine fission* to form propiophenone when heated with hydrochloric acid, while structure (I) cannot give propiophenone.

Thus (II) is a more likely structure for ephedrine than (I).

Probable mechanism for hydramine fission of (II):

Propiophenone

6. Additional evidences for the support of structure (II):

(a) Ephedrine when subjected to Hofmann exhaustive methylation forms 1, 2-methyl phenyl ethylene oxide (III). Formation of compound (III) can be explained only if the structure of ephedrine is assumed to be (II) and not (I). Thus,

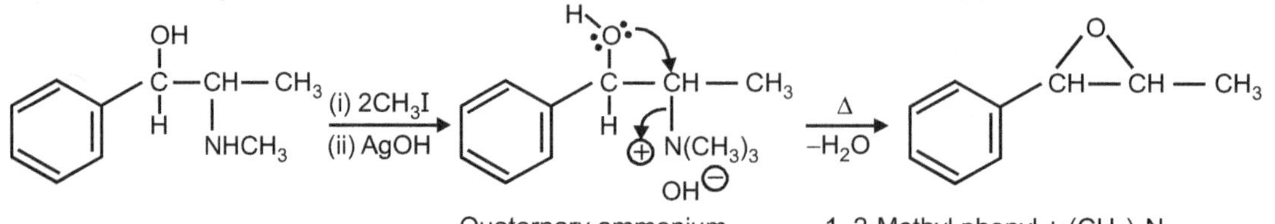

| | Quaternary ammonium hydroxide | 1, 2-Methyl phenyl + (CH$_3$)$_3$N ethylene oxide (III) |

(II)

(b) Structure (II) is further supported on the basis of following evidence. Structure (I) contains one chiral centre and so replacement of the hydroxyl group by hydrogen will result in the formation of an optically inactive compound. Structure (II), however contains two chiral centres and so replacement of the hydroxyl group by hydrogen should still give a compound that can be optically active.

Experimentally it has been found that when this replacement is actually carried out in (–) ephedrine, the product, deoxyephedrine is optically active. Thus, structure (II) agrees with all the known facts and is the actual structure of ephedrine.

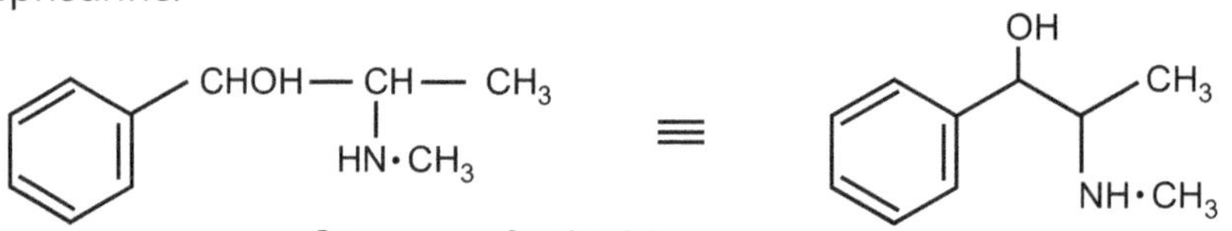

Structure of ephedrine

This structure is further confirmed by its synthesis.

7. (a) Synthesis of Ephedrine by Nagai (1929):

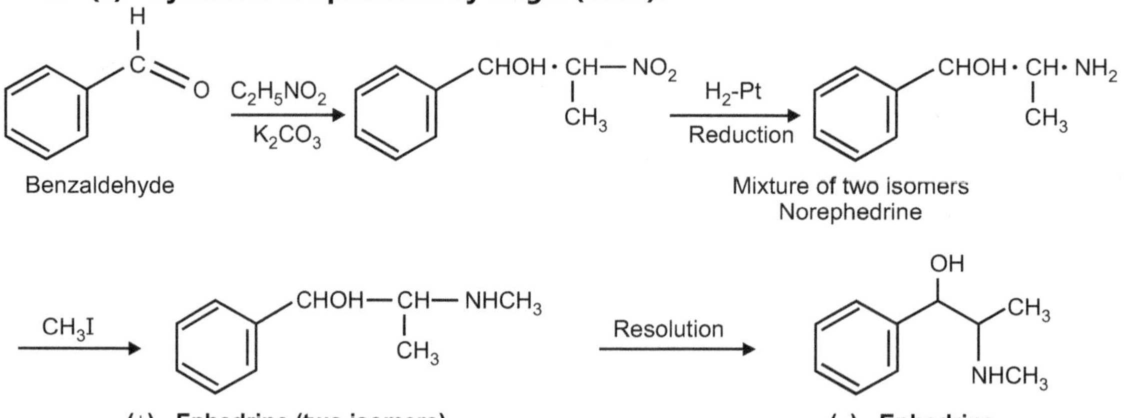

Benzaldehyde

Mixture of two isomers
Norephedrine

(±) - Ephedrine (two isomers)   (–) - Ephedrine

(b)   Synthesis of Ephedrine by Manske (1929):

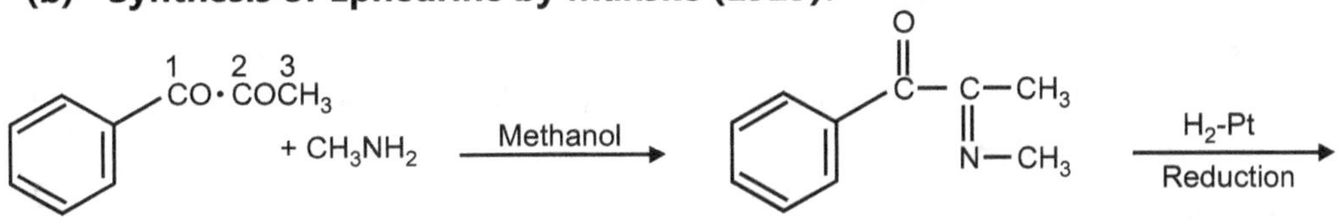

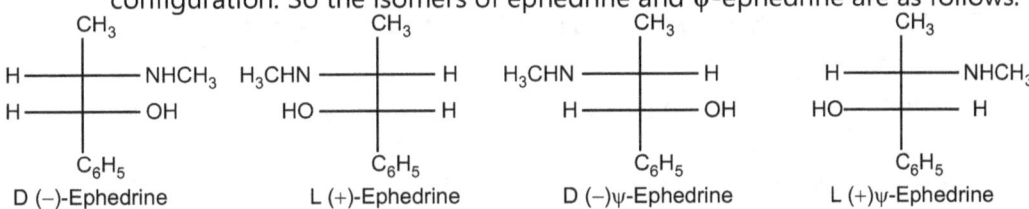

1-Phenyl propane-1, 2-dione
(benzoyl acetyl)

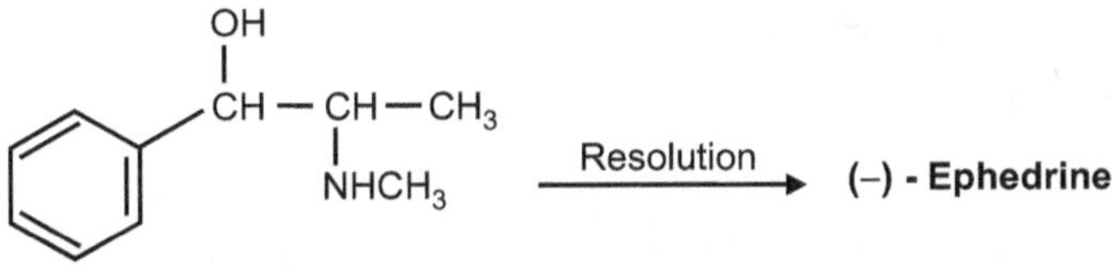

(±) - Ephedrine (two isomers)

8. **(a)   Configuration of (–) Ephedrine:** Since the ephedrine molecule contains two dissimilar chiral centres, four optically active forms (2^2 = 4, two pairs of enantiomers) are theoretically possible. Out of these, two correspond to ephedrine and two correspond to ψ-ephedrine. It has been confirmed that ephedrine has the *erythro*-configuration and ψ-ephedrine has the *threo*-configuration. So the isomers of ephedrine and ψ-ephedrine are as follows:

D (–)-Ephedrine	L (+)-Ephedrine	D (–)ψ-Ephedrine	L (+)ψ-Ephedrine

These configurations are confirmed by experiments.

9. Confirmation of the configuration of (–)-ephedrine, as its hydrochloride has been obtained from X-ray analysis.

Hence, the actual configuration of D(–)-ephedrine is as shown above, or

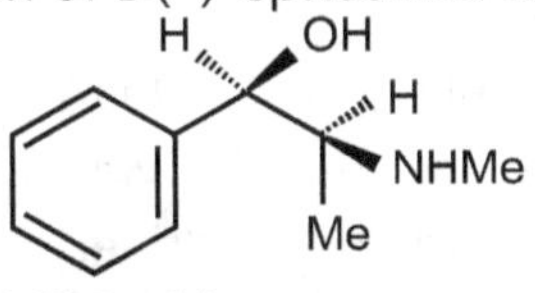

D (–)-Ephedrine

Exercises

1. What are terpenoids ? How are terpenoids classified ? What are the different methods for isolation of terpenoids from natural sources?

2. Discuss the general analytical methods used for determination of structure of terpenoids.

3. What are alkaloids? How are they classified? Describe the general method of extraction and purification of alkaloids from natural sources.

4. Discuss the general analytical methods used for determination of structure of alkaloids.

5. Discuss the structure determination of (i) citral, (ii) ephedrine.

6. Give the synthesis of:
   (i)   Citral,
   (ii)   Ephedrine,
   (iii) Methylheptenone.

7. How are the following conversions effected?
   (i)   Methyl heptenone into citral.
   (ii)   Benzaldehyde into ephedrine.
   (iii) 1-phenylpropane-1, 2-dione into ephedrine.
   (iv)   2, 4-Dibromo-2-methylbutane into citral.
   (v)   Pyridine into 1,3-pentadiene.
   (vi)   Isoquinoline into o-methylstyrene.

8. Write short notes on:
   (i)   Isoprene rule
   (ii)   Stereochemistry of citral
   (iii) Hofmann's exhaustive methylation or Hofmann's degradation
   (iv)   Emde's degradation
   (v)   Von Braun degradation
   (vi)   Zeisel's method

9. How will you prove the following?
   (i)   The presence of two carbon-carbon double bonds in citral.
   (ii)   The presence of α, β-unsaturated aldehyde in citral.
   (iii) The presence of isopropylidene group in citral.
   (iv)   The acyclic nature of citral.
   (v)   The presence of benzene ring in ephedrine.
   (vi)   The presence of $-NHCH_3$ group in ephedrine.
   (vii) Nature of nitrogen atom in ephedrine.
   (viii) Nature of oxygen function in ephedrine.
   (ix)   The presence of secondary alcoholic group $\left(\begin{array}{c} H \\ | \\ -C-OH \\ | \end{array} \right)$ in ephedrine.
   (x)   Configurations of citral-a and citral-b.
   (xi)   Presence of methoxy group ($-OCH_3$) in a natural product.
   (xii) Nature of the side chain in ephedrine.

10. Give significance of the following:
    (i)   Citral on treatment with Br_2 gives tetrabromocitral.
    (ii)   Ozonolysis of citral gives acetone as one of the products.
    (iii) Citral on mild oxidation with Ag_2O gives geranic acid.
    (iv)   Ephedrine on oxidation gives benzoic acid.
    (v)   Ephedrine on heating with hydrochloric acid forms methylamine and propiophenone.

11. **Multiple Choice Questions:**
    (i)   Terpenes with molecular formula $C_{15}H_{24}$ are ____
           (a) Monoterpenes   (b) Diterpenes
           (c) Sesquiterpenes   (d) Sesterterpenes
    (ii)   Common name for 2-methyl-1, 3-butadiene is ____
           (a) α-Terpineol   (b) Limonene
           (c) p-Cymene   **(d) Isoprene**
    (iii) Iodoform test is given by ____
           (a) RCOCH₃   (b) RCHO
           (c) ROH   (d) RCOOH
    (iv)   Silver mirror test with Tollen's reagent is given by ____
           (a) Alcohols   **(b) Aldehydes**
           (c) Ketones   (d) Carboxylic acids
    (v)   Citral is a ____
           (a) Monoterpenoid   (b) Diterpenoid
           (c) Sesquiterpenoid   (d) Triterpenoid
    (vi)   Citral-b on reduction with sodium-amalgam in dil. acid forms ____
           (a) Geraniol   **(b) Nerol**
           (c) Terpineol   (d) Menthol
    (vii) Ephedrine is a ____
           (a) Pyrrolidine alkaloid   (b) Quinoline alkaloid
           (c) Phenylethylamine alkaloid (d) Pyrrolidine-pyridine alkaloid
    (viii) A compound on heating with sulphuric acid forms formaldehyde. This indicates the presence of ____
           (a) – OCH_3 group   **(b) – O – CH₂ – O group**
           (c) – NCH_3 group   (d) – COOH group
    (ix)   An alkaloid when heated with HI at $150° – 300°C$ under pressure produces methyl iodide. This indicates the presence of ____
           (a) – OCH_3 group   (b) – NCH_3 group
           (c) – CCH_3 group   **(d) – OCH₃ and – NCH₃ both**
    (x)   A method applicable to heterocyclic rings with β-hydrogen atoms is ____
           (a) Herzig - Meyer method   (b) Emde modification
           (c) Von-Braun's method   **(d) Hofmann's exhaustive methylation**

■■■

www.ingramcontent.com/pod-product-compliance
Lightning Source LLC
Chambersburg PA
CBHW080822020726
47501CB00009B/2375